SURVIVING
MR. RIGHT

D1564370

SURVIVING MR. RIGHT

Teresa McClain-Watson

sepia

BET BOOKS

BET Publications, LLC
http://www.bet.com

SEPIA BOOKS are published by

BET Publications, LLC
c/o BET BOOKS
One BET Plaza
1900 W Place NE
Washington, DC 20018-1211

All Kensington Titles, Imprints, and Distributed Lines are available at special quantity discounts for bulk purchases for sales promotions, premiums, fund-raising, and educational or institutional use. Special book excerpts or customized printings can also be created to fit specific needs. For details, write or phone the office of the Kensington special sales manager: Kensington Publishing Corp., 850 Third Avenue, New York, NY 10022, attn: Special Sales Department, Phone: 1-800-221-2647.

ISBN: 1-58314-320-3

First Printing: April 2002
10 9 8 7 6 5 4 3 2 1

Printed in the United States of America

One
Robert

He's no Billy dee. That's what my homegirl Vera had the nerve to tell me just as I was about to open the door of her apartment and meet this blind date she had set up for me. He's smart, sharp, as friendly as can be, girl, she assured me, but he ain't no Billy dee.

My first reaction, knowing Vera, knowing all those other blind dates she had set me up with in the past, was to run into the bedroom and bolt the door, but there had not been a steady man in my life in almost two years. When you get to be my age and still available, it's not as if you can be all that particular anymore. You begin settling for what you can get. You rationalize, as I did that night, and try like hell to pretend that your standards haven't lowered but matured with age. So what, you say, if he's not in the same league as the finest man ever to walk the face of anybody's earth? How many people are? He's smart, Vera said, which probably means he's successful. He's friendly, she said, and Lord knows I could use a good laugh. Is he a loser simply because he's no super good looking man like Billy dee Williams? Please. Besides, Billy dee is probably old now and fat and bald. Even Billy dee's no *Billy dee* anymore. Now if girlfriend would have told me not to get my hopes up because he ain't no Mike Tyson, yes, there would probably be a problem. But Billy dee? I could live with that.

I jumped to these conclusions, however, before I opened that door. Then I opened that door. And Lord have mercy Jesus. I looked at Vera hard. "*Ain't no Billy dee?*" I yelled at her. "Child, please!"

I slammed that door so hard I think I broke his nose (Lord knows it was big enough). I was through with Miss V. If her husband Rollie had not intervened I truly believe I would have choked her to death. I could not believe what she had done to me. She knew better. We had been friends for years. Girlfriend knew what she was doing. She knew I could settle for a lot of things (and have settled for a lot of things), but going out in public, on an official date, with somebody you have to look at twice to verify that he is, in fact, a human being, was expecting too much. And I know you should never judge a book by its cover and all that. But damn. The man looked like something the cat dragged in, yanked around, then dragged back out.

But that's how it was going for me in Florida. One loser after another. From Vera to my other best friend, Gina, they kept me busy with blind-date losers. They figured something was substantially wrong with me because I was thirty-four and still single and they were both married, happy, and normal. Vera even told me that I expected too much from men. She often bragged about how she managed to remain married to the same man for almost eight years when I couldn't stay in a relationship for eight months. "Knights in shining armor disappeared years ago, Victoria Coleman," she often said to me, "so you may as well get over it and grab what you can get."

Gina was less diplomatic. "You're cute," she often said, "and you have a wonderful personality. But you ain't all that either." Cold. But true. I was five-ten, for one thing, which was tall for a lady. I'd been told countless times that I favored Diana Ross in her Supremes "You Can't Hurry Love" days. I had that same smooth, walnut-colored skin, that same wide, easy smile, and those big, Kennedy fifty-cent eyes that always looked stunned by the view. My body wasn't exactly like hers, however. Let's just say that mine was a slightly *fuller* version of hers, although I did manage to maintain just the right combination of hips and backside that brothers seemed to crave nowadays. My dress wear wasn't exactly Diana Ross glamourous either. I mean I stepped out in some Donna Karan on a regular basis, don't get me wrong, but I wore Donna Karan pants and blazers most of the time, with slipper-heel stack shoes and an oversize hobo bag to round out the package. My looks, style, everything then has always bordered more on that *something about her* side than pure handsomeness. But I liked what I liked and men with faces only a mother could love need not apply.

My stubbornness, however, still did not erase the fact that I was manless for almost two years, since the night Robert left. He had left before (oh so many times before) and I had vowed not to take him back again before. When he said he was not coming back it seemed to be nothing more than his normal line. I never dreamed he'd mean what he said for a change. That's how whipped I was. I was even sassy about his leaving. "Let the door hitcha where the good Lord splitcha and don't come back!" I yelled.

"I won't!" he yelled back.

That was over a year ago. It was the first time in our six-month affair that he kept his word to me.

I had the deep-down love jones for that man, you hear me? And he knew it too. There is nothing worse in this world than a man who knows when he has a woman whipped. And I was whipped. I was goddamn Lassie on a leash running behind Robert, that's how whipped I was. It got so bad that he started getting bold with his shit. Why should he care? All he had to do was yank the chain and I came running with my tongue wagging.

One night I found him in bed with another woman. He told me that the woman was his cousin. "We grew up together," he said. "There's only one bed in my apartment so we shared." And I, a

well-educated college professor, believed him. No matter what line
he laid on me, what tale he told to me, I believed him. Yes, sir. I deserved everything I got from Robert C.K. Johnson.

I was not living in Florida, but in Washington, D.C., when I first
laid eyes on him. It was one of those blustery cold days in D.C.,
where the insult wasn't so much the weather but the car wrecks and
ensuing traffic jams that seemed always to come along with days
like this. Add to it the fact that Congress was in session, which
meant numerous congressional aides and staffers assisting the traffic gridlock with their BMWs and Saabs, talking on their cell
phones and huffing down cappuccinos as if driving was the last
thing on their minds, and the entire town seemed to converge at
the same point in time on the same city block where my car stood.

I lived on Capital Hill at the time, in a beautiful Victorian row
house that had been converted into a four-unit apartment complex,
but I worked at Howard University, which wasn't that far away but
seemed light-years away when caught in the maze of bad weather
and traffic jams that was my drive to work.

I saw Robert for the first time at Howard. It was the start of a
new semester and I walked into my last class of the day, an elective
course entitled The Role of African-American Women in the
Antebellum South, expecting to find weary-eyed upperclassmen
still unsure why they kept on signing up for these darn history
courses, but I didn't expect to find romance. It was, in fact, the last
thing on my mind. That is, until he walked in.

He stood out from the start. He was one of only three males taking the course and the only male over twenty-one. When he first
walked into the room my eyes blinked and went into slow motion.
He was tall, like me, but had an athlete's stride and swagger that
forced folks to check him out. His brown eyes were large and
moon-shaped and his wide nose and full dark lips were just what
the doctor ordered because I was ready to take him where he stood.

I tried to conceal my admiration of his beauty because he was my student, for crying out loud, but I failed miserably. All he had to do was part those juicy lips and smile that Denzel Washington smile and I was his.

He sat at the front of the class and stretched his long legs so far out across the floor that they were almost touching mine. Once, near the end of the semester, our shoes did indeed touch and I allowed it. My other students had to know of the attraction I had for Robert, and I am sure there were rumors, but it would have been too sensible for me to care. My weakness was good-looking men and he had all the right parts working for him. And he was successful too. Lord have mercy. Not only was the man a member of the practice squad for the Washington Redskins, which I thought was some big deal back then, but he also part owned a local Foot Locker franchise, which meant he was steady and knew how to handle his business. The brother had it all, in other words.

He always found an excuse to stay late after class and we'd talk about everything but the course itself, and by midsemester we were meeting for lunch. Near semester's end it was dinner. During finals week (the night after the final, to be precise) I finally caved and said yes, he could come up for a drink.

He wore a pair of khaki pants and a red polo shirt that night. His short, S-curled Afro sparkled against the dark blue sky. We stood at the entranceway of my apartment building and talked on the stoop. The neighborhood was quiet at night, with rows and rows of houses sitting like two-story boxes pushing out onto a stoop with nothing more than a night-light for their protection. Other than the occasional dog barking or scary cat screeching or teenage gangsta wannabe flying by in some souped-up Oldsmobile as if our little street were the Daytona Speedway, my neighborhood wasn't exactly the place to be. But what I liked about Robert was that he didn't seem to care about all of that. Peace and quiet seemed to suit him just fine, as if just being with me was all the excitement he needed. That was why we stood on the porch talking on and on, about the course, about the Redskins, like two love-struck kids unable to say good night. It was Robert, however, who finally worked up the nerve to get to the point.

"I could really use a drink for the road," he said as if Georgetown, where he lived, were some long journey away.

"Of course," I said gladly, "come on up!"

We walked up, Robert and I, and the closer we got to my apartment door, the more animated his conversation became. The brother was a little too excited about this drink for the road, it seemed to me. If my suspicion was right, and it usually was, brotherman's sudden burst of gaiety was not because of my wet bar but because of a great expectation that he was about to get laid.

That made me nervous. I was comfortable with my body, if not totally pleased, but I wasn't so certain that it was ready for prime time yet. And let's face it, a great-looking showboat like Robert would want his woman to undress before his very eyes—and with the light on. How was I going to handle that? My body was okay, probably even desirable, but I couldn't take that chance. Robert often bragged about how he had dated supermodels before, the kind of figure-eight beauty queens that girls like me hated. In light of that background he probably would not be amused if he saw me naked. He would hit his forehead, have one of those *I could have had a V-8!* moments, and get on down the road looking for the kind of woman more befitting a hunk like him.

My idea of perfect lovemaking is for the gentleman to leave the room while the gentlewoman undressed, hopped into bed, and flicked off the light. The gentleman would then feel his way into the room, get under the covers, and fantasize. If he saw me naked, however, his fantasy would be shot to hell, and all the tea in China couldn't rekindle the mood.

But who was I kidding? Robert was the show-and-tell type just as sure as he was good looking. He would snatch off his clothes at the drop of a hat and expected his woman to do the same. What could I tell him? I'd love to, but turn off the lights first? Talk about a red flag. He'd think I was some transsexual or something. He'd think I had the body configuration of a lumberjack with all of that great need for darkness I was asking for.

But as we walked toward my apartment door I began to get desperate. I liked Robert a lot but I wasn't comfortable enough in our relationship to go all the way with him. I didn't feel as if I knew him. Whenever we were together we talked very superficially, mainly about history, or sports, but never about him. How could I sleep with somebody when I didn't even know what his middle initials stood for?

That was why I had to think of something fast. I thought about that old *my period is on* excuse. That would take care of the first visit, but then what? I couldn't claim to have an eternal period. That would only create problems of a different kind. I'd become the Freak Lady then and he'd be up the road faster than he would have been if I had a penis swinging down there.

I could say I had a headache, but I knew that wouldn't work either. I tried that line many times before, on better men than Robert, but it never worked for me. I tell a man I have a headache, he tells me it's not my head he's after.

Of course there was always the religious excuse, the abuse excuse, or the old, reliable virgin excuse. None, however, have ever worked for me. Especially the virgin excuse. I once told a date that I never go to bed with a man visiting my apartment for the first time. He, therefore, walked out of my apartment, knocked, and reentered. "This is now my second visit," he said and snatched his clothes off.

It wasn't until we reached my apartment and I began to unlock the door that my obsession with the state of my body ceased and turned into a sudden concern with the state of my apartment. I began wondering if I left that newspaper scattered around the living-room floor, for instance. Or what about last night's dinner dish? Did I remember to remove it from my nightstand? What if there was a musky odor in my apartment? I hadn't put up air fresheners in weeks. He might step into my apartment and pass out from the funk. Robert was a neat freak. His dress style proved that. He might look at my untidy apartment and declare me unsuitable.

The apartment turned out to be in worse shape than I imagined. There were piles of clothes in chairs, a half-empty two-liter Diet Coke bottle just standing as if it were furniture in the middle of my living-room floor, open bags of Cheetos and Doritos, and even a bowl of stale popcorn sitting boldly on my coffee table. I was so embarrassed that I wanted to dig a hole right then and there and drop into it. But my untidiness was only half the story. For the apartment reeked of muskiness from day-old food lying about and my stale cigarette smoke that clogged the air and caused poor Robert to cough.

"Are you all right?" I asked him.

He bent over coughing and nodded that he was. "It would help if we could open a window," he said, and added that it was because of his allergies, but I knew better than that. Yet I flew open every window in the house just the same. I lived alone. It never occurred to me to sniff the aroma of the air or clean up behind myself or open a window. Most nights when I would get home from work I would drop my briefcase, flip off my shoes, rummage through the fridge for what I could find, and then eat, smoke, and alternate between watching C-SPAN and reading the latest novel that caught my eye at the bookstore.

By the time I returned from the bedroom Robert was coming out of the kitchen with a glass of water. "Feels better in here already," he said as he raised his glass in an imitation toast to me. I knew he wanted to say, "It *smells* better in here already," but I appreciated his dishonesty.

His coughing stopped completely by the time we settled down on my living-room sofa and began talking. We talked for hours. He was a deep brother, let me tell you. And a history buff out of this world. Although the conversation was good and we seemed to possess many of the same views on political, social, and economic matters, most of the talk never rose to the level of anything remotely resembling intimacy or personal revelations. When Robert did talk about himself he talked about himself as a practice player for the Redskins or as a local businessman. His family background, his current life away from work, or even what his middle initials stood for, never came up. I was pleased by the tenor of the conversation because it didn't seem to be the kind of talk that would lead to lovemaking, but then Robert stood up.

First he gave out an obviously forced yawn and then he began to stretch and contort his body around as if he was just plain exhausted. But I knew what time it was. I'd been around that block too many times not to know what that stretch routine meant. A man stretching as if he's worn out and sleepy always meant one thing in my book: bed action time. But before he could unclench his gorgeous muscles and get a word in edgewise, I blurted out, "I'm sanctified!"

It seemed as if everything stopped. Even Robert stopped stretching midway and looked at me curiously. It was as if he did not know what to say. "Are you?" he asked. "Which church?"

Now I was lost. "Excuse me?"

"Which church do you attend? Unless I misheard you, you said you was sanctified, right?"

"Yes, I did say that," I said. "But I didn't mean that kind of sanctification."

He hesitated as if he was expecting me to explain, but I didn't. I couldn't. "Anyway," he said, "it's late and I've got to go to work tomorrow. It might be off-season but I don't earn the big bucks like the Steve Youngs and the Jerry Rices do. I have to work for a living. But I'll see you around, okay?"

And then he was gone. Just like that. I blew it. I blew it big time. I just let the finest Negro in D.C. walk out of my door because of my foolishness. I showered, pushed my notebooks aside, and got into bed. I did not even turn on my television, that's how bad I felt. But then I remembered he had my phone number. *Maybe he'll call,* I said to myself. *Maybe he'll go home, shower, and give me a call. Then I'll know that the night was not as big a fiasco as I had thought.* A phone call from Robert would be all I needed to have a good night's sleep.

I checked the phone over twenty times to make sure it was on the hook. I cursed myself for not getting his number, but my mother, who held herself out as the Dr. Ruth of Philadelphia, had ingrained in me the idea that a woman was never to call the man first. Otherwise, she said, you'll never know his true intentions. I cursed my mother for giving me that lame advice. I didn't care about his true intentions, I just wanted to hear from him. But by four A.M. I reached the conclusion that he should have made it home by now. He did not call, I decided, because he did not want to call. Or maybe he lost my number. *That's it! Your boy lost the number!* The thought of it caused my heart to leap with hope. But what if he didn't lose it? That thought caused my heart to sink. I should have known, that very night, that Robert C.K. Johnson was bad news. I mean, I was doing all of that crazy stuff already and I barely knew the man. I was better off by myself. I was lonely, yes, and in some ways discontent, but at least I was functional. At least I was doing for the most part what I wanted to do. Now my entire life was on hold because of some man. Child, please. I should have said child, please that very night, turned over, and got my whipped ass some sleep.

I slept all right. But as soon as the day dawned, and when I should have been dressing to go to my office at Howard University, I was dressing in a sleek blue dress and heels preparing to go to Foot Locker.

Gina and Vera, my two best friends, both lived in D.C. at the time too. Gina telephoned me just as I was walking out of the door. She wanted to know if we could meet for lunch. I told her to try me later. My morning visit to a shoe store would be the determining factor.

"What are you talking about, girl? What shoe store?"

"Foot Locker," I said.

"Foot Locker? What, they got a sale?"

"No," I said, being purposely coy.

"Then what's so hot at Foot Locker if it's not a shoe sale?"

"It's a long story, G," I said.

"Aw, shit," she said, "it's a dude!"

"I didn't say anything about a man."

"What's his name?"

I sighed. "Robert C.K. Johnson."

"Damn. That's a lot of name. What's the C.K. stand for?"

I had no idea. I started to ask many times but thought it too personal a question and didn't. "It's personal," I said.

"Oh, you go, girl! Personal, is it? I hear that! Just wait till I tell Vera. She was thinking about hooking you up with this gorilla-looking man Rollie works with. But you went and got you a hunk all by your lonesome. I's scared of you!"

Gina was like that. She wanted me attached more than my own mother did. Her choices of men for me, however, were pretty terrible, although her choices were a little more suited to me than Vera's choices. So all those blind dates later and I was still single. But Gina saw Robert as a hopeful sign because *I* chose him and they knew nothing about it. So Gina gave me her blessings, begged me to phone her as soon as I could, and I was off.

I was in my royal-green, 1994 Toyota Camry and was backing out of the parking lot of my apartment building before I looked down and saw that I had a run in my panty hose the size of a basketball. That meant a trip to the supermarket, a dash into the bathroom for a panty hose change, and then a fast and furious drive of panic and impulsiveness for more whippings from Robert.

The Foot Locker that Robert part owned was a nice establishment in northwest Washington. Located in a strip mall on M Street, the store stood sandwiched between a bike shop and a bakery. It was early, a few minutes after ten, and only a handful of cars graced the parking lot. I sat in my car like a regular idiot and stared at the front of the building. Signs of 10% OFF, 20% OFF, 30% OFF cluttered up the plate-glass window, making it next to impossible to see who roamed around inside.

Robert was there, however. His bright red Navigator was parked directly in front of the store's main entrance. I hadn't come all that way for nothing, I thought, so without any further delay I stepped out of my Camry and headed for the door.

I felt foolish immediately. I felt as if every fiber of my self-respect were slowly unraveling before my very eyes and I were watching and even aiding in its destruction. I started to turn around. Who needed this? But then I saw Robert.

He was inside the store ringing up a purchase for a male customer. He was smiling that wonderful white smile of his and talking with the customer as if that young boy were his best friend. I walked up to the front door and peeped through the glass for a better view. I stood there, mesmerized with Robert. I didn't realize somebody had walked up behind me until I felt a hand on my shoulder. I jumped and turned so quickly that the man behind me backed up and threw up his hands, as if he was the one alarmed!

"May I help you?" he said, regaining his composure only after I calmed down too. He wore a black-and-white-striped shirt with FOOT LOCKER on the pocket so I assumed he worked there and was just arriving to begin his day's labor. I smiled and said that I thought I saw a friend of mine inside the store and I was peeping to get a better look. "Before I went in and made a fool of myself," I said.

"Maybe I can help you. What's your friend's name?"

"Actually, that's not him," I said and went back to my car, cranked up, and drove off. I could see from my rearview that the guy was still standing in front of the Foot Locker door, watching me leave and shaking his head. Women probably gazed through that window every day looking at Robert. And I was doing it too. I decided to forget Robert. I decided to go to my office, grade the remainder of those final exams, record the grades, and do what I had to do to prepare for the next semester.

By the time I returned home that evening and attempted to watch a symposium on C-SPAN about the Bakke decision's effect on Affirmative Action, Robert was on my mind once again. And then Gina phoned. And before I knew it she and Vera were at my front door.

Vera, as usual, took the sanctimonious route. She walked into my apartment preaching, amazed that I would even consider a relationship with one of my former students. "It's unethical," she said. "You could be fired!"

Vera was like that. She was our group's voice of reason. She believed in cuttin' loose and having some fun just like everybody else but there were significant limits to how much fun she was willing to cut loose and have. She was a born-again Christian since she hooked up with her husband Rollie yet she had no qualms about associating with big-time sinners like me and Gina. She did, however, take every chance she had to set us straight, to get us to at least think about getting our acts together, but she never pressured us. "It's like a drug addict," she often said. "They're either willing to come clean or they aren't. But you can't make them come clean."

Gina, on the other hand, was something completely different. Let me put it this way: Nobody, and I mean nobody, was about to confuse sistergirl with Mother Teresa, Sister Teresa, or even Miss Teresa who might go to church every blue moon. She was beautiful by any standard, with long, straight, coal-black hair, apple-shaped hazel eyes, and with a body so sexy that any woman would be proud to claim it as her own. She wore everything designer: Versace skirt suits and heels; Louie Vuitton and Dooney and Bourke handbags; Cazal sunglasses; Cartier watches. But her hazel eyes were her prize—big, bright, and caring. They were sexy but they were also sad, very sad, as if she'd seen too much and couldn't get over it.

Even when she laughed out loud, her eyes were more telling. For if you looked into her eyes in the midst of her joy, you wouldn't believe for a second that she was happy.

But Gina was my girl. She understood my hurt in ways Vera never could. Hell yeah, it was irrational how I was feeling. Hell yeah, I'd been in misery ever since I laid eyes on Robert. And hell yeah, I was hurting as if I were dying. Gina understood that. She was on husband number three. She had been there and back and might be going again.

But Vera, God bless her, was at a loss. "It was only your third date," she said, "and by your own admission the first two weren't real dates at all because he was still your student. What could have possibly happened in that short length of time to have you all bent over with a love jones already?"

"He done rocked her world!" Gina said and snapped her fingers.

"Ain't that much world rocking in this world," Vera said.

"How the hell would you know?" Gina asked. "You're married to a man who specializes in the dead. A goddamn mortician! How the hell would you know anything about somebody rockin' or not rockin' somebody's world?"

"Let's leave my husband out of this, please," Vera said.

"Bump your husband!" Gina said. "Who he suppose to be? I'll leave him in this if I want to leave him in this!"

"What*ever*," Vera said and held up her hand the way those grown teenagers do to disrespect somebody.

She and Gina both were almost thirty-seven years old during my Robert days, but Vera acted and carried herself as if she were far older, even to where I sometimes called her Granny. She used to be gorgeous enough to give Gina a run for her money, but all those years of losing herself to become the good little wife of her husband's dreams had not been kind. She was now razor thin and haggard looking, her once stylish dress and manner now nothing more than a figment of bygone days. She was a Kmart girl head to toe now and was the kind of sister who no longer thought it necessary to flaunt anything, who found my need to wear Donna Karan and Gina's love of Versace too pretentious for her. Give her a store cart and those Kmart Blue Light sales any day. Give her a buy-one, get-one-free special and sistergirl was good to go. She wore long, flowery skirts with the matching tops most of the time, a matching scarf tossed around her thin neck, and flats. Sometimes her hair was in a ponytail and sometimes her hair was in a ponytail with one of those big, flower child flop hats thrown on top.

Gina would complain endlessly about Vera's lack of style, as she saw it, but Vera wasn't thinking about Gina. To Vera, her taste was more refined than Gina's, and she liked her oddness. So Gina gave up complaining altogether since it never did any good anyway. Now she simply looked at Vera and her flowery coverings and shook her head. To Gina, the girl needed help, a makeover to end all makeovers, but she wasn't going to get her blood pressure up worrying about it.

Vera was pretty, in a stray cat sort of way, with small, pensive eyes, a long, narrow face, and a mouth that seemed wider than her little face could handle. She spoke in deep tones, as if she were a contralto opera singer trying desperately to talk as correctly as she sang, but Vera's actual words were more along the lines of a preacher's vocabulary. She never cussed, not even when she was mad as hell, and every time Gina or I lost ourselves in the language she kindly asked us to knock it off.

"I know I'm being irrational, Vera," I said once she and Gina ended their contentious conversation about Rollie's line of work, "but that's how I feel. I like Robert and I wanna see him again."

"Then call him," Gina said.

"Don't be ridiculous," Vera said.

"Call him, Tory. What you got to lose, girl?"

"Her self-respect, for starters."

"Oh, be quiet, Vera. Call the brother up, Tory. He could have lost your number, for all you know."

"I know," I said. "I thought about that."

"He knows where you live," Vera said. "He would have been here if he wanted to."

"I thought about that too."

And around and around we went. We lay across my big bed like three schoolgirls trying to figure out what we were going to do with me. I was a mess. My apartment was a mess. And the man I hoped to truly have a future with aced my exam (and I mean he didn't miss a question!) and hightailed it out of my life as quickly as he had come into it. Vera was telling me to drop that zero and get myself a hero and Gina was telling me not to listen to Vera. "I don't see her dropping her zero," Gina said.

That did it for Vera. She had had enough of Gina's insults, she said, and she would not remain a moment longer. "I'm leaving now," she stood and said in her deepest of voices.

But Gina wasn't repentant. "Then leave," she said.

"I'm talking to Tory. I'm leaving now, Tory."

"Then leave," Gina said again. "Take yo' flowery ass on!"

"Don't go, V," I said. "Please."

But she was at the point of no return. She had to leave. It was an honor thing with her now. Gina won every argument, every bet, every game, and Vera was getting tired of it. I offered to drive her home but she called Rollie instead. "Call me later," she said and I promised that I would.

Vera was barely out of my apartment before Gina announced that she had an idea. Tomorrow was Saturday, she said, and it would be a perfect morning for the two of us to dress and go buy a pair of Air Jordans. I told her that I couldn't, that I tried that already, but she insisted. "Leave it to Gina, girl. I knows how to get results!"

I left it to Gina and went to bed. When the morning came, I jumped out of bed and dressed quickly, as if my life depended on it.

Gina arrived in her white, gold-trimmed Lexus around ten. She had on a pair of green-tinted Cazal sunglasses and was bebopping to some loud rap music as if she were still a teenager. She was, in fact, a well-respected, popular attorney in town, but she still knew how to relax and enjoy herself.

As we rode to M Street, Gina kept trying to interest me in this grand plan she had for me to win over Robert, but I declined participation. I decided that I would be straight with Robert. He was either interested in me or he wasn't. But games and schemes and even Gina's grand plan were not the way I wanted to go anymore. That was why, when we arrived at Foot Locker and found Robert in his back office poring over inventory ledgers, I took the lead, walked swiftly up to his desk, and smiled.

He looked up. My heart dropped and my smile almost disappeared. He was the one. This beautiful Adonis of a man was the one human being I wanted to be with. I felt ordinary in my blue jeans and blazer, emitting what Gina often called the *Tory* look, but I liked what I liked. And Robert C.K. Johnson was it.

He at first seemed almost shocked by my sudden presence in his office, as if I were some *Fatal Attraction* chick who didn't know how to take a hint, but then he smiled. "Victoria," he said with great gaiety, "how you doing?"

"Good," I said with equal gaiety. "What about yourself?"

"I'm cool," he said, offered me and Gina a sit-down, and it was on again. He didn't phone me, he said, because he was stupid busy at the store and wasn't able to have a moment for himself. I understood immediately. But Gina didn't. Robert, appreciating her apprehension, gave an additional, more simplistic explanation. "Honestly," he said, "I forgot your phone number, Vick."

"I thought so!" I said and smiled broadly, my heart soaring with satisfaction.

"Not so fast, Pollyanna," Gina said to me, bringing me back down to earth. Then she looked at Robert. "She works at Howard University and you know it. She's in the book, brother."

That was true too. We both looked to Robert for an explanation, but none came. But it really didn't matter overall. Robert saying that he would have phoned if he could was enough for me. But Gina was not me.

"Well?" she said to Robert.

"Okay," he said. "You got me. I didn't think to call the school. And I couldn't go by her apartment either. It's been a busy, crazy week here at work and I couldn't find the time for anything or anybody really."

"I understand exactly what you mean," I said, putting on my best sympathetic act yet. But Gina wasn't impressed. She looked at me as if I were through dealing. But I couldn't help myself. Robert was still interested in me. I wasn't about to mess that up. Gina could afford to be righteously indignant. She didn't read novels for vicarious excitement or watch C-SPAN just to hear somebody talk. She had her beautiful husband and a beautiful retreat on Martha's Vineyard. I was weary of books and C-SPAN. I wanted more. And I wanted Robert. What he did or didn't do in the past was in the past, as far as I was concerned.

After Gina finally gave up and walked out, Robert leaned back in his chair and smiled. He looked me up and down and then asked if I was free that night. I said that I was without a moment's hesitation, and that response alone sprung my roller-coaster romance with Robert C.K. Johnson into immediate and often devastating overdrive.

Gina was upset with me during the entire ride home, especially when I told her that I didn't have time to go mall hopping with her.

"And why the hell not?" she asked.

"Robert's coming over tonight," I said. "I've got cleaning to do."

Gina went on and on, telling me about thirty times that Robert was no good and I was being irrational and foolish. I paid her little attention. I wanted her to hurry up and get me home. I had things to do for a change.

She stopped her car in front of my apartment building. As I

began to get out of the car, she grabbed me by the arm. When I looked at her, she took off her shades. She looked so serious and concerned that she scared me. "Take it slow, Tory," she said. "Compared to a heartbreak, being alone ain't so bad."

"I know."

"Don't rush it, Tory. Promise me you won't rush it."

"I promise, Gina. I promise."

She stared at me with those sad, hazel eyes of hers and then she released my arm. I stood out in the parking lot and waved good-bye to her. As soon as her Lexus turned the corner and was clean out of sight, I ran to my Camry, jumped in, and hightailed it to the mall. I had to get me a new outfit, new shoes, perfume, the works. I had to buy cleaning products and AIR FRESHENERS and floral arrangements and everything I could think of for me and my little apartment. I aimed to please. Robert was one man I aimed to keep.

He didn't show up. I waited, until after eleven, but he didn't show up. When I finally stopped rationalizing and concluded that it wasn't happening that night, I undressed and crawled into bed. C-SPAN was telecasting a rerun of a *Book Notes* episode where some obscure British writer was going on and on about the virtues of lesbianism. If I wasn't hurting so bad I would have laughed. *There's an idea*, I thought. *Become a lesbian. That'll show every man that ever hurt me that I meant business.*

But Robert was still on my mind. How could he not come? I kept asking myself. How could he not come after all of that apologizing and explaining away? It never occurred to me that he wouldn't show. I thought it was settled. That was why it hurt so bad. I was duped again without even realizing that it was a possibility.

After midnight, when I was truly not the one to be bothered with, the telephone rang. I grabbed it from my nightstand and yelled hello. It was Robert.

"Man, I'm sorry," he said. "I am so sorry."

Yes, you are, I wanted to say. "Where are you?" I said instead. I was by now a total wipeout.

"I'm at the phone booth outside your apartment. I am so embarrassed, Vick, I am so sorry."

"What happened to you tonight? And why are you outside my apartment?"

"I forgot we had a date. I flat forgot. When I thought about it I was asleep in bed, in *my* bed, alone, and I realized, 'Oh my God,' and I drove on over. Please forgive me, Vick. I really am very embarrassed by this."

I thought about it for all of three seconds and then told him to come on up. I started to grab my clothes and do a fast-speed dress-up, but decided to keep my robe on instead. There would be no excuses this time. If he wanted me, he could have me. If he didn't want me, he could have me. It was all up to him. Life was too short and love was too fleeting for me even to try and act as if I weren't willing to play the fool.

Our relationship was never stable, but it had some high points, like the time Robert took me on a cruise to the Bahamas and the time he introduced me to some of his Redskins teammates. But for the most part it was a rocky road. I had an inkling that Robert was unfaithful less than two weeks into our affair. He claimed, every time Gina or Vera or I caught him with another woman, that he was telling his old girlfriends that he was a one-woman man now or she was merely somebody he knew from his school days or she was his cousin. I would end the relationship, then run him down and end up apologizing to *him* for my unbelief. He was a smooth operator, let me tell you.

Neither Gina nor Vera cared for Robert. He was a player and they could see it as clear as day. I could see it too but whenever he came back with a reasonable explanation—or even an unreasonable one—I decided that he, not my eyes, not my instincts, but he was the one to believe.

I wasn't myself anymore. I was trying so hard to be what Robert wanted, which changed every week, that I forgot who I was. Gina kept telling me to slow down, that love that desperate couldn't possibly last very long, but the more I tried to slow down, the more desperate I became. And ended up going faster than I was going before.

But Gina was right. Robert and I were together all of six months when it ended. Oddly enough it ended not with a bang, not with some unbelievable act of infidelity on his part, but with a whimper. Gina called me at work to tell me that she saw him at some snazzy restaurant with another woman. That meant very little to me since Robert had (or claimed to have) numerous female relatives that he wined and dined occasionally. I was beyond my running to check out every potential indiscretion phase and would merely wait to bring it up when I saw him again.

I saw him later that night. He dropped by my apartment on his way home from work to pick up my copy of John Blassingame's *Slave Community*. Robert was an avid reader, especially on black history, but he hated spending money on books. He would just as soon borrow them as buy them and he borrowed practically everything I had on his subjects of interest. But he never returned them. I used to remind him to bring my books with him when he came over, but soon I stopped asking. I figured I should be grateful to have a man who enjoyed history as much as I did. Besides, I rationalized, they were only books.

Robert got the book, talked briefly to me about his busy day at the store, and was about to leave when I thought to broach the subject of this female lunch date of his. It was a minor matter, as far as I was concerned, but Robert refused to explain her away. He outright admitted that he had lunch with a female. "Is there anything else you wanna know?" he asked. His arrogance at first surprised me. He was usually apologetic when such matters came up. But this time he was defensive as hell.

"Who was she?" I asked.

"None of your business," he said.

"What?"

"You heard me."

"What did I do?"

"I'm sick and tired of your shit, you know that, Tory?"

"*My* shit? What about *your* shit? That's what this conversation is about."

"You know what, keep your book, all right?"

"What's the matter with you?"

"Ain't nothing wrong with me. Every time you come with your bullshit you try to put it on me. Well, you can forget it this time."

I don't know why, but something snapped in me. For the first time in our relationship I saw right through his game. He would deflect blame off of himself by putting it on me, only he was deflecting big time that night. "You need to quit," I said to him. "Your ass got busted and you're blaming *me?* Get out."

He looked at me hard, as if he had never heard me tell him to leave before, although he'd heard it many times. "What did you say to me?" he asked.

"I said get out, that's what I said!"

"Oh, you're bad tonight, aren't you? Having a field day, aren't you?"

"Good-bye," I said, hurrying him out. "Let the door hitcha where the good Lord splitcha and don't come back!"

He looked at me hard. "I won't!" he said angrily, threw Blassingame to the floor, and left.

Two

A Moon for the Discontented

It wasn't long after my breakup with Robert that Vera had some startling news. She and her husband Rollie, she said, were relocating to Tallahassee, Florida. Rollie's father, a well-respected funeral-home owner down there, was terminally ill with colon cancer and could no longer fulfill his responsibilities. Although there was a brother already in place who could run the family business just fine, Rollie, in one of his most irritating sanctimonious moods yet, decided that it was his place, as the eldest child, to take over.

Gina and I invited Vera out to dinner for what we thought would be our last night together. It all happened so fast that we could hardly believe it, and although we made many promises about getting together as often as we could, we felt, in our hearts, that this was it.

Gina chose the restaurant. It was called Kumba Bay, a quaint little soul food bistro in Anacostia, and it was one of those black-owned places in the sho' nuff hood that Gina was known for frequenting. I was late, as usual, but was still able to park my car less than a half block ahead of theirs (Gina's white Lexus was parked directly behind Vera's black Lexus). I smiled as I walked past the twin cars, remembering how Gina and Vera both begged me to get with the program and buy me a Lexus too. "For the good of the sisterhood," they said. When I asked, however, if the *sisterhood* would make the payments on such a *well beyond an associate professor's salary* automobile, the proclamation was stymied. "Your Camry's close enough," Vera said.

Kumba Bay was small, nothing more than a storefront building surrounded by a liquor store, a pool hall, and a shoe-repair shop, with gaudy blue paint slapped on above the name and SOUL FOOD DELIGHT! painted in. It wasn't exactly the kind of place you'd choose for a farewell dinner, but Gina loved the idea of supporting these obscure black businesses around town. She outdid herself this time, I thought, as I hurried across the street toward the little eating place. Loud-talking brothers hung out in front as if it was the place to be, and the closer I got to the building, the more I had to endure the usual harmless but sometimes annoying banter those street-corner brothers loved to lay on me: *Hey, mama, what's happ'nin'? You sho' look fine, you know that, sista? You hot. Real hot. You sho' know how to work that thang! Baby got back! Bring yo' beautiful self over here so Papa can make you feel all right! Damn, your eyes big!*

I batted those big eyes, which I was prone to do when I was nervous, and politely but quickly worked my way in out of the cold.

Inside was another story. It was a cheerful atmosphere, for one thing, with young and old, families and couples, enjoying their meals with light talk and gaiety. I stood at the foyer and looked around at the setup. There were rows and rows of small tables with booths against the walls. But there didn't appear to be a seat available. I didn't see Gina or Vera either but that was more than likely because they were in the smoking area in back, so instead of waiting on a waiter and obeying the PLEASE WAIT TO BE SEATED sign, I walked around table after table until I was in the smaller, but no less cluttered, back area.

Gina was on her cell phone having what appeared to be a rather heated conversation, and Vera, in her flowery outfit and scarf and with small reading glasses on, was perusing the menu.

"Hello, Granny!" I said and hugged her neck. She smiled but removed the glasses all the same.

"You're late," she said.

"I know, I know. It couldn't be helped."

"That's what you always say."

"I know."

I took the seat in the middle, which was usually my place in the threesome, and informed the waiter, who had apparently followed me back there, that I would have what they were having.

"Very good, ma'am," he said and left.

"What y'all having, girl?" I asked Vera upon his departure.

"Soda for me, gin for Gina."

"Of course. Sometimes I think the only reason she orders gin all the time is that it's an *A* short of Gina."

Vera smiled. "Nobody's that silly," she said.

"I don't know now," I said, taking my shades and hobo bag and setting them both on the floor next to my chair. "She loves herself and all things associated with that self."

"True. But I still wouldn't go that far."

I smiled and looked around at the small but packed-to-capacity restaurant. It was an old building, with rings in the ceiling from too many leaks, but the staff was friendly and the crowd seemed to be enjoying themselves, so I relaxed too.

"How's the food?" I asked Vera.

"Fair to middling," she said.

"I wouldn't call that a ringing endorsement."

"I've only been here once."

"Well, that's all it takes, honey. You either love it or you don't."

"Oh, hell no!" Gina suddenly said loudly into her cell phone. "Who do you think you're dealing with? You don't know jack about my goings and comings so don't even try to trip that shit on me!"

Gina's loud voice attracted so much attention that Vera leaned over and told her to cool it.

Gina looked at Vera with a big-time look of annoyance on her face. "What?" she asked.

Vera looked to me. She had enough on her mind than to even try to get into a confrontation with Gina. "She said to cool it, G," I said and, motioning with my eyes toward the other tables, added: "The world is watching."

Gina, in one of her shittiest of moods, looked around at the other black faces that stared back at her. But instead of respecting the occasion and chilling out, as all of those faces were suggesting that she do, she jumped defensive. "What the hell y'all looking at?" she asked snappishly and they shook their heads or rolled their eyes, but they all looked away. This was their night out, probably the only one some of them could afford for a while, and they weren't about to let some yucky yuppie like Gina ruin their evening.

Gina then looked at me and Vera. Her sad eyes betrayed the regret she felt after speaking so harshly to those poor folks who had done nothing to her, those same folks she often lauded as the backbone of the black community because they had to endure crap, not only from whites, but from uppity blacks as well.

She rose from her seat, her gorgeous cream-colored Versace pantsuit sparkling against the drab of jeans and jackets that appeared to be the wear of choice inside the restaurant, and urged her phone mate to hold on. "I'll be back," she said to me and Vera and then headed for the exit, deciding wisely to continue her conversation outdoors where the ambience was more conducive to her kind of telephone explosions.

I looked at Vera. "Carter?" I asked.

"Carter," she said. "They're battling over the divorce settlement again. It's pitiful."

It was. But, in a lot of ways, so was Vera. She had changed so much. She wasn't always the fuddy-duddy who couldn't appreciate good times or romance that was totally desperate. She used to be our leader, for crying out loud, the passionate one, the sister with an attitude, but that was before she made it official with Rollie Langston.

I first met her six years before our farewell dinner. I was new in town, taking a job as an assistant professor of history at the University of the District of Columbia after working for two years in Philadelphia, my hometown, at the junior college. We met, oddly enough, right in Anacostia at a campaign rally for some Don King–looking brother who wanted to be mayor. I didn't know jack about the brother and was only attending the rally because I was sightseeing and happened upon the assembled crowd. It was a windy day and the area was filled with blight and trash, and here stood this big man on the steps of the Baptist church urging folks to give him a chance to make their dreams come true. He gave many reasons why we should consider him, mainly because he was tougher on crime—a big problem in D.C. back then—but I couldn't get over his hair. It stood up straight on top of his head, for one thing, and flapped in the wind like brown cotton candy. The brother had to be using some spritz out of this world, I thought, the way it just stood up so high. But Vera took my great attentiveness to her candidate to mean admiration of what he was saying.

"That's right, sister," she said as she handed me a campaign flyer, "we need people like you. We need you to tell your coworkers and everybody you see that Keith Webster is the best man for the job."

I couldn't tell you what she wore that day but she had a fire in her eyes that sparked my interest. I couldn't care less about Keith Webster, but I was curiously drawn to her. "You work for him?" I asked her.

"Not exactly," she said like a Hertz commercial as she handed out more flyers in the area where I stood. "I'm the deputy chief of staff in Delegate Rice's office. Mr. Webster is a friend of hers so I'm just helping out."

There it was. My first conversation with a real live congressional staffer. And it was Vera. I was impressed.

"What about you?" she asked.

"Me? What about me?"

"What are you? I mean, what do you do?"

We both smiled. We hit it off just that quickly. "I teach. I'm an assistant professor of history at the university."

"Which university?"

"You mean there's more than one?" I joked. She smiled. "No, I'm at D.C. right now. Although I hope to get a position I applied for at Howard."

"Howard, is it? I could talk to somebody."

My big eyes became bigger. "Really?"

"Yes," she said, and then she started staring at me.

I looked at my clothing, to make sure everything was secure. "What's wrong?" I asked her.

"I don't mean to sound funny but has anybody ever told you that you look just like Diana Ross? I mean in her younger days, and before all the hair."

I laughed. "Oh yes," I said. "I've been told. But you really can talk to somebody at Howard for me? You really would do that for me?"

She would and she did. She was my first friend in D.C. and I followed her around as if we had suddenly been joined at the hip.

Vera was gorgeous back then, an odd woman who wore dreads and sisterhood beads on the one hand and very expensive, tailored suits on the other. She had compassion and passion that inspired, the kind of unconditional love that kept her in the good graces of everybody who knew her. And although she hailed from a well-to-do family of professionals, she was the kind of person who knew that worthiness wasn't defined by a street address or a degree on a wall.

It was Vera who introduced me to her friend Regina Ridgeway, a woman Vera admired not only for her success as a trial lawyer in one of the best firms in D.C., but also for her undaunted independence. Although Gina was married, Vera would tell me, she kept her maiden Ridgeway name and refused to take on her husband's at all.

"Not even as a hyphenated name?" I asked Vera.

"Not even that, girl," she said, and we both looked at Gina with amazement back then.

We three were so much alike in the things we enjoyed and we hung out together so much that those around us began mocking us as *The Three Blackateers*. Vera found the reference insulting but I was an intricate part of a group for the first time in my life and loved the title. Vera was our leader back then and although she hated the group's name, she loved her role. She was smart, pretty, a congressional staffer. An upwardly mobile sister if ever there was one.

But she married Rollie Langston. They had been dating for a good long time and less than a year after Vera and I became friends he popped the question. I first met Rollie when he worked as a get-out-the-vote coordinator in Keith Webster's campaign. I decided to walk over to headquarters one day to meet Vera for lunch. And there he was, standing at the door like some Mack Daddy, laying that lame *hey, foxy lady, I'd love to know your sign* line on me. I didn't know he was dating Vera at the time and I didn't care. I found his approach, given the environment, so rude and degrading that I felt compelled to tell him so. He immediately apologized, which surprised me, and walked away sheepishly as if even he couldn't believe he'd said that to me.

I grew to appreciate his commitment to the community and his work as a mentor for fatherless boys, but I could never appreciate his old-fashioned ideas about women and their role in society. Rollie and I spent many days arguing about his views, and Gina often joked that he was about as liberated as Archie Bunker, but Rollie didn't care what we thought. He believed a woman should be homebound, slaving over a stove, knocked up, and happy, and if it was up to him, Vera would have been pregnant many times over. But unfortunately and to his great dismay, he couldn't have kids.

But Vera loved him anyway. And just as we predicted, the union changed her forever. He made her quit her job, for one thing, because no wife of his needed to work for a living. When she tried to explain to his crazy butt that it was more than just earning a paycheck that kept her working, he told her never to dispute him in public again. Vera was a smart, well-educated woman from a prominent family of liberals, but her love for Rollie trumped everything else that mattered in her life. She became morphed into Rollie. She became increasingly less tolerant of people and downright spiteful in her criticisms. Rollie referred to me and Gina as sinners and hell-bound folk and she joined in the song too. She could no longer go out with us unless Rollie knew when, where, and why, and our *girls' night out* gig became less and less frequent. Vera declared that it wasn't the way it seemed. She insisted that she was merely changing her ways because of her new understanding of Christianity's teachings on humility. But Gina and I knew better than that. It was Rollie.

Now, six years later, that same Rollie Langston was trying to take our leader away from us for good. I sat at that table in Kumba Bay and looked at Vera, who used to be so vibrant and loving, so full of kindness and affection, as she wilted into an old, settled woman. Rollie's woman.

Vera, as if she could read my mind, responded without looking at me. "Please don't," she said.

"Don't what?"

"Pity me."

"Pity you? Why would I pity you?"

The waiter returned with a glass of gin for me. I guess he could tell too that I needed something infinitely stronger than soda water. When he walked away from the table, I looked at Vera. "Why would I pity you?" I asked again.

"I'm standing by my man. Yes. Mock it all you want."

"But this is your home, V. Why does Rollie have to pack you up and disrupt your entire life like this?"

"His father is ill."

"I know that. But he has a brother already working in that funeral home down there. Why can't he run it? Or why can't Rollie just go down there, help out, and come back? Why does he have to shove you down South when he said himself his brother can handle it?"

"It's not debatable, Victoria. Me and my husband will be starting over in Florida, that's all there is to it. I've got a lot of bad memories here in D.C. This ain't been no paradise for me. I know you don't like Rollie. I know you think his old-fashioned ideas about a woman's place are contrary to everything you believe. But I love him, Tore. And he's a good man. We just need a change, you know? So I don't see Florida as some second-best consolation prize. I see it as a great opportunity for us to start over."

"But Rollie's pushing forty, V. You can't teach an old dog like that new tricks. If he's got those old-fashioned views in D.C., he's gonna have 'em in Florida too. It's not gonna be any better just because you're in a different state."

Vera sipped her soda and then looked at her glass. She looked haggard now. Tired. "Maybe it will, maybe it will not. But at least in Florida there's a chance it'll get better. But if I stay 'round here I know it won't."

She was right. As quickly as the words rolled from her lips I realized how right she was. I was tired too. Of too many unhappy endings and great romances that always end up as day-old bad news; of too many *I'll call you* but they won't, and *I'll be good to you if you give me a chance* but they don't. I had bad memories in D.C. too. Too many bad memories. Why should I hang around for more of the same? Florida, down South, was beginning to sound sweeter the more I thought about it.

"I'm going too," I blurted out before I knew what I was saying. Vera, who was about to sip her soda, stopped midway and looked at me. Then she put the glass down altogether.

"Are you serious, Tory?"

I didn't know if I was or not but ever since Robert left I knew I needed to do something. A relocation may be just the thing, I thought. "I'm serious, girl," I said. "I'm serious as a heart attack."

Vera smiled a great smile of total elation and total disbelief. "Cool!" she said as if that said it all.

"What's cool?" Gina asked as she reappeared at our table. "Because I truly just lost mine with that trifling Carter." She sat down but kept on talking. "You know what that Negro did? He filed papers declaring how our marital problems are all my fault because, and I'm paraphrasing to protect myself, I'm a slut who slept around with every Tom, Dick, and Harry while he was this faithful-as-a-bird-dog good husband who didn't do shit. So please tell me what's so cool because I know it ain't me."

We couldn't respond. Vera was staring at me and I was staring at her. We were both terrified, it showed easily, but we both had a sense of serenity too. Sometimes you can't do it anymore. You can't pretend that tomorrow will bring on better circumstances because you told yourself the same thing all those yesterdays ago but you can psych yourself out just so many times. You get tired of those same excuses. You get tired of lying to yourself and shrouding yourself in so much pretense that you can barely breathe. You decide to get real for once in your life. That great romance ain't happening and that's all there is to it. Or you decide to relocate to Florida and start the charade all over again.

"Hello?" Gina said, waving her hand in our faces. "Excuse me but I'm talking to y'all."

Our trancelike stare broke and we looked at Gina. She was her usual hot-tempered self when she wasn't the center of attention. I knew immediately that she would hate the idea, especially since it would mean she'd be the last remaining member of the group still in D.C. Vera, however, seemed to act as if Gina would be elated with the news.

"Tory's going with me," she said with a grand smile, as if she was realizing for the first time that she wouldn't have to face her new life alone anymore.

"Going with you where?" Gina asked.

"To Florida."

"To Florida?" Gina screamed and Vera, the quintessence of propriety, shushed her.

Gina lowered her voice. "Y'all gots to be jiving!" Then she looked at me. "Tory, I know you jiving, girl."

Then she knew wrong because I was as serious as I had ever been. "Florida State's in Tallahassee, isn't it?" I asked Vera, already planning my suddenly interesting future.

"Yes, ma'am," Vera said. "Florida A and M, a historically black university like Howard, is there too."

"Ham mercy," I said. "This is great. I'll make some inquiries ASAP. I've been teaching at the college level for almost eight years now, I'm sure to get a bite eventually."

"Oh, Tory," Vera said, "this is so wonderful!"

Gina, of course, thought we had both gone nuts. She sat there stunned. She couldn't even speak. Vera looked at her, asked if she was all right. But she didn't say a word. Sistergirl just grabbed her purse and left the building. Just like that. A few months later and she would be right there in Florida with us displaced D.C. folk too. But she wasn't wit it that night.

Tallahassee, Florida, turned out to be just what the doctor ordered. Not only was it a college town known for its big-time football (Florida State Seminoles) and out-of-this-world marching band (Florida A&M's Marching 100s) but it was also the capital of Florida, which meant a lot of activity, which meant Hicksville, USA, it was not. I was relieved.

I arrived in town three weeks after Vera and Rollie. I was excited too, driving into my new life sassy and ready for a change. And it turned out to be a different place, to say the least. It was hilly, for one thing, with slopes and slopes of up-and-down roads that curved too sharp and converged too narrow. The homes weren't upscale town houses or overdone big chateaus, but practical places with big yards and picket fences and kids on bicycles unafraid of being snatched by some pervert or gunned down by some reckless drive-by shooter.

But there was also, of course, the other side of Tallahassee. D.C. had its politicians and Tallahassee had more than its fair share of college kids. They were the energy of the community, or so they thought, even though most of them hovered within the small but busy areas surrounding Florida State University and Florida A&M. They were the ruckus ones on the weekends, especially after a home game at Doak Campbell Stadium where Florida State was the victor and the opponent wasn't some weakling like Wake Forest but another powerhouse like the Gators or Hurricanes. God help the city then. They honked horns and hung out of their car windows, yelling obscenities or bragging about the victory. It was those same students who had the most courage too, who felt it their honor to ride your bumper or blow you off the road or nearly run you over just to cut in front on a mad dash to Burger King. I thought I had gotten away from the bustle when I relocated to Florida. And for the most part I had. But heaven help all lovers of peace and quiet on Saturday nights.

When I first arrived in town I was relieved to know that Vera had done her homework and secured for me a nice condo near the Governor's Square Mall. It was on a dead-end street of transplanted palm trees and live oaks, an apartment-style condominium complex filled with young professionals. My condo was small, one bedroom, with cathedral ceilings, white oak floors, and a balcony that overlooked a man-made lake. The moving people had dropped all of my furnishings in the living-room area and for about a good month after my arrival I was yet sorting through boxes and rummaging through bags, but I loved every bit of my new condo and city and life. The town and my home were perfect, I felt, for starting over.

Vera and Rollie arrived around noon the day after my arrival to give me a tour of the town. I grabbed my sunglasses and hobo bag and took a backseat in Rollie's big Ford Explorer SUV. I had changed, he said, and he couldn't keep his gigantic eyes off of me. I meant to change. My hair was being worn fuller now and I had that bouncy, Oprah look action going on. I worked out daily and went on that cabbage soup diet during the month before my decampment. I had managed to drop eleven whole pounds in what appeared to be all the right places. Now I looked fit and felt fit and was especially thrilled because I did it, not to please some fastidious man in my life, but I did it just for me.

But Brother Rollie could forget that sudden admiration of my beauty crap because I wasn't thinking about his crazy behind. Yet every time I looked up he was looking through the rearview at me. And poor Vera didn't have a clue. She was sitting on the front seat beside her man just talking and having the time of her life, thinking that somehow he would change; that he would allow her to work outside of the home and be herself again; that he would stop his harmless but incessantly flirtatious ways and pay more attention to her for once. She regretted a lot of things: not having children, not pursuing her career despite Rollie's protestations. But she believed deeply that it was just a matter of time before he would eventually come around.

We drove past the Governor's Square Mall (the largest mall in Tallahassee, according to Vera) and up Apalachee Parkway to where it became a dead end into the old State Capitol building. It was midday and Vera beamed when she realized that the governor of Florida himself, along with a pack of state legislators, was at that very moment having a photo-op on the lawn.

"That's the governor!" she yelled. "That's our governor, Tory!"

Whoopdedo, I wanted to say. We were from D.C., remember,

Vera? The other *capital?* The place where the president of all these United States was in view on a regular basis? And she expected me to get all hyped over some *governor?*

But Vera was so excited that I couldn't burst her bubble. She got enough of that from everybody else. "Yeah, child," I said instead. "I see the governor. Ain't it something?"

From the State Capitol we visited the Supreme Court building, an old drab structure that looked desperately in need of renovation. A black man, Leander Shaw, was chief justice once, Rollie said. "Isn't *that* something?"

"Not really," I said. "I shook hands with Clarence Thomas before. A state Supreme Court justice who happens to be black is nothing to me."

"But he was the *chief* justice," Rollie said.

"And?" I said.

Rollie's goo-goo eyes turned bitter. Vera turned to look out of her passenger-side window. A small but noticeable smile crossed her face.

Rollie's bitterness remained as his tour of the town became more and more obscure. Instead of showing me the places I wanted to see, like the universities, for instance, he decided to take me on a tour of places from his past. He showed me the house he grew up in on Virginia Street and the church he was christened in on Call Street and the elementary school he attended on Gadsden Street. It wasn't until he was about to take me to the funeral home where he received his first tutelage that I spoke up. This was nice, I told him, but where was FSU?

He drove to the campus, begrudgingly, and insisted on showing me more the perimeters than the belly of the school. There was the huge waterfall in front of the administration building; the arch that led to the old, brick dormitories; fraternity row, with Rollie, of course, making a point of showing me the sorority house where Ted Bundy killed those girls. "It was like a black cloud over the city," he said.

"How sad," I said, but urged him to move on.

From there we drove over to Florida A&M University, or FAM-U as it was called. It was half the size of Florida State, maybe even smaller, with a slower sense about it. The urgency that seemed to hover around FSU was more steady here, as students came and went at their own pace, walking and talking or just hanging around.

The campus had its share of old, brick buildings too but the main spot, for the students anyway, was what Rollie referred to as The Set.

"The what? Where?"

He pointed to an area on campus that was distinguishable by nothing, where many students simply stood around. "There," he said. "It's called The Set. A college kid's version of the hangout corner."

Leave it to black folks, I thought, to find a hangout corner on a college campus. I would later learn, of course, that The Set was much more than Rollie's definition, that it was a place where speeches were made and information shared and intellectuals converged for good talk and comradery not unlike gatherings at the local café in Georgetown or the coffee shop on Capital Hill. But that was Rollie: a champion of his people and their harshest critic too.

From there we drove past the Museum of Florida History, a nature preserve, and the Tallahassee Community College. I had applied for employment at all of the three schools we toured and was eager to see what I was up against. All three schools were charming, I thought, with FSU dwarfing the size of the other two. But I felt I didn't stand a chance at a good-old-boys, Bobby Bowden kind of school like FSU, and accepting a position at a community college would seem like a demotion. FAM-U, the only historically black university in Tallahassee, was my choice.

Three weeks later and I became their choice as well. Associate Professor of History became my title and I accepted without even knowing what my pay grade would be.

I settled down in Florida. I worked, came home, watched C-SPAN, and loved my life again. I refused to date for an entire year, even after Gina relocated to Florida and tried her best to rekindle my interest. But I wasn't wit it. I was terrified of another bad relationship. I was terrified of losing myself in somebody else again. Even Gina never fully understood how completely I fell in love when I decided to go down that road. The love affair became my life. I couldn't take it easy. I couldn't take it slow. I plunged in every time. Even with a jerk like Robert. I just knew he was the one when everybody and their half-blind mamas could see the truth. But that's me. Obsessive to the core. I don't just fall in love. I crave the love with a kind of desperation that no man can handle. That was why I refused to date. I wasn't about to come all this way to Florida to get knocked down again.

But as the months came and went in Florida and my single status began slowly to start bothering me again, I became terrified, not of dating, but of contentment. What if, I thought, this was it for me? Work, C-SPAN, and the occasional night out with the girls. What if this was as good as it was going to get? I wasn't getting any younger, after all, Gina and Vera both did not hesitate to remind me. "That's right," Gina said on the night of my thirty-fourth birthday party, "you're old as hell now!"

The fear of spending the rest of my life alone gripped me and wouldn't let me go as the months began to pile up in Tallahassee. Even Gina had remarried since she arrived in Florida (to Isaac Becker, husband number four) and I didn't even have a prospect. I didn't want to be alone, that was the bad part about it. I wanted to share my life with someone. I realized it more than ever when I turned thirty-four and that *never been asked* stigma still hung over my head like the black sword of Damocles. Single. Unmarried. Unattached. OLD MAID.

It was fear, then, more than anything else, that drove me to it—but I did it. I informed the girls that I was back in circulation, ready to get into the game of love all over again. It was a terrifying decision for me, given my track record, but I was praying for a good turn.

I got a good turn all right. First there was Malcolm. Gina picked this character. He wanted to break into show business and never hesitated to demonstrate his abilities. He was an airhead when you got down to it, a man who actually believed that Tallahassee, Florida, was the southern version of New York City. When I, foolishly, asked him to justify such a statement, he merely said that he had a "gut feeling" about this and knew, one day, that he would be proven right. So Brains R Us he was not, but he was nice enough and good looking (very), so I tolerated him.

The first date was the best one and it was pretty terrible. Gina introduced us at the Red Lobster restaurant and left. Malcolm then proceeded to serenade me with his off-key, high-pitched renditions of his favorite Broadway tunes. To say the brother sounded bad would be a gross misrepresentation. He stunk. Not only could he not sing a note on key but he often didn't even know the words to the title of the songs, let alone the songs themselves, forcing him to make up words as he went along. "Come to the Cabaret," for instance, was "Come to the Castle Maid" to Malcolm. "Life is a Castle Maid, oh chum," he'd sing, "come to the Castle Maid!"

But when he started singing "Feelings," where his "oh-oh-oh's" were out of tune to such a degree that everybody at Red Lobster was actually laughing at the man, I wanted to crawl under the table. But he meant well and although he was self-centered as hell he treated me a sight better than a lot of my past dates, so I kept on tolerating the intellectually challenged hunk.

And my desperate behind went out on a second date with him. He took me to his apartment this time and put on a one-man show for me. I almost turned and walked back out when he announced his intentions, but I didn't have the heart to do it. He was so excited that I started getting excited too. Maybe his acting abilities were better than his singing ones, I surmised. I was wrong.

The entire show centered on his conversations with "The Man," his pseudonym for a white cop, about police brutality. "The Man" was a chair with a broom standing in it and your boy Malcolm would walk around this chair preaching to the broom about how demoralizing it is when a cop knocks a brother upside his head. "Them licks hurt!" he yelled to the broom.

I crossed my legs and sat there amazed by what I was watching. This guy was either psychotic or just plain nuts, I couldn't decide which. And Malcolm was serious too. At one point he took the broom and started slinging it around the room. "How that feel?" he asked the broom as he slung it against the wall. "You ain't big and bad no more, is you? You ain't Mr. Tough Policeman no more, is you?" He stomped on the broom, got on his knees and snatched straws out of the broom, cursed the broom's breath and talked about the broom's mama. I was so beside myself with anger that I wanted to take that broom and sweep Malcolm's ass out the door for wasting my time like this.

But as I said, he was very good looking, so I endured it. And even agreed to go on a third date with the man-child! But this time I wised up. I asked him, at the door of my condo when he arrived to pick me up, what did he have in store for us tonight? When he said he had just created a Mr. Bojangles soft-shoe routine that was sure to knock my socks off, I took a pass. Forever.

Then there was William. Vera's discovery. And William was surprisingly cool for a Vera selection. He dressed in snazzy blazers and tailored pants, had the *yeah, I'm bad* swagger down to an art form, and had the looks that made him come across as God's gift to women.

He would have been God's gift to me too if it wasn't for his breath. I mean it stank. The first time I sniffed it was at a restaurant. But I figured he probably had onions for lunch and forgot to freshen up. But on our next date and the smell was still there, I began to get suspicious. But it wasn't anything I worried about. I just pretended that my throat was dry and pulled out an Altoid. And instead of offering him one I affectionately dropped one into his mouth. He smiled.

The smell would go away for a while but it kept coming back. One night, when he and I met Gina and her husband Isaac for drinks, his breath was especially horrific. This was Gina's first encounter with William and she was not amused.

"Wait a minute," she said in the middle of our small-talk chitchat. "Somebody got some serious halitosis up in here! Now whoever it is, and you know who you are, you need to drag your behind into the rest room and drink a bottle or two of Listerine because I'm not about to spend my well-planned evening holding my nose!"

I looked down at my drink. I was embarrassed for William but somebody had to tell the brother something. I was too cowardly. Gina was not.

It was his response, however, that sealed the fate of our romance. Instead of standing up like a man and apologizing for his offensive odor, he tried to put the blame on me.

"I told Victoria over and over she needed to get that taken care of," he said, grinning as if he had just told some cute joke.

Gina started to tell him a thing or two, she even geared up by pointing her finger at him, but I beat her to the punch this time.

"Me?" I asked incredulously. "No, you ain't trying to put this on me! Your breath curled my hair the other day, William, I know you ain't trying to act like you don't realize your problem!"

Maybe he didn't. Maybe he honestly thought it was me. But I'm willing to bet he knows the truth now.

Then there was Alexander *Denzel* Moffit. A Gina blind-date selection for me. I thought I had struck gold when I met Alexander. The brother was smart, good looking, and so articulate that he mesmerized me with his words.

But that romance was short-lived too. Alexander, it seemed, had one little problem. He was a woman trapped in a man's body and had every intention of someday getting a sex-change operation. But he, of course, didn't see a problem at all.

"It's cool," he said. "Because I'm actually a lesbian."

I looked at the brother for a full three minutes just trying to figure out what he had just said. He was a man who wanted to be a woman but he didn't want to be a woman to date men but to date women, which he was already doing anyway. He called himself a lesbian but I had another name for him. "Confused," I said, and that was the end of that romance.

But of all the blind dates they had set me up with, Vera's *he ain't no Billy dee* date absolutely took the prize.

That was why I slammed that door of Vera's apartment so hard that I think I broke the nose of the man behind it. I wanted to kill Vera. And if it wasn't for Rollie's intervention I would have. Sistergirl then had the nerve to tell me to calm down, that it wasn't as bad as it seemed. "Then you date him," I said. "You go out in public with him!"

"I told you he was no Billy dee. I told you that."

"But you didn't tell me he was subhuman looking, Vera. Now, did you?"

"Come on, Tory," Rollie said. "Peter's not that bad."

"Yeah, right."

"He's not," Vera said. "And he has a wonderful personality."

If sistergirl only knew how close to death she was, she would have closed her mouth immediately. But she kept going, praising this Peter as if he were the incarnated Christ. Even Rollie praised him, saying how he was really a very nice guy. That was unusual for Rollie. He normally stayed out of it. He normally let me and Vera go through our yelling matches over her various choices of men for me and pretend he had no opinion whatsoever. But even he was praising this Peter. Besides, the poor man *was* standing outside the door. "Okay," I said. "Okay. I'll complete the date with him. But this is the last blind date you will ever, and I mean ever, set up for me. Understood?"

42

"Yes, yes," Vera said. She would have said anything to get me to stay the course.

She hurriedly opened the front door. Peter, who looked like a cross between an alligator and a praying mantis, had already turned and was descending the apartment stairs, his bowlegs bent out so wide that he looked as if he were walking stooped down.

"Peter!" Vera yelled. "Where are you going?"

He was embarrassed, we could tell. "The door was slammed so I assumed—"

"You assumed what?" Vera asked sympathetically. She was mush when it came to lonely people.

"I assumed I wasn't what she expected so, you know . . ."

"Don't be ridiculous," Vera said, going onto the porch to retrieve him. "Her makeup wasn't right, that's all." Vera had lied. I was surprised. It was the first lie I had ever heard her speak.

She escorted him back to the apartment and we all found ourselves safely inside. It was awkward from the start. Vera forgot to introduce us and began ushering us into the living room, talking on and on about how lovely it was that we both were able to make it. Rollie offered sodas (they did not drink) and Vera asked us to excuse her and Rollie while they checked on dinner.

And then there were two: Peter and me. We sat on the couch. He smiled politely in my direction but I had neither the will nor inclination to smile back. He was so hard to look at that I tried to avoid eye contact as much as possible. And then he spoke. "I'm Peter Lawrence," he said. "You must be Tory."

I looked at him. His head was especially big and his eyes reminded me of Clarence the Cross-eyed Lion. I looked away. "How are you?" I said.

"Pretty good," he said and seemed momentarily rejuvenated. But when I did not follow up my greeting with some nice chitchat and the conversation died as quickly as it had begun, he faded back into his quietness.

Vera came back quickly, with Rollie behind her, but even they couldn't lighten the mood. We all sat around that living room as if we had just come from a funeral. Rollie tried to talk about the proverbial weather and Peter Lawrence tried to chime in, but the awkwardness was too entrenched. Every two minutes I had the urge to get up and leave. It was not worth it, I felt. I was wasting my time. Hell, I could have been watching C-SPAN!

"Peter's a schoolteacher, Tory, did you know that?" Vera asked me. Naturally I said no.

"Yes, he is," Rollie said, surprising the hell out of me. "A very good one too."

Peter smiled. "Thanks, Rollie, I do my best."

"You do more than that. Did you know, Tory, that Peter here was named teacher of the year three years running?"

Three years? That *was* impressive. "No, I didn't know," I said as if I was wholly unimpressed. I did not want him to think, even for the slightest moment, that I was interested in him in the least. I did not like to be led on and I was not leading on. We'd eat this dinner, go to this play, and that would be the end of this fiasco, was my motto that night. But Vera and Rollie insisted on lifting up praises of Peter so much that Peter himself began joining in.

"It was tough," he said. "But I made it through, thank the Lord."

"Made it through," Vera said. "Child, please. You graduated with honors. Everybody can't graduate from college with honors."

"This is true," Peter said. "I guess you can say I'm on the smart side."

Well, I hoped so, given his looks. But I didn't care if he was Albert Einstein, I still was not interested. In fact, the longer they went on about his graduating with honors (whoopdedo!), the more determined I was to end the date early. I would stay for dinner (that was fair), but no way was I going to the theater with *him*. No way. I motioned for Vera to follow me into the kitchen and I told her so.

"Don't do this, Tory," she said. "He's a wonderful guy."

"I'm sure he is. But I'm not interested."

"He's not asking you to marry him. He's lonely. He just wants a little company, that's all."

Vera made it seem so simple, and she also made me seem so foolish. What was my problem? He did appear to be a nice, decent fella. Why was I bitching about his looks so much? I was no Vanessa Williams myself. And it wasn't as if we had to make a commitment. There was still such a thing as *just friends.*

So I went along with Vera's assessment of the situation. That was my first mistake. Soon, I even began enjoying Peter's company. That was my second mistake. And by the time we ate dinner and had seen the play, a revival of *Ragtime,* I was in a downright good mood. I even invited Peter over to my house for drinks. And that was my ultimate mistake. He was so excited by my invitation that he took a moment to pray. I found it amusing at the time. I found it even cute at the time. I was naive.

"Make yourself at home," I said as we walked into the front door of my condo.

Peter commented on the beauty of the place (especially the view) and I went off into the kitchen to make drinks. I could not have been gone for more than five minutes. But when I returned to the living room, Mr. Peter Lawrence was butt naked sitting on my sofa. I dropped both glasses of wine to the floor. He looked like Humpty Dumpty in a brown bodysuit sitting there. I was at first shocked. And then I was mad as hell.

"What do you think you're doing?"

"Who, me?" he asked as if he was seriously confused.

"No," I said. "The couch. I'm talking to the couch."

"Oh, this," he said and smiled his gap-toothed smile. "You told me to make myself at home. This is how I hang out at home."

I looked immediately at his penis when he said that. No hanging there.

"Get out of my apartment please," I said, trying not to grab my broom and run him out.

"Pardon me?" he said as if he were a little kid. "What did I do?"

"Get out of my apartment please."

"What did I do?"

"Get out of my apartment, *please!*"

A look of agonizing shame crossed his face. He had read me wrong. He thought my good humor at the theater meant I wanted him sexually. He thought my invitation for drinks at my place meant he was going to get laid. Well, normally it would have meant those things. But Peter Lawrence was not my normal type of date. I could never find him sexually attractive but I thought, given his good nature, that we could be friends. That was why I relaxed around him. That was why I invited him up. It had nothing to do with sex. Yet he thought it had everything to do with sex. I guess I should have told him up front. But given his looks, I assumed he knew.

All I wanted was to fill a void with his friendship. I figured he was lonely and I was lonely and it seemed logical that we could team up occasionally and go to a movie or a play or out to dinner. But for homeboy to have the nerve to get naked in my living room (on my couch!) was too much.

He realized it too as he scrambled to put on his clothes. I'll admit I felt sorry for him but I was still too angry to let any kind of sympathy get in the way. He had exposed himself to me. Every inch of himself. He did not ask me if my eyes could take it, or even wanted to try, he just did it. Tory's a lonely, unattached, thirty-four-year-old female, I'm sure he surmised. Why would she care? Well, I cared. Just one look was all it took.

He tried to apologize for his misjudgment but I would have none of it. Robert and all those blind-date losers toughened me. I was taking very little from men in those days, especially the ones I couldn't care less about. I told Peter I didn't want to hear it, just leave. He left. And then I called Vera.

"If I was about to die on some deserted island somewhere and a guy you believe would be perfect for me was the only one who could save me, let me die, Vera. You hear me? Let me die, girl-friend!"

"It couldn't have been *that* bad," Vera said in her best deep voice.

"Oh, honey, it was bad. Do you know what that choirboy did tonight?"

"What?"

"He walked into the door of my apartment and proceeded to get stark naked right in my living room!"

"You're lying!" Vera was always saying "you're lying!" every time somebody told her something shocking. It was as if she did not really believe anything anybody said to her. You always had to give more details before Vera would bite. I, however, was not in the mood to give sistergirl anything.

"No more dates, blind or otherwise, from you to me, okay?"

"But why would he get naked? I don't understand."

"Good night, Vera."

"I've known Peter for years. He's not like that. You must have told him something."

"Oh, right, Vera. I forgot. I told him to please make himself at home by getting naked on my couch because I would love to see his beautiful body."

"Don't be patronizing."

"No, you don't patronize me. I must have told him something! How could you say that? Yeah, I told him something, all right. I told him to get his Jell-O ass out of my house, that's what I told him!"

And then I hung up the phone. And pulled out a cigarette and turned on C-SPAN. If I didn't date another living soul as long as I lived, that would have been fine with me.

I felt that way, however, before I met the Moon.

It was a Friday night and the entire faculty was invited to the university president's house for a dinner party. I had no intentions of going, finding those pretentious get-togethers about as exciting as some of those blind dates I had to endure. But Arnold Miller, the dean of the College of Arts and Sciences, made it clear that his departments would have "one hundred percent compliance." Of course he could not mandate that we attend some after-hours party, but if we expected to curry any favor with him, we had better attend.

I attended. I arrived late, as usual, and walked into the big house of crystal chandeliers and arch-top chairs as if get-togethers were the joy of my life too. I worked hard to look good, wearing a stylish tobacco-brown Donna Karan pantsuit, a matching pair of stack-heel slipper shoes, and a cute brown clutch. I had my hair done (slicked down with a bouncy-up flip), my nails done, and my toes done. I looked good and felt as if I looked good. But I still dreaded the occasion.

The house was packed with people, almost all of whom I didn't know at all or, if I knew, I barely knew. I immediately searched for Dean Miller. He was the only reason that I came. I had no desire to teach a freshman cram-the-history-of-the-world-into-one-semester course and I was determined to stay in his good graces to avoid such a fate.

When I saw him I hurried to him. He was surrounded, as usual, by other kiss-up professors and professor wannabes who knew that most promotions went through Dean Miller's office first. I wasn't very good at kissing up, my personality was a bit too spontaneous for that, but I knew how to endear favor when I needed to. I spoke to him and his posse, commented on how handsome he looked tonight, and tried to laugh at his ill-humored jokes.

"There was this black man in the Old South who was traveling ninety miles an hour in a fifty-five-mile-an-hour zone," he said. "The state trooper stopped him and asked what was his problem. 'Why are you driving ninety, sir?' he asked. 'Because,' the black man said, 'that sign said ninety was the speed us could go.' The trooper was puzzled. 'Where does any sign anywhere on this highway say ninety miles an hour is the speed you can drive?' The black man pointed to the sign on the side of the road signifying highway U.S. 90. 'See,' he said. 'It says *us 90*.'"

The crowd roared. Dean Miller, pumped, kept on. "That state trooper looked at that black man with wonderment. 'Thank God I stopped you before you got to *us* 115,' he said."

Another roar that was so exaggerated that even the kiss-ups from other groups had to look over. I walked away. All of these intellectual black folks poking fun at those less fortunate wasn't my idea of a barrel of laughs. But that was what these parties were all about. A time for like-minded successful people to get together and gloat. They made it, their suddenly sophisticated manner of dress, speech, and even menu—no soul food allowed!—clearly demonstrated, and tough luck to all those suckers who didn't. And we used to be a village, so in love with our own culture and speech and hipness that we had room at the inn for whosoever wished to come. Come, they now say, but only if you're driving a Lexus-BMW-Jag-Benz, college-educated, well connected, and making the kind of big bucks alien to most black folks in America. It was a new culture now. The culture of go-getter snobs with misplaced priorities.

That was why I loved Gina so much. She made it, she could draw rings around most everybody in the room, but she never checked out. And if she was here and heard Dean Miller's so-called joke, she'd interrupt as only she could and set the brother straight. And the College of Arts and Sciences would never have been the same again.

But I was no Gina. I had a mouth, all right, but in times of controversy it was generally a muted one. Instead of confrontation I pretended I didn't hear the joke or insult and would walk away. Like that Friday night. I grabbed a glass of wine from the tray of a waiter passing by and walked away. Only I walked right into another crowd. A women's group. Their pet peeve, of course, was men.

"All dogs, every one," the woman who appeared to be the leader, given her constant babbling, said. "My daddy was a dog. My grand-daddy was a dog. My brother was a dog. Every man I've ever met was nothing but a dog."

"*Dog!*" I said and they all looked at me as if I were the sister from another planet. I moved on.

I ended up standing alone against the side of the living-room wall, near the gaudy fireplace. I looked around, at those well-dressed brothers and sisters, my peers, and I knew as I had never known before that this was not my crowd. Give me Gina and Vera and even crazy Rollie any day. But not this group. Not these self-righteous, convoluted, get-on-your-last-damn-nerve egomaniacs please. Besides, I had just begun another book, *A Different Drummer* by William Melvin Kelley, and I could have been home relaxing and reading it. That was why I slipped my glass of wine on the tray of another passing waiter and turned to exit.

As soon as I turned I saw him. He was already looking at me. At first I thought he was Judge Joe Brown from the television show. He had the same hairstyle—that soft, short Afro cut, the same pale yellowish complexion, and that same frosty-eye look that made you wonder if he was drunk or had fallen asleep standing up. But he didn't have the mustache or the bulkiness. He had a tall, athletic body and he wore a double-breasted Armani suit with the same ease that most folks wore jeans. Distinguished was his look. A tall, dis-tinguished gentleman. When I realized he was not some television celebrity but a gorgeous man who might actually be interested in me, my heart sang. Finally, I thought. But I had to do this right. I immediately grabbed another glass of wine from the tray of another passing waiter and slowly turned and headed back toward my posi-tion next to the fireplace (perfect positioning, I thought). Yet when I turned back around I did not see Mr. Dreamboat but an odd-looking, mousy professor by the name of Jake Onstead standing di-rectly in front of me.

"Hello, Doctor Coleman," he said and grinned.

I almost jumped out of my skin, but then I thought to use this sudden intrusion to my advantage. Perhaps Jake could tell me all I needed to know about Mr. Dreamboat. His name, age, *marital status*, for instance. I therefore quickly summoned his help, asking him to ease his way from in front of me, *without looking back*, move beside me, *without looking back*, and then slowly turn around and toward the direction in which I was facing.

Jake, being who he was, skipped the first two steps and looked back. I could have wrung his chicken neck. "What?" he asked as if all of my prior directives were just hyperbole.

"I told you not to look back," I said.

"But why?"

"Because," I said. "Over there."

I looked where Dreamboat had been standing, to show Jake what I was talking about, but Dreamboat had sailed. My heart dropped.

"I don't see anything," Jake said, squinting his eyes as he looked around. He was one of those short, bespectacled mathematics professors with the bow tie, part on the side of the hair, pencil pile in the shirt pocket, the works. He was also the most unpretentious man I knew and my favorite person on the staff. But I could have killed him that night.

My big brown eyes focused like laser beams around the room. My dream man could not have gone that far, I reasoned. It had only taken a minute, seconds even, for me to turn and walk toward the fireplace. Nobody, not even Superman, could have booked that fast. And sure enough he was still there, this time in Dean Miller's group, but only he wasn't laughing at the jokes.

"There he is!" I yelled.

"Who?" Jake asked and squinted his already tiny eyes.

"That man over there, next to Dean Miller."

"What man?"

"That man, Jake. Look."

I had to literally take his face in my hands and point it in the right direction. "Oh," he said as if he were suddenly discovering some worthless secret. "Moon McCalister."

"*Moon* McCalister? That's his name?"

"His real name is actually Derrick McCalister. But everybody calls him Moon."

"Why?"

"I haven't the foggiest."

Moon McCalister. It was a name that didn't seem to fit. I would have expected a man as impressive looking as he to have an equally impressive name. Preston Osbach the Third, maybe. Or Hilton Honeycutt the Fourth. But Moon?

"Who is he?" I asked. If his name was the worst thing about him I would count my blessings still.

"He's a local hero of sorts. A do-gooder. He does a lot for the poor, serves on a number of commissions and boards and such. He was once a city councilman for a number of years."

"Really?"

"Yes. He's a real estate developer by profession, however."

"I see. Wealthy, is he?"

"Very. He's also a very good friend of FAM-U's. Contributes much money, time, and, of course, real estate expertise."

"How well do you know him?"

"We're not friends, if that's what you mean. He's just a big man around here, active in the community, that's all. I thought everybody knew the Moon."

Everybody, it seemed, except me. "Is he married?"

Jake grinned. "You don't be kidding, do you?"

"Is he, Jake?"

I was in pain to hear the answer. Jake saw this and cut the jokes. "No," he said. My heart leaped.

"But why would he be," he added, "when every woman in the state would love to get their paws on him?"

He was right. What in the world was I thinking? That gorgeous hunk of a human couldn't possibly be interested in me. Or if he was, his interest lasted about as long as it took me to turn and walk to the fireplace. He was too perfect to want some *nothing to write home about* person like me. And as quickly as I thought about it, my suspicion was confirmed. A beautiful sister in a cute green dress and the kind of heels that made stilettos look flat walked over to him and began flirting all over the place. She knew how to work that thang and was slinging it in every direction. I was out of my league. I looked like Slew-foot Sue compared to her. Why would he want me when he could have some well-experienced seductress? And the way his eyes stared at her without even blinking. He was probably undressing her where they stood. And although he seemed to find Dean Miller's jokes distasteful, her attempt at hurling jokes appeared to be a riot.

"See you Monday, Jake," I said and set my glass of wine on the fireplace mantelpiece. No more heartbreaks for me, thank you.

"Don't leave, Vick, come on," Jake insisted, but by that time I was well on my way.

My car wouldn't start. I got in, turned the ignition, and nothing. It was the first time this had ever occurred. Jake, who had walked me to my car, motioned for me to roll down the window.

"What's the matter?" he asked.

"It won't start."

"What do you mean?"

"It won't start."

"Give it some gas."

"I gave it some gas."

"Give it some more."

"Then I'll flood it, Jake, and I'll need a boost on top of whatever it is that I already need."

"Who told you that nonsense? Pat that gas pedal and turn the ignition."

Jake wanted to play the big man that night, I could hear it in his weak but commanding voice. He once asked if I could be interested in somebody like him, some quirky mathematician, as he called himself. When I told him no, that he was definitely not my type, I expected our friendship, such as it was, to end right then and there. But it didn't. And the subject never came up again.

But it still didn't stop him from trying to impress me at every turn. So I did as he commanded and patted on the gas pedal again and turned the ignition key again. Nothing. Do it again, he said. And then again, he said. I did. And I did. On my last gas-patting, ignition-key-turning attempt, it didn't even try to turn over. The sound of clicking could be heard.

"See," I said as I stepped out of the car. "I told you it would flood."

Jake rubbed the back of his neck. He was a mathematics professor who knew how to figure out a problem better than most. Only his problems always had theories to back them up, and formulas. Cars weren't quite so tame. Sometimes they just didn't want to act right and all the theorems and equations weren't about to change that fact.

I stood at the foot of the driveway, where my car was parked, and looked around at the ritzy environment I had thrust myself upon, knowing how embarrassed I would be for my image-conscious coworkers to come out of that big house and see me nursing a broken-down old Camry. Jake, apparently, had thought about it too.

"I guess we ought to call Triple A," he said.

"Triple A? You aren't gonna look under the hood?"

"For what?"

"To see what the problem might be."

"We know what the problem is. It won't crank."

No shit, Sherlock, I wanted to say. "But why won't it, Jake?" I asked instead.

He didn't know. And I didn't either. Jake didn't even own a car, he walked or hitched a ride everywhere he had to go, so we were forced to looked around for help, at a driveway loaded with cars but void of people. After about half an hour of this, folks slowly started trickling out. We stood like beggars at the foot of our college president's driveway and asked the various professional people as they came and went if they could kindly give us some assistance. They were either in a hurry, had a prior engagement, couldn't, or wouldn't. Jake suggested again that we call Triple A but neither one of us had Triple A or any other type of towing service so I suggested he forget that. And our dear brothers and sisters of the struggle, who probably had the good sense to have Triple A every one, weren't about to get involved. In their village my misfortune was entirely my fault. I should have had towing service, one brother even came out and said. And if I didn't, well, that sounded like a personal problem to him.

But that's when I saw the Moon.

He was standing there, near the front door, smoking a cigarette and looking unblinkingly in my direction. It wasn't until I looked at him, however, that he decided to walk over. But my heart wasn't in the leaping-for-joy mood anymore. If that beautiful figure-eight model he found so humorous couldn't satisfy him, I knew I couldn't.

"What seems to be the trouble?" he asked as he stepped his sparkling wingtip shoes onto the graveled drive near my broken-down Camry. The floodlight that hovered just below the front crest of the president's home shone around him as if an angel had suddenly appeared. Even the gods loved the man.

"It won't crank," Jake moved between us and said.

Moon looked at the car as if he were inspecting it prior to purchase. "Well," he said, "that is a problem." He walked away from Jake's side and ended up beside me. His cologne was so sweet and alluring that I suddenly felt light-headed. I couldn't look at him. I just stared at the car.

"Whose automobile is it? Is it yours?" He said this and looked at me.

"Guilty as charged," I said. He hesitated and then laughed.

Then he began removing his expensive suit coat. Without saying a word he handed it to me. I accepted it, gladly, and pulled it against my body.

"Pop the hood," he said to Jake. Jake, knowing the manner of man we were dealing with better than I did, hurried to obey his command. And Moon McCalister, who couldn't look better if I was to dream him up myself, walked around to the front of my car and lifted the hood. I slyly sniffed his suit coat. I nearly staggered back drunk from the sweet aroma.

"You all right, Vick?" Jake asked caustically as he walked over by Moon.

"Yes," I said like a whisper.

I moved over to where the two men stood. Jake, still trying to play the big man, suggested that it was probably the battery.

"I'm sure it is now," I said and they both turned my way. Moon's eyes gave me a quick once-over, as if he was sizing me up for something, and I quickly looked away, at the car—my crutch that night.

"I kept pressing the gas is what I mean. And then it flooded."

"I see," Moon said and turned his attention back to the matter at hand. From where I stood, which was just behind him, his shoulders were broad and his back straight inside his Italian silk white shirt, and his backside, well, talk about a pair of perfectly rounded buns. Just looking at them made me think of Charmin. But I had to keep my wits about me. The brother was too good to be true.

"It's probably just the battery," Jake said again, "and all she needs is for somebody to give her a boost."

"How old is this car?" Moon asked and turned toward me.

"It's a ninety-four," I said.

"Well," he said, pulling out a handkerchief and wiping his big hands. "It could be anything. The battery, the starter, the timing belt. A number of things. Do you have Triple A, young lady?"

Young lady, I thought. Nobody had called me young in quite a while. *Just how old is he?* "No," I said. "I don't have Triple A, B, or C, or nothing else."

He chuckled. And then he pulled out his cell phone. I looked at Jake with one of those *this guy can't be for real* looks. I mean the brother was going to call his auto club for me. That was decent. But Jake was looking as if it was no big deal to him.

"Hello, Ralph?" Moon said into his cell phone. "This is McCalister. I have a '94 Toyota Camry at Walt Sanders's house. It won't crank. I need you to get over here now and tow it in. Call me on the cell when you determine what's wrong with it. The keys will be on the front seat. Say again? You're in bed? Then get out of bed." And he flipped the phone off.

He ordered Jake to set the keys on the front seat and ordered me to come with him. I immediately realized that he wasn't the kind of man who waited for an answer, or asked somebody to do something. Like with me. He didn't ask if I would follow him. He told me to follow. I was usually very turned off by bossy men. But Moon was different.

With his suit coat still across my arm I followed him like a lapdog across the graveled drive, into the street, and two blocks up from the house. He had that long, athlete's stride like Robert and he didn't seem to care that I could hardly keep up. I looked back at Jake. Jake just stood there stupefied.

A pearl-colored Jaguar was parked alone on the street two blocks away from the president's house. I'd heard of folks parking their cars away from the crowd to prevent door dings, but two blocks away? By the time he opened the passenger door for me, I was about out of breath. I had worked out pretty good prior to relocating to Florida but hadn't seen the inside of a gym since. Two blocks wasn't chicken's feed when you rarely walked anywhere.

It didn't dawn on me that I was getting into a car with a total stranger until I actually got inside and the door was closed. But the beautiful ivory-colored leather seats and the scent of Moon's intoxicating cologne all over the car only intensified my already suffi-cient lack of prudence. That's the kind of power certain men had over me. As soon as I saw them as a possibility, I lost all common sense.

Moon sat down on the driver's seat and cranked up. "My man will let us know when your car is ready," he said. "Okay?"

Now what did the brother think I was going to say? No? "Okay," I said.

And we rode off. Just like that. He could have been another Jack the Ripper for all I knew, but a ride like this with a man like Moon didn't come along every day. It was a chance I had to take.

Three

One Moment in Time

Tallahassee was alive at night as cars honked horns and raced by with the urgency of a rush-hour dash. Everybody was in a hurry, flying by, shooting in and out of lanes, cutting into this fast-food restaurant, that filling station, this side-street liquor store. It was the students, with their souped-up old cars or sparkling brand-new cars, that fueled most of the traffic, but a few of us grown-ups could also be spotted in the swirl of activity that was Friday night.

Moon McCalister drove the speed limit, not too slow, not too fast, and turned onto busy Tennessee Street with the ease of a man who knew where he was going. He had his jazz playing slow, his fingers strumming the steering wheel as if it were a guitar, his mind seemingly miles away from the reality of the ride. I wasn't very animated either, sitting there quietly, my legs crossed and arms folded, but my ride wasn't quite as mellow. There was a lot I needed to know and wanted desperately to ask, but I was still too moonstruck to make any waves.

As his jazz CD came to an end and the quiet lull between songs permeated our space, he looked over at me until I returned his stare. "You all right?" he asked.

"Yes," I responded quickly, smiling too eagerly for the pro I was trying to put myself out as, and he glanced a little longer at me and then turned his attention back to the dark road ahead of us.

I felt so disgusted by my ever-lurking sense of desperation that I could hardly stand myself. Just when I knew it was unsafe to get back into the water, I plunged in anyhow. And this time I met me a live, woman-eating shark, the kind of man who knew the game inside out; who had only to say jump and every woman around would yell *how high?*; who probably had so many females at his disposal that he could cast them aside as easy as picking up a rock and throwing it down. Now I was one of his pebbles. Now I was once again setting myself up for another hapless romance.

I started to tell him to stop the car and let me out, that my heart wasn't strong enough to handle another break, but he spoke before I could say anything. "Thanks," he said, "for allowing me to help you."

It was an odd thing to say, I thought, even a sad thing to say, but I had yet to discover anything ordinary about Moon McCalister. "You're welcome," I said. "Thank *you*."

And those few words greatly minimized my doubts and made me more than willing to take the chance. If I was wrong it would be a heartbreak that could probably rival any that I'd ever had. But if I was right and he was indeed everything he appeared to be, then Lord have mercy because I would be high; because cloud nine would be too low for me.

McCalister Enterprises was a substantial real estate conglomerate with operations in northeast Florida, southeast Georgia, and Alabama. The company had developed a hotel in Georgia, a mall in Alabama, and over fifty subdivisions in Florida, and those were just the recent projects. Derrick *Moon* McCalister, a graduate in architectural engineering from Georgia Tech, returned to his hometown of Tallahassee "many moons ago" to begin his professional career in architectural design. When no one would hire him at the level he wanted, and after traveling up and down the East Coast searching for such a position, he hired himself.

"And that's the story in a nutshell," Moon said as we drove into the parking lot of his office building on Mahan Street. It was located in a small but prosperous-looking business district in Tallahassee, just off Interstate 90. The building was six stories high and made of white brick with massive bay windows tinted black. Chic, I thought. Very modern. The name MCCALISTER ENTERPRISES was written on a huge piece of granite that stood in the middle of the parking lot. Moon had explained to me that we would wait at his office, since he had to go by there anyway, until his mechanic, or his *man* as he called him, notified him of my car's status. I wanted to ask why he was doing all of this for me, but I didn't. I wasn't stupid. I knew why. The figure-eight model at the party probably wouldn't give it up to him so I guess that left me.

We took the elevator to the sixth floor. No one was in the building, not even a security guard, and the silence of the place gave me the willies. But Moon seemed perfectly relaxed alone. He pressed the button numbered SIX and leaned against the elevator's wall. He had one hand in his pocket and the other one rubbing the back of his neck. He didn't seem particularly interested in chitchat so I didn't bother him with talk either. We just stood there, watching the numbers change from three to four to five to six. And then the double doors slid open into an elongated lobby area accentuated by a WELCOME TO MCCALISTER ENTERPRISES sign hanging down by chains just above the receptionist's desk. On the wall to the right of the desk were pictures of Moon and two unfamiliar faces, apparently his partners, with Moon's picture prominently displayed in the middle. DERRICK EUGENE MCCALISTER, JR., read its caption. Founder and CEO.

To the left of the desk were pictures of the threesome again, this time as they played golf with celebrities or shook hands with presidents and prime ministers alike, beaming in their success, so full of life and themselves that they could hardly contain their glee.

But as impressive as the lobby and its hangings were, they were nothing compared to the office behind the desk. "We can wait in here," Moon said and escorted me through a large office that was obviously his secretary's room, to his office. The double doors were opened and it looked as if I were stepping into another world. An oversize cherry oak desk sat in front of a wall-to-wall bay window with a view of the lake that almost took my breath away. I tried to keep my cool, of course, because the last thing hotshot guys like Moon McCalister wanted to be associated with was a woman who gawked over material things. The first thing he'd suspect was that she wanted him for his money. That would be a hard sell to make, however, given his looks, but I still kept my cool just the same.

There was also a large bar in the office, a conference table with chairs, and a couch. He escorted me to the couch. I halfway expected to find a king-size bed in the room too, where Moon would undoubtedly be anxious to visit, but I didn't observe one.

"What would you like to drink?" he asked as I sat down.

I wasn't drinking anything, I had decided. I'd heard too much about that date-rape drug for me to accept a drink in a deserted office building from a man who was nothing more yet than a total stranger to me. "Nothing for me, thanks," I said.

He looked at me curiously but did not try to change my mind. He walked over by the bar and began pouring himself a drink. While he explained to me that the bathroom was in the small room adjacent to the office, a phone began ringing. I hoped that it was his cell phone and therefore his man calling with news about my car, but it was the office phone ringing. It amazed me that somebody would be calling his office at this time of night, considering that we had just popped in, I thought, but Moon answered the phone not surprised in the least.

I now had the time to get my head together. If I was correct and Mr. McCalister was interested only in some sexual gain he could get from me, I had better think up an excuse fast. I was in the big leagues sho' nuff now and I couldn't even think about using my tired excuses on an old pro like Moon. Those tales wouldn't work on a brother like him. Besides, I liked him. I didn't know him but I liked him. And I wanted him to like me.

That was when I decided to do something radical and try the truth for a change. If it didn't work, fine. At least I wouldn't play games with the man. At least my honor would still be intact. Besides, if my abstinence caused him suddenly to have a headache himself and he bade that I go, I would probably be crushed but at least I could go home with dignity, read a good book, and there was always my old friend C-SPAN.

The telephone conversation was contentious from the start. Moon wasn't talking to the person on the other end, he was yelling at that person. "That cantankerous old bastard!" he yelled. "He won't get a penny more, not one red cent! He either sells or we will withdraw at midnight tonight, is that clear? Midnight. Not a moment later!" And then he hung up.

He stood there, drinking his glass of wine, and then he exhaled. He looked over at me and tried to smile, but he looked too weary for smiling. "Sure you don't want a drink?" he asked.

"I'm sure."

"Well, I need one," he said with an almost effeminate shake of the shoulders and huffed down the remaining wine.

As he walked over by the couch he began unloosening his tie. I crossed my legs and leaned forward, bracing myself for what was sure to be the defining moment of our evening. He was stressed from the phone call and probably otherwise tired from the routines of the day. A little sex before bedtime would be just the punch he needed. But I couldn't do it. I couldn't keep spinning my wheels hoping that the dirt wouldn't fly. If I allowed Moon McCalister free passage into my heart, without so much as proving his worthiness, our relationship wouldn't last the night. He would think of me as just another one of his pebbles. And as Mama always said, a man is not going to buy the cow when he can get the milk for free. If I had any chance of developing a real relationship with this man, I knew I had better play hardball and keep my milk to myself.

He sat down beside me, very close beside me, and crossed his legs too. I wanted to tell him that he was the sweetest-smelling man that I had ever smelled but I couldn't tell him something like that. Talk about a show of interest. Hanging an *I want you sexually* sign around my neck would have been more subtle. I just sat there quietly and let him lead the way.

"So," he said and looked at me, "what's your name?"

The surreal aura of the situation suddenly became real and I could have hit my own self upside the head. What was I doing? I had entrusted my car and, by virtue of my presence in this deserted office building at ten o'clock at night, my very life into the hands of a man who didn't even know my name. My mama would die if she knew what I was doing. My mama would have two strokes and die right here and now if she had even a notion of just how irresponsible I really was.

"What?" he asked. "Did I say something wrong?"

"Oh no. Not at all. I was just . . . no, you didn't say anything wrong."

"I see. So what's your name?"

Fool, I wanted to say. "Victoria," I said instead.

"Okay, Victoria. Is there a last name associated with the first?"

I smiled. "Coleman. I'm sorry. Victoria Coleman."

"As in Doctor Coleman, I take it?"

"That's right."

"What field?"

"History."

He nodded. "How long have you been teaching at FAM?"

"A year. No, two. Almost two years." I was awkward as hell. And it didn't help matters that every time I got up the courage to actually return his eye contact I caught him looking more toward my chest than my face.

64

"Are you from Florida?"

"Oh no. Philly. Philadelphia. But I'd been living in D.C. before I took the job at FAM."

"Washington. Good. Good for you."

Another phone call. Another yelling session with whoever kept bothering him. And then he was back on the couch with me. Surprisingly he wanted to know all there was to know about me, from my childhood to this present day.

"And I graduated from Temple."

"Temple University," he said. "Isn't that the school that Bill Cosby graduated from?"

"Yeah, I think so."

"Was he there while you were there?"

Dang, I thought. How old did he think I was? Me going to school with Bill Cosby? Good gracious. This man must think I'm sixty years old! But it did bring me to a question I was dying to ask: how old exactly was *he*? He was gorgeous, well built, good looking, but you could also tell that he had some years on him. When he smiled small wrinkles came around his eyes and every now and then he appeared to be dozing off. I had placed his age in the early- to mid-forties category when I first laid eyes on him. Now I wasn't so sure.

I decided to go for the jugular. "I'm thirty-four years old, which isn't all that young, but I don't think I'm a peer of Bill Cosby's."

Moon laughed. He laughed so easily. "Forgive me," he said. "I didn't mean it that way at all. It was just my understanding that he had gone back to school to get his doctorate, that's what I was referring to."

"Oh," I said. "But no."

"Well. Thirty-four, huh?" he asked. He looked at me with a strange stare as his head leaned back and his eyes were so close to the lids that they looked as if they were closed.

"What?" I asked. "I look older?"

"No. But I would have put you at a different age."

"Really," I said, perking up. "What age?"

"Fortyish."

Good grief, just kill me now! Fortyish? *Me?* I almost got my old self up and walked out. He laughed.

"Just kidding," he shook his shoulders and said and I couldn't help but smile.

And I relaxed. For the first time in my life I actually relaxed on a first date. Of course it wasn't a date exactly, just me responding to his commands, but it was close enough. Yet the conversation didn't float from talk about my age to his age, as I had assumed it would, but from my age to my family.

"I have a baby brother," I said. "He works at the post office in Philly. As for my daddy, I never really knew him. My parents divorced when I was something like four years old. I've seen him a couple of times around Philly but he had a new family and never seemed to have much time for me or my brother. So we depended exclusively on our mother and she came through for us. All three of us are fairly close considering how far I live from them. We keep in touch anyway. And Mom, well, Mom's a trip. She has her own little beauty parlor in Philly and has been known to party hardy with the best of them. She also has a well-established reputation for having a new boyfriend seemingly every other month. They called her *Sixty Days Sally* even when I was a little girl."

Moon laughed. It didn't take much to make him laugh and he was off the chain that night. The way he treated me and the way he talked to that person on the telephone were like a contrast between night and day. But the fact that he treated me well as opposed to the person on the phone didn't give me much solace either. He could be a Dr. Jekyll and Mr. Hyde personality, for all I knew, where sometimes the one becomes the other.

"But enough about me," I said. "What about you?"

His gaiety slowly dropped into an almost frown. He looked down, at his tie, and seemed genuinely disappointed that I would broach such a subject. "What about me?" he asked.

"Your name, for instance."

He looked at me. "You don't know my name?"

"Let's just say I don't feel as if I've been formally introduced to you."

"I'm Derrick McCalister. Didn't I tell you?"

"You told me how you became McCalister Enterprises but you never told me your name."

"Well, I do apologize, young lady," he said and extended his hand. "My name is Derrick McCalister."

I smiled and shook it. "Not Moon McCalister?" I asked.

He frowned. "Yes, Moon McCalister. I guess I'm stuck with that name."

"Where did it come from?"

"It's a nickname."

"Well, I hope so. But I mean where did it come from?"

It was a very personal question, I knew, but I felt comfortable enough to ask it. There was something about Moon that just put me at ease. He had to be the best-looking man I had ever met, let alone spent time with, but I felt as if I were talking to my soul mate.

His comfort level, however, was greatly decreased when the conversation was about him. He fumbled with his tie and seemed to be inwardly debating if he should discuss this with me, and then he exhaled.

"I was at Georgia Tech and was the Yellowjackets cornerback. I was no earlier version of Deion Sanders but I wasn't bad. They even considered me to be the team's leader. Well, we lost a game pretty badly. It was something like forty-nine to nothing and I was pretty pissed. So after the game, in the locker room, some of my teammates were actually laughing and enjoying themselves. I couldn't believe it. We had just gotten creamed and they were joking around? Well, I lost it. I did. And I pulled down my pants and showed them my ass to kiss. They didn't kiss it but I've been the Moon ever since."

I smiled and then burst into laughter. He smiled too. "A man my age with a name like that," he said.

My laughter ceased quickly. I had to seize the moment. "Your age?" I asked.

"Yeah, can you imagine? But anyway, that's my name. Moon McCalister. Born and reared right here in Tallahassee. No desire whatsoever to live elsewhere. As for my parents, who were wonderful, they're both deceased. I have one sister and no relatives that I bother with. I was married once, briefly, and I have a son who lives in New York. He's an investment banker on Wall Street. I rarely see him."

Divorced with a grown son, an investment banker no less. But he still didn't mention his age. But as the conversation continued I began to realize how little difference it made anyway.

His cell phone rang as we were laughing and talking about silly stuff, like who our favorite singers were. I had told him that I loved Motown and all things R&B and then he told me who he liked.

"Frank Sinatra," he said.

I almost laughed. "Frank Sinatra?"

"Yes, I'm afraid so."

"Let's see. He's the scooby-doo-be-doo guy, right?"

"He's much more than that," Moon said, seemingly offended. "Classics like 'I've Got You Under My Skin,' 'I Get A Kick Out of You,' 'My Way,' 'Love and Marriage,' 'Strangers in the Night,' 'New York, New York,' 'Fly Me to the Moon,' 'Summer Wind,' 'The Best is Yet to Come,' 'Nancy with the Laughing Face,' and on and on, just a wealth of great tunes."

Nancy with the Laughing Face? I looked at Moon as if that were exactly where he had just come from. "Nancy with the Laughing Face?" I asked, but before he could respond his cell phone began ringing.

It was his man. My car was ready, he said. Moon asked for my address, which I gave to him, and he informed his man to take my car there and he'd take care of the rest.

"Well," Moon said as he flipped closed his cell phone, "I guess I'd better get you home, young lady."

He stood and so did I. We stood there momentarily, as he appeared to be trying to decide if he wanted to do something with me or just keep it as it was. I wanted both, to tell you the truth. I wanted us to stay just as we were, but I also could feel my heat rising where I stood. If he would have made an advance, despite all of my inward protestations, I could not have said no.

But he apparently decided against it because instead of asking me if he could jump my bones, he asked if I'd mind if he smoked.

After retrieving my car keys from the front seat of my repaired Camry, we walked slowly up the stairs to my condo. He walked behind me and I could feel his stare. I tried to add an extra twist in my walk until I reminded myself that I had better slow my twisting butt down. This was the perfect date so far, I said to myself, *Don't blow it, Tory.* This guy obviously didn't go for the fast types or he would have been with the figure-eight beauty queen from the party instead of with me. *Keep it slow*, I said to myself. *I just might be on to something.*

He asked for my keys and unlocked my front door. "Would you like to come in for a nightcap?" I asked, more out of a great need for the night not to end than for any other reason, but he declined. I felt disappointed by his refusal, as if he thought I was going to spike his drink with the date-rape drug myself, but he looked tired.

"Thanks but no thanks," he said. "I've still got some negotiating to do on this Thomasville deal so I better get back for that. But you stay sweet and I'll see you later."

And we stood there. Me at my threshold and he just in front of me. My hormones were raging. I wanted him so badly I could taste it. A kiss would have killed me. A touch would have knocked me out. So when he hugged me, when he actually pulled me to him and wrapped me in his arms, I wanted to cry. I felt as if my heart were pounding out of control, and it was the best feeling in this world. And when he released me and pulled my face up to his, tears welled in my eyes. I knew right then and there that I didn't just want Moon McCalister. I needed him. I needed him as surely as I needed air. It was a dangerous door I was opening, one filled with uncertainty and darkened rooms, but it had flung too wide to just close back now.

But Moon would not breach our moment. He stared into my eyes as if he wanted me as badly as I wanted him, but he didn't take the chance. He smiled to where those beautiful wrinkles on the sides of his eyes deepened, he gave me the littlest wink, and he left.

I closed the door and leaned against it for what seemed like hours. I could hardly contain my joy. He was everything I wanted. He was decent and kind and tall, rich and smart. And talk about looks. *Billy dee* was no Moon McCalister, that's how gorgeous the brother was. And he spent his evening with me. Me of all people. All my contentment was shot to hell in one night. My routine was about as foreign to me at that very moment as my new love familiar. Just hours before it would have been my pleasure to come home, kick up my heels, and read a book or watch C-SPAN. But that was before. Everything was different now. I couldn't have read a book that night even if I had written it myself and I couldn't have watched C-SPAN even if the congressmen were standing in my very bedroom. I had found the moon. I had found my knight.

He didn't call. I had hoped to hear from him that same night but I knew it was highly improbable. He had to take care of business that night. But he didn't call the next day either. Or the day after that. Or the day after that. By day number four I was a wreck and just about ready to do something out of my head. I called Gina instead.

"Slow down, girl, slow down," she instructed me as I began to hyperventilate on the phone.

"He hasn't called, Gina, why hasn't he called?"

"Why hasn't who called?"

"I do it every time, Gina, every time."

"What are you talking about, girl? Do what every time?"

When I wouldn't respond, I couldn't respond, Gina suggested we meet for lunch. At first I declined but then accepted. I had to tell somebody. I couldn't carry this pain around a moment longer.

We had agreed to meet in the picnic area on Lake Jackson because it was close enough to FAM-U and even closer to the courthouse. Gina had been in court earlier that morning and was therefore dressed very conservatively in a brown skirt suit and heels. I, on the other hand, was in blue jeans and a blazer. The *Tory* look, as Gina called it.

"Now what man has gotten you in such a state as this?" she asked as she wiped off the bench with a handkerchief and sat down beside me. It was a breezy, beautiful day, where the sun was out in force but the cool wind deflated its harshness. A few families were in the park, some having picnics, others feeding the pigeons, but mostly college kids were there, reading books or tossing Frisbees or lying on blankets in love with the great outdoors. I looked at Gina. She looked exhausted, probably from a schedule too full, but it was just like her to make time for me.

"How do you know it's about a man?" I asked with such little conviction that Gina shook her head.

"It's always about a man, honeychile," she said. "Now who is he and what has he done this fast?"

I explained to her how I met this gorgeous hunk of a gentleman at a faculty dinner party Friday night and how he called his mechanic to repair my Camry and how he took me to his office to wait on the car and how we talked but didn't do anything and how he took me home and gave me a little hug.

"A little hug?"

"Yes. And he told me to stay sweet."

Gina looked at me as if I were flipping out. "Stay sweet? What kind of brother talk like that?"

"This brother. And he's smart and great looking and wealthy and he's got class, Gina. I mean real class. He don't listen to this junk music me and you listens to but—"

"Not so fast, sistergirl. What junk music? Brian McKnight don't be singing no junk music. Luther Vandross either."

"I don't mean it like that. But he's classy, Gina. That's what I mean. Different. He listens to Frank Sinatra tunes, for example."

"Frank Sinatra!" she yelled in her best hysterical voice. "Good God, Tory, who is this joker?"

I hesitated. I didn't want to tell his name for fear Gina might know him. She was newer to Tallahassee than I was but she was totally connected. And there wasn't an eligible bachelor in sight that she hadn't had some dealings with.

"Well?" she asked. "What's his name?"

I knew I had to tell her because my plan of action depended almost entirely on her helping me out. But I was scared to say it. He had been my special secret. He was supposed to be mine and mine alone. I had already decided that Moon was a very private man who expected his woman to keep her mouth shut. But I had no choice this time.

"Come on, girl," Gina said, coaxing, "what's the matter with you? What's the brother's name?"

"Moon McCalister," I said and looked at Gina.

She knew him. I could tell by the way she removed her sunglasses. "Oh," she said. "Him."

"You know him?"

"Do I know him? He's only one of the most successful black men in Florida, Tory. Of course I know him!"

"And?"

"And what?"

"You don't have an opinion about him?"

"He's aw'ight."

"And what does that mean?"

"He's an asshole, okay? Satisfied? I met him before, yes. At a dinner party. He's the kind of man who stands out in a crowd, I'll admit that. And he's good looking, no question about that either. So I walked over to him, trying to be friendly, you know, I may have even flirted with him a little. Just playing around. And the brother wouldn't give me the time of day."

"You?"

"Yes. Me. I was so disgusted with him I almost cussed his ass out. He better be glad my husband was there or I would have. But since I didn't have no business flirting with him in the first place I let it slide. But yeah, I know the Moon. And no, I ain't impressed."

Gina didn't know it but she actually made me feel better. He turned Gina down. Gorgeous Gina! And he also turned down that figure-eight model at the party Friday night. But he talked to me. He spent time with me. Maybe he was a different breed of man. Maybe he was one of those rare human beings who actually went for the inner beauty first.

But that still didn't change the fact that he hadn't phoned. "I was hoping he would phone me after that night," I said to Gina but she was not encouraging.

"Girl, you don't wanna fool with nobody like him."

"Why not? He's good looking, he's wealthy. Why not?"

"Because I just don't like him, that's why. He just stands there and stares at you like you're not a human being but some toy and he's trying to decide if he wants to play with you or not. That's why. And he ain't no spring chicken either."

"What do you mean?"

"The brother's almost half a century old, Tory."

"Fifty?"

"Almost. He's about to kick the mess out of the big Five-0."

So he's forty-nine. Fifteen years my senior. I knew he had some age on him but not that much. But it's not as if it mattered. I still would have wanted him even if he was about to kick the mess out of the big Six-0. Of course he was an older man. It took time to develop a persona like his. No thirty-something man was going to have that look of distinction that oozed from every pore of Moon McCalister's body. No way. Age looked good on a man like him. Hell yes, I still wanted him. And Gina could talk the talk until she was blue in the face but I knew what the real deal was. If he had not rebuffed her the way he had, she would still have wanted him too.

"So," I said to her, "is that the only reason you don't like him? Because he's an older man?"

"Because he's a smug son of a bitch. Because he's weird the way he just be staring at people. And I heard he was as ruthless as all get-out. I heard he was a cutthroat business competitor who left you dangling for dear life, girl."

"And where did you hear all of this?"

"From my colleagues, that's who. They know the fool. Think about it, Tory. Check him out. You don't think he got to be one of the most successful black men in Florida by osmosis, now, do you?"

I didn't. The night we were together he was on the telephone talking business and he wasn't exactly kind to the person on the other end. But he was a businessman. He wasn't supposed to be kind. He was in a dog-eat-dog world. You either step up to the plate or take your behind home. He stepped up. I couldn't fault him for that.

"But what about him as a person?" I asked Gina. "What have you heard about that?"

"I told you. Ruthless. He think he's better than everybody else. That's why he wouldn't talk to me. I wasn't good enough for him. Yeah, he'll fool around with you a little because you have a Ph.D. and everybody ain't able, but I heard he gets bored real quick."

So. That was it. My Ph.D. It never occurred to Gina that he could have spent time with me because he liked me. It was my Ph.D. he liked. But she didn't see his eyes. She didn't see the way he looked at me. She could believe that she was every man's dream and I was only Lassie's all she wanted. But I saw his eyes.

"But anyway, girl," she said, "I've got to get back to the office. It's

apparent from the look on your face that I could have told you that
he was an ax murderer and you still would want him. So good luck
'cause you playing with the big boys now, girl. You gonna need all
the luck you can get."

"The reason I called you," I said before she could stand up, "is
that I need your help."

"My help? How?"

"I was thinking you could go with me to talk to him. The way
you did with Robert."

Gina leaned back and looked at me hard. "Are you out of your
cotton-pickin' mind?" she asked.

"But you went with me to see Robert."

"Moon McCalister don't work at no Foot Locker, okay? And he
ain't no Robert."

"Then what am I supposed to do?"

"I don't know, Tory. But he is definitely not the kind of man you
can just run down."

"But maybe I can remind him that I'm somebody he could really
go for?"

"No. Forget it. Now I'm telling you, girl. If you like this joker
you will have to wait this one out. You cannot beg and plead and
run down a man like Moon McCalister. He'll kick you to the curb
so fast your ass won't know what hit it. And that's only if he hasn't
kicked you there already."

I gave her a knowing nod of agreement as if it didn't matter to
me anyway. I knew she was right. That was probably why I hadn't
called him myself. I was in love with a man this time. A real man.
And real men didn't need their women to remind them to be kind.
Or to treat them right. Or to pick up a telephone and give them a
holler.

Four
Peter damn Lawrence

Five days later and Moon still had not phoned. Up until that day I continued to hold out the hope that he was just busy and couldn't get around to giving me a call. But I woke up on the fifth day of this charade tired of pretending. I resigned myself to the fact that Moon McCalister just wasn't interested in me. Period. No more excuses. It was a sad realization to be sure but it allowed me to go on with my life. I was a failure at love, that was all there was to it. And it hurt. It tore my heart apart every time I thought about all those men I loved who never really loved me back. Like Robert. Talk about a zero. He could have told me that the sun was lying in my backyard and my crazy behind would have run back there to see it. And it wasn't his fault, how could I blame somebody else for taking advantage of my own stupidity? I was the needy one, not he. I was the fool who didn't think enough of myself to leave that con artist alone.

And now the Moon. Was he blind? Did he not see those tears in my eyes when he stood at my front door? He saw them all right. He just didn't care. I had to face facts for once in my life. Victoria Coleman and love just didn't match.

So I went back to reading my books and teaching at the university. I almost got back into my routine. Contentment almost re-turned. But that was when the craziness started.

It began with the phone calls. I'd pick up, say hello, and nothing. Not a sound. Every night it happened without fail. My caller ID couldn't identify the calls and star 69 couldn't trace the calls and the call annoyance people said to write down the dates and times that the calls were made. That was easy. As soon as I walked into my condo, the calling started. It ended every night at midnight. But then it started happening at work too. And it always happened within thirty minutes of my walking into my office, as if I was being timed. I'd pick up, say hello, and silence ensued.

Gina said it happened to her all the time. Somebody was always calling her and hanging up too, at certain times of the day, almost every day. She didn't know who it was exactly but she believed it was some woman who wanted her husband Isaac and therefore pulled that phone-and-hang-up routine just to aggravate her. But I didn't have a husband, I didn't even have a man. And if some female was trying to prick my nerves because of that one innocent evening I spent with Moon McCalister, as if it actually meant something to him, she was wasting her time.

So I listened to Gina and just chalked it up to the fact that this was America where crazy people, people with nothing better to do than to aggravate somebody, were at a premium. And I listened to Vera, who also told me not to worry about it. "Just screen your calls when the phone rings," she said. "If that *unknown name, unknown number* message comes up on your caller ID, don't answer it." And I didn't. My unwillingness to participate in the phone game didn't stop the calls altogether, but it certainly slowed them down.

But then I went to the supermarket. Publix had a sale on two-liter sodas so I thought I'd run in after work, grab a few, and run back out. I ran in all right and grabbed a few, but just as I was heading back down the aisle toward the checkout line, Peter *he ain't no Billy dee* Lawrence, also known as Humpty Dumpty, suddenly appeared.

It was as if he was hiding behind a display case waiting to jump out and yell *surprise!* because just as I walked by the display of corn chips and dip, Peter slid his slimy butt in front of me and cut off my path.

"Victoria!" he said as if we'd been friends for years. "How you doing, girl?"

Great up until now, I wanted to say. "Fine," I said instead. "And you?"

"Good," he said and stared his cross-eyes unblinkingly in my direction. "Long time, no see."

"How 'bout that." I began moving away as if I was in this magnificent hurry. "I've gotta run so I'll see you later," I said.

"Yes," he said and turned his whole body around as if he were pirouetting in a ballet. "I'll see you later!"

I could feel his stare as I hurried away. Talk about an oddball. But I didn't think much about the encounter, except how much I still wanted to kill Vera for setting me up with a joker like that, and I never thought for a second that he could actually be my crank caller. He was a pervert the way he undressed on my sofa, but he was an innocent pervert. He thought I wanted him sexually, he thought I had this thing for his Humpty Dumpty behind, that's what fueled his perversion train. Besides, Vera and even Rollie thought the world of the man and he was teacher of the year for three years running at his school. I just couldn't see a teacher of the year wasting his time calling and hanging up, over and over, as if he didn't get it. Besides, it had been almost two months since our blind date. For him to suddenly start calling me out of the blue like that would have been totally off the chain.

But then I saw him at my dry cleaners that same day. I had a routine of taking a few clothes in once a week to my favorite dry cleaners on Capital Circle. But this time I walked into the small store and there was Peter, standing at the counter holding a friendly conversation with Wen Ho, the store's owner. My movement slowed immediately as I held my clothes across my arm and stared at Peter.

"Victoria!" he said again as if we'd been friends for years.

"What are you doing here?" I asked him. Two meetings in the same day was a little too coincidental for me.

"He make jokes," Wen Ho said, taking my clothes off of my arm. "Funny man."

"How did you know I bring my clothes here?" I asked Peter.

"Excuse me?"

My eyes batted incessantly, the way they often did when I was stunned. "Why are you here, Peter?"

Peter acted as if he was stunned too. "I don't understand."

I didn't respond. I couldn't. It was all beginning to make sense. Not a whole lot of sense, but still.

"I'm here for the same reason you're here, I suppose," he said. "I have funky clothes too."

Wen Ho burst into laughter. "See. He funny man. Funny, funny. He should go to the Hollywood."

That wasn't the only place he should go. But if he was trying to stalk me or otherwise bother me, he wasn't showing his true intentions at all. "Anyway, Wen Ho," he said, "I'll see you in a couple days."

"We'll keep working on that stain but the hope not good."

"I appreciate whatever you can do." And then he looked at me. "See you later, alligator," he said and walked out of the door smiling that reptilian smile of his, as if he had this big secret.

I turned to Wen Ho. "You know him?"

"He Mr. Peter. Come in regular."

"Since when?"

"I don't know. Five, six weeks ago. Maybe little longer."

"Oh," I said, and then I felt foolish.

But as the days came and went my foolishness was muted. I started seeing Peter everywhere. I'd go to the post office to check my box and he was there. I'd go inside a few stores at Governor's Square Mall and there he'd be, in every one, speaking to me as if we'd been friends for years. Another supermarket. Another Peter sighting. At first I used to confront him about his just so happening to be in every place that I just so happened to be in, but he always had a comeback. He was picking up mail for a friend, picking up gifts for a coworker's retirement party, buying cat food for his cat.

But his sightings were taking their toll on me. I didn't know what he was capable of. I'd seen too many movies on that Lifetime cable network to know that stalkers can be very unpredictable. As soon as you let your guard down, they attack. Even after Gina and Vera both told me that I was overreacting, that Tallahassee was too small for me not to constantly run into people I knew, I couldn't completely buy their reassurances. Vera said it was like buying a new car. You hardly ever see that particular model on the road but as soon as you buy one, you see that particular car everywhere. In other words, you're looking for the car now. It was there all the time, she said, but I just wasn't paying attention.

Gina told me story after story about how she'd run into this person or that person so many times that she felt as if it was déjà vu. I had a feeling too about my encounters with Peter but my feeling terrified more than enlightened me.

I thought about calling the police, but what could I tell them? This guy I once went on a date with has been following me around? Has he touched you? they'd want to know. Has he threatened you in any way? Has he destroyed any of your property or otherwise trespassed against you? He hadn't. He was too smooth for all of that obvious stuff. But that only meant bad news for me because without some overt action on Peter's part I could forget involving law enforcement.

But to my credit, I thought, I was able to keep it together while at the same time acting like a paranoid basket case whenever I stepped out of my front door, looking around, behind me, checking my rearview every few seconds. And it worked for the most part until Mr. Peter Lawrence decided to bring his scare tactics a little closer to home.

My night class was entitled The Bolshevik Revolution: Was it

Lenin or Was it Inevitable? and I was shocked when I walked into the classroom and saw him seated in the very back of the room, his burly arms folded in satisfaction, his long face beaming from ear to ear. *Oh hell,* I thought. *He's getting bold with his shit now.*

He threw me that night, I must admit. I tried to carry on with the lesson plan but I became so disoriented that my students could not help but laugh. I began grappling for words, an awful display for a college professor, and decided that I had no choice but to dismiss class early.

They would have forgiven me anything when I dismissed class early.

I needed to talk to Peter. He had another thought coming if he had any notion whatsoever that he was going to keep up this game of following me around and harassing me as if he could force me to fall in love with him. I wanted to make it crystal clear to brother-man that he could take that stalker trip and can it because I was not the one.

I waited for the last student to leave before I looked in his direction. He got up and slithered his bowlegged self toward the front of the class. He was smiling and trying to look casual, as if he were just passing by and happened to see a class in session. His smiling and casualness only heightened my anger.

"What do you want?" I asked so bitterly that he stopped in his tracks.

"And hello to you too," he said.

"What do you want, Peter?"

"You know how to make a fella seem welcome, Victoria, you know that? But hey, I know how you feel. We're two of the same people. You, me, the same. I saw it right off. Vera thought she was the one who put us together, didn't she? But we knew better than that. It was fate."

I just stood there. Talk about being unlucky in love. The man I wanted wouldn't give me the time of day. The one I didn't want to be in the same room with couldn't get enough of me.

"But I digress," he said, grinning like a slightly deranged Cheshire Cat. "I came here only to apologize."

"No thank you and good-bye," I said and began gathering up my books. My anger wasn't because of what had happened on our date. That, for me, was history. I was upset because he had come to my job, to my turf, as I, when I had that love jones bad, went to Robert's. And the phone calling. And the following me around. I didn't want to have anything to do with making somebody lovesick over me, especially somebody like Peter Lawrence. And I wasn't going to lead him on either. If he was obsessed with me, I wanted him to leave knowing that his obsession was misplaced, that I wasn't interested in any way, shape, or form.

"Why won't you accept my apology?" he asked, confused.

I stopped all activity and looked him in the eye, to make it clear that I wasn't playing. "Because I don't want to, Peter, okay? I don't care anything about you or your apologies. I just want you to stop calling me, to never again come within a hundred feet of me, to just leave me alone! It's not what you did that I don't like, it's you. You understand that, Peter? It is you. I don't like you. You might be a wonderful person, I might regret bitterly that I let you get away, but I don't care to have any kind of relationship with you. Understand?"

I was a bitch and I knew it. But I meant to be. I wanted your boy to regret the day he ever met me and go on with his life. But he kept smiling like the snake he was, as if I didn't mean a word I said.

"I bet you got a charge out of those phone calls too," he said. "That's why you never hung up right away. See, I know you. We're the same people. I could just see you naked in that bed of yours and your big, beautiful eyes were dilating with excitement! You knew it was me all along and you was jerking off just like I was."

It was unbelievable. He was a schoolteacher. A goddamn teacher of the year. And he was a bona fide psycho stalker. It didn't get any scarier than that.

I started to go off on him again, telling him about his behind with even more unambiguous phrases, but I caught myself. I really didn't know what he was capable of, despite Vera's praises of him, so I didn't think it wise to keep provoking him. I would just leave, I thought. Actions spoke louder than words anyhow.

I threw my last book into my briefcase, gathered up my papers, and headed for the door.

"No, but really," Peter said. "I really didn't come here to apologize."

I stopped and turned. I was too curious to keep going, although, in retrospect, I should have.

"I'm here because I didn't want you to be sitting at home worrying about how you treated me."

How I treated *him?* Was your boy delusional or what? But I let him talk.

"I thought at first, yes, that if I brought up the subject of apologizing, then you would feel better about apologizing to me. But obviously you would rather keep the game going. But I'm not going to get into that right now, we'll have plenty of time to get into that. The way you're standing there in your skintight jeans. You always wear your jeans so tight, you know that? It's like you're toying with me. But that's okay. That's okay. I like it, can you blame me? But I'm not here for that. I'm here because I just wanted you to know that I wouldn't mind terribly if you wanted to have dinner with me."

A train could not have knocked me harder than Peter did that night. I understood clearly how folks got killed so easily over dumb stuff because if I had a gun I would have shot him. I was so beside myself with anger that I just stood there. And good old Peter, this supposedly wonderful man Vera and Rollie both praised and insisted I go out on a date with, took my inaction to mean acquiescence so he kept on flattering himself.

"See, Tory, I know women like you. You might be in love with a man but you're too—how do I say it?—too proud or liberated, yeah, liberated to act on your feelings. But you can tell Papa all about it, baby, 'cause I know how to treat a woman. Okay, I'll do it. I feel you're worth it and I'm sure you dreamed about this moment many times." He actually got down on his knees. "Victoria Coleman," he said, his cross-eyes staring up at me, "will you go out to dinner and preferably a movie with me tonight?"

I shook my head with astonishment. "I would rather read *Beowulf*," I said and left the building.

I went straight home, threw my briefcase on the bed, and phoned Vera immediately. "You set me up with Jeffrey damn Dahmer!" I screamed into the phone at her.

She, of course, didn't get it. "I did what?"

"I'll bet if we went to his house right now and looked in his refrigerator we'd find human heads rollin' around in that motherfucker!"

"Will you please stop all of your profanity?" she asked in her best shocked voice. "Now what are you talking about?"

"I'm talking about Peter damn Lawrence, that's what I'm talking about!"

"Peter? What about Peter?"

"That nigger's crazy!"

"You saw Peter tonight?"

"Yes, I saw him. He's crazy, Vera. And I mean certifiable. Where did you find this guy?"

"I don't understand. I thought you said you weren't going out with him anymore?"

I looked at the phone. What was I doing? Vera was about as nutty as Peter. How would she understand craziness? I realized I was wasting my time and hung up the telephone. I was through with Miss V for a while. She and her blind dates could go to hell as far as I was concerned, for a while.

I showered, got into bed, and turned on C-SPAN. I fell asleep and woke up to the ringing of my phone. When I picked it up, the person on the other end hung up. I was too sleepy to think much of it until, some two or three minutes later, it rang again. And again the person on the other end hung up when I said hello. After two more rings and hang-ups I pulled the phone cord out of the wall. It was Peter damn Lawrence and I knew it. If it wasn't so late and I wasn't so tired I would have found out where that fool lived and done a drive-by on his butt. But when I pulled the cord out of the wall, peace returned. Soon, sleep returned too and I chalked up as a dream what was about to become a nightmare.

I arrived at work late the next day. I parked my Camry across the street from the Arts and Sciences Building and hurried inside the front door. I halfway expected to see Peter Lawrence standing there waiting for me, but thankfully he wasn't there. I didn't feel very courageous that morning. I didn't have the energy for a battle.

I took the stairs to the history department's suite of offices and hurried inside my office, barely speaking to the secretary and clerks out front. But I couldn't help myself. I felt antsy. All I wanted to do was stay out of sight as much as possible and hope like hell that Peter would just leave me alone.

But I was kidding myself. I wasn't settled in my office thirty minutes when the calling and hanging up started again. It got so bad that I told Holly, the history department's secretary, to screen all of my calls. That didn't help because Peter would tell her that he was this professor or that community leader but after I said hello, he would continue to hang up.

After lunch, however, I concluded that I had no choice but to take corrective action. It all started when I came back to the office and saw a nice bouquet of red roses on Holly's desk.

"Nice," I said.

"They're for you, Doctor Coleman," she said, but only she was not smiling. I grabbed the card and looked at it. It read *To the bitch that wouldn't come to dinner.* And it was unsigned.

SURVIVING MR. RIGHT

I threw the card and roses back on her desk. "Cancel my afternoon class," I said and hurried for the exit doors.

Tallahassee, Florida, is a town of winding roads and hills and curves. The fastest way from point A to point B was normally a straight line, but in Tallahassee where curves and dips and traffic slowdowns were almost omnipresent, the back roads were preferable.

I drove fast along the back streets from FAM-U, where the traffic was sparse, to Meridian Road, where Fletcher Academy was located.

I drove onto the school grounds slowly, taking in the beauty and majesty of the small, private school. The building was redbrick with flags flying high and JEFFERSON RAYMOND FLETCHER ACADEMY sitting atop the building in deep, dark lettering. When I drove onto the school grounds I could not imagine somebody like Peter working there. It seemed too quaint and quiet for a sex-obsessed joker like Peter. But I guess that's where you find the perverts. The main place you'd least expect.

I stepped out of the car in a hurry, my heels pounding hard into the pavement as I walked, my hobo bag and blazer flapping briskly with the contrary wind. Although Peter Lawrence had never actually touched me, I felt as if I had been violated. I felt as if my life routine was being uprooted before my very eyes and I was sitting back and letting it happen. I had to make it stop. And I wanted thousands of people around when I told Mr. Lawrence about himself. I wanted his principal and his students and the maids and kitchen help and everybody else around when I made him so ashamed of his conduct that all he wanted to do was jump off the face of this earth. He left that card as if that was supposed to scare me. Yeah, I was scared, all right. I was nearly running to the entranceway I was so scared.

The principal was a tall, heavyset man whose tight polyester

87

pants collected up around his fat thighs when he walked. He came out of his office immediately, at the urging of the secretary when she rushed in to inform him to come fast, that they had a hysterical woman on their hands.

"Good afternoon," he said, extending his hand, although he was something like fifteen feet away from me. "I'm Josh Matheson. I'm the principal here at Fletcher. And you are?"

I was in no mood for formalities but his intense eye contact and long extended hand routine did succeed in calming me down. "I'm Doctor Coleman," I said, emphasizing the *doctor* as I was always prone to do when I needed the extra respectability of title. When he finally made his way up to me, I shook his stubby hand.

"Doctor Coleman, hello," he said. "Welcome to Fletcher Academy. Is there something I can help you with?"

"Like I already told your secretary, I need to talk to one of your teachers and I need to talk to him now."

"I see. That's not a problem. And which teacher is this?"

"Peter damn Lawrence!" I said and all of the ladies in the main office sanctum looked up. I hated busting a brother in front of self-righteous folks like them but I couldn't help it. That brother had no business messing with me. That brother had no business believing that I was going to take his foolishness lying down as if I were some doormat strategically placed for him to step on. I had to do what I had to do. And if a fight was what he was looking for, he found it.

After my *Peter damn Lawrence* line the principal escorted me into his private office under the guise that perhaps I would be more comfortable talking in there. I would have been comfortable standing on top of one of those desks and talking, but I went along with the principal just the same.

"Now," he said after seating me and sitting down himself, "what's this about Peter?"

"He's been harassing me and I want it to stop."

"Harassing you? Peter?"

"Yes, Peter!"

"How?"

"He calls my house and as soon as I say hello he hangs up the phone."

"How do you know it's him if he hangs up the phone?"

"Because I know it's him."

"Did you have one of those tracing devices hooked onto your phone?"

"No. I mean yes. But he's too clever for that. You can't trace the calls."

"I see. Well, did you activate star sixty-nine and Peter's number was the last number that called your line?"

"No. I told you the calls couldn't be traced."

The otherwise friendly principal was taken aback by my snappiness but I didn't care. I wanted Peter.

"If you didn't trace the call and the caller hung up at the opening of your mouth, then how do you know it was Peter?"

"Because I know! Because he's been following me around town too. Because he came to my classroom and told me so. And I told him I would rather read *Beowulf* than go on another date with him."

"*Beowulf*? I don't understand. What's wrong with *Beowulf*?"

I rolled my eyes. If Opie Taylor didn't get Peter Lawrence up in here fast I was really going to make a scene. "The point is, Mr. Matheson," I said, "I refused to date him again and he decided he was going to get me back because of that rejection."

"You dated him then?"

"No. Well, yes, in a way, one time. We went to dinner and the theater once, but he was a blind date and I hated him from the moment I laid eyes on him."

"I see. And based on your going to dinner and watching a play with him, he began harassing you because you did not want to do it again?"

"Not exactly, no."

"Then what exactly?"

"After the dinner and play I sort of invited him over to my place for drinks."

"You *sort of* invited him?"

"I invited him over for drinks afterward. Okay?"

"Yet you hated him from the moment you laid eyes on him?" Matheson asked, as if to make some point.

"Yes. I mean, no. What I mean is, I started to like his sense of humor as the evening progressed so, after the play, I decided to invite him over."

"For drinks?"

"Yes."

"And?"

I felt as if I were at an inquisition. Matheson wanted to know everything. And I told him everything. But he wasn't wit it. He even chuckled when I told him about Peter getting naked on my living-room sofa.

"I'm glad you find this amusing, Mr. Matheson. But it's not funny to me."

"I'm chuckling, Doctor, because I am certain that Peter is not the person responsible for your plight."

"You're *certain?* How can you be so certain?"

"I have known Peter Lawrence for over nine years, Doctor. And I've known him well. Peter Lawrence would not harm a fly. He cares about people. He's one of the most thoughtful, caring men I know. Those phone calls are, perhaps, coincidental, but I assure you that is all they are. Peter is not that kind of person."

I could not believe what I was hearing. Vindictive, obsessive people like Peter don't go around advertising their dark side, didn't Mr. Principal realize that? Jeffrey Dahmer's coworkers thought he was a nice, normal guy. O.J. Simpson's friends thought that he was the nicest, sweetest guy you'd ever want to meet. They're all nice, sweet folks. Until you cross them.

The principal went on to tell me that Peter could not possibly have sent me flowers that day because he was at a teachers conference in Tampa. "He left last night," the principal said as if he never heard of anybody phoning in a flower order. But I didn't argue with the man. I was preaching to the preacher and I knew it. But I did want to ask him one question.

"Ask away," he said in a voice betraying his inner delight at knowing that I was about to leave.

"Did you ever, in all the time you've known Peter, socialize with him after work?"

He had to think about it. Then he said no. I told him I was not surprised, and left. Nothing bothered me more than hearing somebody go on and on about how great somebody else is when the only time they ever see the person is in a formal work setting. How can you know somebody based on that? But Mr. Principal was so certain of Peter. He just knew Peter wouldn't do what I claimed he did. I was wasting my time.

I drove away from Fletcher angrier than I was when I first arrived there. That trifling Peter Lawrence had managed to ruin my night *and* my day. And his boss made it seem as if I was some spurned woman looking to harass *Peter!* That's what I was up against. I found tears strolling down my face as I began to realize what I was up against.

I went to Gina. The law firm where she worked was near the capital, and finding a place to park was next to impossible. I ended up parking some three blocks from her office. But I needed the exercise. The only physical exertion I was doing in the run of a day was lugging a briefcase full of books from class to class. And at home it was worse. Picking up my television's remote control was it for me.

Tallahassee was moving slow that afternoon. The student population was tucked away somewhere, I supposed, because the trees and birds, a staple of the Tallahassee landscape, did not have to take a backseat to the pomp and aggressiveness of busybody students going nowhere fast. The sidewalk was filled with maple leaves, for instance, and I could actually hear them crunch under my feet. It felt good to walk on leaves. There was still some order left after all. Spring still came and maple leaves still blew around like feather airplanes landing under your feet, and birds still flocked around on telephone poles. Everything wasn't as out of control as my life appeared to be.

Gina's office was on the fourth floor of the Crown Point Office Building on Lafayette Street. Her secretary, Brenda, was nice as usual. "She's on the phone right now," she said, "but I'll let her know you're here."

I smiled and sat down. Gina was the new kid on the block in Tallahassee but she was already taking the place by storm. Unlike me, before she left D.C. she made sure she had all of her ducks in a row. A job, a home, a staff she could rely on. She knew what she was doing. And her office suite looked like something out of *Home and Garden* magazine, with plush hunter-green carpet all over the floor, beautiful plants and shrubbery all over the side walls, and African art hovering above like watchful masks. Gina was one of a kind; I discovered that a long time ago. She was one of those sharp corporate lawyers who knew how to play the game with the big boys yet stay down to earth and enjoy herself in the process. Whenever we went out together she never bitched about her job or talked endlessly about its rewards and perks although, I am sure, there were many. But that was Gina. Her father was an attorney, her mother was a high school administrator, and her little brother Joseph was a big-time recruiter for the NBA. Success was a given in her family. There was never any question that she would do well and well indeed. Whereas in my family success was more tenuous. Staying out of jail was success. Graduating from high school was success. Earning a Ph.D. was fantasyland.

Thirty minutes after my arrival we sat down on the blue leather couch in her office. She was immaculately dressed in a short skirt suit and heels, Versace, of course, with newly manicured nails and a new do: a French roll with sister curls on the side. You go, girl, I wanted to say. But I didn't have the energy.

"What's the matter?" she asked, picking up immediately on my sense of drain.

"Peter Lawrence has been harassing me and I don't know what I'm going to do about it."

"Who's Peter Lawrence?"

"That blind date Vera set me up with two months ago. The one I told you has been following me around town."

"Ah yes. Mr. Butt Naked."

"Right."

"What has he done now?"

"In addition to the phone calls and following me around he came by my classroom last night asking for another date, and then today he had a dozen roses delivered to my job with a card attached calling me the bitch who wouldn't come to dinner."

Gina, to my surprise, laughed. I must have been lost in cyberspace somewhere because I certainly didn't get the joke.

"What else has boyfriend done?" she asked.

"What else? Hasn't he done enough?"

"Sure. If you can prove everything you're saying."

"If I can prove it? I have the card to prove it!"

"You have a card that could have been purchased by anyone. You can investigate, of course, and determine if he used his credit card to purchase the roses. But even if you prove that he did, the most that could be said is that he's not much of a gentleman and he may not be a very nice guy. It's hardly enough to go to court on, girl."

"I don't want to go to court. I want him to leave me alone, that's all I want."

"Have you told him to leave you alone?"

"Yes! And I tried to tell him again but his boss claims he's at some teachers conference in Tampa."

"His boss? I thought you said he works at Fletcher Academy."

93

"He does."

"And you discussed this matter with who? The principal there?"

"Yes, I did. I went to Fletcher and—"

"Wait a minute, girl. Wait a minute here. You *went* to Fletcher and discussed this matter with *that* principal at *that* school?"

Here we go, I thought. "Yes, I did, Gina. This has been very upsetting for me."

"But, *Tory!*"

"But, Tory what?"

"You busted a brother in front of all those white folks?"

"What does that have to do with anything? I had no choice. That brother has been harassing me!"

"But you didn't have to bust a brother like that."

Even Gina wasn't on my side anymore. This was not my day. "If he would have been harassing you the way he's doing me, what would you have done?"

"First of all, Tory, it's not harassment. Not yet. It hasn't risen, in my judgment, based on what you've told me thus far, to a level that I would call harassment. The phone calls, maybe, but you can't prove he's the one who made those calls. But if Mr. Lawrence would have phoned me a few times and hung up and sent me a nasty card like that, I might try to get a restraining order against him, which I doubt I'd get, but for the most part I would just forget about it."

"Forget about it?"

"I would forget about it, yes, Tory. And go on with my life. He's just a rejected, dejected Negro, and nothing more. But I would never have gone to Fletcher. Do you realize he's only one of a precious few number of African-Americans at that school? It looks bad, girlfriend, I ain't gonna lie to you. It looks super bad when we air our dirty laundry out like that."

I sighed and pinched the bridge of my nose. Maybe she was right. Maybe I was overreacting. Maybe I should go on with my life and forget that zero as she said.

"You understand what I'm saying, Tory? Some battles just ain't worth fighting. This might be one of those battles. I mean, if he comes back to your place of employment a few more times or continues to follow you around and you can determine that's what's going on, then we can revisit the legal merits of your claim. But if I took to court every joker who has followed me around and harassed me for dates I'd be in court for the rest of my life!"

I smiled. Gina was well versed with men. She should know about such things. I almost told her that maybe she was right. Until I thought about that note and the visit to my classroom that night and all of those sightings and phone calls. And I couldn't do it. I couldn't let some jumped-up joker like Peter Lawrence knock me off stride all night and day and *not* blame him. Then I got mad at Gina. She should have understood.

I got up to leave. She tried to stop me but I snatched away from her. She and Vera and that principal and Peter damn Lawrence could all take a hike. Nobody was going to crap all over me, over and over again, and then try to make me believe that it ain't shit.

My spirits didn't lift when I got home. I could tell something wasn't right when I saw the brown paper bag lying against my front door. I kicked it a few times and started not to open it but curiosity, as usual, got the best of me. I opened the bag. What looked like a huge dead rat was lying inside of it. I threw it down and hurried inside my condo. I was so mad and scared that I called the police. This had risen, in my view, to undeniable harassment.

The officers took their time, especially since I explained to the 911 operator that I wasn't currently under attack and no weapons were involved, but they came. Officers Vytex and Rieters. They inspected the contents of the bag and then walked into my home. I was so nervous that I couldn't stop walking around in circles. I drank Coke and smoked cigarettes and offered a seat to the officers. They declined.

"What seems to be the problem here, ma'am?"

I was confused. "Did I miss something or did you not inspect that paper bag?"

"Yes, ma'am, we inspected it," one of them said.

"I know who put it there," I said.

They looked at each other. "What do you mean? You believe somebody put it there on purpose?"

"Officers, it's a dead rat. Right at my front door. What do you think?"

"Don't get smart with us, miss."

"I'm not getting smart."

"This is an old building. It's not unusual for dead rats to be in the hall."

"Oh, I get it. This particular rat decided to crawl into a paper bag, crawl, while he is still inside this bag, to my front door, close up the bag, and then conveniently die? And I suppose the fact that I had been harassed all week long, last night, and half of today hasn't anything to do with it? Is that how you explain it, Officer?"

The taller officer, Rieters, I think, wanted to know more about my harassment allegation. The smaller officer couldn't have cared less. I, nonetheless, went through the story again, from the phone calls to the card. Rieters started to take notes but the more I talked, the less he wrote. Finally he closed his notebook altogether.

"Get some rest, ma'am. You're probably just overtired. There's nothing here we can justify as a crime."

"Leaving a dead rat on somebody's doorstep isn't a crime?"

"It's not a rat," Vytex said. "Technically it's a hamster."

"And technically I'm getting highly upset with the Tallahassee Police Department and I technically might just file a complaint."

My boldness upset even Rieters. He told me to go right ahead and file, and left. Vytex gladly followed. I slammed the door, double-checked the lock, and went to bed.

The phone calls started up again around 9 P.M. I would say hello and the other end of the phone line would go dead. I tried to cuss

Peter out but he never stayed on the line long enough for me to get the words in. I tried star 69 but was told by some recording that the number could not be traced. By ten I pulled the plug on the phone altogether. I fell asleep but it was a hard sleep, filled with nightmares of a man, a ghastly, perverted man, who wouldn't take no for an answer.

I started to call in sick the next day and just stay home in bed, but I went on in anyhow. My body was drained. I looked haggard and I knew it. Coworkers and students alike asked me constantly if I was all right. I told them that I was. Holly asked me if the dozen roses and card situation were resolved to my satisfaction. I told her that they were. What else was I going to say? She didn't want to hear the truth. My best friends Gina and Vera didn't even want to hear it, why would some secretary who couldn't care less about me want to hear it?

I sat in my office all morning and waited for Mr. Lawrence to do his thing. But he didn't call. When it was time for the mailman I waited by the coffee table in the outer sanctum, waited like a salamander ready to pounce on her prey. Nothing came. No regular deliveries, no special deliveries. I was relieved but I couldn't shake my edginess. Looking back, maybe I did overreact. I mean, I was going nuts, especially after that rat incident. I felt as if I were slowly being drawn into a prison Peter had created just for me and there was nothing I could do about it. His boss was on his side. My best friends were on his side. And their actions spoke volumes to me. In their eyes I was being a bitch because I refused to take Peter's shit lying down. I was being irrational and foolish because I actually had the nerve to hate what was happening to me. I was on my own and it was scary.

That was why I called Moon McCalister. I didn't know what I was going to say or how I was going to say it. But I needed help. Peter wasn't going to just stop his game playing, he was having too much fun. And I'd seen too many shows on A&E's *American Justice* to know that stalkers could be deadly when they wanted to be. I couldn't just sit back and let it happen. Peter could be plotting my very demise, for all I knew.

"McCalister Enterprises," the soft voice on the other end said. "May I help you?"

I almost hung up. But I couldn't. "Yes, may I speak with Moon, I mean Derrick McCalister, please?"

"May I ask who's calling?"

I hesitated. "Victoria Coleman," I said. "Doctor Coleman," I added, to help my cause.

But the soft voice didn't skip a beat. "Just a moment," she said.

I waited for less than a minute before the old girl was back on line. "Mr. McCalister is in a meeting at this time," she said. "But you may leave your number and a brief message and he will return your call as soon as he can."

She sounded like an answering machine who dripped out exactly what McCalister had programmed her to drip out. I wasn't important enough, I suppose, for him to take my call. "No," I replied, "no message. Thank you."

And I hung up. It was crystal clear now. This was one battle I had to fight alone.

After work I went to Publix, loaded my basket with TV dinners and sodas, and drove slowly home. I searched every car for Peter's and every face for his grotesque face. And even going home was not much of a comfort anymore. I didn't know what to expect there either. Another dead rat. Or a dog this time. Or maybe even a snake.

I walked up the stairs to my condo hypervigilant, looking from side to side and behind me as if I was truly a woman on the verge. When two small children burst out of their apartment and ran past me, I thought my heart had dropped through my shoe. I leaned back against the rail just to balance myself again.

When I walked up to my front door and realized there was nothing languishing around in a paper bag or otherwise, I hurried inside and locked up. I fell against the door and tried to regulate my erratic breathing. I was a mess. One man's delusions had managed to devastate me. And for what? Because I didn't want to date his butt? Had he looked in the mirror lately? I know I wasn't the first woman to reject his advances. No way. But I was the one he chose to target. Me.

I set my bag of groceries on the kitchen table and turned to go into the bedroom (my refuge) when I noticed something odd about my kitchen. When I turned around, I saw what I could not believe. My cabinets all were swinging open. A pot of cooked rice, a pan of fried chicken, and a pot of boiled corncobs were on the stove. A note was tacked up on the refrigerator, written in red crayon. I was so afraid that I felt light-headed. On one level, I knew it couldn't be what it appeared to be. How could he possibly have gotten into my apartment? The door lock and the dead bolt both were locked. But on another level, I knew it was exactly as I suspected, especially when I saw that he had left a note. It was just like Peter to commit a felonious act but still have the unmitigated gall to brag about it.

I snatched the note off of the refrigerator and turned quickly. His crazy behind could still be present, I thought. I hurried to my silverware drawer and grabbed a butcher's knife. And then I read the note: *Guess who came to dinner, bitch. Ha ha!*

I clenched the letter in anger and with knife in tow ran to the back of the house. But it wasn't until I saw that my bed had been touched, with my bedspread and sheets flung onto the floor, that I panicked. Terror gripped me as it never had before. It was one thing to follow me around town, come to my job, mess with me from a distance. But he had been inside my home now. He had taken away that one safe haven I thought I still had. That was another matter. I started backing up. This shit was serious now. That high level Gina kept talking about had just been reached.

I ran. I backed out of that bedroom of mine and ran for the front door. I tried to unlock the door as quickly as I could but I was so nervously looking around and behind myself that I kept fumbling with the locks and couldn't get it right. I felt my heart pounding. I felt all of my big talk dry up into a ball of terror and all I could think about was getting away. It wasn't a game with him anymore. The stakes were too high now. If he was caught he'd go to prison for years just for breaking and entering. He knew it too. And he wasn't going to stop there either. You commit one felony, you might as well commit twelve, Gina once said to me, because either way you're going down.

The locks finally unlatched and I flung my front door open. I ran like hell's fleet out of my apartment, out of my sanctuary, but I had barely cleared the corner that led to the stairs when I flew right into the arms of who I knew was Peter Lawrence.

But it wasn't Peter. I knew it when I smelled that sweet aroma and saw the sparkle of the button on his expensive suit coat. Peter wore polyester, not Italian silk.

"Moon!" I screamed when I saw his face.

He looked at me, as if I had startled him too, and pulled me into his arms. I leaned against his broad chest and breathed in as he breathed in, out as he breathed out, and I could have stayed where I stood for the rest of my life.

But then I thought about the matter at hand. Peter. I turned around quickly to make sure he was not coming up behind me. Moon asked what was wrong with me. "And what in the world are you doing with that knife?"

I looked at the butcher's knife that I held in my hand and I broke into tears. I could not believe what was happening to me. I was afraid to go into my own home, I was afraid to be outside of my home, and I was packing a knife to protect my scared behind!

With one arm Moon pulled me to his chest again. "What's the matter, honey?" he asked so sympathetically that I felt my emotions swell higher and the tears flowed more.

I explained, undoubtedly hysterically, that somebody had broken into my house.

"His name is Peter," I said.

"You know who did it?"

"Yes. I know who did it."

"Is he in there now?" he asked, looking toward my condo's door.

"I don't think so," I said. "But I don't know."

He took me by both hands and gently moved me to the side of him. "Wait here," he said and began walking toward my front door.

But I couldn't wait there. I was terrified there too. So I followed him.

He walked into my condo looking from side to side. I wanted to hand him my knife, but I didn't. If Peter jumped Moon, then I could jump him, I thought. But Moon knew what he was doing. He went from room to room in the house, even the bathroom. He looked into closets and actually got on his knees looking under my bed. It was a sight to see, seeing Moon on his knees like that, but that's why I loved him. He was willing to get in the mud with everybody else and get the matter resolved. He didn't treat me particularly well, I mean he didn't even give me a phone call, but just seeing him again, trying to lend a hand, almost erased my pain.

As soon as we both agreed that the coast was clear, as he put it, I dropped down on the living-room sofa. To say that I was relieved would be an understatement.

But Moon was still curious. He walked over to the front door and began inspecting it.

"How did he get in?" he asked me.

"I don't know. The door was completely locked when I came home."

"Did he have a key?"

"A key? Jesus, no. I mean, I didn't give him one."

Moon began rubbing the front side of the door with his hand and then he walked outside and looked up along the back side of the door. When he walked back in he closed it.

"How could he have gotten a key?" I asked. "I never gave him a key."

Moon stood in the middle of my living room, his hands in his pants pockets, staring at me. "It was jimmied," he said.

"But I have a dead bolt. You can't jimmy a dead bolt."

"Yes, you can. With the right equipment. And he's a pro, he left precious few scars. He's clever."

That was the word, I thought. Clever. A man who had everybody fooled: Vera, Rollie, his boss and fellow teachers, even me for two minutes. But that only racked my nerves more. The fact that I didn't have a regular dimwit psycho on my hands, but a clever one, wasn't something that was going to help my sleepless nights.

Moon walked over to the chair in my large living room and sat down. His back was straight, his legs crossed, his hands resting in his lap. He looked forward, at the painting of a little black girl on my wall, but I could tell that his mind was a million miles away. The man was always calculating his next move. It was comforting and nerve-racking at the same time. It was as if he didn't do anything without thinking about it first, counting up the costs, wondering to himself if the end result was worth the price to pay. Great for business, no doubt. But lousy for love. He'd have to size me up the way he checked out a land acquisition before I could get to first base with a person like him. And every move I made would be analyzed in one of those *Is she worth it, is she not?* thought sessions of his. The sad part was that he had probably already concluded that no, I wasn't worth it, and that was why he stayed away, but my own neediness brought him back to me. I hoped my phone call wasn't the reason he came. I hoped he came because he had planned to visit me again all along. But it would have been a helluva coincidence if that was the case.

But it would not have been impossible. Maybe the fact that I had told his secretary my name was enough. He had planned to come anyway but since I had phoned he decided to delay no longer. It was a fool's hope, to be sure, but it was better than none at all.

When it appeared to me that he wasn't about to do anything but sit in that chair and stare forward, lost in his own strategy session, I kindly interrupted.

"Do you think we should call the police now?" I asked.

That was when he looked at me. His bright brown eyes stared deep into my big, dark ones. He looked tired, probably from too much activity at work, and now me and my mess. "Tell me about it," he said.

"About what?"

He did not respond. He continued to stare at me, his head tilted slightly backward, his eyes appearing almost closed.

"Before I met you," I prefaced my remarks, "I went out on this blind date with a schoolteacher named Peter Lawrence. It turned out to be a pretty decent date overall until I allowed him to come up to my place for a nightcap."

His head tilted sideways when I made that statement, as if I had said something odd. I didn't know how to read his reaction. I didn't know if he was surprised that anybody would bother to date me or disappointed that I would bother to date anyone.

"When I came back into the living room with the drinks," I said, "I discovered that Peter had made himself at home. Literally. I discovered that this mild-mannered schoolteacher was sitting naked on my couch." I looked at Moon, half expecting him to laugh the way Gina and the principal did. But he didn't even bat an eye. "So," I said, continuing, "I was livid of course and I asked him to leave at once. He did. I thought that was the end of it. Two months later and he starts calling me constantly and hanging up, or just holding on the line until I hung up. Then he started following me around, taking his clothes to my dry cleaners, visiting the supermarkets and mall stores that I frequented. He came to my classroom asking me for another date, and again I made it clear to him that very night that I wasn't interested in him at all, that I would rather go home and read *Beowulf* than date him."

Moon smiled. I was so glad that he understood the joke that I smiled too. But his smile faded as quickly as it appeared. He wanted me to get on with the story. "Anyway," I said, getting on with it, "the phone calling kept up and then he sent me a bouquet of roses with a card referring to me as a bitch."

His head tilted back and his eyes disappeared behind the lids again. "A bitch?"

"Yes."

I expected him to tell me that Peter was nuts just as I was trying to tell everybody else but he held his hand out in a gesture that made it clear that he wanted me to continue with the story. I was the queen of the aside but he wasn't the king. Distractions were probably a liability in his line of work and he seemed to find such tendencies to go off on a tear about the peripheral issues of a story a weakness. "So he called me a bitch," I said. "By that time I was tired of it so I went to his job, he teaches school at Fletcher Academy, and I told his principal everything. But his principal didn't believe me. I told an attorney friend of mine about it too, but she told me to just forget about it. But I couldn't. After my visit with his principal it seemed as if Peter upped the ante. He left a dead rat in front of my door, for instance. And now this. He's getting bold with his shit now."

Moon frowned. "Watch your language," he said. "Do you think that's attractive, all of that profanity?"

"Excuse me?" I asked, jumping defensive.

"Are you certain this Peter is the only one who could have done this?"

That was when I realized that Peter's letter was still balled up in my hand. I handed it to Moon. "He left a calling card," I said.

Moon opened it and read it. "He's bold, all right," he said in response to the letter. And then he looked at me. "You can pick 'em."

"I didn't pick him. It was a blind date."

"And you always invite blind dates up to your apartment for drinks?"

Actually I did, for the most part. But I couldn't tell him that. "No, of course not," I said. "It was just something that happened."

His look lingered, however, still sizing me up. "Where does he live?"

"I don't know."

"You don't know?"

"No, Moon. We didn't exchange addresses or phone numbers or anything."

We were getting testy with each other. Moon seemed disappointed in me and I was angry that I had disappointed him.

"You said he's been calling you and hanging up. How did he get your phone number to do all of this calling and hanging up business? You're not in the book."

How did he know that? I wondered. "I don't know how he managed to have my phone number. Vera, the lady who set up the date, could have given it to him, I don't know. But I didn't give it to him."

"Okay," Moon said and pulled out his cell phone. He dialed seven numbers and then kept his eyes on me the entire time he waited for the person he was calling to pick up. I tried to look as sexy as I could, sitting up straight so that my sizable breasts would sit up high and proud, but I knew it was useless. I looked haggard and tired. I looked as if I had been through too many sleepless nights and not enough peaceful days. If he found me sexy that day it had nothing to do with my looks.

"Will? Hey, this is McCalister. I want you to do a quick search on a name for me. Peter Lawrence. No, Lawrence. A schoolteacher at Fletcher. That's all I know. Yeah. Address mainly. Call me back on the cell. And I mean within ten minutes."

He flipped the phone closed and sat it on his lap. He was tired of me, I could tell. He leaned back and closed his eyes completely. Since it was a lost cause anyway, I reasoned, I thought I may as well relax. And I did. Briefly. "What brought you over to my place?" I asked, curious if he took the notion himself, or if it was strictly because I had phoned.

"You phoned," he said, "and didn't leave a message."

Figures, I thought. *Why else would a hunk like him be coming to my house?* It was nice of him to come, for sure, but it wasn't as if it meant much. He came because he knew he should have called me by now. He came out of some stupid sense of chivalry, just to make sure I wasn't so lovesick by his neglect that I was on the verge of a suicide attempt and had phoned to give him one last opportunity. Maybe it was my Ph.D. as Gina said. And maybe he was bored already.

His cell phone rang within minutes and Moon picked it up quickly, too quickly, as if he couldn't bear this scene much longer. "McCalister here," he said and then he listened. And listened. And listened. "What's his address? Brevard? Okay. Yes. Listen, Will, I want you to contact Bud Driscoll and have him to meet me over there in about an hour. That's right. No, a friend of mine is being harassed by Mr. Lawrence. Yes. That's probably what it'll take. Okay, Will. Later."

Moon flipped the phone shut. And then he stood up. I stood up too. "You wait here," he said.

"No," I said.

He looked at me, my body first, and then my face. And then he said okay.

Peter lived on Brevard Street, the same street that housed the governor's mansion. He lived in a small, wood-framed structure surrounded by a white picket fence. The lawn was perfectly manicured and the front door awning had a purple sign with WELCOME written on it in bright, semicircled lettering. It looked like the quaint little house of a normal little old lady. I wondered if Moon had remembered the address correctly.

His Jaguar stopped at the curb in front of the house and he

leaned against the steering wheel and stared at the small structure. He was thinking again, contemplating his strategy, and then he stepped out.

I jumped out too. This was one encounter I didn't want to miss. Peter had mocked my entire existence with his foolishness. He had me nervous and scared and uptight about everything and everybody. It would take a real man to slow that brother down. If Moon couldn't do it, then I didn't see how it could be done.

Moon buttoned his suit coat and walked in long strides toward the front door. I brought up the rear, moving slow on purpose, not sure if Peter Lawrence was one step ahead of us and had already concocted a defense. He could lie and declare total innocence. Or he could declare it was all my fault, that I pursued him until he couldn't take it anymore. It would be some lie to tell with a straight face but I wouldn't put it past a man like Peter. He was already known for his great reputation. His friends still defended him as if he were some holy man. Maybe Moon could get taken in by Peter too.

Moon rang the doorbell and, without awaiting a response, knocked with loud bangs on the locked screened door. After several seconds the home's white wooden door behind the screened one was opened and Peter Lawrence stood before us. He wore a pair of thick-rimmed glasses and was wiping his chunky hands on a red kitchen cloth. He looked different, more serious than I had ever seen him before, and he stared through the screen at Moon McCalister as if he couldn't believe his eyes.

"Peter Lawrence?" Moon asked.

Peter glanced at me and then looked back at Moon. "Yes," he said. "I'm Peter Lawrence."

"My name's McCalister."

"Yes, I know."

"And you remember Victoria."

Peter looked at me as if he wasn't certain he remembered me at all. "I've met her before, yes," he said.

"May we come in?" Moon asked and Peter hesitated. He knew why we were there. He was putting on his best golly-gee, innocent-me schoolteacher act, the kind of performance that won him raves among my friends and his colleagues, but he knew that Moon McCalister wasn't visiting his house just to say hello.

"You want to come in here?" Peter asked.

"May we come in?"

Peter sighed and looked at me again. Then he unhooked the screened door.

We walked in slowly, with Peter barely allowing us clear passage as his wide body did not move out of the way but simply turned sideways. The smell of cinnamon met us as we entered and once again it was Peter Lawrence, the everyday joe, on display. Big, Herculean floral-print furniture sat in the home's living room, while beautifully unique blue and green and white vases on cobble-stone tabletops lined the eggshell-white walls. The carpet was a plush mauve with matching sweeping drapes and the small fireplace mantelpiece housed the most striking collection of exotic African art that I had ever seen. The home, then, was perfectly maintained, almost antiseptically beautiful, and I knew then that it was a front too. It helped to shield the real Peter Lawrence in much the same way that his winning personality did. But his game was as phony as a three-dollar bill to me. I only hoped that Moon saw through it too.

And Peter, true to form, started putting on the show big time. He smiled, offered us a seat, even offered us a sampling of his home-baked cookies. Moon sat down on the large couch, and I sat down beside him, but we both declined the cookies.

"Now," Peter said, sitting on the chair in front of us, "how can I be of service to you folks this evening?"

Moon was his regular preoccupied self, looking around at the walls, the artwork, the almost oddly serene surroundings, and his apparent lack of interest in his host seemed to agitate Peter.

"Mr. McCalister," he said, still smiling, still emitting that reptilian slickness, "I don't mean to sound rude but I don't understand what this is about."

That did it. I had had it up to here with Peter and couldn't wait to let him know. "You know what's going on," I said quickly, angrily. Moon looked at me as if he wanted me to cool it immediately, but I couldn't help myself. "Don't try to act like you're some innocent bystander because you and me both know better than that."

"What? What are you talking about?"

"You broke into my house today, Peter."

"I *what?*"

"You broke into my house and you've been following me and calling me on the telephone and then hanging up like some damn fool, and then you sent me that sick-ass card, so don't even go there with that golly-gee, innocent-me routine, okay?"

My fire seemed to take Moon by surprise but he didn't interfere. He just sat there, crossed his legs, and listened. Peter, on the other hand, was putting on an Academy Award performance, denying everything. But he went too far when he tried to implicate me.

"Mr. McCalister, I don't know what she's been telling you but I just went out with her just for something to do, you know what I'm saying? And the next thing I know she's showing up everywhere. Every day I see her. Now this. I'm telling you, it's scary. Now I don't know how well you really know her but she needs to get some help."

I was so outdone I didn't know what to do. I looked at Moon. Moon was staring at Peter. "You know me?" he asked him.

"Excuse me?"

"You know who I am, don't you?"

Peter smiled. "Yes, sir. You're Moon McCalister. You was once a city councilman and I know of the good work you do for the community. Of course if my bank account was as solvent as yours I'd bet I could do a lot of good work for the community too."

"Do I look like a bullshit artist to you?"

Peter's grinning suddenly evaporated before our very eyes. The real brother was slowly but surely emerging. "What?"

"Do I look like a joker, a prankster, somebody with time on his hands?"

Peter did not know what to say. He looked at me and I placed my hands on my hips as if demanding a response too. He looked at Moon. "No," he finally said, "you don't look like a prankster."

"This young lady, seated beside me, is a friend of mine. You've been bothering her."

"No, sir, no, I haven't."

"You've been bothering her. It was probably harmless for the most part. A joke here, a prank there. But you went too far today."

"Look, with all due respect—"

"You went too far today. Which means that the jokes, the pranks, are over. Understand?"

Knocks were suddenly heard on Peter's front door and he turned quickly, too quickly for a cool brother like him.

Before Peter could respond to the knocks, however, the door was opened and a tall man in cowboy boots and blue jeans walked in. His face was long and friendly and his hair, a mat of grayish blond locks, dropped along his back and bounced as he walked. His odd appearance seemed to stun Peter.

"May I help you?" he asked with a tinge of concern in his voice.

"Hello there," the visitor said. And then he saw Moon. "Well, if it ain't Big Mac."

"Come on in, Bud," Moon said, his eyes still fastened on Peter.

"What is this?" Peter asked Moon. "I don't understand what's going on here."

"Mr. Lawrence," Moon said, "this is Bud Driscoll."

"Hello, Mr. Lawrence," Bud Driscoll said and extended his hand. Peter, so in tune with his need to seem like a good guy, actually smiled as he shook Bud's hand.

"He's a lieutenant with the Tallahassee Police Department," Moon said and Peter's smile, once again, disappeared.

"Police?" he asked.

I was surprised too. Bud Driscoll looked more like a throwback from the sixties, a hippie who never checked out, but not a cop.

"Here's what we're going to do," Moon said to Peter. "You're going to leave Victoria alone. And we're going to leave you alone."

Peter looked from Bud to me to Moon and he knew this was no game. But he couldn't let it go. "I don't know what you're talking about," he said.

"If you don't leave her alone, then we'll have no choice."

Peter waited for Moon to explain his *no choice* reference, but Moon stood up instead. I stood up too.

"What do you mean?" Peter asked.

"You work at Fletcher Academy, is that right?"

There was an unusually long pause in Peter's response. Moon was on to something.

"Fletcher, yes," Peter said flaccidly, his voice strength now a discernible whisper.

"Victoria went to see your principal once. Josh Matheson, I believe. Only he found her concerns about you humorous. But I assure you, Mr. Lawrence, he won't find me funny at all."

Peter stood up quickly. Moon had touched a nerve. "What does Fletcher have to do with this?" he asked angrily and then attempted to display a smile that was feeble at best.

Moon, however, wasn't playing the game and refused to respond.

"You can't go to my school, not about something like this. You're not going to my school. Are you?"

Moon continued to stare at Peter without responding, a move that caused Peter's coolness to show rapid signs of evaporation. Soon his agitation, which had been bubbling just below the surface since we got there, finally boiled over. "That's my job, Mr. McCalister!" he yelled.

"He loves his job," I said to keep him on the defensive.

"Loves it, does he?" Bud asked.

"Adores it. They tell me he was teacher of the year three years running."

"Three years?" Bud asked. "You don't say? There probably won't be a fourth year, however. At least not at Fletcher. Or at any other school in Tallahassee."

"Or Florida," Moon said, joining in on the subterfuge.

The sweat began appearing like tiny beads on Peter's forehead. He still tried to smile, to keep fronting as long as possible, but I could tell that he was thinking too, about a way out, about a reasonable and uncontroversial escape.

"What do you want me to say?" he asked.

"The truth would be refreshing," Bud said.

Peter's anger flared again. "Look," he said, "I was just playing around, okay? I didn't mean anything by it. I was just joking around!"

"Breaking and entering, in my line of work anyway, ain't no joke."

"But I didn't," Peter said as if he was getting ready to deny everything once more, but he looked at me and decided wisely to drop that strategy immediately. Then he looked at Moon. "I swear to God I was just joking around!" he said.

Moon stared at Peter. He could not have looked more serious. "No more jokes," he said.

Peter seemed mortified by that look from Moon. He even looked away from Moon, at the carpet, at the artwork on the walls. "Yes, sir," he said.

"Funny thing about jokes," Bud said. "They sometimes work and they sometimes don't. When they work, man, it's a beautiful thing to see. But when they don't, well, you don't wanna know how devastating it can be."

"In fact," Peter said, clearing his throat, "I'd been thinking about moving, relocating to a different school district out of state. North Carolina. I've received offers there. And other places."

"Out of state?" Bud asked.

"Yes. All are out of state."

Bud nodded and looked at Moon. But Moon hesitated, looking at Peter with the proficiency of somebody who knew him inside out. "Well," he finally said, "that settles it then."

Peter attempted to smile but it was half-baked and more out of nervousness than elation. His once confident face was now sweating bullets and his deep-seated anxiousness was betraying his smooth joe routine mightily. He was smooth now, all right. Too smooth by half.

When we arrived back at my condo I expected Moon to drop me off and disappear the way he did before, but he invited himself in instead. And to my astonishment he began helping me erase from my home any reminder of Peter Lawrence and his so-called pranks. We scrubbed down the kitchen and removed and discarded all the linens in my bedroom. It was a sight to see Moon McCalister in rolled-up shirtsleeves, tossing Peter's cooked meal into the trash and then cleaning the pots and pans. By the time we completed our work we were exhausted. I knew then that Moon would grab his coat and go. But he didn't. He plopped down on the couch beside me and actually smiled.

And that was the beginning of our beautiful evening. Moon was actually playful as he sang Frank Sinatra tunes and I sang Whitney Houston tunes and we both sang off-key. We laughed at each other and at ourselves. I laughed so hard that I had to run to the bathroom twice. He laughed so hard that he had to loosen his tie and then remove it altogether. We sat on that sofa and drank sherry and laughed and sang and talked until well after two A.M. Peter Lawrence, to my shock, was a distant memory.

When the laughter and talk seemed to die of its own exhaustion, Moon stood up to leave. I stood up too. I didn't want the night to end, but neither did he by the way he kept hesitating. He stared at me again, as if deciding what he should do, but then he pulled me to him, slowly, and I fell into his arms. He rubbed my hair and hugged me for what seemed like a small eternity. When we released he looked into my eyes.

And then he kissed me. I closed my eyes and allowed his lips to press hard into mine. He held me tighter and kissed harder, as if he wanted to enter me through the mouth. I held on to him and pushed against him and breathed through him. All I wanted at that very moment was to experience the fullness of him inside me.

He lifted me up as if I were a feather and I wrapped my legs around him. I could feel him rising higher and higher the harder I pressed against him. He continued to kiss me as he carried me away, his tongue pushing into mine, his excitement unleashed as if he'd never had it this good.

He carried me into my bedroom and lay me on the bed. He stood there, staring at me, and then he lay down on top of me. He unbuttoned my blouse, one button at a time, and slowly opened it. He looked at my pink lace bra and began kissing the part of my breasts that hung out. And then he lifted the bra up and over my breasts and put my nipple into his mouth. And sucked. My body clenched and pushed up as he went from nipple to nipple, sucking and licking and giving me a feeling that should have been too in-tense to bear. And his cologne and his sweet breath and his touch, lips, and tongue were too much. I became intoxicated on the power of his love alone. I started screaming with joy, I let it all hang out, and my breathing became so erratic that he moved his lips up to my mouth, kissed me again, and effectively took my breath away. His air was my air. His tongue was my life source. I began pulling on his shirt, to remove it, to feel for the first time his bare chest against mine.

But the kissing stopped. He looked into my eyes with a look of wonderment. It was as if he couldn't believe it either. We found each other. We finally found each other. Tears of joy streamed from my eyes. He wiped my tears away.

"Promise me you'll stay sweet," he said to me with love in his eyes, not lust. And he said it so sincerely, as if his very life depended on my response.

"I promise," I said. What else could I say? But that was enough. A smile came on his face and he leaned down and held me tighter. I held on to him and closed my eyes. It was time. It was time for him to remove all garments and enter me. My anticipation grew. My heartbeat quickened. The moment had arrived when my dream would come true and Derrick Moon McCalister would enter my body and we would morph as one.

But it didn't happen. The snoring got in the way. When I stretched my already big eyes far enough to see his face, I realized that he had fallen asleep. Just like that. The bases were loaded but the brother had struck out.

But it was wonderful still. He was with me that night, me, and he asked me to make a promise to him, a promise to stay sweet. It was such a simplistic request that I wondered if I had missed something. But I hadn't missed a thing. He needed my sweetness to calm his ruthlessness. He needed my compassion to keep his in check. In other words, he needed me. This great man, who was sleeping on top of me, who was everything I could have dreamed of and more, needed somebody like me. It wasn't the Ph.D. after all. It was me. Finding water on a deserted island would not have been more pleasurable.

But it didn't last. I woke up, the next day, to find him gone. No note, no explanation, gone. I cried, not because he left that way, but because I allowed it to happen again. A man shows me a little kindness and I'm sending out wedding invitations! I was pathetic. I lay in that bed thinking about how completely pathetic I really was and the more I thought about it the more I cried. But that didn't stop my craziness. For just as quickly as I realized what a hopeless case I was, I started looking at the telephone, praying that he would call.

But the call never came. Not then, not the next day, not the day after that. He didn't tell me he loved me after all. He just told me to stay sweet. But after days and days of nothing from Moon McCalister, being sweet was the last thing I wanted to be. I wanted to be ruthless and heartless like him, able to give somebody hope and snatch it back as soon as he grabbed for it. I wanted to drop in and out of somebody's life as if he never existed, as if the twinkle in his eye was nothing more than stardust, as if I had nothing to do with somebody else's happiness.

I was therefore primed for a change of pace in my life. After Peter Lawrence and his games and Moon McCalister and his disappearing acts, I was up for something different, something adventurous, even if it meant another big letdown.

Five
Sharon and the Preacher

It's a small world after all. There I was, wallowing in my own misery because some man wouldn't call me, and out of the blue comes my old running partner from my days back in Philly. Sharon Williamson. My ace boon coon before I knew Gina and Vera existed. The woman who had kept me in stitches about all her conquests (when she and I both knew that she was a virgin like I was). But sistergirl had a sho'-nuff imagination. And for girls like us, those who were too scared to allow a boy to go all the way, imagining it was as good as the real thing.

I saw her, of all places, at Walmart. I stopped by on my way home from work to pick up a pair of panty hose when there she was, over by the jewelry display case, holding up this gaudy pair of huge earrings. "What do you think?" she asked the saleslady.

"They're gorgeous," the saleslady said.

"Quit lying," Sharon said and threw the horrific-looking earrings back on the countertop. She was an extremely thin woman, wearing a pair of almost high-water suede pants and a small cotton T-shirt. She carried one of those Coach shoulder bags that was so well worn that its leather material had what appeared to be tread marks all over it. She wore her hair extremely short, in a cute man-cut Afro, and her once pretty round-shaped face was now showing the signs of what could only have been a hard life.

She began moving away from the jewelry section when I found myself calling her name. "Sharon?" I said. "Sharon Williamson?"

She turned toward me and stared at me. It seemed, at first, as if sistergirl wanted to pretend she didn't know me. But we went back too far for that to work. So she smiled instead. "Tory Coleman?" she asked. "I'll be damn. Is it really you?"

And that was the beginning. We hugged each other's neck, talked about how good each other looked (a lie on my part, hers too probably), and ended up at the McDonald's inside Walmart, sipping sodas and remembering old times.

We had met in elementary school when I was the new kid and she was the well-established classroom bully. We didn't really become friends until much later, high school, when I started carrying her books around for her. She asked and I did it. The other girls thought I had lost my mind but I liked Sharon. There was always something genuine about her. Most people just saw her as this hardhead who got her kicks bullying around unsuspecting bookworms, but I saw the other side. She was smart and funny and always had a good story to tell. And her dreams weren't wild like everybody else's. She didn't want to be rich or popular or the first woman president of the United States. She just wanted to be happy.

After high school we had both attended Temple University but Sharon had a hard time there. She stayed in the streets with some new friends she had made and her grades suffered. By the start of our sophomore year she was already on academic probation. So she dropped out. She walked into our dorm room and told me that she was not college material. "Who told you that lie?" I asked. She didn't answer. She just packed up her little bags and left.

"That was a long time ago," she said.

"Yeah. Did you imagine that night would be the last time we'd see each other?"

"Heck nall," she leaned back on the loud-colored seat and said.

"I thought I'd be back at Temple the next semester, to tell you the truth. But things got in the way."

She didn't elaborate so neither did I. It was obvious that it had been hell. It was written all over her face. Even her smile, which she attempted to display often, too often, had an edge to it. "But them was some good times, girl," she added. "We was close."

"Yes, Lord," I said.

"We was thick as thieves."

"You telling me. I can still remember the time when you snatched off Roberta Young's wig and ran around the cafeteria with it."

She laughed. "Wasn't she crazy? She was baldheaded Monday, then Tuesday her hair was down to her ankles. And she had the nerve to claim that it was her real hair. Heck yeah, I snatched it off. That baldheaded joker!"

I laughed until my belly ached but the conversation stayed on that superficial level the entire time. It wasn't the same. There was no way we were going to pick up where we had left off because there was too much life in between. Hers and mine. I had my scars from too many bad relationships and she had her scars too, from too much of something. It wasn't until I was set to leave, with that "it's getting late" excuse, that I had the first tangible clue of what girlfriend had really been through.

"Are you living here now?" I asked as I grabbed my pair of panty hose and my hobo bag.

"Yeah," she said. "I've only been here a couple days."

"Oh. Well, give me a call sometime. Where you staying?"

"City of Hope."

"City of who? I'm not familiar with that hotel."

She smiled. "You have not changed a lick, girl," she said. "I was just jiving. I'm around. Staying here and there."

City of Hope? City of Hope *Rescue Mission?* I looked at Sharon. Had it been *that* bad? "You're staying at a rescue mission?" I asked her.

* * *

She smiled. "I told you I was just kidding."

"My God, Sharon."

"What?"

"It's been that bad?"

She sat there and then she shook her head. "It's been pretty bad," she said.

"But what about your parents, your family?"

"My family, Tory? Come on. My mama was a junkie when it wasn't even fashionable. And my dad? The street pharmaceutical salesman? Please. Who he gonna help?"

"There's nobody then?"

"Nobody, girl."

"Did you ever marry?"

"Never been asked. But I got me three kids." She smiled when she said this. "Two boys and a little girl. Michael, Marlon, and Jackie. But the state took them all. That's why I'm here in Florida. For a fresh start. I figure I'll get me a job, a little place to stay, and they'll let 'em come back and live with me. That's all I got to do, they said. Get my act together."

She had said a mouthful. I didn't know what to do. I just stood there, almost in a state of frozen animation. If I had still been talking to Gina I could have called her for advice. Or even Vera. But both of those sisters were on my endangered list. They treated my problems with Peter Lawrence as if I were just overreacting. They never tried to understand how I felt. That was why I hung up the phone when Vera tried to call me again and I wouldn't take Gina's calls. They were a day late and a dollar short with all of their apologies, as far as I was concerned.

But Sharon was a different story. She was in need of a serious helping hand. I couldn't just walk away. Not from an old friend like her. We went back too far. Besides, it wasn't as if my life was bursting at the seams with excitement anyway. Maybe we could keep each other company. Maybe I could help a sister get back on her feet for a change.

"Let's go," I said to her as if I knew what I was doing.

"Go?" she asked. "Where?"

"To get your things. You're going to stay with me."

"With you?"

"Yes, with me. What? Do you have a problem with that?"

She smiled. "I ain't got no problem. But you sure you wanna do this?"

"Of course I'm sure," I said and grabbed her by the arm. I wasn't sure, not by a long shot, but I didn't see where I had a choice. No friend of mine was going to tell me that she was down on her luck, living at a rescue mission, and I would say *see ya, wouldn't wanna be ya*, and just walk away. No way.

I later learned that she had no things to get. Somebody at the mission stole everything she owned, she claimed, and all she had left were the clothes on her back.

That presented a problem of a different matter. She was too thin to wear any of my clothes and her suede pants and T-shirt were not the kind of attire normally worn at job interviews. And it wasn't as if I was independently wealthy. I was basically living from paycheck to paycheck with minor savings on the side. I knew I had to get her some clothes, but I first had to know where her head really was. Because if sistergirl didn't wanna work but just needed a place to crash, then her visit with me would be short-lived. But if she was serious about getting her act together and getting her kids back, then I was willing to do my part. But it was all up to her.

When we arrived at my condo Sharon walked in as if it were something special to behold. The white oak floors, the simple but well-maintained black leather living-room suite, the fireplace, the nook that led to a kitchen of hunter-green and eggshell-white linoleum and a wet bar loaded with few amenities but worth commenting on anyway, and, of course, the view on the balcony, the beautiful, breathtaking view of a somber lake almost hidden from sight by the trees and shrubbery surrounding it.

After all of her adjectives were exhausted we sat out on the balcony and sipped sherry. But she could not get over how large I was living. She knew I would make it, she said, but not like this. "You must be some rich chick," she looked at me and said. I smiled, tried to play the big shot for a minute, but then I got real.

"No, ma'am," I said. "I'm just trying to survive like everybody else."

"Sure, buddy," she said, wholly unconvinced by my humility. "You're a college professor and you have your own condo? Girl, who you think you jiving? You the man!"

I wasn't but I couldn't sway her either way. Besides, my bank account wasn't the issue. Her intentions were. So instead of going on and on about my success or lack thereof, I questioned her about her past. "So," I said, "what kind of work have you been doing?"

She looked at me curiously, as if I was coming on too strong too soon, and she walked over to the porch rail and leaned against it. "Why?"

"Not that I'm trying to be nosy, Share, but I thought we could have a better chance getting you some work if I had an idea about your work history, that's all."

"Oh," she said. But she still didn't answer my question. She looked over the balcony, at the lake, and again commented on the view. She walked around, folded her arms, and talked about the weather, the architectural design of the building, my hairstyle. We talked about everything but what we needed to discuss. I was still broken up over Moon and not yet ready to fall back into my book reading, C-SPAN-watching routine, so I let the conversation remain on the nostalgia tip. I actually enjoyed the talk. And Sharon proved to be an excellent listener. Even about my problem with Peter and my trials with the Moon.

"Where is this Peter now?" she asked.

"Out of town, I hope. He's out of my life anyway. And I'm very grateful to Moon for that."

"But why won't this Moon person pick up a phone and at least give you a call if he was willing to get rid of Peter for you?"

"I don't know. He told me to stay sweet and that was it. Just when I think we've made a connection, you know, he takes off. It's happened twice already. I guess he's just not interested in me."

"I guess not," she said. She didn't offer advice, however, which I appreciated; she simply listened. The only snide remark she made at all was when I told her about his music preference. "Frank Sinatra!" she yelled. "He need to quit."

But by the next day she was out of my life too. I woke up, looked on the couch expecting to find her there, but sistergirl was gone. Just like the Moon before her. I just stood there and shook my head. Even she couldn't bear my company. Even she preferred a rescue mission to me.

My self-esteem, by this time, was shot to hell. I felt as if my life was a disaster. I couldn't keep a man, friends, anybody. I thought about therapy, I really did. I thought about paying some shrink to lay me on her couch and let me spill my guts to her. But what could she tell me? She'd probably declare me nuts for real and recommend inpatient care. I even walked over to the math department and asked Jake Onstead if he knew a good therapist. He told me a therapist wasn't what I needed. "You need help, Victoria," he said. "You need to try Jesus."

I smiled when he said that, knowing it was a joke, but Jake wasn't kidding. It wasn't exactly the solution I had envisioned. But it was better than what I had. So I tried Him.

I read my Bible, which helped, and started visiting different churches throughout the city. One elder in a Mormon church showed me pictures of a group of very old looking white men and told me that except I join his church and allow one of those men to lay hands on me, I won't be going to heaven. Well, I thought, I won't be going back to *that* church, and I got the hell out. Any church that claimed to have the inside track on getting into heaven raised red flags for me.

The Muslims were no better. Those were some intense brothers at that mosque I attended, some seriously intelligent brothers. A group of them sat around a table while the rest of us sat in the audience supposedly mesmerized by their ability to quote Bible passages and demonstrate the superiority of the Koran on every point. To me it was absurd the way they took scriptures from the Bible and twisted and turned them to satisfy their own preconceived notions of life as we know it. And in the end, when every chapter was completed, it became all about race; all about the white man this and the poor black man that and how Allah teaches this and how Christianity teaches that and it was more like a comparative institution class than a church service. Since I wasn't looking for a history lesson, especially not that kind, I decided to leave.

"Can't take the truth, dear sister?" a brother asked as I approached the exit door.

"Apparently not," I replied and kept going.

I ended up at a Baptist church. The Zion Hope Missionary Baptist church. It was a big, redbrick structure on a slightly elevated hill near the campus of Florida State University. College students by the truckload were there, but the driving force of that establishment was its old-fashioned, tambourine-beating, sister So-and-So Big Mamas. They ushered me in, asked if I would fill out a visitor's card, told me that they were so glad I came, and then quickly tipped away.

The place was packed wall-to-wall with folks by the time I arrived. The choir was singing, which meant that everybody was on their feet. I immediately felt welcomed as I squeezed in between two nice young ladies who were clapping and singing along with the choir. Everybody seemed so happy and content that I stood up and joined in too. I felt as if I were at a rock concert, the way the music played and the way everybody stood up clapping and having a merry good time. It had been years since I last stepped foot in somebody's church and I knew right away that such a long absence was a big mistake. This was where I belonged. This was where I could forget about Peter, Vera, Gina, Sharon, and the Moon, stars, and rain, and just enjoy myself for a change. No wonder black folks went to church so much. It was like getting high. It was like an artificial high that made you want to burst through the sky.

I looked like the weather witch when we sat down, however, with the sweat pouring from my face and my hair doing pretty much what it wanted to do, but I didn't even care. I tried to shape it a little for beauty's sake but as soon as the next song began, I was on my feet again and so much for the shaping.

We were up and down and clapped and sang for over two hours before the pastor got up to preach. According to the program they gave me at the door, the sermon was to be administered by the Reverend Malcolm C. King, their wonderful pastor. He turned out to be a good preacher, I'll give him that, but I didn't see what was so wonderful about him. He was a short, compact man, black as a shoe, with a bushy midsize Afro and a bushy mustache that connected to a pair of very long sideburns. He had big, bug eyes that stretched every time he wanted to emphasize a point and he gave off a general persona of a very stern, no-nonsense man.

"God is able!" he yelled after reciting the various and wondrous things the Lord had done for him or a church member or a preacher formally known as a big-time sinning man. "Don't tell me God ain't able!"

After the sermon, and during the altar call, I found myself hurrying to join that church. The members actually applauded my decision, some even standing on their feet as if they knew a critical case when they saw one. I almost cried I was so happy. This appeared to be just the shot in the arm I needed. Even a homeless woman didn't want to be bothered with me. But I didn't mind. The church wanted me.

After signing up me and two other ladies, the church secretary ushered us into a suite of offices upstairs. She told us to wait, that the pastor would be with us momentarily. The protocol dictated that whenever someone joined the church they had to meet briefly with the pastor so that he could explain the church's philosophy and find out a little about us. We waited almost an hour. We talked among ourselves with the other two ladies growing extremely impatient as time went by. "When he does show up," one of the ladies, the most verbose of the two, said, "I'm going in first. I ain't got time to hang around this church all day. I got things to do."

"Me too," her cut partner, who wore one of the biggest hats I had ever seen, said. "I got next!"

That, of course, left me to pull up the rear. But I didn't mind at all. I was beginning to feel a little better, which, for me, was the point.

But time was becoming a problem. I began to wonder if they had forgotten that we were back there. I decided to check it out. Talk about timing. As soon as my mind told me to stand up and see what the delay was about, Pastor King came lumbering in. He immediately extended his hand to me. "And you are?" he asked.

"Tory. I mean Victoria," I said. I was suddenly nervous and out of sorts. He looked very different up close.

"Come with me, Victoria," he said and I followed him. I looked back at the two ladies yet in waiting and they gave me a look something cross. This was not how they said we were going to do it. The fast-talking lady was to go first. Then the lady with the big hat. And then finally me. Just by standing up to find out more information, I had thrown the entire plan off course. But what could I do? Tell the pastor of the church that no, I can't come yet because the fast-talking lady called for first first? He would think I was some kind of idiot if I told him that.

His office was small but nice enough with a big, metal desk and two chairs for visitors. He motioned for me to sit in one of the chairs and, to my surprise, he sat in the other chair. He leaned back, crossed his legs, and rested his elbows on the chair's arms. He was exhausted. His eyes, which looked so big and buglike to me in the sanctuary, now looked soft and droopy and, I must admit, sexy. Yes, sexy! But I knew he was a preacher so I had to recuse myself from checking him out the way I was prone to do. I instead concentrated on the spirituality he radiated and his charisma, although I couldn't help but notice how muscular he was. *Dang*, I kept saying to myself, *he looks good!*

He talked for maybe five minutes straight about the history of the Zion Hope Baptist Church and what every member was required to do (attend five classes for new members, attend Sunday school regularly, be of good, moral character, etc.). He then asked if I thought I could do these things. I told him yes eagerly. He then looked me dead in the eyes. "That includes premarital sex," he said.

I looked at him as if he were a mind reader. "Excuse me?" I asked innocently, although I knew full well what he was talking about.

"We do not sanction in any way, shape, or form premarital sex. We view it, indeed the Bible views it, as an abomination before the Lord. If you can't abstain, then marry. For it is better to marry than to burn."

I wanted to fall out of my chair. Why would he say such things to me? I bet he wasn't going to tell the woman in the big hat all of this. Why tell it to me? Did I have a sign on my forehead notifying the world that I was in heat and wanted some? Besides, what made him so certain that I wasn't married already? I had my left hand hidden from his sight, he couldn't have assumed I wasn't married by the absence of a band. How then? So I asked him.

"You don't emit the spirit of a married woman," he said.

"Oh," I said. That's some deep shit, I wanted to say.

"Now," he said, "tell me about yourself."

I had decided before I went in that I was not going to mention the fact that I was a college professor and had my Ph.D. I had some warped idea that if I was to tell how successful I was, those poor church folk would fall to their knees and try to worship *me*. My plan, then, had been to be a down-to-earth, everyday person. But that was before I saw the preacher up close and personal. I'd never known a good-looking man I didn't try to impress. So before he could even finish asking me to tell him about myself I was telling him that I had a Ph.D. and was a professor of history at Florida A&M University.

"I see," he said, wholly unimpressed. "We have quite a few FAM-U professors as members here. There's Doctor Akbar, Doctor Malbury, Doctor Lusaid. Maybe you know some of them?"

"Only by name," I said. I felt arrogant and foolish. But the reverend didn't seem to mind. He even smiled at me.

"Where are you from? Are you originally from Tallahassee?"

"Oh no," I said again with marked arrogance. I could not believe my missteps. "I mean, no. I mean, Tallahassee is a wonderful town but I'm just not from it. That's not to say that I would not have liked to be from it but . . ." I was a babbling idiot and the reverend knew it. He looked down, at his hands, as if he wanted to spare me the agony of having a spectator witness my *life's most embarrassing moments* moment. "I'm from Philly," I finally said.

"Ah, Philadelphia. The city of brotherly love. Nice."

And then he asked me to tell the next person to come in on my way going out. I was not ready to leave so I awkwardly rose. He stood too, he was a perfect gentleman, and watched and smiled at me until I was clean out of sight. I told the fast-talking lady that she could go in now. She gave me a cold, hard stare, and then I left. I somehow had the feeling that I had missed an opportunity. I didn't know what that opportunity was, just that I had missed it.

A week later, on a Saturday morning, Sharon Williamson was knocking at my front door. She said she came to apologize for leaving the way she did but she had to go and straighten out some things. My better instincts told me to slam the door in her face but I was trying to walk that Christian walk at the time, so I let her in.

She plopped down on my leather couch as if it were a picnic table bench at Walmart, her well-worn Coach bag dropping to the floor as her feet hit down. Before I could take a seat beside her she looked up at me intensely and asked if she could stay with me until she found a job. "I'm ready now," she said with certainty. "I got things straightened out and I'm ready now."

I was skeptical. "What did you have to straighten out, Share?" I asked her.

"Things, stuff," she said, pulling out a cigarette. "You know."

I didn't know but I also didn't pursue it. I was still on such a religious high that I began to think that maybe my helping out Sharon was a part of some divine plan, some great plan within the scheme of plans of the Almighty Himself. It was a plan, all right.

It started that evening when I took her shopping. I had decided to buy her the bare necessities: a dress for work and church interchangeably, a pair of dress shoes, a casual outfit and shoes, and lingerie.

First of all, sistergirl didn't appreciate the fact that I wanted to take her to Walmart to find some lingerie. She wanted to go to Victoria's Secret. And the nice pair of tennis shoes that I wanted to purchase her from Payless Shoe Store was a joke to her.

"*Pro Wings?*" she said. "What kind of name is that? I ain't never heard of no *Pro Wings*. You better get me some Air Jordans or K-Swiss or Reeboks up in here or we can forget it!"

Then forget it, I should have said, but I didn't. I bought her what she wanted. She sat in my car with her bags of name-brand clothes and shoes that cost more than what I normally purchased for myself, and didn't even say thank you. But Sharon was always a proud woman, so I let it slide.

The next day proved just as taxing. I thought it would be a good idea for us to go to church together, since I had gone out and bought her a dress specifically for the occasion, but she was not interested. She was laid out on my leather couch in my quiet living room as if she were a sack of potatoes taking up space. I shook her and told her it was time to get up for church.

She opened her eyes, mad as hell. "What?"

"It's time to get ready for church."

She looked at me as if I were stone crazy. She was speechless. So I repeated myself. "It's time to get ready for church, Share," I said.

She continued to stare at me, her eyes unblinking, her face so pissed off that I thought she would do me harm.

I left and went to church. It was crowded, as usual, and Pastor King was as feisty as ever. He preached about Lot's wife and the danger of looking back. It was an uplifting sermon and everybody in the sanctuary was on their feet before it was done. The lady seated next to me kept commenting on how great he could preach. Finally, I agreed with her. "Amen to that, sister," I said.

"Can't he preach?" she asked again. "And he's so good lookin' too. It's amazing how a man that good lookin' ain't married!"

When she said he wasn't married I stopped in the middle of a clap and looked at her. It felt as if something had hit me with a sledgehammer. *Ain't married?* That wonderful, charismatic creature *ain't married?* I kept turning it over and over in my head. Your boy ain't married? He is without wife? He is available? He is an eligible, available man? I couldn't believe it. I wanted details, like why not and was he ever married, but I didn't know that sister well enough to ask her all of those questions. Besides, women can smell competition a mile away. She and what I estimated to be about fifty other women in that church had their eyes on the good reverend.

"Are you all right?" she touched my arm and asked. I finally released my suspended animation.

"Yes," I said. "Fine." But I sat down anyway.

After getting over the initial shock of his availability, I realized almost immediately that I had some serious work to do. A man like that didn't come easy. He wasn't single by accident. He was fastidious. He didn't settle for anything. His demands were probably so high that they were outrageous, that was why boyfriend was without wife. But the reality of it didn't scare me away. I had Moon McCalister in my life once. I had high standards too. And if my competition was going to be a third of a whole church, then I was ready, willing, and able to take them on. "Bring them on!" I said to myself as I shook the reverend's hand at the exit door and proceeded toward my car. He didn't know it at the time, as he stood at that door and thanked me for attending service, but he and I were going to make some beautiful music together, soon and very soon.

My entire drive home was focused on the reverend and what I could possibly do to win him over. I know it seemed crazy, trying to jump into another relationship after falling for the Moon, but what else was I going to do? Stop living? Pick up the chastity belt and become a eunuch just because of one man who didn't have enough sense to know that he had himself a good sister? That wasn't about to happen. It was hard in this world alone. And like a miracle out of the blue, without my even thinking about it, Pastor King came along. I was going to snatch up that brother if it was the last thing I did. I was due a good relationship. Hell, I was due a grand wedding and a wonderful marriage too! I was tired of failed relationships. Pastor King was no Moon McCalister in the looks department, I'll admit that. But he dwarfed him on the question of character. And that's what I decided I needed. A man of character. A man who, by his very nature, just couldn't break a woman's heart.

Sharon was just waking up when I walked in the door of my condo. I slammed the door shut on purpose, causing her to excitedly jump awake. Her hair stood on top of her head and her eyes were as big as mine. Girlfriend looked bad. But at least she was up.

"Oh," I said, "did I wake you?"

She looked at me as if I were crazy. "Yes," she said and sat up on the couch. "What time is it?"

"Almost three."

"Damn," she said. "I must've been tired."

Or lazy, I thought. I went into the bedroom and changed. She had to go. I didn't seem as interested in helping out the divine plan that Sunday the way I wanted to help the day before. I had something on my mind now. I had strategies to plot and battles to win and I didn't need Minnie the Moocher hanging out distracting me. I decided, changing clothes, that it would be more convenient for me to give her the money to get her own place right away (like that next day) than to wait until I was able to find her a job and then wait still longer for her to get paid. She was already an expensive friend but, I decided, getting her up from around me was worth the expense.

I told her about it at dinner. We put two TV dinners in the microwave and took a seat at the kitchen table, waiting for them to heat. She was even mad about that.

"I ain't never been crazy about no TV dinners," she said.

"Oh really?" I said. Chick had some nerve, I tell you. "Then why don't you go buy you something that you like?"

"I would if I could," she said. "Can you loan me twenty bucks?"

Sistergirl was through dealing. I almost told her something real good, like if it wasn't for me she would be hanging out in a gutter eating something substantially less tasty than a TV dinner, but I let it go. I could never stand a person who helped somebody out, then threw it in her face every two minutes, even if she deserved to have it thrown there. So I let it slide. But it sure as hell made it easier to say what I originally had to say.

"You got to go," I said.

She looked at me and frowned. "What?" she asked.

"Two women under the same roof ain't cuttin' it."

"What are you talking about? I barely been under your precious roof one full day! What are you talking about?"

She was right. We had a rough day yesterday but very little contact today. But things had changed for me. I met a man. Well, I didn't exactly meet him in the traditional sense, but I found out that the man I found attractive was single. And if all went well, I didn't need some woman up in here preventing me from bringing my man home. She had to go. "I'll help you get a job and a place to stay," I told her, "but as far as staying here with me, I don't think so."

She waited a little while and then she smiled and shook her head. "It's a man, ain't it?"

Damn. I couldn't conceal shit from anybody. "Yes, but—"

"Yes, but nothin'," she said. "You're just like the rest of them, you know that? You'll sell your girl to the devil, your own homegirl, because of some crusty-ass man you just met! And what's gonna happen? It's gonna last two damn minutes like all those other relationships of yours lasted, and then you'll need me again. Well, guess what? I ain't gonna be around next time!"

She got up and went into the bedroom. I got up and rushed behind her. She was telling the truth and nothing but. And I felt like hell.

"Look, Sharon, you're right, okay? But I can't help it!"

"Oh, don't even go there," she said as she threw in a bag the new dress I bought her. "You can help it. You can damn sho' help it! But that's cool, you know. I can't give you none of that bed action, I know. But why the hell you wastin' your time goin' to church and tryin' to be so religious if all you want out of a relationship is a little bed action? Hell, you ain't nothin' but a ho if that's what it's all about!"

It was more than that, way more, but I felt foolish even thinking about telling her that it was. I knew I should have just left the room and let her leave mad. After all, I didn't put her in the predicament she was in. I helped her for one day to stay out of her predicament. I fed her, bought her a brand-new dress, and that was the thanks I was getting? I knew I should have let her go. But against my better judgment again I begged her to stay. I even offered to take her out to dinner to her favorite restaurant if she would only stay. She sat on the bed and thought about it (can you believe that?) and finally agreed to stay. But only on one condition.

"What's that?" I asked.

"I live here and I leave here on my terms," she said. "Okay?"

I even agreed to that. Can you believe me? This homeless person had more control over me than I had over myself. I was a mess. I was a sorry excuse for anything remotely resembling an independent woman.

Gina called a few days later. She, at first, tried to act as if nothing had ever happened between the two of us but when she could tell that I wasn't going for it, she got to the point. It seemed she and Isaac, hubby number four, were having a dinner party two weeks from Saturday night and she was wondering if I would be interested in attending. I told her that I would think about it and hung up the phone. I was a bitch and I knew it. Gina and Vera were my ace boon coons from way back, but I was treating them as if they had snatched a man from me or something.

It didn't hurt, however, that I had Sharon. After that Sunday afternoon we became real tight again. Forget that every job I offered to take her to check out, she didn't like. Forget that every day I came home from work she had my house looking as if a tornado had been through it. Forget that she was selfish, inconsiderate, lazy, and had thrown me completely off my rhythm and into a funk with her. She knew what I needed and she played it to the max. For as soon as I tried to set her straight or kick her out or give her an ultimatum, she launched into a discussion of Pastor King and exactly what strategies were I going to employ? I was, by that time, so lust struck and unfulfilled that I totally lost my train of thought and fell for her bait. I knew what she was doing, but I was powerless to see it for what it was. I wanted the preacher. I needed that preacher to fill the void Moon had left. And anybody willing to listen to me talk about how badly I wanted him, and help me develop a strategy to get him, was all right with me.

The week that followed was a tough one. I tried numerous ways to get the good reverend interested, but he barely gave me the time of day. Every time the church doors were opened I would call and see if Pastor King was in. If his secretary said yes, I would hang up the phone. Then I would somehow show up at the church. I would claim to have a question about some biblical reference or I would claim to want to join this auxiliary or that board, and he would gladly oblige my requests. But it never went beyond that.

One night after Bible study I got up the nerve to ask him out for coffee, but before I could get a word out edgewise an emergency with a member came up and he had to leave. I was getting nowhere fast. And I knew I had to hurry and come up with something because the ladies around the church were quite suspicious of me and knew, by their looks and head shakes, that I was no more interested in some Bible verse or joining some auxiliary than they were. From what I heard, they had been trying for years to get the inside track and had failed every time. What made me so special to just come off the street and try to claim their man? My determination, that's what!

But even with that great determination I was still in no better position to win over the preacher than anybody else. But my hopes changed one Friday night when Sharon, of all people, came up with what I thought was an ingenious plan. It was deceitful and wrong and filled with the kind of manipulation of events that most folks would frown upon, but it was a masterful plan. She was to phone the church and ask to speak with the reverend. She would then tell him that he needed to come to my apartment expeditiously because I was suicidal and she didn't know what to do. I was to look beautiful when he arrived and sweep him off his feet, giving him credit for being my rescuer. Sharon would stay around to help perpetuate the lie; then she would get lost for a few hours. Coming up with such a scheme was a stroke of genius, I thought. But that's how out of whack my sense of reason had become. A pathetic con artist like Sharon was my mentor.

She phoned just after we estimated church would end and, sure enough, he came knocking at my door. I was lying on the sofa, my feet up, my damsel-in-distress look holding steady. I was dressed in a beautiful blue pantsuit and my home smelled of lilacs on a summer day. It was perfect.

He walked in hurriedly. When I looked up and saw him he looked even more attractive than I had remembered. My heart fluttered. Finally my potential future husband was in my living room. I felt as if I could die and go to heaven at that very moment and would be perfectly suited for the occasion.

Unfortunately I had died and gone to heaven with company because coming into my living room behind the reverend were two wide-framed Big Mamas from the church, Sister Kelley and Sister Blakely. They knew what my game was before they stepped foot in my house, I could see it all over their faces, those sisters could smell a rat a mile away. I felt like a fool. But it was too late to turn back now. For if I changed my tune, then they would know for sure that it was all a scam.

"Reverend King?" I said as if I were surprised to see him.

"I didn't tell her y'all was coming," Sharon told them as if she knew all along they *all* were coming.

"Sister Coleman," the reverend asked excitedly, "are you all right? Your friend said you was having some trouble here, that you was suicidal."

I had to put it on thick right about now, and I knew it. I forced myself to cry (it's easy when you're as pathetic as I was) and I looked down. The plan was for the reverend, at that moment, to walk up to me and pat me lovingly on my back. But before I knew anything, Sister Kelley rushed up to me and grabbed me by the arms while

Sister Blakely rushed up and grabbed me by the hips. They slung me off the couch and started dragging me around the living room.

"Get up, child!" Sister Kelley yelled. "We got to get them pills out of you!"

Those Negroes knew I didn't have any pills in me but they slung me around that living room all the same. I slung past Sharon but she was laughing so hard that she had to turn her back. That wonderful, majestic pose that had taken me damn near ten minutes to concoct was gone. I looked like a rag doll the way they snatched me around that room. I was getting so angry, not to mention dizzy, that I almost snatched away from those sisters and beat the hell out of them. But I doubt if that would have helped my cause. That was why I, instead, in as sweet a voice as I could manage, told them to knock it off. "I didn't take no pills," I said softly. They, of course, pretended as if they didn't hear me. So I said it a little louder and then a little louder still. When I realized they were determined to drag me around until doomsday if they had to, I got ghetto on them sisters and snatched away from them. "I didn't take no goddamn pills!" I screamed. They smiled.

I looked at the reverend. My heart was in my shoe. But he looked at Sharon instead. "Is that true, young lady?" he asked her.

She looked at him, said, "Yes, it's the truth," and then turned around grinning. I couldn't believe her. All of that laughing and grinning only made me look like the biggest liar this side of living, but Sharon didn't care. It was all a big joke to her and she certainly let Pastor know it was. But he, being the dear man he was, didn't let on for one moment that he was disappointed in me. He even helped me back to the couch.

"Sit back down, sister," he said. "It's gonna be all right."

It sho' nuff was all right after he touched me. He touched me! I felt so good I started smiling. But Sisters Kelley and Blakely had radar detectors and could sense that I was loving the reverend's touch. They politely but forcefully pushed the reverend aside and took over the touching of me. Sister Kelley started rubbing my hair and making a point of messing it up while Sister Blakely kept thumping me in my back in the guise of comforting me. They weren't going to stop until every strand of my hair was pointing in every direction conceivable and my back was damn near broken.

"God don't like suicide," Sister Blakely said.

"He don't like ugly either," Sister Kelley added.

"You kill yo'self, child, you gonna go straight to hell. You hear me now? You'll toast in hell you keep this up!"

I looked at Sister Blakely. She was having a field day with me. She and Sister Kelley both knew that the entire scene was a fraud and they were milking it for all they could. Even Pastor King began to get suspicious. He walked over and kneeled down. His big eyes looked at me with a mix of concern and contempt. Those church ladies were winning him over, I could tell. All of my hopes for a life with him were slipping fast.

"Sister Coleman, why are you doing this?"

My heart sank. He knew! "Doing what?" I asked.

"Contemplating suicide! It's wrong. Don't you know you can't be forgiven for such an ungrateful act?"

"I know," I said with such a look of pity that he touched me gently on the shoulder. Naturally Sister Kelley saw the touch.

"I don't know what you up to," she said and the reverend and I both looked at her, "but black folks don't be committing no suicide. Now I may not have all the edumacation you got but I got enough sense to know that!"

"What are you getting at, Sister Kelley?" the reverend asked her.

"Uh-huh. Ask her. She know what I'm talking about."

He looked at me. Sister Kelley really knew how to do it, I had to give her credit. She really knew how to mess your game up. It was a good thing that the reverend was there or it would have been on. Me and Big Mama would have been two fighting Negroes up in my condo that night.

Finally the reverend said, "This is about a man, isn't it, Sister

Coleman?" and I closed my eyes in shame. When I reopened them Sharon was over in a corner bent over laughing. She knew how to mess your game up too. She and Sister Kelley would have made a good tag team.

But Pastor King kept talking. "It's always about a man. This is one of the most unfortunate things about my ministry. You ladies have got to learn that there's more to life than having a man or pursuing a man or lamenting over not having a man."

"She lamentin', all right," Sister Kelley said. "And I bet you right, Reverend: It's about a man. But ask her who the man is."

The reverend did not look away from Sister Kelley (thank God!). He frowned at her. "What difference does that make? A man is a man. Who he is hasn't anything to do with it."

Amen! I wanted to say.

"Even when the man is you?" Sister Blakely said and I could have died! I could not believe she would say such a thing. I never told that witch about my feelings for the reverend. It was true that my every behavior indicated that I was up to something, but she wasn't *certain* of it. How could she make such a bold statement without being certain? And she called herself a Christian!

The reverend stood up. He was visibly upset. "I want you and Sister Kelley to leave now," he said to Sister Blakely. Both she and Kelley got mad.

"We ain't done nothing but tell the truth," Kelley said.

"Good evening, ladies," the reverend said.

They both hemmed and hawed a little longer but when they saw that the reverend wasn't playing, they sailed their suspicious behinds out of my house. Their little espionage trip failed. God is good.

I looked at Sharon. It was her time to sail away home too. But that sister wasn't budging. She even took a seat in the chair. She didn't want me to be with the reverend, who was she kidding? I get him, then I wouldn't need her anymore and she knew it. She concocted this suicide ploy to end my desire for King once and for all.

She expected everything we planned to backfire. And it almost did, let's be for real here, but not totally. At least not the part of the story that mattered: i.e., the reverend stayed.

But my triumph was short-lived. For he was angry with me too. He sat down on the couch beside me. His kind eyes and sincerity made me feel bad. I could tell at once that he was not the kind of man you schemed to get. His spirit was too pure. It wouldn't work in the end.

"You did not mean to commit suicide at all, did you?" he asked me point-blank.

I sat up and decided to deny everything. "What do you mean?" I asked.

"Respect me enough, or at least my position, to tell me the truth."

It touched me deeply when he said that. I was being disrespectful to him, the cloth, God, everything that is supposed to be holy and right. How could I do that? How could I burn so greatly in my own lust and desire not to understand how low-down and dirty all of my carrying on was? I was willing to lie and cheat and God only knows what else to get that man. And he was a man of the cloth! How could I do that to a man of the cloth?

Tears began to drop from my eyes. I cried partly because I felt bad but also because I wanted him to be moved by my contrition. He wasn't.

"I'm the pastor of a very large church, Sister Coleman, with many members who have serious needs. I preached two funerals this morning and officiated tonight's service that included a very long and taxing altar call. I was very tired. But then I received a call from your friend who told me to come immediately because you were attempting to commit suicide. I came immediately. I dropped everything else I needed to do and came. I could tell by the reactions of certain of my members that it was probably a hoax, but I came." He then turned his body toward me and looked me squarely in the eyes. "I'm not interested in a relationship with you or anyone else, Sister Coleman. Pastoring Zion Hope is all the emotionalism that I can stand in my life. I don't want or need a mate. That is why I'm not married. It's a choice that I made, it is a vow I made to God. Next time, be careful what you try to conquer."

He tried to say more, mainly about how deplorable I was deep down, but I couldn't take anymore. I guess he realized it and so he got up and left.

I went into my bedroom and fell across the bed. This was too much. Nobody but some depraved human being like me would be so crazy as to even consider deceiving a preacher into a romance! How low could I go to think *that* was all right? He probably thought I was some nymphomaniac coming on to him the way I did with that grand scheme of Sharon's.

Sharon. I forgot about her. What was with all of that grinning and carrying on? Sistergirl knew it wouldn't work—she was a slick witch from way back—she knew a bad scam when she saw it. And she pulled me into it anyway.

I got off of that bed and went back into the living room. The more I thought about how she played on my loneliness, the angrier I became. She was in the kitchen, seated at the table, hogging down a ham and cheese sandwich. Girlfriend looked satisfied. Girlfriend looked as if she had the world on a string pulling it in whichever direction she chose.

"Have some?" she asked, offering me my own food. She had some nerve, I tell you.

"You knew it wouldn't work," I walked up to the table and said.

She played dumb. "What you talking about?"

"Don't play crazy with me, okay? You knew that suicide ploy wouldn't work, that's why you thought it up!"

She smiled and shook her head. "I had my doubts about it, yeah," she said. "But you got so excited and kept telling me how brilliant I was for coming up with it so I figured maybe it could work. I mean, you're the one with the Ph.D. and you was calling it 'masterful' and 'ingenious.' So, hey, I figured you would know."

"It was masterful and ingenious all right. Now I have to leave a church I love."

"I'm sorry about that but, hey, you know?"

She was on one of her *hey, you know* kicks now, which was bugging the hell out of me, and every time she said it I wanted to claw her eyes out.

"We tried it, Tory. You wanted to try something and we tried it. But don't blame me because it didn't work out."

"Hell yeah, I'm blaming you! You didn't have to do all of that skinning and grinning and just give it away!"

"Them church ladies knew what you was up to, that's why I couldn't stop laughing. And I'm sorry if you're offended by that but, hey, you know?"

"But if you couldn't control yourself you should have got up and left."

"Now look here, sister," she said, thoroughly offended, "you ain't gonna stand up here and put all this shit at my feet! He didn't want yo' ass, all right? It's as simple as that. He looked at you, said no thank you, ma'am, and got the hell out of here. It ain't my fault he didn't want you."

She was on a roll. Oh, sistergirl had the head bobbing and the fingers snapping and she was on a big-time roll. But just watching her angered me. That was why I yelled for her to get out of my house as fast as her big, lazy feet could take her. She looked at me.

"Oh. So you want me to leave now?"

And I thought she was on the stupid side. "Yeah, I think that's what I'm getting at," I said, playing dumb too.

"Okay. All right. Uh-huh. Yeah. No problem. Ain't no problem. Soon as morning come, I'll be gone."

"No, ma'am. Now. I want you out now."

She looked at me as if something were wrong with me. I became a little worried because I didn't know if the streets had taught her how to be violent too, but I held my ground. She had to go and go right away, before I did what I usually did and changed my mind.

She left. Without another word she walked out of my house and life seemingly for good. As soon as the door slammed shut I leaned against it. I thought I would be relieved when she left, but I wasn't. I was just lonely again.

That weekend turned out to be one of the worst weekends of my life. I walked around, sat around, looked out my windows. But mostly I ate. I must have gained five pounds that weekend. I knew, by Sunday night, that I had to get out of this funk or it was going to destroy me.

That was why I called Gina. I was ready to forgive all because I needed her. Her husband answered the phone. He said that Gina was out of town on business (she was trying a case in Kansas) and she wasn't due back until midweek. He reminded me about the party they were having in a couple of weeks and told me they would not rest until I arrived. "It's Gina's first dinner party since she's been in Florida," he said. "She's depending on your presence."

I thanked Isaac for the invite and told him that I would try my best to make it. I was lying, of course, since I had zero intentions of going—especially going manless—but I wasn't about to tell some husband of Gina's all of that.

I called Vera too. I got the recorder. I had forgotten. It was Sunday night. She and Rollie spent all day and night in church on Sundays. Even their recorder bespoke of their great faith as they recited Bible passages and played gospel songs before the beep. When the beep did finally come, I hung up. So much for reconciliation, I thought.

My breakup with Sharon lasted all of five days. On Wednesday, while I was in my office attempting to understand why more than half the class missed question number four on my weekly quiz when it was not, in my view, ambiguous at all, Sharon walked through my door. I looked up. She was nicely dressed in the dress that I had bought her and had her hair looking reasonably decent.

"Your secretary lady told me to come on in," she said. "I hope you don't mind."

"No," I said.

"I was wondering if them jobs I turned down before was still available 'cause I'm ready to work now."

That was good news. I had to see it to believe it, however, but it was a good start. "I don't know," I said. "But I can check."

And we were on again. Jake Onstead's office needed a part-time clerical person to do the filing and Sharon, with her very limited skills, was perfect for the position. She was hired and could start work the following day. She also moved back in with me. Why was I continually making the same mistakes over and over? I couldn't say. It could have been anything. Loneliness. Desperation. Or just plain stupidity. But I did let her move back in.

And it was all good at first. We talked a lot about the old days in Philly (again) and talked long and loud about how no-good most of the men we had dated were and how we were so much wiser to their ways and how we wished we knew then what we knew now because if we did we wouldn't have given most of those losers a second look. It was all good. Until that next day when Jake Onstead paid a visit to my office.

"What do you mean she quit?" I asked him.

"She told my secretary that she was leaving and she left. She did stay long enough, however, to say that we was to mail her paycheck to your address."

I couldn't believe it. "Her paycheck?"

"That's what she said. For those two or three hours she worked for us."

I spent maybe ten minutes apologizing to Jake. He was a kind, gentle man whom you never wanted to disappoint. He helped everybody out and the first time I asked him to help me by hiring

Share, she quit on him. And after only a few hours! I couldn't believe it.

I also couldn't wait to get home to set your girl straight. But she was one step ahead of the thought police, as usual. She met me at the door as I walked in.

"I got a job," she said.

At first I was surprised. Then I was curious. "A job?"

"Yep. A courier job."

"Courier? What kind of courier's job?"

"You know. A transporter. I transport mail for this private company and they pay me up front, cash in hand."

I took a seat on my living-room sofa. She had her bedclothes on the floor and my entire front room looked like a pigpen. "Wait a minute," I said. "How can you be a courier or transporter if you don't even have transportation?"

She smiled and sat down on the sofa next to me. "That's where you come in at," she said.

I sat up tall. I figured I was coming in there somewhere.

"I told them I could work only on the nights that you don't have class and they said okay."

I was truly baffled. "Wait a minute, Share. What does my having classes or not having classes have to do with your job?"

"On the nights that you don't have classes, then you can drive me around to make my drops. I would take your Toyota myself and drive it but, you know, I ain't got my license straight."

It was so far-fetched, so beyond reasonableness that I burst into laughter. I laughed and laughed. Sharon, herself confused (that's how far gone sistergirl was), started laughing too. We laughed and laughed. Then I straightened up, told her hell no, and took a shower.

That very night Sharon and I were picking up packages from shady characters named Snoop and Turk and Ice Pick and Mad Dog and dropping them off to equally shady characters with equally shady names. I stayed in the car for the most part but by the fourth drop-off and pickup I had to be a fool not to know what was going on. We were in a part of Tallahassee known as French Town, for one thing, where criminal conduct was not an unusual occurrence, and it was the time of night where any self-respecting courier would have long since clocked out. Sharon, my old homegirl, had done it to me again. She wasn't a part of some legitimate drop-off operation, but was dropping off dope or money or both to those underworld gangstas just as sure as the sky was blue. When I came to this realization, however, Sharon had apparently come into something too because she ran back to the car and jumped in.

"*Go! Go! Go!*" she yelled, hitting her hand on the dashboard and looking back, terrified.

I cranked up without asking why but before I could make a move I heard a big crash behind me. When I turned around I saw where a big brick had sailed through my back windshield and put a hole the size of a basketball in it. The brick landed at the foot of my stick shift and Sharon and I both looked at the brick and then at each other. I heard a male voice yell ". . . want my damn money!" but I didn't see him because I was gone in the blink of an eye.

I didn't realize we were being followed until I turned the corner out of French Town. Then I saw the real danger. About four men in an old Plymouth were driving behind us swerving like maniacs. The shooting didn't start until we were on Tennessee Street. I swerved around corners and ducked in and out of traffic and cussed Sharon and my own stupid behind and cried and complained and screamed for mercy from on high until a police car from out of nowhere started chasing our pursuers, causing them to turn and travel in the opposite direction. But before I could even think about relaxing, another police car started chasing me. Sharon told me to gas it, that we could "lose the cop" if I would pick up speed, but I looked at her instead. I was crazy but I wasn't *that* crazy. I pulled over to the side of the road.

SURVIVING MR. RIGHT

* * *

We were allowed one phone call. I looked at the desk sergeant at the Tallahassee Police Department and exhaled. I wanted to call Gina, since I knew I would be needing representation, but I didn't want to waste my call if she was still out of town. I could have phoned Vera, because I knew I would eventually need bail money, but I couldn't bear hearing her sanctimonious lectures tonight.

"I ain't got all night, lady," the desk sergeant said. "Now who's it gonna be?"

It seemed inevitable that I would try it, so I did. "Moon McCalister," I said self-assuredly. Why not? I thought. He had the money. Bailing me out and finding me adequate representation was the least he could do after sleeping in my bed. The sergeant, however, looked at me as if he could not believe the name that had dripped off of my tongue.

"Moon McCalister?" he asked. "The councilman?"

"The former councilman, yes," I said and pulled out his office phone number.

I did not talk to him, only his answering service, but I left the message with her. I was relieved and disappointed at the same time. But that's what kind of night it was.

Another officer escorted me back to the cell, a small box of a place where Sharon was sitting as if she was terrified.

She stood up when I walked in. Her face betrayed mightily her inner uneasiness as she rubbed her arm and stretched her eyes. "Did you get somebody?" she asked anxiously. But I did not answer her. I lay down on the small bed instead.

"What's the matter with you?" she asked. "I told you to gas it, I told you to keep going."

"Why did you steal their money, not to mention their drugs? Did you actually think you could get away with that?"

"Yeah, I could've got away with it."

147

"Spare me, Sharon, all right?"

"I could've got away with it if you didn't act like you was drivin' Miss Daisy and took yo' ass on!"

Now it was my fault. And it was, in a way. I was an accessory to all kinds of felonies, thanks to my buddy over there. And all she could think about was how she didn't get away with it. All she could think about was how, if I would not have agreed to drive her around in the first place, she would still have her freedom.

Less than an hour later Lieutenant Bud Driscoll, Moon's hippie friend, walked up. "Victoria?" he asked, not certain if it was me.

"Yes," I said and stood to my feet. Sharon stood too.

He motioned for the guard to unlock the cell door. "Come with me," he said. Sharon proceeded to follow.

"Just her," he said.

I followed him down a long corridor and into a small office area. He sat on the edge of the desk and offered me a seat. I sat down. He pulled out a cigarette and offered me one. I gladly accepted.

"So," he said, "you're Mac's girl."

"Yes," I said. I wasn't, actually, but if pretending I was would get me an advantage I was more than willing to play the game.

Bud folded his arms and shook his head. "He's on his way," he said. "And he ain't no happy camper."

I leaned back in the chair and closed my eyes. I hated that I had to call him at all, especially on nonsense like this. I know his answering service lady thought I was out of my mind. Tell Mr. McCalister that I'm in jail and need his help. I bet he couldn't believe it. He already didn't want to have anything to do with me under normal circumstances. But this? I felt like crawling under Bud's desk. What kind of irresponsible human being was I? First I'm involved with some psycho stalker who breaks into my home and makes my life a living hell and now I'm making narcotics drop-offs with a shady lady who couldn't care if I was dead or alive.

It was unbelievable the way my life had turned. Florida was supposed to be my new beginning. It was a new beginning, all right. A new beginning of the same old nonsense, only farther south and more outrageous.

I apparently fell asleep sitting in Bud Driscoll's office because when my eyes reopened, the Moon stood in front of me. He wore a light blue warm-up suit and a pair of Nike high-tops. He looked young and vibrant. But Bud was right. He wasn't happy at all.

"Hey," I said and attempted to sit up straight in my chair.

"*Driving the getaway car?*" he asked with a look of sheer bewilderment on his face.

"I didn't know what was going on," I said in a plea for mercy.

"You're a well-educated woman but your judgment, Victoria, leaves a lot to be desired."

He knew how to hit me where it hurt. I looked away from him. His judgment wasn't the best either, I wanted to lash back. What decent man of sound sense would get out of a woman's bed, after kissing her and her breasts so passionately, and never bother to call her again? But I let his comment stand because he was right. My legal predicament and his moral one weren't exactly of the same magnitude.

He looked at Bud. "Who was this woman she was driving from the scene?"

Bud picked up a pad. "Sharon Williamson," he said. "Also known as Sharon McPike. Also known as Sandra Alexander."

Moon looked at me as if he wanted to be certain that I heard every word. "She has a rap sheet."

"A mile long, Mac. From you name it to you name it."

Moon shook his head. "And this is the friend you would risk your freedom for?"

"I didn't know we were breaking the law," I said.

"What do you mean you didn't know? What do you think she was doing in French Town at night? Picking up care packages for the boys back home?"

He was hot. I'd never seen him so animated.

"I didn't know it was drugs. She told me she was making deliveries for a courier company."

"And you believed her?"

I sighed. "Yes."

He shook his head and stared at me in a pathetic sort of way. "How did you hook up with her anyway?"

"I knew her from Philly," I said. "I was just helping her out."

"They live together," Bud said caustically, "according to the arresting officer."

Moon frowned. "This woman lives in your home?"

"No," I said. "I mean yes, but only because she was an old friend down on her luck, that's all. I hadn't seen her since undergrad school. I called myself helping her to get her kids back."

Bud laughed. "That's what she told you? And you bought it? Damn, lady. I got some swamp land over in Lake City that I'll let you buy real cheap."

I ran my hands through my hair. Sammy Davis Jr.'s voice rang in my ear, singing "What Kind of Fool Am I?" because that was exactly how I felt. Like a pure fool. A child could have seen through Sharon's game. A blind child at that. But not me. Not Miss Ph.D. I was helping a sister out. It was all a part of some divine plan. Yeah, right.

If Moon's chastisement and Bud's jokes were designed to get me to see the light, they were wasting their time. I saw the light. I saw myself in that light. And I had FOOL written on my forehead in big, bold, semicircled lettering.

But if I thought my enlightenment somehow meant that the trial was over, I was only kidding myself. Moon continued to stare at me, his head tilted back, his beautiful eyes almost hidden from sight. *He rescued me from a crazed man, now he's got to rescue me from a crazed woman.* And all he asked me to do was stay sweet. I couldn't even do that right. But I didn't aim to do it right. I couldn't forget that night. I couldn't forget the fact that he didn't say good-bye to me. Just got up and walked out. No explanation, no phone call later that would have settled everything. So I turn to career criminals and men of the cloth to help fill my days and nights. It was bad decisions after bad decisions but I didn't see where I had a choice. It wasn't as if there were this wealth of options for me. Reading books and watching C-SPAN was old now. I couldn't keep going back to that. I wanted what other women had. I wanted a man, a male companion, another human being on my side. Even if it meant listening to the advice of a homeless street thug on how to win myself a preacher, I wanted me a man. I didn't give up on normalcy. Normalcy gave up on me.

Moon's staring act lasted a good long time. He was sizing me up left, right, and center. Why he even showed up was a mystery to me. It was obvious that he had already decided that a relationship with me wasn't worth the effort. But he came anyway. Talk about an enigma. Moon McCalister. The quintessence of the enigmatic male.

"What will it take to drop the charges?" he turned and asked Bud Driscoll.

Bud stood up from his desk. He was a man easily in his mid to late fifties who looked to be too old for all of this excitement Moon kept thrusting upon him. "Drop the charges, Mac? Come on!"

"You've got to, Bud. Her reputation is at stake."

"Her reputation? Are you kidding me? I didn't see her thinking about no reputation when she was hightailing it up Tennessee Street! I'm telling you, Mac, your friendship is coming at too high a price for me. I can't keep doing this shit! They already hate my guts around here. They already think the only reason I'm still on the force is because I'm a friend of yours. You can't keep putting me in a position like this, I'm telling you. Drop the charges? Are you jerking me around or something? This isn't some simple misdemeanor. This chick committed a felony tonight!"

Moon took his fingers and ran them through his short, soft hair and he turned and began pacing the floor. Even I didn't expect him to try and get the charges dropped for me. Bail was the best I was hoping for.

Moon leaned against the back wall and folded his arms. Even as casually dressed as he was he still stood head and shoulders above anybody else. "That girl, her friend, are there any outstanding warrants on her?"

"Yes. Plenty."

"Where?"

"One in Tennessee. One in Virginia. Four in Pennsylvania. All felonies. All drug related, including possession with intent."

"Drop the charges here and extradite her to Pennsylvania."

I shook my head. Was Moon out of his mind? There was no way Tallahassee was going to drop the charges on Sharon. She stole money and drugs from a drug dealer, granted, but the drug angle elevated it to a criminal act. I knew why Moon suggested it. If they dropped charges on Sharon they would have no choice but to drop them on me. But if they kept Sharon incarcerated, then her testimony at trial could only devastate my so-called reputation. But Bud wasn't as certain as I was. He looked as if the suggestion was actually worth some consideration.

"I don't know about drawing up any extradition papers on her but the state attorney may drop charges against Victoria if she's willing to testify at trial against her friend."

Moon looked at me. The idea carried some promise. But I didn't know if I could live with the terms. "Testify against her?" I asked Bud.

"Yeah. Of course. What do you think this is? A faculty meeting? You committed a felony here tonight, lady. Drugs were in your car. Stolen property was in your car. You've got to pay one way or the other. And either both of y'all go down or she goes down alone. That's the choice."

I nodded. This is what it came down to. Her against me. I could barely stand the sight of Sharon by now. She used me and abused me all for her own selfish gain. But she was my friend once. My best friend. I couldn't just save my skin by sacrificing hers.

"Well?" Moon asked.

I looked at him. I appreciated the way he put his neck out there for me, even if I couldn't understand why he did it, but this was a road I was not willing to travel. "I can't," I said.

Bud sighed and threw his hands in the air. He saw me as this hopeless case. Moon just stared at me. I wasn't quite certain what he saw me as.

"Okay," Moon finally said as if he was proud of my response. He then looked at Bud. "Extradite Sharon," he said. "There's no other way."

"Do you realize what you're asking?"

"Yes."

"It's not up to me and you know it. We'll have to get the state attorney's office in on this and they won't go for it, Mac, I'm telling you."

"Who's on shift tonight? Anderson?"

"No. Barker."

"Get him on the phone."

"It's eleven o'clock at night."

"Get him on the phone."

"I'm not disturbing Doug Barker at home because of your girlfriend's ill-advised romp with danger."

"Get him on the phone."

"This isn't some petty parking ticket, Mac—"

"Goddamnit, Bud, get the man on the goddamn phone!"

Bud stared at his friend. And Moon stared at him. One day, it was inevitable, Bud was going to say no. The sad thing was that his right to decline to jump through hoops for Moon McCalister would mean the end of their long-term friendship. It was just that slim a thread they hung on to. One false move and the line would be severed forever.

Bud sighed, looked at me, and then picked up the phone and called Doug Barker. It took another hour of phone calls back and forth but the charges against both me and Sharon were dropped. And Sharon would be extradited to Pennsylvania where her fate was well beyond the control of us Florida hicks.

"Let's go," Moon said to me when the final decision to drop all charges was handed down. And I, like the good little whipped puppy that I was, went.

Six

Honeymoon

He did not take me home. We drove, instead, to his waterfront estate on the outskirts of Tallahassee. It was after midnight when the car drove off of Highway 319, down Harvey Mill Road, to a long, dark, isolated street filled with big, elongated homes on at least ten acres of land apiece. A large, swamplike lake surrounded the back of the homes, and wind-tossed trees of all stripes, from spruces to live oaks to chinaberries and magnolias, clogged up the highway and gave the area the look of a nature trail rather than a neighborhood.

Moon's house was farthest away, around a series of sharp curves at the end of the road. It was a dark, quiet-looking two-story ranch home that stood in stark contrast to the squall and bluster of the trees and lake. It had a country simpleness about it that immediately drew me to it. I expected a mansion with security guards and cameras and bloodthirsty rottweilers roaming the grounds, not this understated, almost ordinary home of charm and elegance. But it was just another example, it seemed to me, of how completely contradictory Moon could be.

His Jaguar drove past the opened picket fence and down the winding gravel path that led to his front porch. I stepped out quickly, not waiting for him to open the door for me, as I hurried to feel soil again and the wind blowing against my brown face: Freedom. I stood there, in his driveway, looking up at the big house and down at the backyard water view, and a serenity came over me that I had not experienced before. It was my first visit to this place but I felt as if I were home; that I was exactly where I ought to be.

Moon stepped out too, but instead of hurrying to his destination as was normally his way, generally leaving me to hurry up behind him, he walked around the car to where I stood, and smiled. "Well," he said, "now you know all my secrets."

"It's beautiful," I said. "So peaceful."

He looked up at his home and nodded in agreement. "It was pretty run-down when I discovered it ten years ago. I had to literally redesign the entire scope to get it in accordance with the modern world. But it was worth every moment of sweat." He then looked at me. "Let's go around back," he said, but not in his usual commanding voice. It was more a suggestion than an order this time. And I gladly obliged.

We walked along the side of the house to a large backyard that led to a beautiful but blustering lake. We sat at the shore, against the backdrop of a half-moon and picturesque blue sky. I lay back on my elbows and could not believe the beauty that surrounded me like an aura of invincibility. It was peaceful at Moon's house; the waves that roared and wanted only their majesty to be heard insisted upon it. The strong breeze blew back my hair and I felt, lying there in my blue jeans and blouse, that I was more sexy than I could ever have tried to be.

Moon crouched down beside me and picked up rocks and flung them into the lake. His warm-up suit was hardly his best wear but he had never looked sexier to me. I knew I needed to temper my feelings, because I wasn't sure if I could stand another letdown, but they were too intense to control. I felt as if I had nothing to lose. I felt as if I was on the brink of total devastation tonight, thanks to my buddy Sharon, but God had mercy and reeled me back in. Everything else, in my mind, would be anticlimactic.

Moon was about to throw yet another rock into the water when I asked him a simple question.

"Why?" I asked.

He stopped himself and looked down at the object in his hand. He was in his contemplative state again, I could tell. He almost turned to look at me, but he didn't. "What?"

"Why didn't you phone me? How could you just leave like that?"

"It couldn't be helped."

"What do you mean it couldn't be helped? Do you realize how much you hurt me? How could you just do me like that?"

He hesitated. "I was in love once," he said and then, as if satisfied that his confession didn't kill him, he tossed the rock into the lake. And looked at me.

I didn't know what to say, so I just blurted out the first thing that came to mind. "Your heart was broken?"

"Oh yes. Big time. She was the love of my life, you see. Never met a woman like her. She could do no wrong in my eyesight. But she broke my heart, Victoria. That's the problem. And that's why I've been very cautious since."

He picked up another rock and flung it into the lake. "You do funny things to my heart, that's why I didn't call you. When I look at you it's as if I'm looking at a part of me. My heart goes out to you, isn't that strange? From the moment I saw you at the faculty party to this very night I haven't been able to shake the feeling. I've tried, by staying away from you, not calling you, but every time you've called for me it's as if I couldn't get to you fast enough. I felt this way only one time before in my entire life."

It was a beautiful moment, hearing him admit his feelings for me, but it was terrifying too. "Who was she?" I asked, too curious just to enjoy the moment.

He looked away from me, to the darkness of the lake before us. "Somebody I met in Baltimore on a business trip."

"And you've been alone ever since?"

He nodded. "You can say that, yes," he said and looked at me.

I tried to smile, to keep the moment free from the burden of my own desperation, but I couldn't pull it off. I loved Moon McCalister. I loved him with everything within me. I had to convince him that I was different; that I could never willfully break anyone's heart. But if I rushed him, if my desperation showed, then I would lose him. I knew I would. And losing Moon McCalister was no longer an option.

Regal was the only word to describe the interior of his home. We walked in through the back door, through the beautiful yet almost sterile looking kitchen, as if no cooking had ever been done in there, but the full effect didn't hit me until we entered into the living-room area where the massive chandeliers and custom drapes swept the ambience from quiet country into elegant privilege. His taste in furnishings was astounding, from art deco to Victorian eclectic to modern classic pieces such as his arch-top chairs. Amazingly it all came together in one beautiful whiff of perfection.

The crystal staircase was artwork in and of itself as it wound around into a beautiful glass walk-up. I looked at Moon. "I've got to meet your designer," I said.

"Glad to meet you," he said and extended his hand.

We did not linger long downstairs, although he did show me his library and conservatory, but we both knew that sight-seeing wasn't what this was about. We walked upstairs, slowly but deliberately, and ended up on the second-floor landing that led to a room at the end of the hall. Moon's room. We walked slowly toward that door, that big, white wooden door that stood between our hearts and our heads, and Moon moved slightly behind me. He was still cautious, still unsure if I was a woman of substance or just up to no good, but I walked with fire under my feet. I knew what I wanted and that door led to it. He was going to throw that caution to the wind, I believed, when I got through with him.

I opened the door and stepped into a huge bedroom with a fireplace, two wingback chairs, and a king-size bed that stood like a throne in the chambers of my lord. This was where Moon McCalister slept, I thought. This was the place where that beautiful man laid his head at night. I looked back at him, as he walked in slower, his gorgeous face shrouded in uncertainty, his body tight with fear. It was surprising, I must admit, to see him this way, a man with all of his strength seemingly afraid of that thing called love, but it was refreshing too. He wasn't perfect. That was reassuring.

That was why I took his hand and led the way. We weren't children ready to explore each other's body, but two grown-ups, ready to experience the next level, able to understand that nothing ever worked if you didn't take the chance.

We walked to the side of the bed, hand in hand, and turned and faced each other. I moved up to him and unzipped his warm-up jacket. It opened and revealed a bare chest, no hairs, no matted grease, as smooth as a baby's bottom. I looked up at Moon. He was not fully relaxed yet, but he placed his hands on my elbows.

I kept moving, pulling down his pants and watching them as they dropped along his ankles. He was a man who wore briefs, not boxers, and his were so tight that his penis looked as if it was bunched in and could not contain itself inside much longer. So I let it out. Gladly. His briefs dropped to his pants and his penis whipped out and bounced in front of me. I looked up at Moon. He smiled as if he was actually embarrassed. But the brother had nothing to be ashamed about. He stood before me tall and gorgeous, his soft, black hair, his shoulders broad and strong, his stomach flat as a pancake, his penis long and thick like a just-ripe banana without the curve.

He took off his tennis shoes and stepped out of his pants and briefs. He acted as if he knew as I knew that there was no turning back now. We were about to cross that Rubicon going in the right direction, where it was all up to us now, not fate, not manipulated circumstances. Whatever was going to happen from this moment on would happen while our eyes were wide open and our sense of free will still vibrant and in control.

He moved as close to me as my breath and unbuttoned my blouse. He took it off and then pulled me gently against his bare chest. We touched, chest to chest, the warmness of the closeness sweetly suffocating. He reached behind me and unhooked my bra, allowing the straps to slide down my thin, brown arms with the bra dropping to the floor. I looked down at the bra, as it curled around my feet, but he took my chin in his hand and held my face up to his. *Don't look down*, his eyes insisted. *Look up, at us. Enjoy us. Keep your head high and enjoy the ride!*

He removed my jeans and panties, the last vestige of our past relationship, and then he dropped to his knees. He kissed me and rubbed me with his tongue. He separated my legs and licked my inner thighs. I quivered as he touched me, as he moved up my body, to my belly, to my breasts, until he stood up. He lifted me and laid me on the bed. And got on top. He opened my legs wider and entered me slowly. I hadn't experienced sex without a condom in years, but I experienced it with Moon. And he knew what he was doing. He pushed into me harder and harder, sliding inside me like a warm, gentle massage. My hands squeezed his arched back as he pumped against me. My body rolled with the feeling that encapsulated me, the hope of my lifetime taking over every fiber of my being, and we got in sync, up and down, in and out, side to side, moving as kindred spirits in rhythm with the beat of our hearts.

The next morning it seemed like déjà vu. I woke up to find the bed empty, Moon's presence nothing more than a sweet scent inside my nostrils. I panicked and jumped out of bed. Not again, I thought, not again! I was completely unclothed so I grabbed my blouse and threw it on as I ran across the landing and down the crystal stairs. I was too impertinent to think rationally, or look at other possibilities, or even to button my blouse.

"Moon!" I yelled as I cleared the bottom stair. Please, Moon, be here, I wanted to scream. Don't trip this shit on me again!

"In here!" he yelled and I raced toward the sound of his voice. I pushed open the door of the kitchen, still in a state of total panic, until I saw his face. He stood at the stove, in his tight briefs that more than displayed his huge endowment, stirring eggs. I exhaled. He looked at me, standing there, even more unprotected, my blouse concealing nothing but my back, and he removed the pan from the burner.

He walked to me, slowly, and pulled me into his arms. My blouse dropped from the sheer weightlessness that overtook my body. He pushed me against the table and lifted me onto it. I closed my eyes and leaned back. My body craved his and I waited for the moment to come again. And it came. He lifted his body into mine and pulled me closer. He pumped against me and I pumped against him. I screamed and he moaned. It was exotic and rapturous and completely beautiful. Another moment to end all moments. Another day in paradise. How could I ever get used to this?

He cooked me breakfast. Eggs, bacon, *grits*, and toast. We ate in the bedroom, in front of the fireplace. We ate and laughed and talked about everything. He even laughed at my close call with Sharon. "What were you thinking?" he asked, but I could do nothing but laugh.

I felt as if we could go on like this forever. It was a Friday morning and we both should have been at work but work was the furthest thing from our minds. We enjoyed each other. We experienced highs of love with the reassurance that nothing could stop us now. I was scared, to be sure, but the timing was perfect. I was ready to take on the world. I was ready to give my heart completely even if it meant yet another wrenching disappointment. I would have traded a lifetime for that one night with Moon. I would have traded every good turn my life ever took for that one night that allowed me pure, unmerited, selfish happiness for a change.

What I didn't know at the time was that my happiness was just beginning. Moon was a man of action. He didn't talk to me about places, he took me there. On one weekend trip alone, for instance, we took a private jet to California where we spent an entire afternoon shopping in Beverly Hills. I ended up with more Versace and Gucci and Givenchy than Gina could have dreamed about. No more jeans and blazers for me, thank you. Enough of that *Tory* look, as Gina liked to call it. Victoria Coleman was finally getting with the program. Victoria Coleman was stepping out in the big leagues now!

From the West Coast it was back to the East Coast, New York City this time, where we enjoyed *Cats* on Broadway, a walk along Fifth Avenue, more shopping, and a visit to the Waldorf-Astoria for a night of rest, and other things, and then the journey home.

Moon talked business on the phone as his jet hovered above the Atlantic Ocean. I leaned back on the leather seat and watched him do his thing. Although he seemed as happy as I was and thrilled to be with me, there was still something cautious about him. His laughter, for instance, was always tempered with somberness, as if he couldn't dare to allow himself too much pleasure. And at night sometimes, when he should have been resting with the reassurance that he knew his way around the bedroom, he'd get up and stare out over the terrace for hours, just staring into the darkness as if somebody were calling his name.

There was a broodiness about Moon McCalister, then, a kind of unrelenting sense that he was undeserving of his good fortune, but he would never allow me to pierce the wall. I asked him what was wrong on many occasions but he would say nothing was wrong, or he was fine, or he'd tell me to go back to sleep.

"What kind of automobile do you like?" he asked as he hung up the phone and looked at me.

"Automobile?" I asked. "What do you mean?"

"What's your favorite kind of car?"

"Oh," I said. "You mean like my dream car?"

"That's usually what favorite means."

"Let me see."

"And please don't say Lexus. That is one car that is well represented in our community. Too well, in my view."

I smiled. Thought about Gina and Vera and their twin cars. "No, I wasn't going to say a Lexus. I think I prefer a Mercedes, if it was up to me. Yes, no surprises here. I've always dreamed of a nice, comfortable Mercedes Benz."

We stopped down in Miami Beach, at this elegant car lot where the manager knew Moon by name, and drove home to Tallahassee in my brand-new, sports convertible, flame-red Mercedes Benz SL500 AMG. Talk about a dream.

We arrived at my condo late that Saturday night. "I'll dispose of this," he said, looking at my old Toyota Camry, a little beat up and worn (especially after my night with Sharon), but it had served me well.

"Certainly," I said, without showing the least bit of loyalty to this well-served car of mine, removing my books and papers gladly from its trunk and backseat as I couldn't take my eyes off of my brand-new Benz.

Moon kissed me on the mouth, got in the Camry, and told me to be ready by ten in the morning.

"Ready? Ready for what?" I asked. Another coast-to-coast fun ride?

"Church," he said and drove away.

* * *

The First Timothy Church of the Pentecost was a small building near FAM-U on the downslope of a hill. Moon took my hand and helped me out of his Jaguar and we walked slowly toward the door. It seemed odd that a man of his standing would attend a church this small but he dismissed my surprise with a hunch of the shoulder. He drove by it two years ago, he said, and decided to stop in. The people welcomed him with open arms and they didn't know him from Adam. He liked the anonymity and stayed.

Now it was my turn, I thought, as we walked up the three steps to the entranceway and entered in together. Would they welcome me with open arms or be disappointed that I snatched who had to be their most eligible bachelor? Most people would look at me and Moon and wonder why he would be attracted to me. I expected no different pondering from the women of First Timothy.

They welcomed me with open arms. "King Derrick has brought his queen into our midst this morning," the pastor, a large woman in a sheet dress, said. "Come on in, sister, come on in!"

The entire church stood to their feet and applauded as we made our way up the aisle. Some of the females gave me a second look but it didn't feel disrespectful. They probably felt the way I once felt—that Moon was out of their league and they were simply checking out the kind of woman who had the nerve to be with him. I was proud to be that woman. Moon made me feel as if I were the most gorgeous creature alive and no other human being could supplant me as his chosen lady.

The church service was good but long-winded. The pastor spoke from Revelation about the church of Laodicea and she used as her subject, "Don't waste your time on a lukewarm salvation."

"Be hot to trot, be too cold to scold, but don't be in between," she preached. "Don't live in Laodicea, saints. Don't let your fire go dim. Stay on fire for Jesus. He said in His word that he would never leave you alone but you got to stay on fire. You got to stay on fire. You got to burn with the need to get happy every once in a while. I'm happy, church! I'm filled with fire. Oh, hallelujah, church. Get up on your feet and praise the name of Jesus. Praise Him. Praise Him. Praise His Holy name!"

And everybody in the church was on their feet in praise. Moon lifted up his hands and closed his eyes. He was happy too. I looked around the church, at how everybody, from the oldest to the smallest child, knew how to praise the Lord. And I knew that my misgivings about the women in the church were wholly misplaced. These females had more important things on their minds. They wanted to live for Jesus. They wanted to be the best they could be. They may not have had much and they may not have known what the inside of a college looked like, but they were Christians in the purest sense of the word.

After service, and while we were all still pumped up from the sermon, we followed a small caravan of cars to Mother Stewart's small house in the country. According to Moon, every Sunday after service they piled into their automobiles and made the short journey to Mother Stewart's place.

"Why?" I asked him as I reclined in the front seat of his car and watched the older model Fords and Chevys speed off in front of us.

"Why?" he asked. "Simply for the best fried chicken this side of living. That's why."

I laughed. You look at Moon McCalister from afar and you see this truly stuck up brother. But once you get to know him you find somebody completely the opposite of his persona. It was a pleasant surprise for me as each day seemed to bring us closer and closer.

Mother Stewart's house was down a long, dirt road and behind a small creek. It had the rustic appearance of a log cabin and sat alone surrounded by big live oak trees. Moon parked, much to my shock, right in the thick of things. His normal custom of parking as far away from other cars as possible, to, I assumed, avoid door dings, went out the window when he hung out with his church folks. He parked next to their old Bel-airs and Monte Carlos and one woman's old Pinto as if he were in Beverly Hills parking next to a Rolls. He knew these people, I suppose, and trusted them, and if they did indeed ding his car it would be completely and understandably accidental.

They turned out to be my kind of crowd too. We sat on picnic benches in the backyard and feasted on fried chicken that made you want to cuss out the colonel for wasting your time. "I was eating Popeyes and KFC when I could have had *this*," I said to Mother Stewart, a woman almost as large as the pastor and with a heart as big as her body. She grinned a little clever grin and reminded me to eat the rest of that meat on that drumstick.

Moon sat next to the pastor and seemed totally engrossed in some information she was giving him, while I sat next to two women who knew how to take care of business. They were eating that chicken so fast that they stopped only long enough to catch their breath. They would lean back, exhale, and then stoop back over for more good eating. The woman across from me ate very sparingly. Her interest tended more toward me than the food. When I looked up she was staring directly in my face.

"So," she said as if she was simply waiting for me to look her way, "you're Brother Derrick's friend."

I smiled but didn't respond. What did she want me to say? She knew I was his friend. I guess sistergirl had a thing for him too, and was highly disappointed that my *nothing to write home about* behind was with him, but that wasn't my problem. He could have chosen her just as easily as he chose me, that was all I knew.

When she realized I wasn't about to chat with her about my personal relationship with Moon, she looked off into the distance as if somebody were saying something to her and then got up and left our table. One of my big-eating partners, the one sitting to the left of me, elbowed me. "Don't mind Miss Lady over there," she said in reference to the girl who had just left. "There's always a busybody in every crowd, girl. She need to get herself a man of her own; then she wouldn't be so concerned about yours."

I laughed. She was right. Life was too short to spend it worrying about other people's hang-ups. That was why I relaxed, grabbed yet another drumstick, and without giving my waistline so much as a second thought, proceeded to get down too.

Seven

A Reversal of Fortune

Two months later and the flame was still red hot. Every time I saw him I wanted to hold him. Every time he looked into my eyes I wanted to fall into his arms and stay there until the twelfth of never. Love like this was so new to me that I often had to ask myself if it was really me; if this great run of luck was really mine to have. I expected, at any moment, for the wall to cave in. I looked for it, took some solace in knowing that it was just a matter of time. But it didn't cave.

He took me to New York again and to a business conference he attended in Seattle. "This is my lady Victoria," he said to his fellow real estate developers and I beamed the way Miss America beamed when her name was announced. That was what I loved most about our relationship. It wasn't just me with all the enthusiasm. Moon was just as giddy about our affair as I was. Sometimes he would look at me and tears would well up in his eyes. Other times he would call me on my job just to hear my voice. No man had ever been that kind to me. They'd put on a little show early on, for the first few dates, but as soon as they got what they wanted, namely a little bed action, the show was over. "I'm not ready to make a commitment," they'd say. Or, "I don't think we have the right chemistry." Of course brotherman wasn't thinking about no chemistry when he was doing his thing on the bed, but that was the level of relationships I had been dealing with. That is, until I met the Moon.

And it was never left up to me. That was another big problem in my relationships. It was always up to me. They never knew where they wanted to go for dinner. "Where do you wanna go?" they'd ask. They never could decide on which movie to attend. "Which movie do you wanna see?" they'd ask. It became so bad that I started eliminating the drama altogether by just picking a restaurant and movie ahead of time. Then they'd complain that they weren't consulted, which created a whole new argument and even more drama.

Moon took care of all the arrangements. He was the perfect planner. If we wanted to have dinner at a nice Italian restaurant or an elegant lunch at a quiet French hideaway, he'd pick up the telephone and take care of it. There were no debates, no protestations, no drama. He was even set to plan our vacation, a cruise to Tahiti, but something rather extraordinary occurred that effectively put the brakes on what we thought would be a quiet summer.

It was a Friday evening at Moon's house. Moon was seated on the bed with his back against the headboard attempting to review a land acquisition proposal. He had on a pair of shorts and a T-shirt and wore reading glasses that made him look bookwormish. I was lying on the bed, my feet toward Moon, watching videotapes that we had rented. I was dressed comfortably too, in one of Moon's big shirts, and was crying up a storm over the movie I was watching. It was our night in, just the two of us, and I loved every moment.

"What are you watching?" Moon asked and I turned and looked at him. He was staring at the television by peeping over the top of his glasses.

"What?" I asked in a voice nearly hoarse from crying.

"Why are you watching something that brings tears to your eyes?"

"Because it's so romantic!" I said and burst into tears again.

"That doesn't make sense, Victoria. A good movie is supposed to uplift you, make you happy, not have you crying so much that you can barely see straight."

"But they made a pact."

"Who made a pact?"

"Cary Grant and Deborah Kerr. They said they would meet again in six months at the top of the Empire State Building but if the other person doesn't show up, then it would be because their love affair just wasn't meant to be."

"Let me guess: Cary Grant didn't show and Deborah Kerr's all bent out of shape. Women."

"No, no. Cary Grant did show up but Deborah Kerr couldn't. She was struck by a car and was paralyzed. She was on her way to the Empire State Building but she was looking up at the building in anticipation and the car hit her."

Moon laughed. I looked at him. "What are you laughing at?" I asked.

"That movie, that's what."

"Oh, it's funny to you that Deborah Kerr got hit by a car? It wasn't like she wanted to get hit. She couldn't help it. She was looking up at the Empire State Building and didn't see the car."

"That's what she gets for looking up."

"Moon! How could you say that? She was paralyzed and everything. And Cary Grant thought she didn't show because she didn't love him anymore. Isn't that awful?"

"It's awful, all right."

"Ah, forget you," I said and turned back to my movie.

I felt his hand on my ankle but I assumed it was just an affectionate touch. Then I felt my body begin to slowly slide down, toward the headboard, my shirt slipping up, revealing my naked backside. I turned and Moon smiled. "Come here," he said.

I'd seen that look before. Many times before. That was why I didn't hesitate in coming to him. He removed his papers and I sat on his lap. He caressed me and wrapped me tightly in his arms.

171

There was something reassuring whenever I was with Moon. He knew what he was doing. Some brothers needed a little prodding. They needed you to guide their hands to exactly the right spots. But every spot Moon touched was the right one. It was an exhilarating feeling when he touched me. My entire body would draw up into a ball with the anticipation that something special was about to happen.

And it happened again that night. First he held me until my body was so relaxed that I could have fallen asleep. And then he kissed me. He didn't French-kiss or play otherwise crazy games with his tongue in my mouth. He just kissed me. Soft and gentle and long. Kissing was something I rarely enjoyed because the men I used to know always wanted to sling their saliva-filled tongue down my throat as if such roughness was supposed to demonstrate just how passionate they were. But Moon always took it slow. Slow and easy. He never rammed or slung or banged. He never yelled nauseating expressions like "come to Papa" or "here's Johnny!" or "hold on to your hat because the hurricane has arrived!"

But Moon experienced my body, as if he was discovering something new every time. Our lovemaking wasn't some ego trip for him, some pathetic display of male prowess. We made love. We took the time to be with each other, to fall madly into each other's heart.

After kissing me continuously he laid me on the bed and removed my shirt. I closed my eyes. His hands and mouth massaged my breasts with the gentleness of a morning fog. He kissed my stomach and held me down. And then he entered me. I could feel my feet push down against the bed as the euphoria of his caressing tongue caused me to lose control. I pushed back against the headboard and grabbed hold of it, an almost primal scream releasing from my innermost being as my heart pounded against my chest and my soul prepared to break down. I was the most fortunate woman alive. I had a man. A real man. And he didn't need me or anybody else to tell him how to get a groove on.

SURVIVING MR. RIGHT

* * *

We were back to our old routine, Moon reading over papers while I watched more videos, when the doorbell rang. I looked at Moon and Moon looked at me. No uninvited guests ever came to his home, and especially not on a Friday night.

"Who could that be?" I asked, but he did not respond. He sat there, his back against the headboard, his reading glasses once more perched on his nose, and waited to be alerted by his manservant Walter.

Walter had been in Moon's employ for over nine years and was paid consistently although he was rarely called in to work. The only reason he was there that Friday night was that we had decided to stay home that evening. Moon wanted him available in case we needed something special cooked or some errands that needed taken care of. But we hadn't counted on company.

"Excuse me, Mr. McCalister," Walter bellowed out over the intercom, his baritone voice almost unrecognizable, "there are two gentlemen here to see you, sir."

I sat up on my knees.

"Who are they, Walter?" Moon asked.

"A Mr. John Rogers and a Mr. Van Weaver, sir."

Moon nodded as if he knew the men but instead of giving instructions he fell into a contemplative stare.

After a few moments, Walter chimed back in. "Are you available, sir?" he asked.

"Yes," Moon said as if he had, at that very second, made up his mind. "Show them into the library. Tell them I'll be there directly."

"Very good, sir," Walter said and signed off.

Moon stood up quickly and began dressing for the occasion. I stood up too.

"Who are they, honey?" I asked.

"If my memory serves me correctly, they're strategists."

"Strategists? What kind of strategists?"

173

"Put on some clothes and come see for yourself."

We dressed quickly, he in a Brunswick sport coat and a pair of khaki pants, me in a denim jumper dress and sandals.

By the time we walked downstairs and into the library the two gentlemen in question were receiving tea prepared by Walter. They stood quickly when Moon arrived.

"Moon, hello," the taller of the two said as he set his cup of tea on the tray and extended his hand.

Moon walked over to him and shook it. "Hello, John."

"And you remember Van, don't you?"

"Sure, Van, how you been?" Moon shook Van's hand too. He then stood erect. "This is my lady Victoria," he said and I beamed.

I shook both hands as they announced how pleased they were to meet me. And then we just stood there. John was a black man and Van a white one and both men appeared to be in their mid to late thirties. They both seemed slick to me, too polished for my taste, having that televangelist look of confidence and self-importance that made me wonder how Moon could ever have associated with them, although Moon didn't seem in the least offended by their presence.

He offered them seats and we sat down too, on the couch opposite them. "So," Moon said, "how can I help you gentlemen?"

John and Van looked at each other as if to decide who would go first. John took the lead and moved toward the edge of his seat. "As you know there are a lot of rumors flying around about a lot of things, but specifically about the state of Mayor Ross Austin's health."

Moon nodded. What did that have to do with the price of tea? I wanted to ask.

"The reason we're here, Moon, and please excuse us for disturbing you at home, but Chairman Spiceland wanted us to get to you before any press people did."

"Who's Chairman Spiceland?" I asked.

"The chairman of the local Democratic party," Moon said. "But,

John, I'm as lost as Victoria here. Why would Spiceland need you to get in touch with me?"

John looked at Van. Van picked up the torch. "We received a beforehand notice tonight," he said, "that Mayor Austin, due to very ill health, will be stepping down by summer's end and will not be able to fulfill the remaining two years of his term."

Moon leaned back. The picture was crystal clear to him now. I was still lost. "I see," he said.

"It's a historic opportunity," John pushed back toward the edge of his seat and said. He was definitely the jumpier of the two. "There will be a special election, of course, but the full weight of the DNC will be behind you. And Mayor Austin has made it clear that he'll support the party's choice. The time is now for this to happen, Moon. The time is now. The Democrats are tired of talking about diversity in this town. They want to put their money where their mouth is and Spiceland and many others feel this could be our best chance at making it happen. And let's face it, Moon, there's no other African-American in Tallahassee with your kind of stature. You've served on the city council before, was even council president before you decided not to seek another term. And you're a respected, well-known community leader and a very successful businessman. The perfect candidate for this kind of election."

Moon exhaled. And then he shook his head. "Do you realize what you're asking me?"

"We're asking you to make history," John said. "You'll become the first black man ever to be elected mayor of this town. That's the gravity of this. This kind of opportunity comes around maybe once in a hundred years. We're asking you to seize it, Moon."

It seemed surreal what they were talking about. *My Moon McCalister as mayor?* It seemed like such a big joke that I began looking around, expecting at any moment for somebody to jump from behind a chair and yell for us to smile because we were on *Candid Camera*!

But Brother John was too serious for that to happen. And so was

Van, who told Moon to look at the practical aspects of why they wanted him, of all people, to run for mayor. "Think about it, Moon," he said. "You're as popular a figure in Tallahassee as the mayor himself. People know you here. They saw the work you did on the city council for everybody, regardless of their race or political affiliation. They see you as a man of principle, not party, a man of conviction. Nobody else carries that kind of instant credibility. You're an honorable, decent man, Moon. That's what they see."

Moon had long since fallen into his contemplative mode. He sat there staring at the men before him as if he was weighing the measure of their character against their rhetoric. They were campaign strategists, slick political handlers, not some defenders of historical integrity. They saw Moon McCalister as a proven winner, a man who didn't take on fights he couldn't win, and they wanted a piece of the action. I saw it all over their anxious faces and I knew Moon saw it too. But their motives didn't appear to be his focus.

"What's in the minus column?" he asked.

Van looked at John. "We don't follow you," John said.

"Mr. Weaver here has just recited all of these wonderful attributes of mine. What are my negatives?"

"That's the beauty of this whole deal," John said, "you don't have any negatives."

Moon became suddenly agitated. "Bullshit," he said.

Both men seemed taken aback. "Excuse me?" John asked.

"Bullshit, John. I have a ton of negatives and you know it."

John smiled. "Listen, brother, everybody has their faults, but yours are so minor . . ."

Moon removed his hand from around my waist and pointed his finger at John. "Don't fuck with me. Okay?"

John's bubbling self-confidence shrank like a violet before our very eyes. That Moon Mystique had done him in. He was exposed for who he really was, which was something along the order of a sheep in wolf's clothing.

Van, whose confidence was waning too, knew that the ball was in his court. His partner had messed up big time with that flimflam blow job he tried to run on Moon and now the convincing was all up to him. What he didn't know at the time, and I was just beginning to figure out, was that Moon had probably made up his mind before he even walked down those stairs.

"Okay, you're right," Van said. "You are considered ruthless by some in the business community, maybe even cutthroat, but they aren't the mainstream voters we're going after. To the everyday joes and soccer moms, ruthlessness comes with the territory of being a successful businessman."

"I've been divorced," Moon said as if he hadn't heard a word Van had just recited.

Van looked to John for help. Wrong place, I thought. But John had learned his lesson. He decided to play it straight this time. "We know that," he said.

"I have a son in New York who won't give me the time of day, who believes, with some merit, that I'm among the same species as a snake in the grass."

"We know that too. You're arrogant and hard-hearted and otherwise no John Boy Walton. We know it."

"And you still want me?"

"We still want you. Look, Moon, we aren't putting you up for pope. We just want to put a little color in city hall."

Moon actually smiled. Truth, for once, his whimsical expression seemed to say.

Our guests left around midnight. They had laid out a scenario so compelling that I found myself totally engrossed in every detail. In one week's time Ross Austin, who had been mayor of Tallahassee for almost eighteen years, would announce that he would retire at the end of the summer. At that same press conference he would introduce the public to a man he would declare was perfectly suited to take up the torch and finish his term. And Moon would be by his side.

But the story leaked overnight and by the time I woke up the next day, back home and alone in my bed, missing Moon's touch terribly and still trying to digest the news of the night before, Gina was calling to congratulate me.

"For what?" I asked, barely awake. I had spoken to Gina only briefly in the last three months. I phoned to apologize for missing her dinner party. She accepted my apology, we talked about general stuff, like the new case she was handling and if my relationship with Moon was still on or was it off, but it wasn't the same anymore. Our lives weren't interwoven the way they were in D.C. It became harder and harder for me, her, and Vera to make room for each other and after that fiasco with Peter Lawrence I stopped trying altogether. Now she was calling me the day after one of the most significant days of my life and I was at a loss to know what on earth she was talking about.

"Come on, girl," she said. "You ain't got to act like it's some mighty secret anymore because the shit done hit the fan and it's blowing all over the place!"

I pressed my forehead and frowned. "What time is it?" I asked.

"It's one in the afternoon," she said. "I just heard about it."

"Gina, what are you talking about?"

"Mr. Moon McCalister. Soon to be Mayor Moon McCalister."

I woke up then. "How did you find out about that?"

"See there? I told Vera you already knew but she said you would have told us about it because you ain't never been able to hold water, let alone a secret like that."

I sat up in bed. "But how did you find out?"

"The news, honey. It was on the twelve o'clock news. Mayor Austin is thinking about stepping down and he's handpicked Moon McCalister to complete his term, that's what they said on the news."

Those weasels, I thought. Those strategists, handlers, whatever they wanted to call themselves. One of them leaked the story after going through that elaborate strategy session. It was a great plan, I thought, a masterful undertaking. But now the story was out too soon. That changed everything. The whole purpose of waiting a week before the Austin announcement was to get as many Democratic leaders in line behind Moon before any other candidate had an opportunity to even consider challenging him. That way all of our efforts could go toward defeating whatever Republican challenger we had to face. Now all of that planning, all of that careful timing was quashed because some loudmouth had dropped the ball. "I'll call you later, G," I said, "but I need to talk to Moon."

"You know, you're acting like you don't know me and Vera anymore since the Moon came into your life, but that's cool, that's cool. I know what love is like. And I'll get off the phone and let you call your honey but only if you promise to attend my little birthday party."

"That's almost a month away, Gina."

"You can't blame a girl for planning early. Just promise you'll be there. It's my thirty-ninth."

"I promise."

"Cross your heart and hope to die?"

"Yes, Gina, I promise I'll be there."

"And bring the Moon. Those stiff-shirt colleagues of mine would get a kick out of that, especially in light of this awesome news."

"I'll be sure to ask him, Gina. Now I'll talk to you later."

"Okay. I love you, girl."

"Love you too. Bye."

And I hung up. You can always tell a relationship is in trouble when you find yourself saying "I love you" because you have nothing else to say.

I attempted to call Moon but the lines at McCalister Enterprises were jammed and not one of my calls could get through. I called him on the cell but his voice mail picked up. I called him on his car phone but his voice mail picked up. I called him at home but Walter answered and, without giving me a chance to get a word in edgewise, said that Mr. McCalister had no comment and hung up the phone.

I gave up and got out of bed. I walked through the living room out onto the balcony, wearing one of Moon's big shirts, and I leaned against the railing. It was a lovely day. The sun was shining brightly, and the gentle breeze was blowing back my hair and making me ever alert to this new and adventurous time in my life. Gina congratulated me as if Moon's good luck was mine too. Although I felt as if I were completely a part of him, I knew I had to be realistic too. I loved history. I was a student and teacher of history. And this entire idea of the man I loved making the kind of history that his election would make was almost mind-boggling to me. I could not allow myself to become some selfish, neglected female who was carrying on as if she didn't know what time it was. Moon's election was essential, in my mind. Moon's election would be more than a victory for him and me. It would be a victory for all of the disenfranchised who tried and gave their all but never quite made it; for our parents and grandparents who marched on that battlefield called civil rights just for a moment like this.

That was why, after the strategists left last night and the noise of talk turned into deep quietness as we pondered the responsibility before us, I held Moon and told him that I would not stand in the way of history, that if he decided to go down this fated course I would march right beside him and become his greatest defender. Moon, who didn't appear to be burdened at all, smiled. "You sound like Martin Luther King," he said.

The phone began ringing and I hurried from the balcony, ran into the living room, and picked up the phone on what appeared to be its final ring. It was Vera. "Hey," I said.

"Hello. I just wanted to offer my congrats as well."

"Thanks," I said, although I definitely felt that she, like Gina, was congratulating the wrong one.

"I don't really know him but I think he'll make a fine mayor and you'll make a wonderful mayor's wife."

A mayor's wife. I thought about that. But talk about prematurity. Moon hadn't even intimated at proposing to me, let alone actually carrying out a wedding. If the truth be told, he had yet to tell me that he loved me.

But I let Vera have her say. But she suddenly found that she had nothing more to say. "Well," she said, "that's all I wanted."

"Thanks for calling," I said. You're welcome, she said. And that was that.

I hung up the phone and headed for the kitchen. I would brew some coffee, I thought, and then try to get in touch with Moon again. But as I walked across the threshold of my small kitchen, my work was done.

"Moon?" I said in such a voice of incredulity that he frowned. He was standing at the stove placing fried sausages on a dinner plate.

"Good morning," he said. "Or should I say good afternoon?"

"How long have you been here?"

He thought about this. "About three hours."

"Three hours! Good Lord. Why didn't you wake me?"

"You needed your rest. After last night I knew you would need all of the rest you could get." He looked at me. I smiled. Good thing I had given him a key, I thought.

"You're cooking?"

"Yes. Have a seat."

He walked over to the table and placed two linked sausages on a plate in front of me. He was well dressed in a tan, minicheck Armani suit that gave off the impression that he was about to sit down to a business meeting rather than lunch. "Sausage for lunch," I said.

He smiled. "Couldn't find any boloney."

I laughed, pushed my hair up, and let it drop. I knew I looked like hell but Moon didn't seem to mind. I ate his sausages while he sat across from me and stared at me the entire time. The atmosphere in the house was tense. He hadn't hung around for three hours just to feed me. He was concerned, unlike I had ever seen him before, and he knew like I knew that all of those leaks and misinformation was just the beginning.

We ended up out on the balcony. He unbuttoned his suit coat and sat on the metal chair, motioning for me to sit on his lap. We stayed there all day, taking catnaps and enjoying the peacefulness of the lake, neither of us daring to shake that peace with any talk whatsoever about that fateful night we had just endured.

But my curiosity was stronger than his. By evening time, and while he was yet asleep, I went into the bedroom to watch the six o'clock news. I had to see for myself what all the fuss was about. It was not the lead story but it was the third one in line. "And in other news," the young anchorman said, "Mayor Austin's office is denying reports tonight that he will step down by the end of the summer because of rapidly declining health. Although his spokesman confirmed that the mayor's cancer is, in his words, 'serious,' he insisted that no decision regarding the mayor's ability or desire to remain in office has been made. There's also word that this man, real estate developer and former city councilman Derrick McCalister, has been rumored to be the mayor's choice of successor should he step down. Although McCalister would not comment on the rumors tonight, he did issue a statement this morning wishing the mayor a full and speedy recovery."

And that was the story in a nutshell. A great strategy turned into the kind of back and fill, make-it-up-as-you-go routine Democrats were famous for, just because some bonehead couldn't keep his mouth shut. "Damn leak," I said aloud and Moon, who, to my shock, had been standing in the doorway, told me not to be so gullible.

"It was a necessary move," he said.

"What do you mean?"

"It was a necessary move."

"You know who leaked the story?"

"You can say that."

I stared at him. "*You* leaked the story?"

He did not respond.

I shook my head. This was incredible. "But why, Moon? We had a great plan. A perfect plan. And the mayor was willing to give us a week to get it together. Why would you mess it up like this?"

"Because it's my ass, that's why! I've got to know what I'm up against. If the reaction to this so-called unprecedented move is viscerally too negative, then the rumor was nothing but a rumor and that's the end of that. It's called floating a trial balloon, Vicky. It's business."

I nodded although I didn't really understand it. I saw this opportunity as a time of triumph. In my eyes it was all about history and instilling pride and hope into the hearts and minds of those folks who never got a piece of that pie called the American dream. Moon saw it as a business proposition and maybe nothing more than that. It was disappointing to see his ruthlessness up close and personal but he was a businessman after all and to his credit, he never pretended to be anything but.

The media onslaught slowed down by midweek as Moon continued not to comment and the mayor's office continued to deny that a decision had been made. Strategy sessions were ongoing but I stayed out of the loop. Moon, Ross Austin, and everybody associated with the situation were all reluctant trailblazers. The historical merits of Moon's election would be, for them, a tool to help ensure victory rather than a rallying cry to help ensure inclusiveness. But to say that I was angry or even mildly upset with Moon would be inaccurate. I was disappointed that he didn't see it my way but I understood why he didn't. Besides, I reasoned, the ends would justify the means. Getting elected was the issue. Making history was the point.

I was back at work at FAM-U, sitting behind my desk attempting to grade papers, enjoying the fact that I actually had a life beyond my relationship with Moon. But Jake Onstead was there, sitting on the edge of my desk, attempting to sell me what can only be described as a bill of goods: a ten-dollar raffle ticket for his church bazaar.

"Ten dollars, Jake? That's ridiculous."

"It's for the church, Victoria. That used to mean something."

"And it still does. But raffle tickets are a dollar a pop, not ten dollars. I'm not giving ten dollars to anybody for no raffle ticket. You can forget that."

He was about to make his case again when my secretary buzzed in over the phone's intercom system announcing the arrival of Miss Trundle.

I looked at Jake. A new professor maybe? But Jake hunched his shoulders.

"Miss who?" I asked my secretary.

"Trundle. Amanda Trundle."

"What does she want exactly?"

"She says it's about Dexter."

"Dexter?"

"Derrick," a female voice said to my secretary but loud enough for me to hear.

"Derrick," my secretary said. "I stand corrected."

"I see," I said. "Send her in."

Jake smiled and stood up. "Seems Mr. Derrick has been a busy boy lately. First the mayor wants him and now this woman."

"I'll talk to you later, Jake."

"And you still won't consider purchasing one ticket from an old pal like me?"

"Not for no ten dollars I won't."

Jake pushed his glasses up on his flat face and stared at me with one of those *I'll remember that* looks. But he was the furthest thing from my mind. A woman was here to see me about Moon. She could have been a reporter, I thought, but for some reason I doubted it.

When she walked into my office I knew immediately that my suspicion was right and no way was that woman some roving reporter. She was a short, petite woman with large, green eyes, soft brown skin, and long, straight hair that settled around her narrow shoulders in a bouncy underthrow. She was exactly the kind of woman I always envisioned a man like Moon would love. Beautiful, glamorous, bursting at the seams with that full-of-herself self-confidence. An aura of attractiveness oozed from her like a day-spring of perfection. Whereas a man's attraction to me had to entail a whole lot more than looks alone, a woman like Amanda Trundle didn't have to possess a brain in her head or even any sense of decency in her style, yet every man in Florida would be honored to have her by his side.

That was why my heart dropped when I saw her. Moon had spoken of her only once, but he referred to her as the love of his life. He didn't call her by name, she was just this woman from Baltimore, but I was certain that Amanda Trundle was the one. And now she was back, in the flesh, in all of her coquettish, smiling, hair-jerking seductiveness. I didn't stand a chance.

Jake politely spoke to Miss Trundle and then excused himself. He turned when he got to the exit door and mouthed the word *Wow!* to me behind Miss Trundle's back, making it clear that even an old bookworm mathematician like him found her irresistible. He also shook his head in pity for me, mouthed the words *Good luck*, and left.

"Hello, Miss Coleman," she said, speaking ever so softly as if I was about to become her next conquest.

"Miss Trundle."

"Amanda, please. I'm not *that* old. May I?"

She was asking if she could sit in the chair in front of my desk but

I was too engrossed in what her sudden appearance in my life meant. Apparently accustomed to such staring and misdirected inattentiveness, she took the liberty to sit down anyway.

She wore a sleek, very short black dress that dropped along her small body as if it were stitched on. She crossed her legs when she sat, revealing perfect legs that would have made Tina Turner proud. And like Tina, she could have been sixty years old, for all I knew, but she was in such great shape that I declare she didn't look a day over twenty.

"This is a very nice university," she said. "Kind of drab, but nice. I've seen it before, when I used to come to town to visit Derrick, but this is the first time that I've been on its grounds. I'm impressed."

I leaned back and exhaled. I wasn't about to engage in any small talk with sistergirl and I wanted to make it clear to her right away. *Cut the crap*, my facial expression descried, *because, given the circumstances of the visit, I ain't wit it.*

But she was a spoiled little brat who seemed determined to play the game her way, at her pace, by her rules. My impatience and righteous indignation meant nothing to her.

"Of course I'm from Maryland so I've never spent any significant amount of time at a Negro university."

Negro? Check her out. What century was she from? We hadn't been Negroes since Jim Crow. And what did being from Maryland have to do with anything?

"But I understand they're decent enough little schools for those of us who may not be able to make it into the legitimate colleges, even with Affirmative Action, which I find amazing. But nothing surprises me anymore. I remember when I completed my courses at Radcliffe and was considering going to a different school, Yale, maybe Princeton, for a graduate degree in law, and oh my goodness. One of your schools, Howard or Hampton or one of those names, had the unmitigated gall to write to my parents' home in

Baltimore and offer me, *me*, a scholarship to attend their law school. My father almost went into cardiac arrest when he read that letter. What would his daughter, a graduate of Radcliffe, no less, look like attending some coon school? I tell you we had a grand laugh over that particular letter!"

She was a fool. It was clear as day. And my theory was right. Moon certainly wasn't attracted to Miss Stuck Up over there because of her bubbling, down-to-earth personality. It was strictly a physical thing. No wonder he said she and I were as different as night and day. Just listening to her made that crystal clear. But she was once the love of Moon's life. He said so himself. This kind of human being once stole his heart. It surprised and disappointed me at the same time.

She continued ragging on the *coon schools*, as she called them, showing the full extent of her ignorance with every word she uttered. It was her nice-nastiness that got to me most, however, the way she appeared to give tepid praise to some historically black college and then make it seem as if an elementary school were a more challenging place for learning. When she, in fact, spoke of how sweet it was that less fortunate minorities had somewhere to go to better themselves but then proceeded to compare their college education to her childhood boarding school days, I had had enough.

"What do you want?" I asked her sternly, trying desperately to sound as harsh as I could. Her soliloquy stopped in midsentence and your girl suddenly developed a fondness for the culture she despised because she gave me the best *check this Negro out* expression that she could muster.

"As I was saying—" she said, determined to continue her denigration of all things black and poor and otherwise beneath her, but I cut her off again.

"I wish I had this mountain of time to spend here with you but I've got exams to grade and a class to teach in less than an hour. So I ask you again: what do you want?"

"As I was saying," she said again, "there is a time and place for everything. Everything fills a need, a void if you will. Like you in Derrick's life."

Finally the point, I thought.

"Derrick is a good man, he's a wonderful man, and when I left him he was devastated. He loved me, oh, he loved me so much. His love suffocated me, it was just that strong. Now I don't know how much he's told you but our relationship was a very deep, wrenching relationship. He even proposed to me. That's right. I was on the verge of becoming Mrs. Derrick McCalister, that's how deep our relationship was. But I left."

She hesitated after saying this, as if the realization of what she walked away from was still a bitter pill to swallow. "I left him," she continued, "and it hurt him to his core. Then a few months later he meets up with you. But it can't possibly mean anything to him. He still loves me, there is no doubt in my mind about that. You're just somebody to help him forget his pain. That's all. And who knows? Derrick is a good man. Maybe he's not using you. Maybe he actually cares about you. But there's a problem. You see, Miss Coleman, FAM-U is a fine institution, I'm sure. But it's no Radcliffe. You're a fine individual too, I suppose. But you're not me."

Her self-confidence allowed her to speak with total sincerity. She was not making some idle boasts to make me feel jealous or just plain unworthy. She wanted to break me down. She wanted me to understand in no uncertain terms that I was out of my league, that I was unquestionably the wrong jockey for a horse like Moon.

"Are you trying to tell me," I asked, nervously this time, my barely discernible confidence almost gone, "that you and Moon are still together?"

"Has he been cheating on you, in other words? No. He has not. He's not that kind of man. But I've decided that what Derrick and I had was too wonderful to toss away. I want him back, Miss Coleman, that's what I'm telling you."

The awful truth. The wall that I was waiting to cave in caved.

Not only was I now in competition with another woman but I had to compete against Miss America, Miss Radcliffe graduate from a family of such esteem that they could laugh in the face of a great university like Howard as if it were some school for the misbegotten. A woman of background and breeding. The perfect rich man's woman. The perfect politician's wife.

I leaned back in my chair. Miss Trundle was shrewd if she was anything. Love had something to do with her presence back on the scene but power, namely the kind that comes with being a mayor's wife, had more to do with this triumphant return.

She stared at me obliquely. "You look out of sorts, Miss Coleman," she said, to rub it in.

"How am I supposed to look?" I asked, offended by her fake concern. "You waltz into here proclaiming your right to possess the man that I love deeply and I'm supposed to look like I couldn't care less? I'm supposed to say, you go, girl, and smile as you destroy my life?"

"Of course not," she said, still feigning interest in my plight. "But it is your love for him that brought me to you first. He has no idea that I'm even in town. I came to you because I knew you would understand."

"Understand? Understand what?"

"History."

Talk about confusing the issue. Sistergirl was good, I'd give her that. Here she was taking what was nothing more than some passion play on her part and turning it into some great, lofty cause. "What are you talking about?"

"According to my spies you're a professor of history, are you not?"

"What spies?"

"My friends here in town, who keep me posted on the goings-on. Are they correct? You are a history professor?"

I shook my head. Why fight it? I thought. "Sure. Yes. I'm a history professor."

"That's why I'm appealing to you." She stood up and began pacing around the room. For leverage, I assumed. "As you know," she went on to say, "Derrick is probably going to run for mayor soon, that's hardly a secret anymore. And given the situation it will definitely be the rave. That would be an accomplishment indeed but it would also mean quite a responsibility. Not just for him but also for the woman he chooses to be by his side. Now Derrick is forty-nine years old. He's much older than both of us. But he's nobody's fool. He's a businessman first and last, make no mistake about it. And he hates to lose."

I frowned. "What does any of this have to do with me?" I asked. I had a darn good idea but I wanted to hear it directly from the horse's mouth.

"The woman Derrick chooses," she said, ignoring me entirely, "cannot be some country bumpkin blinded by the lights of the big city. She must be politically savvy and well connected. Derrick is about to make history and every move he makes must be calculated and recalculated. He'll be the prize everybody wants to see and many people will want to destroy. His woman will need to know how to win friends and influence bigwigs without them ever knowing that they were being played. She can't just be cute. She must be seductive. She can't just be attractive. She must be the kind of woman that men crave. In other words, Miss Coleman, you are not that woman."

I should have stood up and heaved her out of my office right then and there. I should have told her that what Moon and I had was special, that he was his own man and it was up to him to decide if I was that woman or not. I should have bragged to her about the times we spent together, when we went to New York and Seattle and California. He was committed to me, I should have screamed. He loved me.

But I didn't say a word. I couldn't. Every sentence Miss Trundle uttered was a sentence that I had played around in my head from the moment those strategists had entered our lives. Being a politician's wife was no game. It required skill and, as she said, savvy. I didn't have either attribute and I would be the first to admit it. That was why I stayed still and let her talk. The whole idea of being in the eye of the storm of Tallahassee politics terrified me. And my visitor could see it all over my face.

"This is just the beginning, Miss Coleman. You know it and I know it. Mayor today, governor of Florida tomorrow. And then there will be no turning back. We can't squander this opportunity. We can't let our own selfish desires get in the way of history. That's why I came to you. Judge it for yourself. This is our defining moment. You or me. Who's it going to be?"

I felt as if a sledgehammer had knocked me down. She was right. God, she was right. Moon was going places. He was just that special. And he was going to need somebody like her to calm the waters that were certain to rise up. What could I do in a situation like that? Amanda Trundle had more seductiveness and sagacity in her finger than I had in my entire body. There was no competition. There was nothing to judge.

But I loved Moon. That was the problem. I couldn't sit back and let him go. Not even for history's sake. I wasn't strong enough to do that. But my little guest had an answer for that too. She even had a plan.

"I know that Moon still loves me. A love like ours, that lasted almost five years, never just goes away. And I know in my heart that if I came back into his life he could not resist me. But I don't want to take him by force because he feels some burdensome obligation to you. I know Moon. If everything isn't lined up just right, he'll forget the whole thing, history, all of it. That's just the kind of man he is. If the odds are against him he just won't take the plunge. That's why he can't be the one to decide. We've got to decide. And you've got to let him go. There's no other answer. And I believe if you were to see his face the first time he sees me again, you'll know without a doubt his true feelings for me and you'll walk away no questions asked."

No questions asked, she said. I'd just walk away the way she did. She didn't know me. She didn't know how desperate I became when love was in play. She didn't know that these "few months" that I'd had with Moon were a lifetime for me. And I couldn't let that go.

I stood up. "I'm sorry, Miss Trundle, but you have the wrong one. I love Moon and he loves me. And that's all there is to it."

She stood still and stared at me. Her look was sinister, methodical. She was about to play hardball. "The truth of the matter is, Miss Coleman," she said, "you don't exactly have a choice."

"Excuse me?"

"If you won't step aside, then I will have no alternative but to take matters into my own hands. I will leak to the press, as soon as I leave this office, that Derrick McCalister, the man the Democrats wish to put up as their great black hope, is nothing more than a woman beater who brutalized woman after woman like some manipulative psychopath. And to back up this claim my representative will give names and phone numbers to the press and when these women are contacted they will admit without hesitation that Derrick McCalister beat the shit out of them."

At first I was too stunned to speak. Her coldness astounded me. She was more than willing to destroy the man she purported to love just because she couldn't have her way. "What are you talking about?" I finally asked. "Moon McCalister could never hit a woman."

"I will also have witness after witness testify to Derrick's shady business dealings, and many will call for an investigation, a hearing, and a total dismantling of McCalister Enterprises."

I couldn't believe my ears. "You're serious, aren't you?"

"He'll be persona non grata all up and down the East Coast."

"But it's all lies. What shady business dealings?"

She didn't skip a beat. "I'll think of something," she said.

I shook my head. This was too much. "You're talking about

Moon McCalister, okay? I know him. He's an honest businessman, he's no crook. And he could never mistreat a woman."

"You know he never could and I know he never could and those women who we'll line up know it too, but the voting public don't know it. That's the point. It's the domino effect. The pile-on. The press will eventually discredit each and every one of those women. Easily. But in the practice of law we offer this very sage advice: don't allow the opponent to even attempt to give misleading information to the jury because you can't unring that bell. The damage will have already been done. That'll be Moon's plight too. He couldn't get elected paperboy after that."

"You'll destroy the man you claim to love just because you won't be by his side?"

"I will emasculate him, Miss Coleman, make no mistake about it. I will destroy him as a politician and a businessman. That reputation he worked so hard to achieve will be obliterated overnight. He won't know what hit him when I finish with him. I'm the one, don't you understand that? I'm the woman he judges all the others by. That gives me certain leverage. He won't be able to withstand another heartbreak from me. Don't you get it? And don't think he'll come running to you again, because he won't. He'll be a shell of a man when it's all said and done. He'll want to lie down and die, Miss Coleman, not run to you, when I'm done with him."

I sat back down. The devil wore a black dress, a sleek black dress, and she was on fire with hate. "But how could you destroy him if you love him?" I asked, still searching for some humanity in the woman.

"I love him, but my mind is made up. I've got to have him. And if I can't have him, then I'll make damn sure that nobody else will. I'll use his love for me against him if he resists me, I'll do it in a minute. But you needn't worry. He won't resist me. He can't."

I felt as if I were in quicksand and every word she spoke pulled me farther and farther in. He loved her the way I loved him. I knew what that was like. Everybody else was window dressing compared to him. But that fact alone made me feel so helpless. If I refused what she was trying to do, she promised to destroy him personally and professionally. And it was already obvious to me that a woman like Amanda Trundle, who already proved that she could break Moon's heart and think nothing of it, did not make threats she was not more than willing to carry out. Moon would be destroyed or I would. That was her bottom line. We were the pawns in her twisted little game of life and either way the wind blew, one of us was going down.

I choked back tears as I watched her operate. She moved like a cat, from one side of the room to the other, calculating every step, so certain of her superiority that it angered me. I wanted to lash out at her and kick that devil back to hell where she belonged, but I couldn't. She had all the power. She had all the control. It was going to be me or it was going to be Moon. Period. And she knew as I knew that I could never let it be Moon.

"I've got to know that it's what he wants too," I said with little enthusiasm.

"You will," she said eagerly.

"I don't want you to hurt him again."

She paused as if my concern for Moon were touching to her. "I know you don't."

"I've got to know that this great love he's supposed to have for you is the real deal, not just some figment of your imagination."

"He's invited you to the Baxters' dinner party tomorrow night, right?"

"Yes," I said.

"Good. I have an invitation too. Do you have a cell phone?"

I sighed. She had it all figured out. "Yes," I said.

"Give me the number."

"Why would I give you my cell phone number?"

"After you and Derrick are comfortably placed inside the Baxters' home, I will call you on the cell. You'll excuse yourself to the ladies' room, but stay around to watch me in action. Because that's when I'll make my entrance and Derrick will see me. But don't keep your eyes on me. Keep your eyes on him and his response to me."

It sounded so cold and calculating. But it was a plan that had to be. I still would have to see it to believe it but that was only a testament to my weakness. Because it was as clear as day that a woman like Amanda Trundle, who once broke the heart of the greatest man on earth, meant business. It was a necessary plan and she wanted me to see it for myself. It was a plan that was as necessary a part of my existence now as the dull, unrelenting pain that slowly crept through my broken heart.

I was to meet Moon at the Baxters' house by seven. Minnie and Gerald Baxter were two of the most admired community activists in Tallahassee. Gerald was the current president of the Chamber of Commerce and Minnie was recently honored as Tallahassee's woman of the year. Whenever they decided to put on a shindig, everybody came.

Since Moon was no slave to punctuality either, I managed to arrive first. The Baxters lived in Mariner's Point in a Tudor-style split-level home with a driveway in the round and a side lot for dinner-party traffic overflow.

It was drizzling rain when I arrived and the security officer, overdressed in a big, yellow raincoat, motioned for me to drive my Mercedes all the way near the back of the fence. That would not do. If I needed to make a clean getaway, I didn't want to wait for cars to be moved out of the way first.

I thanked the officer but opted to pull one of Moon's numbers and park up the block. That's when I saw Moon. He was stepping out of his Jaguar and slipping into his suit coat. It was easily Armani, since that was all he wore, and as soon as he saw me he threw up his hand and smiled.

I parked behind him and stepped out of the car. I was dressed in Versace for a change, an eggshell-white pantsuit with matching scarf and bag that Moon had purchased for me, and he immediately shook his head in acknowledgment as he hurried over to help me lift my umbrella.

"You look very pretty, Victoria," he said and kissed me lightly on the lips.

"Thanks," I said but the umbrella was more my immediate concern. It was one of those oversize big FAM-U umbrellas that didn't want to act right and Moon stood over me pulling on it and attempting to bloom it out. I looked up at him. He smelled sweet and looked as if he were on top of the world. He was, in fact, in one of the best moods I'd seen him in.

"You okay?" I asked him.

"Yes. I'm fine. Why?"

"You just seem so bubbly."

He laughed. "Well, I've had a good day, Victoria."

"Really? The mayor is ready to announce?"

"Not that. I was finally able to give the go-ahead on a new mall in Ft. Lauderdale. It's been years in the planning."

"Oh. Congratulations."

"Thank you."

I felt more odd than elated, however. He had never mentioned such a project. If it was *that* big a deal, why hadn't he? I wondered if there were a lot of things he had never mentioned to me, like the true nature of his relationship with Amanda Trundle and if his feelings for her had really ended as I had thought.

We walked hand in hand toward the Baxters' home. It was one of those ritzy, old-money kind of neighborhoods where high-security fences and roving cameras kept mischievous folks at bay. Moon held the umbrella over my head as if I was some prized possession of his and he even started whistling a tune. For the first time in our relationship he was annoying me. This was the worst night of my life, a night that could spell the end of my dream, and he was whistling. He should have felt bad too, I thought, even though he had no clue about my predicament.

Gerald Baxter greeted us at the door. He was a short, jovial man who prided himself on keeping the common touch, and he seemed surprised that Moon didn't bring some glamour queen with him but some ordinary college professor like me.

Within moments of our arrival, however, Moon was whisked away by numerous guests as if he were the main event, and I found myself mingling haphazardly, looking at my watch, and wondering why Amanda didn't hurry up with the show.

But then my cell phone rang. I looked at the number, *666*, which was the code Amanda Trundle had selected. Fitting code, I felt, looking at the numbers, since it was also the mark of the Antichrist.

But I had a charge to keep. I looked at Moon, who was immersed in a conversation with a small group of businessmen, and then I headed down the long hall that led to the downstairs bathroom. I did as Amanda had plotted and stood near the stairs waiting for her great arrival.

And, man, did she arrive. All that was missing was the blowing of the horns and the red carpet. She didn't walk in beauty, the sister *was* beauty. She was decked down in a flame-red hot-mama outfit that didn't look slutty on her at all. It was a short, skintight dress that highlighted every curve on her body where not one curve was out of place. Every man in the room gave her a second look, even Gerald Baxter, who nearly tripped over his wife getting to her side.

After much talk and reverie, she moved ever so deliberately in Moon's direction. He was still in conversation with his colleagues when he turned and saw her. He stood frozen at first, as if he had been overtaken by a mirage, and then he smiled. Greatly.

"*Mandy!*" he said like an exhale.

"Hello, Derrick."

And they just stood there, the two of them, looking gorgeous and superior to all who stood by. Moon was not contemplative the way he usually was when situations confronted him. He didn't have to think about how he felt. He knew how he felt. And without much prodding from her he gently and lovingly pulled her into his arms. My heart dropped. My fear was like a penny in my throat, and it was choking me, and I wanted to swallow it but I couldn't, I wanted to spit it out but I couldn't find the way. So I choked. He was holding her, the man of my life was holding the woman of his, and it wasn't me.

He immediately pushed her away from him, but this wasn't out of some sudden realization that his action might actually hurt me, but for a better look at her, and it was then that she gave the most remarkable hair-flipping-back, shoulders-lifting-up, belle-of-the-ball routine that I had ever seen. She was the sex goddess at work and she knew what she was doing. And Moon, not immune to that fact, pulled her back into his arms.

I saw his face as he held her, the way his eyes squeezed shut as if the idea of her returning to him was a dream come true. This was the woman he loved. Amanda was right. He loved her. I closed my eyes too. My short time in his life appeared to be a distant memory fading fast.

I went home and got into bed. I wanted to be angry with them but I couldn't pull it off. Love was a crazy thing. It'll knock you down sometimes when you least expect it. Moon was perfectly happy with me, perfectly content. But Amanda wasn't around. The love of his life wasn't lurking in the shadows. If Amanda would have been there, he would not have given me the time of day. That was how I had to look at it. That vamp Amanda Trundle took away the most important person in my life, it was true, and I hated her for coming back. But I had to look on the bright side. At least she stayed away long enough to allow me to have those few, glorious months with Moon. At least she did that right. That's the only way I could look at it if I wanted somehow to manage to make it through another day.

My phone started ringing just before eleven P.M. I guess it took that long for him to realize that I was no longer by his side. He called three times in a row. And then, less than half an hour later, he was unlocking my front door and coming in.

I jumped up and locked my bedroom door. I could not bear to see his face. He called my name over and over and then began knocking on my bedroom door. "What is the matter with you?" he asked in a voice so strained it scared me.

"Go away."

"Why?"

"Please."

"I will not leave until you tell me what's going on."

"Where is she, Moon?"

"Where's who?"

"Amanda Trundle. *Mandy?*"

He did not respond right away. A bad sign. "She's somebody I used to know," he finally said, but he said it halfheartedly.

"The love of your life, right?"

"She used to be."

"She still is, Moon. Face it please and don't take me through this. I saw you at that dinner party. I saw the way you pulled her into your arms."

"What's that supposed to mean? Because I was glad to see her, does that mean I want to fuck her?"

"Just leave," I said. "Please!"

He was angry with me, probably for not giving him more credit than that, but he left. And he was not the kind of man who begged for second chances. I knew that he was not coming back. He dropped out of my life as quickly as he had dropped in. I was supposed to feel better. I did my bit for history, and that fact alone was supposed to be my point of comfort. He could now go on, with the love of his life at his side, and conquer city hall and the world too if he wasn't careful. It was a noble thing that I did for him. But I didn't feel very noble that night. I didn't feel very obliging. I just felt bad.

Eight

Ace Boon Coons

The night of Gina's birthday party, I thought, would be the perfect opportunity for me to see if there was still a chance that my girls and I could be tight again. I figured after Moon and Amanda Trundle I could use a little normalcy once more. By the time I dressed in a nice but purposely enticing red evening dress and heels and stood at the big white door of Gina's big white house, I didn't know if I was coming or going. My judgment was shot. My sense of independence and my self-confidence were reduced to zero. I needed my homegirls. I needed to know that there was still something about me that was at least a semblance of who I used to be. Nobody could give me that but Gina and Vera. When you came down to it, they were my family. When you came down to it, they were all I had.

I was looking fly, I must admit, when I rang that doorbell. My dress was well up my behind and I knew if I stood the wrong way or turned too fast, something very private was going to show. But I put it on anyway. I wanted to look attractive again for a change. Ever since my breakup with Moon I had been wearing my skirt suits and conservative business attire as if it was my honor to look as unapproachable as I possibly could. But I was tired of that matronly look. I wanted to be the floozie for a change and if a little ass showed in the process, tough. I was going for broke.

A petite, straggly-haired woman in a blue maid's uniform answered the door. I used to try to be friendly with the help, but the help always seemed to find my kindness patronizing and would never give so much as a polite smile to me. "I'm just doing my job, lady," a butler once told me when I commented to him about the professionalism with which he handled his business. They aren't fools. They know what time it is. They would rather be attending the party than serving it. That's the deal.

The crowd was another story. Nobody was going to mistake this bunch for the kitchen help. Everybody looked wealthy and full of themselves as they walked around Gina's spacious crib in their Italian suits and exclusive gowns, wearing jewelry so intensely sparkling that it looked as if a fireworks display had suddenly popped off. The ladies stood impressive like well-maintained trophies, smiling ever so politely as they worked hard to keep their make-up even and their hairdos fresh. And the men, the husbands and boyfriends, stood around in clusters, laughing too hard for old times' sake but taking every opportunity to check out each other's taste in female.

I looked out of place among them and I knew it. But it wasn't as if I cared. I wanted to be the slut that night. I wanted to be the talk of the room. And it worked for the most part because everybody, eventually, turned and looked my way. The women, naturally, were abhorred by my ostentatious flaunting but the men seemed appreciative. That was good enough for me. Females always made me sick with their indignant expressions when another female upstaged them, but they could keep it to themselves that night. I walked around like the Queen of Sheba, twisting my hips from side to side as if I had a condition, and every time a man paid me a little attention, I laid it on thick as jelly then.

My behavior was out of character for me but everything was out of character for me by that time. I probably needed psychiatric help but was just too proud to seek it. Everything got on my nerves. Every*body* got on my nerves. I walked around that room wondering where Gina dredged up the kind of people who attended her party when they were probably wondering the same thing about me. They looked to be some of the stuffiest folks I had ever seen. Where did sistergirl get them from? Did she have them flown in or something? I walked around wondering and flaunting and smiling and winking until it was almost comical to the folks in the room. By the time Gina noticed me, I had wooed the crowd so and had made such an utter fool of myself that she approached me with the quickness, grabbing me by the arm and escorting me to her study as if she was rescuing me, which, incidentally, she was.

When she closed the study's door she stood in front of me and shook her head. I was behaving like some reckless teenager and I didn't mean it, but I couldn't help it either. And, as usual, some man was the reason. Another heartbreak for Victoria Coleman. Another to-die-for romance gone south.

But Gina didn't criticize me or give me one of her lectures. She just smiled.

"Girrl," she said as only Gina could, "I thought you was gonna shake it off!"

I smiled too. "Was I or was I not playing the floozie tonight?"

"You was playing it, girl. Playing it like a game!"

We did a female high five, which was a slightly lower hand slap than the male version, where the hands clasped together rather than slapped. That was when I really looked at Gina. She didn't look like her usual self. Her sad, hazel eyes had a faraway look about them, as if her body were there but not her soul, not her being, and although she still appeared to be easily the most confident person in the building it was a shaken confidence, as if something had happened that forced her to live on autopilot rather than her trademark spontaneousness. She looked like Erykah Badu that night in her African garb head to toe, as if her thirty-ninth birthday was some kind of coming-out party for her. Even her big, wooden earrings and brown wooden beads seemed odd on her. I almost asked if she had turned Muslim on me, but she apparently saw my stare and answered before I could part my lips.

"It's just a change of pace, that's all," she said. "Versace just went African for a night, that's all."

I smiled.

"And what about you?" she asked.

"Me?"

"Yeah, you, with that hoochie mama dress on. Where you think you at getting all ghetto on me like this?" Then she smiled. "But I'm glad you did it, girl. Teach those high and mighties a lesson. Ain't they something?"

"Yes, Lord! Why did you invite people like that?"

"Good question," she said. "I guess those are the only kind of people who would bother to come to a party of mine. My style doesn't exactly spark the masses."

She tried to smile but she couldn't pull it off this time. The realization that at thirty-nine you're only liked by people you despise was too painful to just smile about. But it was a truthful observation. Gina didn't suffer fools well and she had the patience of a guillotine operator. She'd chop first, usually with her tongue, and ask questions later.

"But anyway," she said, "I'm sorry about you and McCalister." I shook my head, as if to say, "Me too," without saying it. "Are you all right?" she asked.

"Not really. But I will be."

"Well, if it's any consolation you look very nonmournful."

I smiled. "Thanks."

"And who is this Amanda Trundle anyway? What rock did she crawl from under?"

My sentiments exactly. "She's some chick from Baltimore. Somebody he used to know."

"And he left you for *that?*"

I told her a million times that it was I who broke up with Moon, not the other way around, but she, like everybody else, didn't believe me. But it wasn't as if it mattered anyway. Besides, Moon McCalister was the last thing I wanted to talk about. It had been a month since I last spoke to him, a whole month, and this was my first night out.

"I just want to enjoy your set, girl," I said, "not get all wet eyed over some man."

"I know, girl, I'm sorry. But I'm just so disgusted by it, you know? I never been crazy about no Moon McCalister, you know that, but I didn't think he would hurt you like this. And the way they're still denying that he's going to run for mayor, leaving that sick man twisting in office until they get their acts together. It's just un-Moon McCalister like, you know what I'm saying? I really thought the brother was above petty politics. But I heard through the grapevine that an announcement is forthcoming."

Great, I thought. Now I had to see Moon and Amanda parading themselves all over the television screen like guinea hens posing for the cameras. It was more than one human being should have to take.

Then we just stood there, Gina and I, and suddenly tears began to flow and we fell into each other's arms and cried like babies. I didn't know what exactly caused Gina to break, her cry was too heartfelt to just be in support of my pain, but I knew without asking that the root of her despair was a man too.

Finally, after what seemed like a long period of bawling, we released each other's grasp. I laughed because Gina's makeup was running and she reminded me of the rock star Alice Cooper. She laughed because my makeup was running too and I reminded her of some equally ridiculous character. Then she shook her Erykah Badu head. "We need to quit," she said.

And she was right. I needed to quit. I needed to realize that Moon McCalister was probably at this very moment having a good old time with Amanda Trundle—while I was letting them ruin *my* good time? Please. "Let's cut this bullshit, girl, and get back to the party," I said, leaving, not even knowing if Gina was following and not even caring that I looked like hell.

The party was dreadful but I stayed until its conclusion. Isaac, Gina's husband, was nice enough, when he eventually showed up, and he seemed to have more of a flare for the occasion than Gina did. Gina wasn't good at working crowds. She was more a one-on-one kind of person. She would often spend long stretches of time with one person or a small group of people while the rest of her guests simply walked and looked around as if they couldn't wait to get out of here. I even heard some talk about how boring the party was and how desperately they wanted to make up an excuse to leave. "Then leave," I wanted to tell them. "You'll do us all a favor."

I instead took a seat on the couch with an odd assortment of women who didn't know how to socialize, who came to the party alone and would leave the same. They talked very little and did a lot of looking around at the other guests. When we became bored with the view, we started talking to one another. But when the conversation quickly shifted from small talk, like what was up with the Rattlers and Seminoles, to how badly they wanted a man, I got up and walked away. I was tired of hearing that stuff. I'd been searching for Mr. Right for almost seventeen years, ever since I graduated from high school. You'd think he would have snatched me up by now. But no. Always the bridesmaid, never quite the bride. And Moon. How could I even think about finding somebody to replace him? How could somebody do it? I would forever judge them by him and it would be an unfair comparison every time and it would be a disastrous way to live in the end.

That was why I walked away. That was old news now. Moon was out of my life, gone, ready to embark on his own historic journey. He wasn't thinking about me, why should I live the rest of my days worrying about him? That's why I moved on. I had to. He moved on, probably forgetting about me the way you forget about a bad experience. If I was wrong about his love for Amanda Trundle, why didn't he come back and tell me so? Was our relationship so fragile that he could cast me aside just because I made a mistake? That's a shabby way to treat the woman you're supposed to love. But it was my fault. I allowed the treatment. I knew long ago that a man will treat you the way you allow him to treat you. And I was out of that allowance game. I was done.

The party ended well before midnight, which was a bad sign. I wanted to help Gina clean up but she told me to forget that. "I don't pay the maid to watch you do her work," she added.

She seemed more relieved than disappointed when the last guest left. We chilled out on the couch in the living room for a while, Gina, Isaac, and I, until Isaac's pager went off and he had to leave. A business run, he said. I looked at Gina as he walked out the door. "At this time of night?" I asked.

She ran her fingers through her long hair. "That's what the man said."

"But it's almost midnight. What business could be that important that it has to be transacted at midnight?"

Gina looked at me and smiled. "Just chill, honey," she said, holding up her glass and cigarette as if she were conducting some imaginary band. "Just relax and enjoy the chill."

And we did. We lounged on the couch smoking cigarettes and drinking wine and listening to old-school R&B on the radio. The Dells came on singing "Stay in My Corner" and we both jumped up at the same time, snapping our fingers as if we weren't drunk and swaying from side to side with the rhythm of the beat. We tried to best each other singing every high note, and Gina, who was plastered, even tried to handle the baritone. Then the Isley Brothers came on with "Summer Breeze," and the Delfonics with "Betcha

By Golly Wow" and Teddy P's "Turn off the Lights" got us crazy too. We danced and drank and laughed so much that we finally dropped to the sofa in sheer exhaustion.

I was nearly asleep when Gina jumped up again. "Come on, girl," she said. She had her hobo bag in one hand and a cigarette in the other. "Let's go."

"Go where?" I asked, putting on my shoes.

"Vera's."

"Vera's?"

"We're going to visit Miss V."

"Gina, are you crazy? It's after two o'clock in the morning!"

Gina looked at me. "And?"

We left. Gina slung her Lexus out of her driveway and drove as if she was constantly on the verge of losing control. I asked about fifty times if I could drive but she insisted that she was not drunk and she knew what she was doing. "I don't get drunk," she said as she sped through a red light. I began begging her to stop the car but she wouldn't. Finally, when nothing else worked, I opened the car's door as if to jump out.

"Are you out of your mind!" she yelled and slammed on the brakes. I took over the controls.

We arrived at Vera's place in one piece, thank God, although I wasn't crazy about all of this late-night driving. Every horrific wreck that I'd ever seen on the news occurred around two A.M.

Gina lived in Dalton Estates on the west end of Tallahassee, while Vera lived outside of Tallahassee, near Lloyd, to the east. We knocked on the door and rang the bell repeatedly before lights finally came on and Vera and Rollie opened up.

"What's happened?" they asked as they allowed us passage into their apartment.

We laughed. They looked like Ma and Pa Kettle in their battle-worn housecoats and talking slippers and both of them had a look of sheer fright on their faces. This was well out of their routine. They were not used to late-night visitors. They were certain that something bad had happened. But Gina quickly relieved their fears when she said that nothing was wrong. "We missed y'all tonight at the party," she said and fell down on their living-room couch. "Why didn't y'all come to my party?"

Rollie looked at Vera as if to say, *Get rid of these clowns and get rid of them now*, and he went back to bed. Vera watched us and shook her head. I fell on the couch beside Gina. "You two are pathetic," she said. And then she smiled. "The slut and the African. I'm through wit y'all!"

Me and Gina looked at each other and then burst into laughter. It was Vera the way she used to be. Not Rollie's tight-ass wife, but the girl who could whoop it up with the best of them. "Welcome back, V," I said and she plopped down on the couch beside us.

It was good to be back. We laughed and talked about old times and laughed and talked about older times and laughed and talked until we ran out of things to say. Then we talked about the new stuff.

"I'm sorry," Vera said, "that I ever introduced you to Peter."

"Oh, here we go," Gina said. "Don't start getting damn sympathetic on me now."

"I had no idea he was like that, Tory, honest, I didn't. It must have been awful for you."

I shook my head. "He's out of my life now, thank God."

"And I heard about your split-up with Moon McCalister. I'm sorry."

"Yeah. Me too."

"Why did y'all break up?"

"None of your damn business," Gina said, the wine and her own natural feistiness getting the best of her.

"Well, excuse me for living," Vera said.

"You're excused," Gina replied.

"And Gina told me that you had got yourself caught up in some drive-by shooting," Vera said.

"Damn," Gina said, "just tell her every word I ever said to you."

I looked at Gina. How did she know about my great adventure with that criminal Sharon Williamson?

"Your friend Jake Onstead kept me posted," she said.

I smiled. Jake was one of the best. "It wasn't as bad as it sounds."

"Good," Vera said.

"It was worse, girl," I added and she and Gina both looked at me. "I thought I was in some B movie the way it played out."

"What happened?" Gina asked as if she had been wanting to ask it for a long time. "And who was this Sharon person?"

I told them everything, about my first encounter with Sharon at the Walmart and about my last encounter with her in jail. "I became the getaway driver," I said.

They laughed so hard that they cried.

"She had me going, girl. She told me she wanted to straighten up her life so she could get her kids back. Of course I later found out the sister don't even have no kids. But she was a good liar, I'll give her that. She even had names for these imaginary little ones and everything."

"Names?" Vera asked between laughs. "What were their names, girl?"

I hesitated, not particularly anxious to display how easily I could be duped. "Michael, Marlon, and Jackie," I said.

Vera and Gina fell against each other laughing. "Sistergirl had her some Jackson Five children," Gina said, "and Tory still fell for it!"

"What happened to Tito and Jermaine?" Vera asked and Gina jumped down from the couch and dropped to her knees in laughter.

I laughed too, although it had hardly been funny when I was going through it.

"What were you thinking, Tory?" Vera asked.

"She wasn't thinking," Gina answered. "That's the problem. She should have known that some crack head like Sharon was trouble from the moment she laid eyes on her."

"I did and I didn't. But she was from Philly. She was my home-girl. I knew her since my school days."

"Correction," Gina said, "you knew her *during* your school days. You didn't know shit about her since."

That was true. Sharon Williamson was nothing like the person I had known in school. Sistergirl was so far out there in that drug world of hers that she didn't care what happened to her, me, or anybody else, just as long as she got what she wanted.

We hung out in Vera's living room until it was dawn. That was a first for Vera. She was not a night person in any way, shape, or form. She and Rollie were infamous for their ten o'clock bedtimes and the thought of her staying up all night with two of her slightly inebriated friends was antithetical to everything she knew. But she hung in there. I loved that sister for that. She listened to my mini-saga with Sharon and my almost romance with the preacher as if I were telling her a sweeping, marvelous tale. She even popped popcorn. It was wonderful. I could not have dreamed up a better time.

We said our good-byes in hugs and tears. We promised never to fall out of friendship again. We were like little kids. We were saying things like, "I promise to be your best friend forever," and, "Let's never go to bed mad," and all of that pathetic, feel-good stuff I used to think only desperate people said. Yet, in a way, we three were desperate. We were desperately seeking normalcy; desperately seeking to know that no matter what happened, there would be somebody to turn to, somebody who would be there when the world just wasn't interested.

Two days later I received a call from Gina. I was at work, in my office, looking over some test questions for an upcoming exam. I had just taken off my reading glasses and was pinching my temple when the telephone rang. Gina's call was at first received casually by me, as I jokingly told her that it must be nice to have a job where you didn't have to work, but she didn't laugh. That was the first sign. Then she started calling Isaac all kinds of names without bothering to tell me exactly what was flaming her fire. That was the second sign. Gina never, ever had a lot of negative stuff to say about her husband. He wasn't perfect, but she didn't get her kicks pointing that out either.

"What's the matter, G?" I asked.

"I know now," she said. "I suspected he might have some play on the side, but I didn't have the proof and I wasn't about to confront him unless I had proof. Now I've got it. I know where he's been going every night."

"What are you talking about?"

"I know where his bitch lives and I'm on my way there now."

I stood up. I knew Gina. She had the kind of personality that could be pushed over the edge by something like this. "Where are you?" I asked.

"In my car. I'm on my way there now."

"Wait!" I yelled. "Please. Let's meet somewhere first and talk about it."

"Time out for talking, girlfriend. Time for action now."

"Gina, please. Let me go with you. Okay? Come and pick me up, I'm ready."

She thought about this long and hard. Then she said okay, for me to meet her on The Set pronto. I agreed.

She showed up later than I thought she would. My sense of panic apparently had calmed her down. Her hair was combed straight back in an under flip and she wore dark sunglasses. Every male on The Set turned and stared at Gina as her Lexus swerved in to collect me. She didn't have to dress like a slut or do some outrageous activity to get a man's attention. All she had to do was show up. I wish.

According to Gina she was bored late last night so when Isaac fell asleep on her, she decided to rummage through his things. She ripped through his pants and wallet and found a lot of interesting tidbits, such as receipts for flowers he didn't order for her; hotel receipts; and, to top it off, a receipt for a Bahamas cruise she didn't know shit about. She checked his cell phone bills and found one particular number that he dialed quite often. At work, she investigated further and found out that the number belonged to one Margaret Horn. Furthermore, Isaac claimed that he was going to Pensacola for the day to handle some company business. Gina called his office. Isaac's own secretary didn't know anything about any Pensacola trip. He was on vacation, she said. By that time Gina was through dealing. She had her suspicions before, she told me as we drove along, but now it was verified. He had a mistress. And she had to see it to fully believe it.

This Margaret woman lived in a town house on Thomasville Road and Gina almost stopped her car in the middle of the street when she saw Isaac's dark green Isuzu Rodeo parked in front of the woman's house. I tried my best to discourage her, because nothing good would come from a confrontation like this, but Gina wasn't thinking about me. She wasn't one of those spurned women with wild vengeance on her mind. She was calm and practical. She had to know, she said, and she could not rest another day until she knew for herself what was really going on.

"What are you going to do?" I asked her.

She grabbed her big pocketbook from the backseat (more out of habit than necessity, I thought). She then looked at me through her dark lenses. "I want to see what sistergirl wants with my husband," she said with a matter-of-factness that stunned me.

We walked up to the door and Gina rang the bell. It was a neighborhood that reminded me of Georgetown in D.C. Quiet, clean, and so all-American. But like all such facades, there was a heathen in the midst.

To our shock Isaac answered the door. He was so bold with his game that it astounded me. He, in fact, was eating on some carrot and was smiling and talking when he opened the door. He and the Mistress were apparently having a grand old time.

When he saw me and Gina, however, his grandness became somewhat muted, as if he were suddenly constipated. His chewing stopped and his gay expression turned sour. "Regina?" he asked as if it couldn't be.

I frowned. It felt bad to bust a brother like Isaac. He seemed like such a good guy, such a down-to-earth brother that I often complimented Gina on her choice. "Looks like you picked the right one this time, girl," I would tell her. "Seems that way," she would say.

It was clear that Isaac never even considered that his little tryst would ever come to light. He thought he could live his double life forever and a woman as self-centered and confident as Gina wouldn't dare or care enough to investigate. He was wrong.

"Hello, Isaac," she said, still refusing to take off her shades. "Having a Bible study, are we?"

"Nall, nall, it ain't like that," he said, thinking quick on his feet. "This is my coworker's house. We were going over some figures for a presentation I've got to give over in Pensacola later today."

"Oh. Your coworker. Then I'm certain this coworker would not mind if we came in."

Before Isaac could say if the coworker would mind or not, Gina barged on in. She was the power of their relationship. Isaac, in fact, looked like a wimp in front of Gina. I always suspected that he viewed Gina as some kind of trophy woman, something beautiful and enticing to stand against his plainness and drabness. He was probably always a cheating dog. You couldn't look at him to tell it, but I suspected that this was nothing new to him.

We barged in, Gina and I, and took what we considered our rightful place in Margaret Horn's living room. And an enchanting living room it was, filled with an amazing array of French Empire furnishings, eighteenth-century paintings, and numerous lithographs. She was probably another trophy woman for Isaac, and like Gina, she was a trophy woman with rare and expensive tastes. Isaac and Gina were wealthy, but this Margaret woman's command of style was, quite frankly, something to behold.

214

Isaac kept the show going, talking about his secret lover as if he actually thought we believed that he was there on business. Your boy couldn't have been thinking straight. Why would we come there, if it was to be explained that simply? Surely he had to figure that Gina had the goods on his butt or she wouldn't bother to show up at his lover's door. But old Isaac had probably been unfaithful for so long that he forgot how deplorable, how low-down and dirty his actions really were. Only a fool or a mighty slick man would have thought that his charade could go on in the face of what was before him. I looked at Isaac and couldn't stop shaking my head. But he kept on talking, about this coworker. What was the brother thinking?

"Where is the coworker?" Gina asked as she stood in the middle of the beautiful home. She looked around at her competition's abode and the more she looked around the angrier she became. But to her credit she kept her cool.

"Where's who?" Isaac asked.

"The coworker," Gina said.

"Oh," Isaac said, walking toward the stairway. "Yes, I'll get her." He then stood at the bottom of the stairs and yelled for her to come on down. "Margaret," he yelled, "could you take a moment away from our budget analysis and come down and meet my wife and her friend? I told her how we were coworkers and she wanted to meet you!"

I smiled and looked at Gina. I couldn't believe Isaac could be that dense. Even G had to shake her head at that one. I mean your boy must have given old Margaret more hints than Vanna White gave her game show contestants the way he carefully set the scene for her grand entrance. But Gina kept her cool.

We three stood quietly in the living room until a long pair of thin legs came climbing down the staircase. By the time we could see the entire body, Gina's body language immediately turned defensive as she widened her stance and folded her arms. And there finally stood her competition, the woman of the hour. Miss Margaret Horn. A tall, bosomy, blond bombshell.

215

Gina took off her shades and checked her out. And then she shook her head. "I know better than this," she said.

"Yes," Isaac said as if he were clueless to Gina's outrage, "this is my coworker Margaret Horn. She's an accountant in my office."

Gina nervously twirled around her sunglasses and lingered in her look at Margaret. Then she looked at Isaac. "Nigger, please!" she yelled. "You mean to tell me you've been cheating on me with this white ho here?"

Margaret took exception to Gina's characterization and cocked an attitude too. "I beg your pardon?" she said and placed her hand on her hip. But Gina was not the one to be bothered that day. She put her hand on her hip too.

"You heard me, bitch," she said.

"Settle down, Regina!" Isaac commanded. "I told you she was my coworker."

"Coworker my ass! How stupid do you think I am?"

"Excuse me but I don't appreciate your using profanity in my home," Margaret said and Gina stomped her feet and looked at her sidelong. Even I had to check her out.

"What?" Gina asked in total disbelief. "You don't *what?*"

It was incredible to me too. But you had to give girlfriend credit because she was truly a high-class husband snatcher.

"Let me make sure you understand what is going on here," Gina said, moving her fingers around as if she were demonstrating sign language. "You are having an affair with my husband. Do you read? Do you comprehend? Do you realize that where I come from a woman who has an affair with another woman's husband is nothing more than a trash barrel, the raunchiest street-corner ho? My profanity usage, my dear, is the last of your problems, okay?"

The real Gina was beginning to emerge. No more emotionless freezer queen stuff. She was coming out of the ice. And Isaac, foolish Isaac, was panicking big time.

"Regina, you're overreacting," he said. "Now I don't know what you've been told or what's going on in your head but Margaret and I are coworkers only. That's it."

Gina looked at Margaret. She knew the type. She knew that Margaret loved this scene because it appealed to her kind of womanhood, her deep female desire to snatch somebody's man and revel in the triumph. "Is that right, Stretch?" Gina asked the very tall blonde.

Margaret took the bait. "Who are you calling Stretch? I can't help it if Isaac prefers me!"

Isaac turned red. He was black as a shoe but I declare he turned red. "Wait a minute," he said to his coworker. "What are you doing? We're coworkers working on that budget analysis for the Tampa trip, what are you talking about?"

Gina smiled and nodded. "I thought it was the Pensacola trip. But it don't matter because you the trip, you and this tall drink of water over here. So tell me again what it is y'all been working on, Isaac, huh? What the fuck y'all been working on!"

And when Gina said that, something snapped in her. She dropped her big pocketbook to the floor and actually lunged at Margaret. If it had not been for Isaac's intervention, I do believe Gina would have snatched sistergirl's eyes out. But Isaac grabbed her arms just in time and pulled her back. She tried but she couldn't loosen his grip. Margaret was astounded. She stood with her hand on her heart as if she had never seen such beastly behavior. She could sleep with somebody else's husband, I supposed, and that was all right. But profanity and a little violence were verboten in her puritanical, Brady Bunch eyes. Give me a break!

Gina eventually calmed down and stopped struggling with Isaac. She didn't cry, she was still tough, but she was mad as hell. Margaret was mad too. "I want them out of my house," she said, instructing Isaac. But Isaac was too busy slowing down Gina to pay her any attention.

"Let's go, G," I said to Gina. We really needed to leave the woman's house. Besides, she was all hot with Miss Margaret over there when it was Isaac's behind she really needed to kick. I mean, nobody put a gun to his head and told him to fool around. He was the one who owed Gina loyalty and commitment, not Miss Margaret. She didn't owe Gina shit.

But Gina didn't see it that way. She was hot with both of them, but especially the other woman. She kept looking at Margaret standing there in all of her triumph, and the need to feel flesh returned.

She lunged at Margaret again, only this time she managed to touch flesh and push her to the floor. Margaret fell back hard, with her baby-doll hair flying down over her face.

Isaac again pulled Gina away, but only he didn't attempt to slow her down. He, instead, went to aid Margaret. He fell on his knees beside her and asked over and over if she was all right. He even put her head in his lap in an effort to nurse her, although it was obvious that nothing was really wrong with her. When Gina saw him, however, she stood in amazement. How could he appease a witch he barely knew over his own wife, a wife he had to beg and cajole into marrying him? She could not believe it. I grabbed her arm to hold her steady. We needed to leave. We needed to get Gina's pocketbook and get as far away from Isaac and his coworker as we possibly could.

But Gina was too hurt to go. She needed answers. She needed to let Isaac know how badly he was treating her. My own experiences with men taught me long ago that such noble acts were always misdirected. Men who cheat couldn't care less about how badly you hurt. They're too wrapped up in their own feelings to concern themselves with yours. But Gina wasn't accustomed to being cheated on. She was usually the problem in the relationship, not the man. All of this unfaithful husband trip was entirely new to her.

"How could you?" she asked Isaac as he gently rubbed his woman's glorious blond hair.

He looked up at her. He wasn't a man torn between two women. He knew exactly who he wanted. "Go home, Regina," he said. "We'll talk later."

"Talk later?" Gina asked. "Are you out of your fucking mind? There ain't gonna be no later. You wanted you a white woman trophy and you got you one. That's it. No more discussion needed. But you lost me, and you best believe that."

Isaac was too in love with Margaret to argue. He simply shook his head. Gina shook hers too. "You of all people," she said. "You used to scream in anger when you saw all those black men with those white women on their arms, talking about how they were defaming all the beautiful black queens they could have had. Now you go out and do the same thing."

"It's not about race," Isaac said. "I didn't want it to come to this. I didn't tell you to come here. I tried to spare your feelings. But I love Margaret. And her being white has nothing to do with it."

"Don't even try that," Gina said, slinging her own hair back in place. "It has everything to do with it and you know it. You bought the hype, brother, and that's all there is to it. You grew up seeing the American image of beauty on all those Ivory soap commercials and your ass fell for it. Now you got you an Ivory soap doll. Well, I hope you and her Ivory ass will be happy because you and me are history. You hear me? And I mean ancient history! Now we'll see how comforting her Ivory skin is, because, lover boy, you have lost the absolute, undisputed best!"

Everything seemed to stop when Gina finished her speech. Margaret looked at her, Isaac looked at her, and I looked at her too. She wanted to cry, the tears were on the tips of her eyelids, but they didn't fall down. She merely stared at her husband as long as she could and then she grabbed up her hobo bag and left. I looked at Isaac and Margaret, down on the floor like Romeo and Juliet, and it all seemed so useless. Isaac was supposed to be one of the decent brothers, a man who understood the devastation of infidelity, but he was just like the rest. He talked a good game but in the end he couldn't cover the bet. Another lip-service brother if ever there was one.

I started to share my feelings with him, but I didn't say a word. I left too, hurrying behind Gina before she really did something drastic.

We drove out to the park at Lake Jackson and watched the birds search for food. It was a nice day, with just the right combination of breeze and sun, but Gina was not in the mood to notice. She sat there and stared out at the lake that was as still as a rock, and kept shaking her head every time she even thought about that scene back on Thomasville Road.

"I can't believe he did this to me, Tory. That's why it hurts so bad. I never expected it. I mean, I suspected he might have been fooling around here and there, I haven't been a Girl Scout either, but he's in love with somebody else. That ain't just no physical thing he got going with Ivory Soap. He love that bitch. He chose her over me." She looked at me when she said this, as if she wanted some reaction, but I didn't know what to say.

"And he pull this shit now. Now of all times. He picked a fine time to leave me, Lucille."

I tried to smile. "Well, at least you don't have the four hungry children and the crop in the field."

She looked at me as if she wanted to smile at that Kenny Rogers song retort, but she seemed to realize all of a sudden that it was too real to laugh about. "Not four," she said. "But maybe one."

It sounded like Greek to me. "What?" I asked her.

"I'm pregnant, that's what. I'm thirty-goddamn-nine and pregnant, that's what!" Gina said this and stood on her feet. She began pacing, lifting her hair up and dropping it down, folding her arms, then letting them go.

I sat stunned. Gina? Pregnant? I never thought I'd hear those two words together. Whereas I loved children but just didn't want to have any of my own, she despised the little creatures, as she called them. Her lifestyle, her style period, was totally at odds with motherhood. "You're pregnant?"

She nodded.

"When?"

"What the hell am I gonna do, Tore? I got a baby in me."

"But, when did you know? When did you find out?"

"Yesterday," she said. "I had been feeling lousy lately so I went in for a checkup. My doctor called me and told me the only thing wrong with me was that I was gonna be a mommy. I almost cussed his ass out when he told me that. Me? A mommy? So I called it a day and went home. But I just couldn't bring myself to tell Isaac, or anybody really. So when he went to bed, I couldn't help it. I had to know what was going on. I had to know if he was worthy to be the father of my child."

"What do you mean? He *is* the father. Isn't he?"

"Of course he is. But he's also a cheating dog, you hear me? His shit ain't no accident, T. He didn't happen to stumble across Miss Ivory and fall in bed with her. He knew exactly what he was doing." And then she said, "Damn!" and got mad all over again.

I thought about Gina's advice to me at times like this. Every time Robert or any of my other boyfriends would get busted cheating on me, Gina was always quick with the advice. "Leave his ass!" she'd say. "I wouldn't put up with that nonsense another day!"

"Leave him," I said. "I wouldn't put up with that mess another day."

Gina probably didn't realize that I was feeding her back one of her own lines but it didn't matter because sistergirl had already made up her mind. "No," she said wryly, "I'm going to rededicate my life to him. Of course I'm gonna leave his ass, what do you take me for? That nigger ain't getting away with this! I'm going to divorce him and bleed him for every dime I can bleed him for, that's not even the issue. I'm through with that. My problem is this baby."

"What's the problem, Gina? You'll have a beautiful, healthy baby, I'm sure. With or without Isaac."

She looked at me as if I were speaking gibberish. "What are you talking about?" she asked. "I'm not rearing some baby by myself. Are you crazy? Are you out of your cotton-pickin' mind? If Isaac's out the door, so is his baby. This *his* baby. I'm not struggling for no nine months having *his* baby, and then raising it by myself while he's living it up on Thomasville Road!"

"What are you talking about, Gina?"

She stopped pacing and stood still. She unfolded her arms and tossed her hair back. "It's not turning out right, Tory. This is not the way it's supposed to turn out. I thought after I divorced Carter and came down here to Florida it was going to be different. Our new beginning, remember? But what the hell is this? I could have had any man from here to the panhandle and I pick Isaac. Brilliant me. Didn't even love his black behind. But he loved me so much. He couldn't be without me. He'd do anything for me. And he leaves *me?*" She shook her head as if she could shake away the sting of her now devastating reality. "This ain't right," she said and finally, finally the tears began to flow.

We left Lake Jackson as the sun began to set. I drove but drove straight to Vera's. If it was an abortion your girl was hinting at, I was not the one to consult. My feelings, it seemed to me, ran too deep. I would be biased and unreasonable and have Gina making decisions for her life based on my own prejudice. That would be wrong. She deserved better than that. Vera was the one she needed to see.

When I stopped the Lexus in Vera's parking lot, Gina looked at me coyly. "What's this?" she asked.

"We need some spiritual guidance here," I said flatly.

It was true and Gina knew it. That was why, I supposed, she did not argue with me. Vera was a lot of things but she was always a good Christian. She would always give you straight advice. It would have been malfeasance if I didn't take my best friend to a person that would tell her like it is when she most needed to know. And for all her big talk, I think G appreciated that. We ended up arm in arm when we knocked on Vera's door.

There was no answer. "She probably went to hang out with Rollie," Gina said.

And before she could protest, I put us back in the car and drove the short distance to Rollie's funeral parlor. Sure enough, Vera's black Lexus was parked right in front of the door. Gina, however, just knew I was crazy when we pulled up to the small building, but I pretended as if I didn't realize her surprise.

"I know you're kidding," she said to me.

I stepped out of the car. "Come on, Gina. We'll see her and go."

I made it sound so simple. If the truth were known, I hated funeral parlors and places like it more than Gina did. But we had business to take care of. I didn't want Gina to jump up tomorrow morning and try to do something crazy without first knowing that she had heard from Vera on the subject. Vera, as far as I was concerned, was an expert on things moral.

"Morality hasn't anything to do with it," Gina said as I explained my reasoning to her. "I ain't in the mood to be preached to, Tory, and especially not at some damn funeral parlor."

"It won't take but two minutes, my goodness. Vera is your best friend too. She has a right to know what's going on."

That line worked because Gina, after giving it some thought, got out of the car and went into the building with me.

It was spooky and quiet as expected. Soft organ music was being played in the background. We walked slowly down the long narrow, sanitized hall, looking into the various small rooms that we passed, until we saw Rollie in his casket room talking to a woman who seemed unable to make up her mind. Rollie was speaking very softly, explaining that the price of the casket was the lowest on the market. Every time I saw Rollie in his funeral director's role, I cringed. He was really very scary looking to me. His eyebrows were thick and long and his face had a chiseled, almost deformed twist to it. He was tall and lanky and stood hunched over. If I was that woman I would have taken one look at him and run in the opposite direction. But she seemed to trust him. She seemed to find his unattractiveness comforting.

He never looked up, not one time, to see that Gina and I were standing in his hallway. Vera, in fact, was the first to see us. She was stepping out of a side room on her tiptoes, closing the door behind her so gently that she had to make facial expressions to ensure its quietness. Naturally I took the opportunity to yell out, "Hey, girl" and damn near gave her a heart attack.

"My Lord," she whispered as she placed her hand over her heart and walked toward us. "You almost scared me to death!"

"I'm sorry," I said smiling.

Vera had to smile. "Girl, you ain't about nothin' good."

"What's in there?" I asked, pointing to the side room Vera had stepped out of.

"A wake," Vera whispered and said. "Come with me."

At first we thought she was taking us into the room where the wake was taking place. Instead, she took us to a small office at the end of the hall. Rollie's office. It was a sparse room with an oversize, real wood desk and one long bookshelf filled with various books on Jesus and death and dying. There was also a small, leather couch and Gina and I raced to it. Something about a funeral parlor made you feel more secure off your feet. Vera laughed as she closed Rollie's office door. "Don't worry, girls. We haven't had a live burial in years!"

"That ain't e-much funny," Gina rolled her eyes at Vera and said. She was still miserable, and still looked like hell, but she was doing everything in her power to function. But Vera knew as I knew that something was terribly wrong.

She grabbed Rollie's desk chair and placed it in front of the couch. She sat down. "What is it now?" she asked.

Gina looked her up and down. "Excuse me?" she asked.

"You look like something the cat dragged in, what you think I mean?"

Vera had a strong old-woman way about her. She was a thin, tall woman, with a long, thin face. Although her ponytail hairstyle and small body frame indicated youth and vitality, there was something in her persona that was definitely matronlike. She cared about people. Whenever you came to her with a problem she would lean forward, look you dead in the eye, and listen as if there was nothing more important in this world than hearing what you had to say. Gina often found her style annoying or, as she put it, "too damn sympathetic," but when she sat in front of us that night in Rollie's office, and leaned toward Gina, and looked her in the eye, Gina didn't talk about being annoyed or anything like that. She burst into tears.

Vera was shocked. Gina rarely cried. She looked at me.

"Tell her, G," I said.

"It's nothing," Gina said, wiping her tears and frowning as if she was mad that she had cried at all. "I'm just tired."

"What's the matter?" Vera asked, confused. "What's happened?"

"Nothing happened. I'm tired, Vera, okay?" She then closed her eyes and blew her nose. She was worn down. She would die if she had to discuss what Isaac did to her once more. So I told Vera the story, and Gina sat back and listened too, as if it didn't concern her really.

Like me, Vera was floored by Isaac's infidelity. Your boy had everybody fooled. She moved over to the couch, squeezing between the two of us, and put her arm around Gina. "It's not the end of the world," she said. "It hurts but thank God you found out now. All of us have cried over a man, trust me on that. It's just your time to cry."

Gina, however, took offense to her comments. "Excuse me but I am not crying over no man, okay?"

Vera turned and looked at me, then she looked back at Gina. "I thought Tory said you found out that Isaac was cheating and y'all went over to the girl's house—"

"I'm pregnant, okay? Satisfied? Now you know the news. So run and tell that."

Vera actually smiled. "What did you say?"

"She said she's pregnant, Vera."

Vera looked at me. "She said what?"

"She's pregnant, Vera."

"Pregnant?"

"Pregnant, girl."

"Oh my God!" Vera said almost hysterically.

"Well, damn," Gina said. "It ain't all that surprising!"

"But you hate children."

"I don't *hate* children."

"Yes, you do," Vera and I said together, in complete unity.

"But you're right," Vera said. "We've got to look on the bright side here. And yes, it is a shocker, given your age."

Gina looked at Vera. "What you mean *my* age? I'm younger than your old butt."

"By two months, Gina."

"Well?"

"You don't have to be insulting because you're pregnant. Women older than you get pregnant every day, I'm not saying they don't. But you've always been so dead set against children and to suddenly decide to have one now, at *this* stage in your life, that's what I'm talking about."

"I've never been dead set against other people's children. I've just been dead set against having a child of my own. And I'm still dead set against it."

Vera frowned and looked at me. Then she looked at Gina. "What you talking about, Gina?"

Gina gathered the nerve to look Vera in the eye. "I don't want this baby," she said.

"You don't want the baby? But . . . you're pregnant."

226

"I know that, Vera."

"Then I don't get it."

"Like hell you don't!" Gina said, forgetting, I assumed, where she was.

"You're pregnant. It's nonnegotiable."

Gina looked at Vera. "And who died and made you boss?"

"You're telling me that you're going to have your own baby killed. What do you expect me to say?"

"I expect you to mind your own business."

"It's a baby, Gina!"

"It's none of your damn business, Vera."

"Then why did you come here if it's not my business?"

Gina looked at me. "Ask Mother Teresa over there."

Vera looked at me but I could do nothing but shake my head. She then looked around at the books on Rollie's shelf and pulled down a thin paperback. *Oh, great,* I thought. *I wanted her to talk to Gina but she decides to give her a book to read instead.* I almost stood up and walked out of that room right then and there. But I should have known V better than that. Sistergirl pretended that she wasn't thinking about Gina. Then she handed me the book.

"What's this?" I asked.

"It's called *Life is Enough Alone.* It's just a lesson in learning that you can't help somebody who don't want your help."

Gina looked at the book. I decided to play along.

"I agree," I said. "I was afraid to even talk to Gina about it because I knew it would be like I'm talking to a brick wall. Thanks, girl. I'll read it. I'm gonna wash my hands of this whole thing. And when those nightmares start, she better not even think about calling on me."

"That's what the author of that book says. She says you have to mean what you say though."

"Oh, I mean it. Who? I sho' nuff mean it! I been there. I've had friends to tell me about how that stuff can play mind games on you for the rest of your life. You don't see that part on TV. It's simple.

Y'all hatch 'em and we snatch 'em. Simple. But ain't nothing that easy."

Vera stood up as if that was the end of the conversation. I stood up too. We played up that ridiculous book big time, even to where Vera told me that I should recommend it to my students. Gina shook her head. We were hamming it up pretty good but it appeared to be working.

"What y'all think?" she asked and then she looked up at us. "Y'all think this is easy for me? Y'all think I don't know how painful this decision is gonna be for me? Isaac has left me. And I'm pregnant. I know what it's all about and I don't need no damn book to tell me either!"

She started crying again. Vera and I both sat down beside her and put our arms around her. I had never seen Gina so out of it. She had loved and left so many men down through the years that I guess we assumed she was untouchable with that love thing. But sistergirl had met her match today. Not only was a man involved but a baby too. She had never been on the other side of the coin, until now. And she bested me and Vera by leaps and bounds.

After we hugged and cried together, all three of us leaned back on Rollie's leather couch. Every time we were in pain, every time we couldn't seem to function anymore, it always had something to do with a man. We were thirty-something, successful women. We weren't children anymore. We weren't some wallflower virgin girls all goo-goo eyes over some man. I leaned up and looked at my best friends. This was crazy.

"This is crazy," I said. Gina wiped her eyes and looked at me. Vera looked too.

"What's crazy?" Vera asked.

"All three of us are pushing forty—some of us are pushing the mess out of it, in fact."

"Watch it, girl," Vera said.

"We've got to learn something sometime. We've got to know from jump that if we decide to fall in love with a man, any man in this lifetime, it might not work out. But then we always act so shocked when it don't work out. Why?"

"Because we hope it works out," Vera said.

"But we know it probably won't."

"But we hope it does."

"But nine out of ten times it won't. So why do we keep hoping?"

"Because it might," Vera said again, rather exasperated by my psychobabble.

"But it usually don't. But why do we keep on trying?"

"Because we're damn fools!" Gina said sharply and Vera and I looked at her. Then suddenly and almost necessarily, and with Gina herself chiming in, we laughed.

Nine
On the Rebound

He was to pick me up at seven. I should have known something wasn't right with this brother of Vera's when, at exactly seven P.M., I heard knocks at my front door. I nearly freaked. What in the world was he doing at my door on time? I wasn't used to that. I am a slave to CP time, you hear me? Just because the date was scheduled for seven didn't mean seven *exactly*. Not in my book, anyway. If he wasn't a doctor and I wasn't in need of a little wining and dining, I would have told your boy to come back in a couple hours. Or never. But he was a doctor. A medical doctor. It's not every day a girl has an MD knocking at her door.

But that didn't change the fact that I was nowhere near ready. I had taken my shower and was in my bedroom, moving slow, puffing cigarettes, and singing about that midnight train to Georgia with Gladys Knight. I was still wondering if I was ready for this dating game business again anyway. Vera assured me that it wasn't exactly a date. Her brother, Dr. Daniel Patrick Gurchess, was on vacation from his practice in Phoenix and he wanted to go out on the town for once. Since Vera did not care for the nightlife and Rollie was not willing to help, she asked if I could do the honors. I agreed. Just like that. And why not? Moon had gone on with his life, announcing his candidacy for mayor the day after my thirty-fifth birthday. His announcement was nearly a month ago but I remember it as if it happened yesterday. He was on every local newscast that day and Miss Amanda Trundle was right by his side. I was surprised that she wasn't Mrs. Amanda McCalister yet, since that was ultimately her goal, but that was just a matter of time too.

I cried the night he announced his candidacy. Not because I wasn't there, beside him where I had hoped to be, but because he was there, tall and handsome, accepting Ross Austin's endorsement and making every Tallahassian proud. Sometimes, on my less than charitable days, I would wonder what on earth was wrong with me when I gave up somebody like Moon. Was I nuts or what? Had some big object dropped on my head and rendered me imbecilic?

That's why I came to the conclusion that there was nothing noble about my gesture to step aside. It was fear. It was the fear that I wasn't up for the job, that I wasn't what he needed in his new life. He needed a mover and shaker, somebody willing to wheel and deal on behalf of her husband with unrelenting forcefulness. I didn't fit the bill. Amanda Trundle fitted it perfectly.

That was not to say, however, that I wasn't amenable to a phone call from him. I was. If he had phoned during the days just after my decision and asked that I reconsider, I would have. I loved him that much. But he didn't phone. He didn't come by. He seemed genuinely hurt that I would even think that he wanted Amanda more than me and he just walked away. And went on with his life. So I had to get on with mine too. That was why I accepted Vera's invitation to paint the town with her brother the doctor. I was single, not content yet, but comfortable with my life now; I had nothing to lose.

But I never expected him to be on time. I doused out my cigarette, began hurriedly taking a few of the rollers out of my hair, and ran to look out of my front door's peephole. All I could see was a suit and tie. *Dang*, I thought, *that brother's big!*

232

"Could you give me ten more minutes?" I yelled through the door and placed my ear up against it to hear the response.

"It is seven," he said.

No shit, I wanted to say, but I kept my cool. It wasn't his fault he was on time. I guess not all colored people are on colored-people time after all. "I realize it's seven," I said. "But could you give me ten more minutes?"

He hesitated as if he had a choice and I could see him pull his wristwatch up toward his eyes as if to reconfirm the time. He then said okay. And I got busy. I ran back to my bedroom, slung off my robe, dressed quickly, and began taking more rollers out of my hair when the knocking on the door started again. I looked at my watch. Naturally, it was ten after seven. I was just about ready to tell your boy something, but I decided against it. With some of those big rollers still in my hair, and my face totally devoid of makeup, I merely went back to the door, opened it, and invited him in. I looked like hell but I didn't care anymore. Who needed this? If he was in that big a hurry, then fine. He could paint the town without me. My toughness, however, turned to mush when the doctor walked into my house.

He was tall, dark, handsome, gorgeous, unbelievably sexy. He was no Moon McCalister, of course, but he was closing in fast. He had jet-black skin, Richard Roundtree black, and his face looked like a perfectly chiseled model of perfection. His eyes were sun-shaped and brown, his nose wide and flat, his lips full and juicy, his teeth as white as his skin black. His strong motherland features immediately drew me to him. Here stood a good-looking brother, I thought. And his body. Let me tell you. His shoulders were broad, his chest so big that it looked as if it wanted to burst through his shirt, his arms, thighs, everything about the brother was buff.

And then he had the nerve to have on a seriously expensive baby-blue double-breasted suit that only enhanced his blackness. I was expecting a VW and got the Benz. I had to take a step back just to keep from passing out.

"I'm Daniel," he said in a Barry White baritone. "You must be Victoria." He extended his big hand. I shook it and smiled, all the while regretting that I had opened the door without being fully prepared. I was so mad at myself I didn't know what to do. Mr. Gorgeous had just walked into my house and I was looking like Aunt Jemima. I wanted to kick my own ass for opening that door. But it was too late to turn back now. I told him to please have a seat, I'd soon be with him, and hightailed it out of the room. I figured I had five minutes. I figured he would at least give me five minutes to come back out looking as if I was somebody at least halfway worthy of a hunk of meat like him.

He took me to a Barry Manilow concert. Not that I had anything against Barry Manilow, but dang. *Barry Manilow?* This is what he calls painting the town? Give me Luther, Gladys, even The Captain and Tenille. But *Barry Manilow?* I almost laughed when he told me his plan. But I didn't. I wanted him to really like me for some reason. I wanted him to conclude his evening with me convinced that he'd just met the woman of his dreams.

Why I wanted this was another story. I had no idea why. I wasn't ready for some hot and heavy romance. My heart still dropped whenever I saw Moon's face in a newspaper article. What in the world was I going to do with another man in my life? But, as usual, my reasoning never quite rose to the level of good sense when a good-looking man was involved. All I saw was the man. All I saw was me and the man making good love in the comfort of our own world.

Barry Manilow, then, became my all-time favorite entertainer too. "Oh yes," I said to my pleasantly surprised date as we walked up the steps of the Leon County Civic Center. "The way he sings about the Copacabana and wears those big, frizzled shirts to prove his point. And the way he sings about how he's music, him, not

Luther, not Gladys, but he's the music because he writes the songs that makes the entire world sing. I tell you."

"Wow," Daniel said as we walked across the center's threshold. "This is wonderful that you would like Barry Manilow just as much as I do. This is real music, you know? American music. All of that rap and hip-hop and jazz and blues, they can have it. But Barry Manilow? Now his kind of songs are what I call music for the soul. Don't you?"

"Oh yes," I said and walked on in.

I was laying it on thick, you hear me? It was like a game to me and I was determined to play along. Even inside the concert hall I skinned and grinned and clapped until my hands hurt, listening to that elevator music as if no better melodies had ever crossed my path. Daniel looked at me astounded, as if he was wondering if he had really found his soul mate. He was having the time of his life.

After the show we drove over to an out-of-the-way, ritzy French restaurant that sat like a tugboat on the water. "I come here every time I'm in town," Daniel said as we were seated against a wall that had boat oars and life jackets hanging down like artwork. "Best cuisine around," he added.

"You know Tallahassee better than I do," I said and smiled. "I've never heard of this place."

Daniel did not return my smile. He was a very serious brother. Other than the occasional excitement he displayed on seeing Barry Manilow, he rarely showed any kind of animation. Why I was even bothering with a man like him made me question my sanity. He was not my type by a mile. But he was good looking and looks, for me, could sometimes cover a multitude of faults.

After Daniel ordered the drinks our conversation, such as it was, fell into total silence. He looked at the walls, seemingly appreciative of the odd artwork hangings. He looked up even higher, at the ceiling, then back down, at the other guests. And he looked down at his Rolex watch. If I wanted to get that brother interested in me I knew I had to act fast. He was a by-the-book kind of guy. He probably had already figured out how long our meal would last and what time he would take me home. I didn't want to go home. I wanted to go to his hotel room. It was crazy but it was true. I wanted to show the doctor that I knew how to operate too. But first I had to loosen him up. That wasn't going to be easy. I was no Barry Manilow, after all. I couldn't serenade him with the kinds of words more befitting a Broadway musical than a night primed for lovemaking.

"So," I said, "you're a doctor."

He looked at me and nodded. And that was it. His response, however, wasn't exactly what I was looking for. I had hoped to work in the fact that I was a college professor at FAM-U, a doctor in my own right too. But Daniel wasn't the one to play along. But I pressed on.

"Earlier, Daniel, while we were driving to the concert, you said that going out on a date reminded you of your college days."

"It does. The awkwardness, the nervousness, the fear of the unknown. It's not something I relish, I assure you."

"I know what you mean. I'm sweating like a cow myself."

I laughed. He looked at me with an odd tinge of contempt, as if my buoyancy was annoying to him.

But I kept at it. I wanted him to like me. I felt like a kid who desperately needed a parent's attention and would do whatever it took to get it. It was pitiful but that was how I felt.

"So, what college did you attend?" I asked him.

He threw a few peanuts into his mouth. "Dartmouth," he said.

"Good school," I said. "I'm surprised that FAM let a smart man like you get away, you would have certainly been worth recruiting."

He looked at me as if I had a growth on my nose. "FAM-U recruiting me?" he asked. "Don't be ridiculous."

I smiled. "I think FAM-U is a fine school. I happen to be a professor there."

"Yes, Vera told me," he said without revealing the slightest interest in what I was saying. He then looked at his watch. Again.

"Service is slow tonight," he said. "This is well beyond my bedtime as it is. I may have to take a rain check on this dinner if no food is forthcoming, like right away."

I offended him. Just like that. I made one comment out of bounds and he was ready to sail me home. So let him. I was getting too old to play these kinds of games anyway. The brother wanted to elevate himself above me because his college education was more along the elite school line, then let him help himself. But I wasn't playing along.

"A rain check's fine," I said and he looked at me curiously. He thought he had a man-starved sister on his hands, one who was more than willing to take his crap lying down. Well, I was a little sex starved after getting it from the best and now getting nothing, but I wasn't *that* hungry.

He hesitated. My response wasn't expected. Yet even though he seemed to find my lack of desperation becoming, he apparently concluded that I still wasn't worth staying up for. He called over the waiter, informed him that we would not be staying for dinner, expressed dismay over their slow service, and we left.

He drove me home very quickly, as if he didn't realize that speed limits existed for a reason. He turned his Cadillac Catera off of Monroe Street and onto Appalachee Parkway, zooming past the Capitol so fast that I had to ask him to please slow down. It was well past his bedtime, I knew, and he wanted to get rid of me so that he could get to bed, but damn. It wasn't worth dying over. On top of that he had the nerve to play Barry Manilow songs during the entire drive. "Looks like we made it!" he shouted out with Barry as if his off-key behind could really sing too, and the sound alone made me want to cut off my ears.

He was a self-centered, uppity bastard, I could see it as clear as day. But he had that look thing going for him. That was the problem for me. I wasn't used to casting off good-looking men. I used to run them down until I couldn't run anymore, or, at least, until I caught them. But I was at a time in my life where I wasn't ready to give up my ability to function so easily. I would hope that it would now take more than good looks to get me off and running. The man had to want me too. Being with Moon taught me that much. If the guy didn't show interest in me, then fine. I wasn't interested either.

But old nature is hard to die. I guess that was why I stepped out of the doctor's car in front of my condo and instead of telling his uppity butt to hit the road, good riddance, see ya later, alligator, I asked if he wanted to come up for a drink. He said no and not very politely either. His shitty attitude annoyed me to such a degree that I was ready to read boyfriend up and down. But his body got in the way, his big black body sliding onto the seat of his Catera, and I became mesmerized by the image. It was a crime to look that good, I thought. So my annoyance left and I simply bade him farewell. He reminded me so much of Robert in appearance that it astounded me, but he was on a different plane. Robert's looks drove me to obsession. Doc's looks would drive me to my death. No thank you, I thought to myself as his car cranked and headed south. If my days with Robert taught me anything they taught me that desperation never landed you anything but trouble. And just like Robert, Vera's brother the doctor was nothing but.

I wasn't fifteen minutes in my condo, however, when I started thinking about trouble. I tried to snap out of it, by showering and watching C-SPAN, but nothing worked. I kept imagining him in my bed, the same way I imagined Moon before we hooked up. His long, black, naked body would drape across my satin sheets and beg me to give him a thrill. And I would thrill him as I had never thrilled a man before. I was in heat. Believe it or not, my crazy behind actually became convinced that I had to have Daniel.

I threw the book I was reading, Peter Wood's *Black Majority*, on my nightstand and phoned Vera. Naturally she was asleep.

"If he's there, pretend I'm somebody else," I instructed her.

Sistergirl was too sleepy to get it. "What? If who's here?"

"Who? Mr. Universe, that's who! Your brother. Brother Daniel, remember?"

"Oh," she said in her deep, contralto voice. "Him."

"Yes, him! Why didn't you tell me he looked that good, girl?"

"He's all right."

"Oh yes. I forgot. He *would* be all right to you. But if he was ugly, oh boy!"

"Looks aren't everything, Tory," she said.

"Don't say my name!" I yelled like a fool. "Is he there?"

"Of course he's not here and stop yelling at me."

"He's soo good looking, Vera. I couldn't believe he was your brother!"

"Thanks a lot."

"That's not what I meant. You know what I mean. He's . . . you know what I mean!"

"No, I don't know what you mean. But I'm sure he does."

"Why you say that? He's conceited?"

"Totally, girl. Oh, he knows he looks good. You, me, and nobody else can tell him he doesn't look fine."

"He's got plenty women too, doesn't he?" I could feel myself getting scared. I don't know why, but I just assumed he didn't fully appreciate what a gift he was to women. But according to Vera he knew full well. I didn't stand a chance.

"I don't know anything at all about his love life. He asked me to find him a date for some concert he wanted to attend and he wanted somebody who still enjoyed good music. So I thought of you. That's it. Me and Daniel have never been what you call close."

"He's not married, is he?"

"Now you know I wouldn't set you up with a married man, brother or no brother. No, he's not married. He's never been married, I know that much."

"Oh Lord, he's gay!" I screamed it out. It was as if I suddenly found an answer to his lack of interest in me. But Vera, never one for fantasy-dwelling, disabused me of that notion right away.

"He's straight, all right," she said. "You can rest assured of that."

"Then why hasn't he been snatched yet?"

"Ain't no woman gonna put up with Daniel's bull. Child, please. He'll have you crazy before sundown."

Too late, I thought. "What kind of bull are you talking about?"

"You'll find out. Keep hanging with him. You'll see what I mean."

Actually, I already saw what she meant but I couldn't let her know that. He was stuck on himself, any fool could see that. But I wasn't interested in seeing all that right now. Not now. I still couldn't get his firm, big body out of my mind. That was all I could see. I must have been nuts letting him get away so easily. I could think of fifty women off the top of my head who would have killed to be in my position. Vera had to help me. I know I told her never again to so much as think about setting me up with a man, but girlfriend *had* to help me!

"Forget it, Tory."

"Please, Vera, just this one more time."

"No! You blamed me for that mess with Peter. I'm not going through that again."

"But this is your brother, Vera. This is different."

"Ain't no difference. Don't even try that. And besides, I know Daniel. He's from another world. You don't want somebody like him."

"I want him. I swear to you I want him. Just set us up for one more date, that's all, and I'll love you forever."

"No!"

"Vera, please!"

"No, and I mean no!"

"Okay, okay. Dang. You ain't got to get all hot to trot about it. But, Vera, please!"

I must have begged your girl for half an hour. She was dead set against it, I mean bitterly so, but she eventually gave in and agreed to set up another date.

"I can't promise you he'll go along with it," she said. "But I'll ask him."

That was all I wanted to hear. "God bless you, Vera."

"Yeah, right. You're bestowing your blessings on me today and your curses tomorrow. Child, please. Let me get off this phone!"

By noon the next day I had heard nothing from Vera. I was scared that he had turned her down and she was too upset to call and tell me. But I had to know. Her brother was totally occupying my brain until I couldn't concentrate on anything. In my morning class I even called one of my students Daniel. She looked at me as if I were crazy.

"Daniel?" she asked, totally confused. "I'm not Daniel. Who are you calling Daniel?"

"Did I say Daniel? I'm sorry, dear. I meant Daniels. I thought your last name was Daniels."

She, ignorant to my inner thoughts, accepted my response and went on to continue her explanation of why the Romanov dynasty came to an end. "They ain't had no common sense," she said. "They let what everybody could see was a crazy man lord it over their son and when the writing was on the wall and the end was near, Tsar Nicholas decides he's going to war? Where I come from he would be what we call touched in the head."

Another student agreed. "If them Romanovs were black they would have took all the royal treasures, put them in rows and rows of foot lockers, and as soon as the dark hit haul themselves and their jewels up out of there!"

"But no," the I'm-not-Daniel girl piped in, "they had to stay and face the music. They had to go down fightin'. They went down, all right. They didn't have a lick of common sense!"

241

After class I expected to walk into my office and find a message from Vera waiting on my desk. But nothing was there. I hurried out into the secretary's office. She stated that neither Vera nor anyone else had called for me, that was why she left no message on my desk. As I walked back into my office and slowly closed my door, I heard her tell another secretary, "She's in love again," and then they snickered.

I sat behind my desk and put on my reading glasses. I tried to look over my lesson plan for my night class. I tried, anyway, but it didn't work. I took off my glasses and leaned back. I guess there was something funny about a woman my age still on the chase. This was what teenagers did. Yet I was well over thirty and still at it. I guess if I was younger I would be laughing too. But I wasn't younger. I was well over thirty. And when you get to be my age and still searching for messages from the sister of a man you desperately want to date, it isn't funny at all. Sad, maybe even pathetic. But hardly funny.

But given who I was I didn't take my expansive insights and mend my ways. I called Vera.

Her answering machine clicked on. I hung up and called over to the funeral home. Rollie answered.

"Langston Funeral Home," he said in a deep monotone, as if he practiced how to talk like that to help soothe the bereaved. "May I help you?"

"Hello, Rollie, this is Tory. How you doing?"

"I'm just fine, Tory," he said. "And you?"

"I'm good. Listen, is Vera there?"

"No, she's not. She's over at Jerry's."

"The restaurant?"

"Yes. She and Gina are having lunch, I believe."

"Thanks, Rollie," I said. He was old-fashioned and had that male chauvinistic pig thing going big time, but I was beginning to realize how fortunate Vera really was. He was a hard-working man with generally good intentions. His concept of a woman's role in society was a little nuts, in my view, but at least he believed in something, at least he didn't let trends and fads determine what he believed.

Thirty minutes after my conversation with Rollie my crazy behind was walking into Jerry's restaurant with my hobo bag thrown across my shoulders and my self-respect not far behind.

The place was packed with hungry office workers from the Capitol, where the restaurant was located. They ate fast and talked loud. I wondered why Gina and Vera would want to eat there, since it provided elbow room at best, but it was just like Gina to do it. She was always trying to push me up to go to all of these different eating places with her, regardless of the location. I often told her no and we would compromise. Vera probably didn't care either way.

"Hey, girl!" Gina yelled at me from across the room. The place was loud but Gina had a voice to transcend even a crowd's noise. The customers looked from her to me and I hurriedly moved over by her. Vera sighed, as if she just knew why I was there.

"What are you doing here?" Gina asked, pretending to be in the dark.

I played along too. "I was passing by," I said.

"Sit down, girl. I started to call you for lunch but one thing led to another and I flat forgot."

Gina didn't forget. She enjoyed having lunch alone with either me or Vera every now and then to keep her leadership grip on our threesome. They probably were in the middle of talking about me like a dog for all I knew. But I didn't care. They were cool with me. They were annoying when they wanted to be, and gossipers big time, but when the chips were down and I needed somebody, they would be there. That was all I needed to know.

I sat down and rested my bag on the floor. Vera was in the middle of eating some fried chicken and mashed potatoes combo and Gina was playing at eating a large garden salad. I would give my left arm to be able to eat like Gina. Birds were greedy compared to her.

"That looks good, Vera," I said, looking at a crispy chicken breast sitting on her plate.

"Have some," she said, pushing the plate toward me.

"Oh no," I said. "I don't seem to have an appetite today."

I never had an appetite when I had a love jones. I was too out of sorts to eat. I ate, but it was always in spurts, usually when I had won my conquest and was resting in the laurels of having a man in my life again. As for Mr. Daniel the doctor, well, my conquest had not even begun.

Gina finally gave up on her salad and dropped her fork. "Forget this," she said. "This lettuce taste like it's been cooked in oil or something. Where's that waitress?"

Gina was always finding something wrong with every dish of food she has ever eaten in public. It never failed for her to call the waitress over and complain about the carrots or tomatoes or onions or cucumbers or whatever else she would eat. This time it was the lettuce.

"Y'all call this lettuce?" she asked the young hapless waitress who was trying to balance about four plates of food on a wide, round tray and four tall drinks on a small narrow tray. The waitress looked at the lettuce, which looked fine to her (and me for that matter), and she looked back at Gina.

"Excuse me?" she said.

"Y'all call this lettuce?"

"Yes. It's lettuce. That's what it's called."

Gina hesitated, as if the girl's response was insulting to her. But then she continued. "Do y'all make it a practice to cook your lettuce before serving it?"

The waitress, her pale pink skin becoming increasingly red, looked over at me, then back at Gina. "I don't think they cook it," she said. She couldn't have been more than eighteen the way she looked. She was probably a freshman at Florida State, trying, like any other red-blooded American, to work her way through school. She didn't need to be bothered with Gina's mess that day.

But Gina couldn't care less about that girl. According to Gina, if anybody wanted to be a waitress and collect her tip, they had better be able to make right a wrong. If they couldn't do that much, then they, to Gina, were in the wrong line of work.

"Taste it please," Gina told the young girl.

Again she looked at me, then back at Gina. "Ma'am?" the girl said.

"Taste it, since you're so certain it hadn't been cooked."

Vera jumped in. "That's not what she said, Gina."

"Let me handle this," Gina said to Vera without looking away from the girl. The girl, flustered, set down her drinks and took Gina's salad plate and placed it on the edge of her big brown tray of plates.

"I'll bring you another dish, ma'am," she said.

Gina looked her up and down. "Are you dense, or what? Why on earth would I ever want to eat anything from this rat hole ever again? You'll bring the manager over here, that's what you'll bring me."

"Gina, that's not necessary," I said.

"Yes, it is necessary. I paid good money for that meal. They aren't going to handle me. Bring that manager on. I want him to know how his staff messed up my lunch."

"I didn't have nothin' to do with it," the girl said, getting defensive. "I just serve the food, I don't cook it."

Gina looked at me and Vera and smiled. Then she looked at the girl. "Just get the manager."

The girl sighed with silent anger and left. Gina pulled out a cigarette. "Want one?" she asked me.

"No," I said. Then I added, "You didn't have to offend the girl, G."

"I'm sayin'," Vera agreed.

"I ain't thinking about y'all," Gina said. "I didn't offend that old silly girl and y'all know it."

"Yes, you did, G," I said.

"No, I didn't either."

"Yes, you did," Vera said.

"Then too bad! White folks make me sick when they think they're so much smarter than everybody else. Like she could just tell me she didn't cook it and that would take care of everything. Child, please. I have to encounter those types on my job every day of the week. I'm not taking it at lunch too. This my time. I have a say on who mess with my universe on my time."

She was still reeling from Isaac's affair with Blondie. She never talked about it but it was a part of every snide remark she made. He left her for a white woman. That was all she saw: a white woman. Nothing else. And this white woman had her husband while she sat up there agonizing over what she was going to do about the baby inside her. A baby. No man but a baby. Gina was through dealing.

I very much wanted to ask Vera about Daniel and his response to her suggesting he take me out again, but not around Gina. She might have been disgusted with her life but she was still Miss High and Mighty when it came to uninterested men. She believed in shaking that tree a little to see if anything would fall, but if, after shaking the tree, nothing fell, then she also believed strongly in hitting the road. "Don't force a man to want you," she loved saying. "You'll be like a dog chasing a car. You might catch it, but then what?"

She was right. But I still wanted another chance at Daniel. I shook the tree, I admit that, but I felt within my soul that I just didn't shake it hard enough. Something would have fallen, I felt, if I would have shaken it harder.

I tried to give Vera some eye signals so that she could indicate to me what Daniel said, but she wouldn't play along. It was Gina, instead, who noticed my signals. "What's the matter with your big-behind eyes?" she asked.

I shook my head. "Nothing at all," I said.

The manager finally showed up after about a full five minutes. He was a short, biracial-looking man—presumably black and Asian—and he seemed agitated before he even got to our table. When he got there, he folded his arms but smiled just the same. "Is there a problem here?" he asked.

Gina doused ash into the tray on the table. "I should think so," she said.

"And what seems to be the problem, ma'am?"

"I ordered a garden salad. That's all. A simple, everyday garden salad. I get back a greasy plate of, hell, I don't know what it was. All I know is that it was impersonating a garden salad."

The man nodded. "You may get another salad or your money back, ma'am, those are your choices."

He was cold and direct (and probably overworked and underpaid) and Gina wasn't impressed.

"I want my money back," she said, "and I better get an apology too."

The man gave Gina a quick once-over and undoubtedly wanted to apologize in a way Gina wouldn't soon forget, but he walked away instead. It was not the best business move to make, but what did Gina expect him to do? Grovel? People live on the edge every day. They can take your shit some of the time but nobody can take your shit all of the time. He couldn't take it. So he left. I would have done the same thing.

Gina, however, was offended as hell. "Arrogant bastard," she yelled after him. "Tiger Woods–looking motherfucker!"

"Will you please watch your language?" Vera said angrily.

But Gina was too annoyed to watch anything at that moment. She started to get up, to follow the manager and continue her tirade, but I grabbed her arm. "Let it rest," I said.

She at least sat back down. "The owner of this sorry excuse for a restaurant will be hearing from me, and they can bet that. I even oughta file a lawsuit."

"On what grounds, Gina?" Vera asked. She was tired of Gina's hysterics and was picking up her pocketbook and pulling out her keys as if she was ready to go.

But Gina was still preoccupied with the manager. Nobody, but nobody upstaged her. "Let me find out who's the real boss of this joint," she said and headed for what I assumed to be the kitchen area. Gina always said the best way to get information on the high and mighties was to pump the help. They always had it in for their bosses. They would be happy to help you out, she said.

"I guess she's going to pump the help," I said, using Gina's terminology exactly.

Vera knew it too. "I'm sure that's what she's doing."

I took her departure, however, as my opportunity to pump Vera for information. I asked her straight out. She hesitated. I knew what that mean. "He said no," I said.

"Not exactly," she said.

That was hopeful. "Then what did he say?"

"He said *hell no!*" She said this and looked me dead in the eye. Then she smiled. "Girl, I'm kiddin'," she said. "That Negro said yeah. Of course he said yeah. You're the only somebody ever wanted to repeat a date with him, of course he said yeah."

I threw my fist in the air the way those basketball players do when they dunk over an opponent. I felt triumphant. But I needed the details before Gina got back, so I settled back down. "When?" I asked. "Where?"

"Friday night," she said. "I told him you would cook him dinner."

My smile dropped into a frown. "You told him *what!*" I yelled. "I can't cook!"

"Well," Vera said, "now is the time to learn, isn't it?"

Vera was a smart lady who knew what she was doing. She probably had to promise him a free meal just to get him to go along. I didn't need to know if that was the case, but I still wanted to know. So I asked her. She laughed. "Something like that," she said.

Any other self-respecting female would have told Vera to tell her snobbish brother to kiss her grits, but I guess I wasn't all that self-respecting during my rebound days. As with all the other handsome men I dated, Daniel's looks gave him certain privileges with me. If he wasn't super good looking and still had to be convinced to date me, I would have kicked that joker to the curb as quick as looking at him. But he wasn't unattractive, he was drop-dead gorgeous, and I wasn't kicking him anywhere but in my bed in that little old condo of mine.

I had two days before my big date to get my cooking act together. That was saying a lot, trust me. If I wasn't eating a TV dinner, or eating out, I wasn't eating. The closest I ever came to cooking a meal was back in college, when some of my girlfriends and I cooked spaghetti. It burned. I was in trouble.

I called Gina. She wasn't much of a cook either, but she knew how to wine and dine a man. I closed my office door and sat back at my desk. My night class didn't get started for another hour so I figured a little friendly advice from an old pro was in order.

She pretended to know nothing about it. She voiced surprise that Vera would have a brother that looked as great as I was claiming. "I gots to see this brother," she said.

"He wants a home-cooked meal, Gina, what am I going to do?"

"Tell him to go home and eat this home-cooked meal and call you when he's finished."

She *would* say something like that. "What can I cook him?"

"You? Cook? You're joking."

"It's no joke, Gina."

"When you learned how to cook, girl?"

I shook my head. This conversation was useless. "I can't cook, Gina. That's the damn point, all right?"

"Now wait a minute."

"I'm sorry. I was out of bounds. I just . . . This is important to me, okay?" I was about to cry. I couldn't believe it. It was Moon and Robert and all of those other hunks I've loved before all over again. I was obsessing over some man who already let me know in no uncertain terms that he wasn't particularly interested in me at all. Yet I wanted him. Ain't that crazy? I wanted him because he was cute and big and I was lonely and that was all that mattered. I wiped the singular tear that rolled down my face and frowned. I wished to God it wasn't all about men. I wished to God I didn't have to put myself through this craziness every time an interesting male crossed my path.

Gina took pity on me (I was *that* pathetic) and tried to help. "I know!" she yelled into the phone. I moved the receiver from my ear. "There's this wonderful caterer I've used now and again who'll be happy to completely prepare a full meal for you, and at a reasonable cost too."

"I can't."

"Why the hell not? He'll never know."

"Yes, he will when he wants that wonderful meal again."

"Then you'll cater it again."

"No, Gina. I want this relationship to be right. I want it to be right and honest."

"Now look, girlfriend. You know I ain't got nothin' against romance and love and all that good stuff we live for, but slow down. From what Vera tells me, her brother the doctor ain't all that."

"Yeah, we really should listen to Vera. She's the one who tried to hook me up with Peter, remember?"

"Here we go again."

"So her definition of *all that* ain't *all that* either."

"I give up," Gina finally said. "Do what you need to do. Talking sense into you when it comes to a good-looking man is like talking sense into a Nazi. Do your own thing, girl. But as for cooking, I can't help you. Hell, go buy one of those Betty Crocker cookbooks. Who would know more about cooking than Betty?"

I hung up the phone, thought about Gina's suggestion, and then hurried to the bookstore. There was one Betty Crocker cookbook, a newly revised and updated version of another Betty Crocker cookbook with something like a thousand recipes in it. I clasped the red paperback against my chest and thanked God for Gina. If I couldn't find a decent meal with a thousand to choose from, then something had to be seriously wrong with me.

Something apparently was seriously wrong with me because I was having a devil of a time finding a recipe I wanted to try. My night class was short because I couldn't keep my mind off of the task at hand. In fact, my plan was to dismiss my students as quickly as possible and then call in sick tomorrow. I figured I needed at the very least all that day to cook and recook my selected recipe before I ever thought of trying it out on Daniel. In fact, Gina and Vera both agreed to come over tomorrow evening and act as my designated tasters. If they didn't like it, then it was back to the drawing board. But if they liked it, then, hey, I was set.

I made all of these plans, however, before I checked out those recipes I was up against. I went home from class that night, cuddled up in bed, and opened Miss Betty Crocker. My plan was to cook something, you know, high-class international, but all I read were common old American recipes, like roast pork or oven-fried fish or baked spaghetti. "*Anybody* could cook those," I said aloud, "what kind of book is this?" But I kept reading anyway. I was convinced it was too late to buy another book and start over, so I decided to find a recipe and add my own international flavor to it. It took reading until three in the morning, falling asleep, and waking up at seven in the morning, and showering, dressing, and hightailing it to Publix for all my needed ingredients. And I slaved and slaved over that stove, you hear me? I mixed and baked and stirred and stewed. It was one of the worst experiences of my life. All this for a man, I thought. But then I remembered he was a great-looking doctor man. I kept baking.

By the time Gina and Vera arrived, my meal was ready for tasting.

"Good," Vera said as she walked into my house, "'cause I'm famished."

"What you got?" Gina asked but I told her to wait and see.

"Wash your hands," I said, "and come on down!"

They dutifully washed their hands and then quickly took their seats at my dining-room table. It was ostentatiously decorated with a beautiful candelabra and a large bouquet of red, yellow, and white roses. Gina liked it. Vera thought it was a tad much.

Then the dish came out. I set the main course on the table first and removed the gold-plated cover. It turned out to be, hopefully, venison sauerbraten with wilted spinach.

"What is this?" Gina asked as she arched her eyebrows and leaned back.

"Venison sauerbraten with wilted spinach," I said.

"Venison what?"

"Come on, Gina, it's a popular dish."

"Popular? Where the hell at? Germany?"

I sighed. I was flustered. "Just taste it," I ordered. "You too, V."

Vera tried to be polite but her frown gave her away. "Sauerkraut, you said?"

I wanted to take my apron off and go upside both of their heads. Vera I could understand. She was born and raised in the Pentecostal church and hung around those church picnics and banquets and ate soul food all the time. But Gina surprised me. She was a well-traveled girl. She knew every type of food imaginable. Yet she was playing crazy too. Now I knew I wasn't no Julia Childs, but damn. I cooked it right. It looked just like the recipe in the book.

"It looks just like the recipe in the book," I said.

"We're sure it does," Gina said. "But that don't mean it looks good. And you're planning to give this stuff to a brother? I don't think so."

I was dumfounded. "What's the matter with it?"

252

"Number one," Gina volunteered, "it stinks. Number two, it looks like shit. And number three, where's the ham and potato salad and collard greens and cornbread and peach cobbler? Come on, sister, this ain't no Brady Bunch!"

I sat down at the table with them. Gina, as usual, hit it right on the head. What was I thinking? I'm no cook. Even an uppity joker like Daniel could see that. And that venison dish with all that spinach piled up around it *did* look like shit. Gina was right. But that didn't make me feel better. It just reminded me of how over my head I really was. I didn't go through this much crap for Moon McCalister, why in the world was I going through it for Daniel?

"Let me prepare the meal for you, girl," Vera said. But Gina said no.

"Why not?" I asked. I was out of options. *Somebody* had to cook the meal and, given my glaring failure, it wasn't going to be me.

"You've got to cater it. V's brother, I'm sure, knows V's cooking very well. Cater it. That's the best way. And when it comes time to serve, throw that junk in the microwave and be done with it. All this test cooking and slaving over the stove is ridiculous. And from what Vera tells me he ain't e-much worth it. Give yourself a break this time, girl. All he want is a meal. Ain't none of his business who cooked it."

I nodded. Then I panicked. "But who could I get to prepare me a meal in less than twenty-four hours? What catering company will go for that?"

"Catering company?" Gina asked as if she was truly through with me and my foolishness. "What damn catering company? A girlfriend of mine gonna hook you up, child. That man want some soul food, believe me."

"I don't know, Gina. He seems partial to more international kinds of foods to me."

Vera laughed. "Don't let that French cuisine act fool you, Tore. Daniel will eat anything. Feed him some collard greens and roast beef and your boy will be good to go. Trust me on that. I grew up with him. He might be a big-time doctor now, but he's always begging me to feed him collards whenever I see him."

I had to wave my hands in the air as if I were in church. Vera telling me that Daniel was black at heart was music to my ears. "Yes, Lord!" I shouted and they laughed. But it was true. I found some relief. As usual, though, I went around the world to get around the corner but at least I got there. *I'll leave the cooking to G's friend*, I thought, *and then I'll be free to concentrate on other things. Like my hair, for example.*

I had perm-straight hair that I often enhanced with about two inches of weave for fullness. I wore my hair in a simple, down-and-fluffed-under hairdo that gave me a fairly good, dependable look. But good wasn't good enough if I expected to win over a man like Daniel. I needed a superior do, something even stuck-up Daniel could appreciate. On our first date he never once commented on my appearance. That was unacceptable. I needed him to want me. But first I had to give him a reason.

"Hello," Gina said. "Earth calling Victoria. Do you read, girlfriend?"

I looked at my two girls and smiled. I had forgotten all about them. "I'm sorry," I said. "Just trying to tie up some loose ends in my mind," I said.

Vera touched my hand. "Take it easy, Tory, please. Daniel is a wonderful brother and I love him to death, but he's also very hard to get along with. And there's very little you can do to change that. He was that way all his life."

"I know," I said. "I just want to try and do it right, that's all. If it doesn't work out, then, hey, what else is new? If it does work out, then . . ."

They waited. "Then what?" Vera asked.

I shook my head and closed my eyes. It was too perfect for me even to imagine. "Then wouldn't that be something?" I said.

Gina raised her glass of water up to me and Vera nodded. They understood. I was a reasonable adult who was going into this thing with my eyes wide open. But it never hurt to dream. It never hurt to think that maybe this man above all those other men would be the one.

Gina told me to make sure I didn't feed that meal of mine to the neighborhood cat. "It'll be cruel and unusual punishment," she said as they gathered up their purses and prepared to leave.

"Very funny," I said, walking them to the door. "But I won't anyway."

They laughed, said their good-byes, and left. I hurried into my bedroom and called Bobby.

Bobby was my beautician or, as he enjoyed saying, my hairstylist. He was good and popular and I often had to break down doors just to get an appointment with him. And he hated last-minute stuff. The last time I tried it I had to lie and tell him that somebody died and I had to go to the funeral. That was the only thing that saved me the last time.

"Forget it, girl," he blared into my phone receiver.

"Bobby, please," I begged. He was the best and he knew it. But, damn, was he tough.

"I can't do it, Tory. I told you about that last-minute mess. I'm not wit it."

"But this means everything to me. Please! I wouldn't call you if I didn't have to!"

"I am booked. I'm sorry. I am overbooked. I couldn't work you in here if your life depended on it."

He held firm. I called him a bastard and hung up the phone. Bobby was the kind of person you could call a bastard, hang up on, yet he'd treat you as if you were his best friend the next time he heard from you. But he had rules that he wasn't going to break. I guess his scheduled clients appreciated that.

But I didn't need him to be strong that night. I needed him to say yes he'd do my hair for me. But I was wasting my time. I called Gail, my backup beautician, instead. She was neither popular nor all that good so she was always available. "Sure," she said when I phoned and asked her. "I'll get my perm kit and be right over!"

The date was set for eight and I was ready thirty minutes ahead of time. I knew your boy by now and I wasn't going to pull my "can you give me ten more minutes?" routine again.

At exactly eight o'clock I heard knocks at my front door. I was dressed to kill in one of my beautiful white evening dresses that hugged around my hips and gave me a model shape look; my eggshell-white pumps that gave me two more inches on my height to almost match Daniel's; and my hair, well, my hair was about the way it always was in that straight-down, curl-under look. But it was full and fresh and about as good as Gail could do. I was grateful.

"Daniel!" I said as I opened the door. "You're on time!"

He seemed taken aback by my gaiety and attempted only a curious-at-best smile. "I'm always on time," he said.

I had decided that I would completely ignore all of his little sly remarks and keep up with the happiness. He was a smart, shrewd man who was probably using rudeness and insults as a test, to see if there was a woman somewhere with the gumption and mental toughness to put up with a man like him. Since I had already decided that I was that woman, I was determined to pass his test. "Come on in!" I said. "It's good to see you again!"

He walked in hesitantly, looking back at me to make sure I wasn't having some manic episode that would ultimately lead to my pulling out a shotgun and blowing both our brains out. But I didn't care what his initial reaction was. I was looking at the big picture. And in the big picture I had to be able to withstand his fiery darts when they were slung, lest all of my game plans and high hopes would be lost in the cross fire.

He walked slowly into the living room and stood by the sofa. He was gorgeous of course, wearing a beautiful but conservative Brooks Brothers suit and a pair of fancy wingtip shoes. His coal-black face was firm and strong and his deep brown eyes stretched with approval when he looked around at my living room. The last time he was in my home he looked around with total disapproval. Yet now he seemed pleased although nothing had changed from the last time. I knew then that my game plan was working and I was having an immediate positive impact. "May I sit down?" he asked.

"Please. Yes."

He unbuttoned his suit coat and took a seat.

"Dinner will be on the table in precisely seven minutes," I said, given his great desire to know the plan every step of the way. He smiled appreciatively.

"That sounds good," he said.

I walked slowly into the kitchen and began readying the food Gina's friend Paula had prepared. I had placed everything in the microwave just before eight to have it hot and ready before he arrived, and all I then had to do was place it on the table. I placed it on the table, lit the candles, and asked him if he would join me.

We ate, and we talked very little. I got that part of my game plan from Vera. She warned me not to run my mouth during the eating portion of the evening. "He hates it," she said. "He likes it quiet when he eats."

I gave him quiet with a capital Q. A dropping pin could be heard in the space. Paula had cooked some collard greens, ham, macaroni and cheese, and potato salad. It was probably a bit much for a Friday-night dinner, but Gina told me to let Paula handle it. "She's never lost a customer yet," she said.

Gina was right. Daniel ate his plate clean. Then he leaned back and held his flat but slowly expanding belly. "That was delicious," he said. "You must have slaved over that stove for hours to come up with all of this."

I smiled. "Ah," I said, "it was nothing."

I wasn't lying and he never questioned it. By the time I had placed the plates in the dishwasher and he had made his way back to the sofa, the dinner part of the evening could have been heralded as nothing less than successful. He even took off his shoes and set them neatly against the sofa. When I walked back into the living room and saw his shoes, I wanted to shout, "Lord have mercy!" But since that wasn't in my game plan, I didn't.

"How about a little music?" I asked as I walked over to my sorry excuse for a stereo system. It was a good five years old and about as cheap as they come. But I didn't listen to music enough to invest big bucks into something I rarely used.

My CD collection was just as lame. I had my share of CDs by Whitney Houston and Toni Braxton and, of course, my old-school R&B folks, but that Manilow concert should have warned me that none of those sisters and brothers in my collection were Daniel's kind of folks.

"What is that?" he frowned and asked when I decided on Whitney's "Didn't We Almost Have it All?"

"Whitney Houston," I said.

"Yes, but when you said you were going to put on some music I was assuming you meant Stravinsky at the very least."

I sat down beside him. "I take it you're not an R and B fan."

"It has its place. But not for me. I'm into baroque and have been for quite some time."

"I see. You're a man of the classics. I like Tchaikovsky myself."

"Oh please," he said just a little bit miffed. "That's what everybody says when they don't know what they're talking about. They hear his *Nutcracker Suite* when they are children and grow up thinking they now have a firm knowledge of what is known by them as classical music. Please."

I started to tell that brother to wait a minute, I also liked Chopin and Debussy and Rachmaninoff and Mozart, but that would have been exactly what all those other women would have said. Then he would have hit me hard with his overwhelming knowledge of classical music as against my weak but functional one. No thanks. I had to keep my eye on the prize. "So you're Vera's brother," I said obviously rhetorically.

He smiled weakly. "Yes. I thought we had already established that."

"We had but I was just . . . well, you know, you guys are so unalike."

"I've heard. But we're not that dissimilar."

He had to be kidding but I didn't pursue it. In fact, I didn't pursue anything that evening, which meant numerous dead times in our conversation. We sat beside each other but we did not touch and he rarely talked. So I decided if a move was going to be made it would be up to me. I took his big hand and touched it with my little one. "Are you a surgeon?" I asked. "You have such nice hands."

He smiled. All that brother wanted was a little tenderness. "No," he said. "A gynecologist."

"Oh. The pregnant ladies."

"Right."

"Do you have any children of your own?"

He looked down. "Actually no," he said. "Didn't work out that way for me. What about you?"

That was the first time in our two-date relationship that your boy bothered to ask me anything about my personal life. When I told him no, I had no kids either, he beamed. He was interested in me, I could tell. We were as different as day and night, but I was willing to change. Ain't that something? I wanted a man so badly that I was willing to take the personality I took thirty-five years to cultivate and cast it to the dogs. And how could I even consider another big-time relationship after my time with Moon? It was crazy but it was happening. I wanted somebody in my life. Moon's companionship had spoiled me. Although after the breakup I thought I could make it just fine on my own, something was changing in me. Now being alone just didn't seem like a plausible option anymore.

The night ended on a positive note, with Daniel wondering if I wanted to go to a Willie Nelson concert in Jacksonville tomorrow night. Hell no, I would have said any other time. *Willie Nelson?* Is this brother for real? "Sure," I said instead, and we shook on it.

259

After he left I got in bed and tried to do a little reading, but I was too excited. I put the book down and called Gina. She wanted a blow-by-blow and I gave it to her. Big mistake. She criticized everything that I didn't say but wanted to say, especially when he denigrated my music tastes. "I can't believe that joker's a brother of Vera's," she said.

"He's taking me to Jacksonville tomorrow night."

"Really? At least that *sounds* like fun. But knowing that brother, it won't be. What's the occasion for the J-ville trip?"

"A concert."

"Interesting. Whose?"

I muttered, "Willie Nelson," under my breath.

"What?" Gina yelled.

"Willie Nelson," I said out loud.

"*Willie Nelson?* That cracker with the ponytail? You gots to be jiving!"

"I'm not kidding, Gina," I said, getting annoyed. I could now see how Daniel had such a tough time with his own people. Some of them, like Gina for instance, wanted all of us to be in lockstep one behind another. God help you if you don't like R&B. God help you if you have a little classical and country in your bones. Moon could have his own peculiar taste, like Frank Sinatra, and get away with it because he didn't take crap from anybody. But brothers like Daniel were doomed to the Uncle Tom, color-struck, Oreo labels for life.

Gina wanted to talk longer about Daniel and his faults but I wasn't wit it. I told her that I had to go and I hung up the phone. She didn't understand how narrow-minded she really was. Daniel, I felt at the time anyway, was opening my eyes to the fulness of life where it was all right to be different, and where being different didn't automatically mean being arrogant or stuck up or uppity or whatever the euphemism of the day may be. I lay in bed without a book or C-SPAN for the first time in a long time. Suddenly my thoughts of Daniel were more than enough to keep me occupied. And I was in the kind of lovesick mood where I would have told Gina and Vera and anybody else that yes, I'm in love with a man who doesn't like R&B, rap, or jazz, who doesn't think Tiger Woods is a sellout, and who doesn't give a rat's ass about what other people think about his own cultural tastes. And they could be disgusted by my choice if they pleased because at the end of the day and in that dreaded midnight hour, I might not have my self-respect anymore but at least I could proclaim with my heart joyous and my mind relaxed that I got a man! Pitiful. But, hey.

We left Tallahassee at noon the next day. Jacksonville was only a three-hour drive but Daniel wanted to make sure we didn't arrive late at the concert and couldn't get in, causing him to do all of that driving for nothing. "I don't like blank trips," he said.

I wanted to tell him not to worry, that I was certain there would be plenty of seats left no matter how late we arrived, but I didn't say a word. I was Miss Compliance that night. Nothing was going to rattle me.

He played Willie Nelson's song "On the Road Again" over and over the entire trip to Jacksonville. I wanted to yank out that CD and ram it upside his head. By the time we were passing through Lake City, he started singing along with the CD. I wanted to jump from the car.

"I have heard a lot of singers in my lifetime," Daniel said, "but Willie is my boy, you hear me? He can sing!"

I nodded my agreement. "Yes, he can. The way he, the way he pronounces every word and then keeps coming back to that *on the road again* phraseology. It's amazing."

"You know, you're the first woman I've dated in a long time who understands what I'm trying to say here. The phraseology, that's what I'm talking about. You're a very smart lady, Tory, you know that? I can call you Tory, can't I?"

"Certainly," I said. "And I can call you Danny, right?"

"No. Wrong. My name is Daniel. It isn't Danny or Dan or any other name you can think up. It's Daniel."

His nasty response took me by surprise but I smiled and continued to crochet (yes, I had a crochet kit with me, thinking it would add credence to my good little woman act). I refused to even think about what I was doing. It was as if I were in a blinding storm and Daniel were my rescuer. He wasn't much, I reasoned, but he was saving my black ass.

It was my first time in Jacksonville. It dwarfed the size of Tallahassee but there was more room for the traffic and it therefore didn't seem as congested. We ended up going too far, across the Matthews Bridge and over into the Arlington area of town. We then had to recross the bridge, exit around Alltel Stadium where the Jaguars played, and were finally led to a big building in the round: The Jacksonville Memorial Coliseum. And to my shock we were not the only African-Americans there (although it was close. There were two other couples). And Daniel loved every minute of the concert. He laughed and jumped up and down and clapped until he started rubbing his hands from the soreness. He was like a kid. That was why I enjoyed it too. Can you believe that? I never dreamed I would be enjoying a country-western show with a doctor on a Saturday night in Jacksonville, but I was. I even started jumping up and down and acting a fool too. And I didn't feel self-conscious about being there or anything like that. It was fun. Everybody who went was there to have fun.

We went to dinner after the concert and then across the Fuller Warren Bridge into Baymeadows, to the Embassy Suites Hotel. Daniel, surprisingly, had reserved us a room. One room. Together.

It was what I had wanted so I was, at first, very pleased. But as we walked across the lobby and took the elevator to the third floor, I began to feel nervous, as if I was doing something wrong. The memory of Moon was still very much a part of me and the thought of another man touching my body was a very scary thought. But I wanted Daniel too, and I needed the touch of another man. So my nervousness aside, I did not resist the plan.

Daniel, to his credit, was a real gentleman that night. He even offered to move into another room if I was uncomfortable with the arrangement. Even when I told him no, this was fine, he still didn't move it along. He took his time, walking up to me and kissing me gently on the lips. He then walked me to the bed, laid me down, and started taking his clothes off. I removed mine too as I lay there, but I couldn't take my eyes off of Daniel's midsection. I couldn't wait to see the size of his willie because I just knew it had to be a beaut.

It was a beaut, all right. So small it looked like a sawed-off little pencil with one of those elementary school erasers on top. I knew better than this. That big brother, that big, buffed brother with a weeny? With a dog dick? I lay there and shook my head. All of that desire, all of that dried-up horniness went out the window. What in the world did he think he was going to do with that little thing? It had to be the smallest one I'd ever seen. And the way he was smiling and standing there all naked and proud like some Hercules made me want to vomit.

"You're beautiful, Victoria," he said to me after perusing my body.

"Thank you," I said and looked away.

He then began rubbing his hands together. "Are you ready?" he said with a grand smile.

I looked at him as if he were crazy. Ready for nothing, I wanted to say. "Yes," I said instead.

"I said are you ready?" he said again, with even more animation.

"Yes," I said again, with even less.

"I said," he hollered out, "are you REA-DY!"

"Yes!" I said. Damn! I wanted to say.

He jumped on the bed, jumped, mind you, on top of me, and just knew he was going to sling that naked little wee-wee into me without protection. But I corrected him immediately.

"You did bring a condom, right, Daniel?"

He looked at me. "A condom?"

I looked at him. "Yes. Of course."

"It don't feel the same to me when I put a condom on. But you don't have to worry about that. I'm a doctor. I'm clean."

I shook my head. "I have one in my purse," I said.

He hesitated, as though he wanted to get an attitude about it, but then he checked out my body again and got real. He put on the condom.

Then he did his thing. Pumping and grinding as if he was really doing something. I lay there and let him have his fun. I even threw in a few oohs and aahs just to hurry him along. But it took him forever. He talked up a storm, saying, "Oh, you gonna make me come!" about twenty times before he actually came. As his hollering escalated and his body clenched, I started acting as if I were coming too. I hollered and pinched his back and lifted my legs up and down as if I were fully out of control. Anything, I thought, to get this over with.

Afterward he let out one big fart and then lay on his back as if he had just run a marathon. He was completely satisfied. I was satisfied too, in a less than expected way. I knew he wasn't good in bed, but sometimes you just can't have it all. Besides, I liked sex a lot, and no way was I going to fake orgasms every time we did it, but sex was something that I could easily do without in a pinch. I wanted the man first. I could teach him how to do me later.

Our relationship took off from there. I don't know, and maybe it was just me, but I found Daniel to be one of the most intensely intellectual guys I had ever dated. He was humorless and serious all the time, but there was never a boring moment with him. We went to little obscure movies like *The Remains of the Day* and *Waking Ned Devine*, and African-American art exhibitions, and symphonic concerts. It was heavenly. Even the sex got better. He had planned to spend only three weeks of his two-month vacation in Tallahassee and his remaining time in California where he had other relatives. But he canceled his California trip altogether and stayed in Tallahassee with me. In fact, toward the end of his vacation I took a few days off to spend all day and night with him. Vera joked to me that she believed her brother was falling in love for the first time ever and I told her it was no joke because I was falling in love too. I was lying to Vera actually because I was *already* in love. I had fallen for Dr. Daniel Patrick Gurchess and was willing to quit my job in a heartbeat and relocate to Arizona just to be with him.

It was just a matter of him asking me to do so. That was why when he phoned me on the day of a banquet we were set to attend and told me that after the banquet he had something "very serious" to talk to me about, I hung up the phone and jumped for joy. And called Gina.

"He's gonna propose!" I screamed into the phone.

"What? Already? That's fast, girl, I've got to hand it to you. But, hey, you're no child. You know what you're doing."

Actually I didn't. I was too caught up in the fact that I had a life after Moon to worry about the consequences of a life with Daniel. Moon wasn't out of my system by a long shot. Strangers could be talking about him and his candidacy and something inside of me would quiver. How could I even think about marrying somebody else? And this fast?

But that was exactly what I was thinking about doing. Daniel had his faults. I mean, the brother needed a big-time attitude adjustment and I was experienced enough to know that he probably would never change. But he seemed to genuinely care for me. And at my age and at this time in my life, that was enough.

"You don't sound too thrilled about my news, G," I said.

"I just hope it works out for you, that's all. I know how things haven't in the past and I just hope you're not overcompensating here."

"Overcompensating for what?"

"The Moon."

"Child, please."

"You're catching Daniel on the rebound, girl, on the fly. Those rebound romances rarely work."

"It's not a rebound romance."

"So you're telling me that Moon McCalister is out of your system?"

"Completely."

"The man of your dreams, the love of your life is out of your system already?"

"It's been months, Gina. He went on with his life and I've got to go on with mine."

"True."

"Daniel is a totally different kind of person than Moon. I can't compare the two. All I can do is try to be happy."

Gina understood. "Enough said. It's your life and I wish you well, dog. But as for me I've got a deposition to get to. I'll see you tonight. You and he are still coming to the NAACP banquet, right?"

"We'll be there. Daniel wasn't too excited about attending anybody's banquet, especially the NAACP since they're too left-wing for him. But when I told him that you had purchased the two tickets for us at no charge he warmed up to the idea. So we'll be there."

"I take that back. It's not your life. It's your funeral. Bye, girl, I gots to go."

And she hung up. I should have known then what kind of mistake I was making. Gina wanted me happy and married as badly as my mother did. But she wasn't thrilled at all. Me, of all people, getting all hyped about marrying some pompous black Republican who didn't even support the NAACP. To a politically astute woman like Regina Ridgeway it was blasphemous. To me, especially at that moment in my life, it was just another prime example of the intolerance of black folks.

I hung up the phone too. I was at work, sitting behind my desk, happy and scared at the same time. This was a golden opportunity for me, I thought. A wonderful opportunity to finally be a married lady. But there was also a side of me that knew that it was the right opportunity but maybe with the wrong man.

The banquet was held at the Civic Center and it was packed with the movers and shakers of the Tallahassee community. Daniel and I arrived on time, which was becoming common for me now, and I was astounded to see Vera in attendance too. She was decked down in a beautiful blue gown and blue slipper shoes and she hurried over and hugged us both.

"Y'all look like the perfect couple," she said when she released us. Daniel brushed off his gray tux and resumed what he often called his dignified stance. I looked down at my attire, a black strapless gown that Moon had purchased for me at Giorgio's during our Beverly Hills shopping spree, and thanked her for the compliment. I then looked at her.

"And look at you," I said, "all pretty and sexy and grown-up looking. And no flowery skirts and matching scarfs! Girl, please. I'm surprised Rollie's not foaming all over you at this very moment."

"He couldn't make it."

"You mean he let you out after dark alone?"

She smiled although the smile was hardly a sincere one. "Quit playing," she said.

"What in the world kind of music is that?" Daniel frowned and asked in reference to the soft Grover Washington Jr. jazz instrumental blaring over the speaker system.

"Music," Vera said.

"Yes, but what kind of music?"

"Music," Vera said again.

"Well, I find it rather loud and annoying."

"I'm sure Grover Washington would find you the same, Daniel, but you don't see him coming out of that record criticizing you."

I wanted to laugh but I was afraid of offending Daniel.

"What a nonsensical thing to say," he said. "I think there's a reason Rollie keeps you indoors after dark."

Vera gave her brother a look most cross and was about to zing him back when I noticed Gina coming toward us.

"There's Gina!" I said overenthusiastically to deflate Vera's need to set her brother straight. "But who is she with? Oh my God. Tell me I'm dreaming. Tell me that is not Isaac."

"It's Isaac, girl," Vera said.

I was stunned. "When did they get back together?"

"Last week sometime. Can you believe it?"

No way. Not Gina. Not after all of that advice she had given me down through the years about unfaithful men.

"She's not overly excited about her decision," Vera said, "if that's any consolation."

It wasn't. Not where Gina was concerned. She caught Isaac red-handed and still took him back? If my boyfriends even intimated at being unfaithful she would tell me to run, don't walk, but run away from that relationship. Now she was running back to hers. It almost seemed inexplicable.

But Vera was right. Gina was not pleased as punch. She walked beside Isaac as if he was some last-minute choice for a date and all she wanted was for the night to hurry up and end. Even when she walked over to us and said her hellos she moved from Isaac's side immediately and stood between me and Vera.

As Isaac and Daniel greeted each other and began making general conversation, V and G and I backed off into our little threesome. I asked Gina why.

"Why what?"

I didn't respond. She knew what I meant. That was why she frowned and her hazel eyes closed and quickly opened again, as if the realization of her life choices was still sinking in. "He's my husband," she said as if that said it all.

"Those three gentlemen before Isaac were your husbands too," I said. "And they didn't do half the stuff Isaac has done. But he cheats on you, defends his woman against you, and you take him back? You never did anything like that before."

Gina looked at me with an anguished stare. "I wasn't thirty-nine before," she said. "I'm thirty-nine years old. These men want young thangs now. They don't want some old broad like me. And I'm pregnant too. Hell yeah, I took him back. I even begged his ass to come back to me. Am I proud of myself? No. But I don't see where I had a choice."

This was what it all came down to. We were doing exactly what we always said we would never do: settling for what we could get. Vera just by staying with Rollie. Gina with Isaac. Me with a man like Daniel. We were maturing women now and it wasn't a game anymore. We were horrified of being alone; horrified that we would wake up one day and realize that all of our opportunities for that great romance were in the past. Gone. Never to return. Second best doesn't look so bad up against that reality. A pompous, arrogant bastard like Daniel showed enormous promise as compared to nothing.

Daniel seemed bored the entire night. He complained about the food, the speakers, the ambience of the room. We all sat at the same table—Gina and Isaac, Vera, and Daniel and I—and on numerous occasions Gina appeared ready to tell Daniel a thing or two. But she didn't. She was so not Gina that night, so muted and restrained that I kept wanting to ask if she was all right. But just as I got up the courage to do so, and even leaned toward her, Daniel threw his napkin on the table and asked if I was ready.

"Ready?" I asked, thoroughly confused.

"To go," he said.

I was in the middle of my dinner, had, in fact, my fork raked down in the rice pilaf ready to bring it up again, but I smiled and said yes, I was ready. Gina and Vera both looked at me, but neither one of them said a word.

We stood up, said our good-byes, and headed for the exit doors. If tonight was the night that he would propose to me, then I was ready for the fireworks to begin. I was desperate. No question about it. I was a thirty-five-year-old woman determined not to be alone another night.

But something happened on the way to the exit. Moon McCalister walked in. I stopped in my tracks as he stepped in front of me. Suddenly we were toe-to-toe. His Ferragamo wingtips, my point-toe heels. Together again. My very soul shook.

Before I realized it Gina and Vera had come up behind me. They couldn't see my face from where they had been sitting but seeing the Moon was all they needed to see. They knew, despite my insistence to the contrary, that I wasn't all right with my breakup with Moon and I needed support on seeing him like this. I, they undoubtedly knew, needed serious backup.

Daniel stopped walking and looked back at me. To him Moon McCalister was just another brother walking in and my sudden freeze didn't make any sense. But I didn't care. I was watching the Moon. He remained my tried-and-true example of everything a man should be. And when his bright brown eyes met mine and we locked into an embracing stare, the pain of what could have been melted my heart. I had to fight with all I had to hold back the tears. I had to actually force a smile on my face to avoid collapsing to my knees in embarrassing self-pity.

"Moon," I said as if it took my last breath to say his name.

He leaned his head back and stared at me, his eyes almost hidden from sight. "Hello."

I kept up the smiling, it was the only defense I had. "What a thing to see you here."

He did not respond. He just stood there, more than gorgeous in his periwinkle-blue tuxedo, and stared at me. I missed that stare. I missed the way he'd always tell me to come to him and then he'd pull me to him. Daniel didn't care for displays of affection, or that *touchy, feely* stuff, as he called it. But I still craved Moon's tenderness. He knew how to do me. He knew how to hold me in his arms and make me forget the world and all of its harshness. I needed him. And it hurt. It hurt so badly that my fight to hold back tears almost failed.

But then Amanda Trundle came in and took her rightful place beside him. "The governor's wife just drove up," she said as she walked in, behaving like the stargazer she was. And then she saw me. Moon didn't skip a beat.

"Hello, Victoria," he said as if we had not been locked in a stare at all and I were just another face in the crowd.

I played along too. It took every ounce of strength that I had but I gathered it. "Moon, hello," I said so nervously that it sounded as if I were talking underwater. And then I cleared my throat, which only made my awkwardness worse.

"This is my lady Amanda Trundle," he said. "Amanda, Victoria."

We shook hands as if we had never laid eyes on each other before. He called her his lady the way he used to refer to me in public. She was his lady now. Not me. Her. It was now confirmed. That fact alone brought me back to earth. He was sharing his life with another woman and I was about to be proposed marriage by another man. If that didn't convince me that our rendevous with destiny was over, nothing could.

The only thing for me to do, then, was do as Moon did and introduce my beau to him. But Daniel, being who he was, beat me to the punch.

"Moon McCalister?" he asked, extending his hand and grinning from ear to ear. "It is a mighty great privilege to meet you, sir. Mighty great. My name is Doctor Daniel Gurchess and I want you to know that your candidacy is an inspiration to us all. I'll vote for you if it's the last thing that I do, sir, and I'm not even a Tallahassee resident or registered to vote anywhere near this region of the country." He said this and then let out a laugh so loud that people around us turned briefly.

"Nice to meet you," Moon said coolly and politely removed his hand from Daniel's firm grasp.

"And Miss Trundle, did you say?" Daniel asked Amanda. She seemed pleased that I was seeing her with her man again and she smiled and shook Daniel's hand.

"Yes," she said, "but please call me Amanda. And you're a doctor, did you say? A professor or—"

"Oh no," Daniel said. "I'm a real doctor. I'm a physician."

"I see," Amanda said, obviously impressed. They stood there, Daniel and Amanda, smiling broadly at each other, seemingly admiring the conceit they saw in the other. A perfect match if ever I saw one, I thought.

Then Amanda looked at Gina and Vera, who still stood behind me. "I'm sorry," she said, moving toward them, totally reconfiguring the group to where Moon ended up standing beside me. He moved closer to where his arm was lightly touching mine. I nearly passed out.

Amanda extended her hand to Gina and Vera. "Hi," she said, "I'm Amanda Trundle."

Gina looked at the hand but Vera shook it.

"Hello," Vera said. "I'm Vera Langston and this is Regina Ridgeway."

Amanda, on hearing Gina's name, stopped shaking Vera's hand and looked at Gina. "I thought I recognized you. Regina Ridgeway, the attorney?" she asked.

"Yes," Gina said.

"It's an honor to see you again. You may not remember but I was one of the attorneys in the Pasco lawsuit that you defended in Baltimore. Our client, Pasco Oil, had a team of sixteen lawyers and there you were alone, defending the little guy, and you won. You were one heck of a litigant, I must say. My colleagues had great respect for your abilities. They were calling you the female Johnny Carson."

"Cochran," Gina said.

"Excuse me?"

"You mean the female Johnnie Cochran."

"No, I distinctly remember them saying Johnny Carson."

"But he's a comedian. He's not a lawyer."

"And your point is?"

Gina rolled her eyes and looked at me. *I know*, I wanted to say.

But Amanda didn't skip a beat. "Derrick," she said, backing back until she was beside him again, effectively squeezing me out, "you have such nice friends. We simply must invite them to the celebration."

"What celebration?" Vera asked.

"Derrick's bash. His fiftieth birthday celebration. It'll be next Saturday night at the McCalister compound."

"At the what?" Vera asked.

"Moon's house, girl," Gina said.

"We want all of you to come," Amanda said. "Don't we, Derrick?"

She was still playing games, still putting him on the spot. But he played along anyway. "Certainly," he said.

And she went on and on, talking about this big bash she was putting on for Derrick as if it were going to be a presidential ball. She seemed so smug, as if she was getting her kicks rubbing it in.

I looked at Moon. He seemed uncharacteristically in the background, letting Amanda do her thing without displaying a tap of interest either way. I wondered if he was well, if dealing with a political campaign, a business, and Amanda Trundle was too much for one man to bear, even a man like Moon. But if it was it wasn't

273

showing. He stood by his woman and allowed her to gloat in the spotlight, her enormous beauty and charm mesmerizing everyone in our group. When I looked away from Moon and turned my attention toward Amanda too, Moon turned his attention toward me. I felt his stare, and relished it, but I couldn't find the courage to allow my eyes to look into his.

But Amanda was the center of this universe. She kept on talking and talking with boundless energy. It wasn't until the governor's wife walked into the room that she finally shut up. She insisted again that we all attend the big birthday bash for the birthday boy, as she put it, and then she with Moon moved on to bigger things, to rub elbows with the closest thing to royalty in the room: the governor's wife.

"You okay?" Gina whispered to me as we watched them walk away. I nodded that I was.

We said our good nights to Gina and Vera again and they went back to their meals and Isaac.

"You know Moon McCalister?" Daniel asked eagerly.

"You can call it knowledge," I said.

"Why didn't you tell me? He's all but a shoo-in to become the next mayor of this town and you know him and never said anything?"

"He's a Democrat, Daniel. I thought you said you hated Democrats and their communist leanings."

"I do," he said, "but that's *Moon McCalister!*"

I shook my head. "Yes," I said. "But let's go."

We headed, once again, for the exit doors. It was air that I needed now, and a quick and immediate escape. I could still smell his sweet cologne in my nostrils. I could still see him lifting me onto him, over and over again. That was why, when I was about to take my first step out of the room, I couldn't resist. I looked back. I casually turned my head toward Moon McCalister just as he was turning his head toward me.

* * *

At home in my living room was where Daniel broke the big news. He wanted to propose, all right. He wanted to propose that he and I live together in unholy matri-sin.

I sat on my sofa with my arms folded and my face undoubtedly displaying the look of someone extremely pissed off. "What?" I asked him.

"I want you to relocate to Phoenix and live with me."

"Live with you?"

"Yes!" he said with a large smile on his face as if he were giving me some great prize.

"How?"

"How?"

"Yes, Daniel, how?"

"Well, you pack your bags and—"

"I mean how are we going to live together? As what? Boyfriend and girlfriend?"

"Of course," he said. Even a child would have figured that one out, I'm sure he wanted to say.

I shook my head. I should have known better than to give my heart to this fool. What a night. I had to suffer through seeing Amanda Trundle with Moon again and now this. It was not a good night.

"What's the matter?" he asked, totally confused by my reaction.

"What's the matter? What about my damn ring, that's what's the matter!"

His gaiety suddenly turned solemn, not because of my desire for a wedding ring, but because I had cussed. "I didn't know you used profanity," he said.

I leaned forward and placed my face in my hands. My fine-tuned image as the little woman crumbled before his very eyes on the strength of one four-letter word. The absurdity of the entire relationship crystallized in my head. Moon was the best and I didn't have to lose my self-respect to love him. Now I had Daniel Boone over here, a man I despised from jump, but I was knocking down doors to please him. I shook my head. "What an asshole!" I said out loud. I meant me but Daniel didn't care whom I meant. He stood up, astonished.

"I'll bet there's a lot I don't know about you," he said.

I lost it. Just like that. On top of his wanting me for nothing (and that's all that living-together shit was about), his being insulted because I cussed was too much. I had had it. How could he lead me to a mansion and then offer me a mobile home? Man, please. I told your boy about himself that day. I loved him, in a sick, perverted way, but enough was enough. Besides, he didn't love me. He loved the image of some puritanical woman that I was conveying. He didn't even know me. Because if boyfriend would have known me, he would have sailed his ass back to Phoenix without so much as even thinking about asking me to shack up with him.

But by the time he left my apartment that day, he knew me. Every insult he had ever hurled at me was thrown back at him. I remembered shit so old he didn't even remember ever saying it. But that only demonstrated his problem. He would say things, awful, denigrating things just to hurt people, and then forget about it. But the people he hurt didn't forget. Oh, I went on that day.

He cocked an attitude too. "I'm glad I didn't ask you to marry me," he said like the spoiled little brat he was. "You're nothing like I thought!"

He was right, I was nothing like he thought, but that still didn't stop me from taking him by the seat of his pants and running him out of my front door. I knew I was going to be hurting after that, but I did what I had to do. No man was worth all of that skinning and grinning and knitting and Willie Nelson and Barry Manilow bullshit he had put me through. I couldn't take another minute of that nonsense. I could do bad by myself.

He tried to phone me later that night and apologize but I couldn't see myself turning back. He was no Moon McCalister and Moon was now my measuring stick. I should have known better than to fall for somebody who didn't let me be me. The whole affair was a joke. He wanted a Venus de Milo doll, not a self-assured woman with opinions. So I gave him Venus. It helped him, I mean it boosted your boy's already inflated ego to newer and higher heights. But it left me cold and empty and reeling from the mere thought of losing my entire personality to keep a man like Daniel, a man who, ultimately, wasn't worth sweeping out the door. That was why, when he tried his lame apologizing, I hung up in his face. He had taken my self-respect to its lowest low. Now it was my time to take his down a rung or two.

He tried to phone a few more times but I kept hanging up in his face. On his fourth try I picked up the phone with vengeance in my voice. "Don't try that harassing shit on me!" I yelled. "Ask your sister what happened to the last Negro who tried harassing me!"

He apparently asked Vera because he didn't phone a fifth time. I surprised the mess out of my own self the way I so quickly dropped that zero. Seeing Moon McCalister helped. I went from the Moon to the pigpen. That was too low to go. That was a monumental drop. And even after I lowered my standards for him and played his game perfectly, he still didn't think I was good enough to marry. I was thirty-five and had never been asked but I decided then and there that I wasn't settling anymore. If it meant that I had to jump through another hoop just to get me a man, then I wouldn't be getting one. I was too old, too sick, and too tired to be jumping through anymore hoops.

But the beautiful thing about life is that it keeps on going. It was a few days later. Jake Onstead rushed into my office with some rather shocking news. I was behind my desk, feet propped up, newspaper spread open, not particularly happy but content with my lot in life. If my life pattern was any indication, one of two things was about to happen to me: very bad news was coming or very good news. My life rarely ran in neutral. Fortunately for me, it was good news for a change.

"Let me be the first to congratulate you," Jake said excitedly.

"Good morning to you too, Jake," I said, not even bothering to look up from my newspaper. "And for what am I to be congratulated?"

"Professor of the year," he said and I immediately looked up. He pushed his glasses up on his flat face and smiled. "The student body has voted you professor of the year."

"Me?"

"Yes, you."

"But . . . why?"

Jake smiled. "Why not?"

I thought about it. Yeah. Why not? Why the hell not? Given the kind of year I was having, I deserved a good turn. I may have been a total wipeout in the love department but at least I was succeeding at *something*. But I still didn't believe it. I even asked Jake if he was sure he hadn't made a mistake. I enjoyed teaching and I thought I was good at it, but for me to be awarded professor of the year was not the kind of honor I ever thought possible. But now it was here, according to Jake, I was the winner. I actually felt a surge of emotion and threw my fist into the air. Winning was something that I had lately grown unaccustomed to. I didn't know quite how to take it.

But it wasn't as if I had time to learn. Within an hour of Jake's announcement my phone was ringing off the hook and professors and students alike were in and out of my office with rounds and rounds of congratulations. Professor of the year. From Daniel Gurchess to this. Talk about a reversal of fortune. From nearly jumping off a cliff with an egomaniacal idiot like Daniel to becoming the recipient of an honor that personifies responsible citizenship. It was a reversal in the right direction.

Gina and Vera heard about it later that night. They came over to my condo feigning anger over not being told by yours truly. I was in bed, the excitement of the day giving me a big-time headache, and after I allowed them in and listened to their unable-to-keep-a-straight-face diatribe, I returned to my bed. They followed, going on and on about the insensitivity of some people and how you never really know a person until they win professor of the year and try to act all hot to trot with it. I couldn't help but smile as they went on and on. They knew I needed a lift too. And they were thrilled beyond measure for me.

When they realized that I knew their game inside out and was actually enjoying their little charade, they fell in bed with me and shook me as if we were children at a slumber party. "Professor of the year," Gina said as if that said it all. "Everybody ain't able," Vera added.

And then we lay there, the three of us, looking like oversize baby dolls, enjoying without pettiness or envy the surprisingly good fortune of one of us.

It was a bittersweet moment, the three of us together. We had come a long way from our days in D.C. But we had a long way yet to go. We thought it would be settled by now. We thought we would move down South and take the place by storm. But life got in the way. And it took us instead. Now we were sailing, all right, but not on yachts and sailboats that bespoke the good life, but on every wind and wave, going where we thought we were too proud to go, sinking to newer and newer lows. I looked at Gina, our self-appointed leader, and she was at a crossroads too. She was pregnant and pushing forty, her once highfalutin self-assurance a little less strident now, her continued marriage to an unfaithful husband more out of desperation and the fear of being alone than anything like love. And Vera, still with Rollie, still listening to his ancient advice on womanhood and taking it in stride, still caught up in the whirlwind of the ideal of love rather than the reality. And then there was me. The hapless of all. Thirty-five and still looking for that great romantic knight, the one who would sweep me off my feet, the one who once had to be the picture of perfection but now just had to be a man.

This was our life now. From The Three Blackateers to this. We were smarter now, philosophical even, trying daily to climb out of the doldrums of our own discontent, happy sometimes, lonely many times. It wasn't exactly the life we had planned for ourselves when we relocated to Florida, to be sure. But it was all we had.

Gina started talking about Isaac and his latest conquest, as if she needed to prove to me that my life wasn't as terminable as hers. She even laughed about the other woman and how her husband was scraping the bottom of the barrel now for dates. Vera, however, failed to see the humor. "Why do you stay?" she asked when Gina's laughter died down and we could go there.

Because it's better than nothing, Gina probably wanted to say. "Why do you stay?" she asked Vera instead.

"Probably for the same reasons that you stay with Isaac, or that Tory stayed with Daniel as long as she did. I love him, that's why."

"I doubt if you could put Tory's relationship with Daniel in that category," Gina said. "Daniel was a lost cause."

Vera smiled. "What?"

"They broke up because he's a Republican."

"That's ridiculous. People don't break up over politics, what does that mean? Tory had many reasons to break up with Daniel, believe me, but I'm sure his political affiliation had nothing to do with it. That wouldn't make sense."

It made sense. Vera's decision to stay with Rollie for reasons she didn't even understand made sense. Gina's decision to stay with Isaac because she was thirty-nine and pregnant and terrified of being alone made sense. All of it made perfect sense and all of it was nonsense.

"What don't make sense," Gina said, "is that you would stay with a man like Rollie, who wants you to be his wife and nothing else when you know you want more out of life than that. Now that's what don't make sense. That's some crazy shit there."

"Gina, let's just chill, okay?" Vera asked. "Let's just for once forget about the craziness of my life, yours, and Tory's, and chill. Okay?"

Gina shrugged her shoulders as if it didn't matter to her either way and I raised my hand in an imitation of a toast. "Sounds like a plan to me," I said and my girls, both of them, raised their imaginary glasses too.

Ten

Thank God for C-SPAN

It turned out to be a beautiful day after all. I was up by eight A.M., dressed by nine, and on my way to the manicurist. From there it was one store after another one, from the Governor's Square Mall to the Tallahassee Mall to Norwood. One bag became three bags became sixteen bags. I was buying clothes and jewelry and shoes as if I were born to shop. It was Saturday, the day Moon McCalister turned fifty years old, and I was treating myself.

I was also searching for a birthday gift. His girlfriend made a special point of sending me a personal invitation to his big birthday bash, even after her verbal one, and I felt obligated to at least get a gift. But that wasn't as easy a task as it seemed. I felt as if I were walking on pins and needles. The gift couldn't be too personal or in any way suggestive, so that left precious few options. Even a tie could have some spicy connotations if you're looking for that sort of thing. And given Amanda Trundle, she was.

So I got him a book: *Peter the Great* by Robert Massie. One of my all-time favorites. Moon appreciated history and what the past says about the present almost as much as I did. I knew he would appreciate the book.

Since I wasn't about to attend any big bash given by Amanda Trundle, invitation or no invitation, my plan was to carry the book, beautifully wrapped in diamond-patterned silver paper, to Moon's office and leave it at the front desk. Moon would undoubtedly drop by, if he wasn't there already, and the guard at the desk would give him my gift. It was an impersonal way to do it, but facing him or his insufferable girlfriend wasn't exactly my idea of a good move.

And it worked. Initially. I walked into the lobby of McCalister Enterprises, left my gift with the guard on duty, and walked back out into the parking lot. It was a nice day, kind of lukewarm and breezy, and only a handful of cars graced the lot. To my relief Moon was nowhere to be seen. My relief, however, was short-lived.

"Miss! Miss!" I heard someone yelling behind me as I opened my car door. I turned around and it was the guard, running toward me.

"What's the matter?" I asked as he approached.

He bent over, to catch his breath, and then he stood erect. "You're to wait here. You're not to go anywhere."

"Excuse me?"

"I got a call from upstairs. They said I was to hold you here until Mr. McCalister could get to you."

My heart dropped. Moon was in the building? "Are you sure you've got the right person?" I asked nervously.

"I'm positive. They said to stop that lady. I said what lady. The pretty lady in the yellow blazer, they said. That's you."

"But—"

"Apparently Mr. McCalister saw you from the window upstairs."

I looked up, at the huge white-brick building with its bay windows tinted black, unable to see anything but glass, so I closed my car door and waited.

Within seconds the front, double doors of McCalister Enterprises flung open and Moon came hurrying out. He looked around until he saw me. When he saw me he ran toward me. He was in white shirtsleeves, no tie, a pair of light blue pants, and he was actually running toward me. My heart should have been leaping for joy when I saw him, but it wasn't. It was beating too fast.

When Moon made it up to me he thanked the guard for holding me there. The guard thanked Moon, for no known reason, and then hurried back toward the building and his duties at the desk. Moon looked at me and smiled. I relaxed.

"Hey there," he said.

"Hey yourself."

"I saw you from my office window. Upstairs."

"Yes, the security officer told me."

"And I thought I'd come down and say hello. Well. Hello."

He smiled nervously. I didn't know what to do.

"What brings you out this way?" he asked.

"Oh. Your birthday actually. I wanted to drop off a gift."

"For me? How nice."

"A book. It's nothing spectacular. It's only a book."

"I'm sure I'll enjoy it."

"I hope you do."

Moon nodded. He looked down, at my shoes, and then up at my face. "You look good, Victoria. I wanted to tell you so the other night. You've really blossomed."

I smiled. What a way to put it. I've blossomed. "Thank you."

"And congratulations on your award. Professor of the year, I understand. That's a great honor. A much deserved honor."

"I was surprised, that's for sure," I said. And still surprised, I wanted to add. Of course there are those on campus who would disagree vehemently with Moon's assessment. They believe I didn't win the award because I was a gifted instructor the way they viewed themselves. They believe I won because I was easy and the students liked me. Well, hey, I told them, I'll take it. Being well liked was an honor to me. And if the students found my classes manageable, then that was an honor too. I wasn't teaching molecular biophysics, after all. I was teaching a little history. Just a little information about our lives to keep us from repeating the same mistakes again.

Which brought me back to Moon. His praises aside, I knew I had to keep my wits about me. I couldn't keep making the same mistakes. He was a good man who knew how to pay a compliment to a woman. It was an innocent gesture on his part, as far as I was concerned, and nothing more.

"Well," I said, with that in mind, "I'd better go."

"Are you?" he said quickly, with just a tinge of desperation in his voice. "I mean, you are coming tonight. Aren't you?"

"No, I don't think I'm going to be able to make it."

He appeared extremely disappointed, which shocked the mess out of me. "I see," he said.

"I've just got so much to do and a party, well, I'm just not in the party mood these days."

He nodded. "Know what you mean," he said. Then he seemed to come up with a better idea. "How about something to eat?" he asked.

"I had a salad at the mall, thank you."

"A movie then. Go to a movie with me."

I smiled. "You hate movies."

He smiled too. "Okay, no movie, you've got me there. But you can't fault a guy for trying."

I shook my head. This was not the Moon I was accustomed to. He was upbeat, animated, maybe even a little flirtatious. It was as if he turned fifty and immediately loosened up. His somberness, which used to be his trademark, was nowhere to be found.

"Where're you headed next?" he asked.

Good question, I thought. "The flea market," I said.

"The flea market?"

"Yes. The modern-day version of the swap meet."

"I know what a flea market is. I just never knew you to go to one."

"Oh, there's a lot of things I go to now, Moon," I said, trying to flirt a little myself.

"I see," he said, looking down, at my chest, "you're a regular daredevil now."

"Absolutely. I even hired me a personal trainer. He starts Monday."

"Ah."

"Yes. I've gots to get in shape."

"You are in shape."

I shook my head and opened my car door. "Not to me I'm not."

He moved closer to my door. "Then why don't I tag along? To the flea market, I mean."

I turned around. Moon McCalister *tagging along?* What had Amanda Trundle done to the man? Next he'd be wanting to work out with me or go mall hopping with me. Anything to be with me. With me? I looked at Moon. "Are you all right?" I asked him.

He tried to smile but this time he couldn't do it. "It's just this turning fifty business," he said. "I don't know if I can pull it off."

He looked at me. His somberness was back. And it returned in the form of reality. He wasn't looking for any hot and heavy romance, that was the last thing he needed. He was just looking for a friend.

"Have you had lunch?" I asked him, remembering the time he cooked sausages in my kitchen.

"Me? No," he replied.

"Good," I said. "Let's go get you something to eat."

His spirits lifted immediately, which floored me. I felt as if I was coming to *his* rescue, for a change.

But he took charge, locking up my car and escorting me to his. He was parked in the back of the building, away from the crowd. We walked together slowly, talking about simple things, like the funny weather we'd been having lately and traffic jams. And the more we talked and relaxed, the more I began to imagine things, like the peace that overtakes me when I'm with Moon, and how wonderful it would be if we could actually be friends.

We settled down in a small coffee shop on Capital Circle where they made a mean chicken caesar salad, but Moon barely touched it. Finally he gave up altogether and leaned back.

"Sorry," I said, pulling out a cigarette.

"About what?"

"The salad. I thought you'd like it."

"Oh, it's fine. My appetite just isn't what it used to be."

"I wish I could say the same for mine. I had a garden salad for lunch, in the name of fitness, you know, now I'm craving a cheese-burger. And I don't mean some two-bit, run-of-the-mill burger either, but a big, sloppy, melts-in-your-mouth double-decker hungry-man burger!"

Moon laughed. "Then why did you come here if that's what you wanted?"

"Because this is exactly where my big behind needs to be. Drinking a decaf espresso and chomping on rice cakes."

"And smoking a cigarette to top it all off."

I looked at my cigarette and shook my head. "I know. Me and my bad habits. I know."

Then The Temptations singing "Just My Imagination" blared out over the shop's music system, and I started moving from side to side and snapping my fingers. "Oh, I love that song!" I said, and Moon smiled. I closed my eyes, got in tune with the beat, and even started singing a few of the words: ". . . running away with me."

When I opened my eyes again and looked up, Moon was staring at me.

"What?" I asked and smiled.

"You've been doing all right then?" he asked as if he was disap-pointed.

I hesitated. It depends on what you call all right. I've been functioning. Living. Getting by. "Yeah," I said. "I think so."

"Good. It certainly seems like you're doing just fine."

I smiled, puffed on my cigarette, and wondered where Moon was going with this. He was never the kind of man who telegraphed his moves, and as soon as you thought you had him cornered, he changed direction on you. Today was even worse. He'd talk about very impersonal things for a long time and, as soon as the conversation appeared fated to remain superficial, he hit you with the personal stuff. I didn't know what to make of it. I didn't know which move was the smokescreen and which was the heart of the matter.

"I'm getting by, Moon," I said. "I can't say that everything's perfect because it never is, but things are manageable."

"Where's the doctor?" he asked.

"The who?"

"You know. The *real* doctor."

I laughed. "Daniel. Back home in Phoenix, I reckon. Or still here. Hell, I don't know."

"There's been a breakup?"

I nodded.

Moon shook his head. "Nobody wants to stay together anymore," he said.

"Not true. It would have been my pleasure to stay with you."

I nearly died. I could not believe those words came out of my mouth. I looked at Moon. He was looking down at his food, but then he looked at me.

"Then why didn't you?" he asked.

I sat frozen. I actually thought I had it in control. I thought I could hang out with the love of my life as if he were just another pal of mine. But the feelings ran too deep, and without much provocation and when I least expected it, they surfaced. Now I was on the spot. *Tell him everything*, my heart was screaming. *Tell him that you let him go because you had no choice, because that snake Amanda Trundle had schemed and connived to where there was no other choice. Tell him everything. Tell him!*

But I couldn't. It would mean the end of everything he had worked so hard to achieve. Election day was less than a month away. All polls showed him ahead of the Republican challenger by as many as eight percentage points. If I exposed Amanda now and she honored her threat to destroy him with lies and innuendoes, he may not be able to recover before the election. And it would all be lost. And for what? He still wouldn't necessarily want me.

"Why didn't you, Victoria?" he asked again.

I sipped espresso. "Why didn't I what?"

"Stay with me."

I tried to smile. "It was for the best," I said.

"Whose best?" he asked, but then he nodded. He couldn't afford to pursue it either.

"And how is Amanda Trundle these days?" I asked and then studied his reaction.

He took his fork and lifted a chunk of chicken from the salad plate, looked at it, and then dropped it back down. "She's okay," he said with little enthusiasm, and then he pushed the plate of food into the center of the table. "So," he said, as if relieved to change the subject, "what's next?"

I leaned back and doused my cigarette. "Well," I said, "I still need to get to the flea market."

"Then let's get hopping!" he said smilingly and pulled out his wallet. "What are you going for? To browse?"

"No, to buy some plants. They're having a buy-one, get-one-free sale on artificial plants and I wanted to snatch up a few."

"Artificial plants?"

"Yes. I thought they'd add a touch of safari to my home."

Moon laughed. "They'll add a touch of something, all right," he said, and threw a twenty on the table.

*   *   *

290

I settled on four hibiscus plants, all completely similar, all eleven inches rather than the thirteen inches I had hoped to buy, but all of the thirteens were gone.

Moon paid for the plants and carried them out to his car. I laughed as he opened the back car door and then hesitated. The idea of those cheap, dusty plants lounging around on his pristine ivory-colored leather seat wasn't something he was particularly excited about. Even his once perfectly clean shirt had been stained with dirt spots just from carrying the plants to the car. He looked at me, at how I was laughing at his hesitancy, and he couldn't help but smile.

"I must really love you," he said as he grabbed the plants and began laying them across his unprotected seat.

I stood behind him, still smiling, but confused as hell. *He must really love me?* How could he say that? During the entire time we dated he had never once, directly or indirectly, said he loved me. But he was saying it now so effortlessly; saying it now when a chasm as wide as the greatest divide, namely Amanda Trundle, separated us. It seemed so incredible, so painfully touching, but it also seemed unfair.

We went to my condo to drop off the plants, Moon not seeing the point to dirtying up two good cars, and once I arranged them around in my living room he nodded.

"Okay," he said, "I see your point now. They do indeed add something. Looks good."

Then we stood there, the two of us, in a kind of *don't let this end* linger, just standing there looking too long at hibiscus plants. Moon placed his hands in his pockets and I thought he was going to ask if I was ready to go. He asked, instead, if he could have a glass of water.

I gladly obliged, hurrying to the kitchen to pour water, unable to keep my mind from racing with possibilities. Maybe he was trying to tell me something. Maybe he and Amanda were no longer an item but he just didn't know how to tell me. When I asked him about her at the coffee shop he responded almost bitterly, as if he had figured out for himself that she was worse than the lowest thing crawling, a real-live barracuda, but he just couldn't bring himself to tell me.

But as the water reached the brim of the glass and I turned off the tap, I settled back down. Moon McCalister didn't play games. If he and Amanda weren't together anymore he would have told me at the coffee shop. I smiled and shook my head. I almost did it again. I almost carried myself away into a wishful-thinking trip where everything is contingent on words unspoken and gestures with ambiguous meanings and rampant speculations. I needed to get a grip.

And I would have. But when I turned from the sink to hurry back into the living room, Moon was standing behind me. I walked right into him, causing the water to leap out of the glass and land right on his shirt. I covered my mouth in dismay. But he smiled.

"I am so sorry," I said. "I didn't see you standing there."

"It's all right," he said. Then he looked at me. And I looked at him. He removed the glass from my hand, set it on the countertop, and pulled me to him. I fell against his warm, wet body and closed my eyes. He hugged me tenderly because he understood how much it meant to me, and when he should have let me go he didn't. He pulled me closer and held me tighter. We stood there together, in my kitchen, embracing and breathing heavy, and I was unable to pull away. But I had to. I had to. I let him go.

He seemed rattled when I pulled away from him and he started looking around, at everything, anything, but never at me. "I guess we better be getting back," I said, and he finally glanced my way. And then he quickly agreed.

We left the condo and walked slowly across the parking lot to his car. The entire drive to McCalister Enterprises was quiet and depressing. There were a million things we could have said, a zillion things. But not a word was spoken. We're bound by the choices we make and it doesn't matter if those choices are inconvenient or unsettling or wrong. Moon made his choice when he left my home all those months ago and went to Amanda. I had accused him of wanting her, an accusation he completely denied, but he decided to prove me right anyway by going back to her. That was his choice. When I decided to listen to Amanda, when I entertained her scheme to steal Moon from me, that became my choice. They were both life-altering choices that came down to one quick move in one direction or another, when it could easily have gone the other way, and everybody involved was now forced to live with the consequences.

Moon parked his car beside mine in the parking lot of his office building. He hesitated before getting out, his hands still gripping his steering wheel, his once upbeat demeanor now lost in his own somberness. Then he got out of the car, walked around to the passenger side, and opened the door for me. I stepped out gingerly as well, treading carefully, unable to shake the realization that our entire future came down to one fateful night and one wrong choice.

As I stepped out of the car our eyes met. At first he seemed taken aback by me, as if I still did funny things to his heart, but then he spoke. "I think I'll be proposing marriage to Amanda tonight," he said halfheartedly, as if he couldn't believe it either.

I stood mute. I would have smiled, to conceal my pain and deflate my shame, but I didn't think to smile. I just lingered longer, not knowing what to do or say, and then I walked to my car, got in, and cranked up. I saw Moon in the rearview as I drove away. His body was turning and then walking toward his building, but walking as if in slow motion, his arms flailing back and forth, his stride halting, cautious, uneasy. He was getting away again. And I was letting him go. Another day of decision. Another choice made. I stopped the car.

I slammed on the brakes, jumped out, and ran to Moon. I yelled his name, I cried his name, and he slowly turned my way. When I started talking, the words didn't just ease out, they popped out, like firecrackers, and suddenly I had a lot to say. And I told it. I told it all!

"You can't do it!" I yelled as I approached him. "She's not who you think she is. She was willing to destroy you, Moon. She was willing to destroy everything you stand for just to have her way. She doesn't love you. She loves what you can do for her. She had 'em lined up, Moon. Woman after woman. They were going to tell horrible, terrible lies about you. They were going to ruin your chance to serve this city and help the people who need help the most. She was going to destroy you if I didn't step aside. I had to do it. She said you loved her, that you loved her more than you could ever love me, and that night at the party it looked like she was right. So I had to let you go. But she's a snake, Moon. She's not good enough for you. You deserve somebody who loves you for you, not for what you can do for them. And Amanda Trundle, no matter what, isn't that woman!"

Moon stood stunned. He just stared at me. His frosty, sleepy-eyed look was gone. His eyes were wide open now. I wanted him to hold me. I wanted him to tell me that I did the right thing. But he didn't.

After standing there paralyzed for two solid minutes, he nodded and placed his hands in his pockets. "Okay," he said almost dispassionately, his voice almost a whisper, and then he turned and went into his building.

Gina and Vera arrived by eight-fifteen that night. They were both dressed to a tee with Gina in her dynasty green pantsuit and Vera in her lavender pantsuit. I was still dressing, in the bedroom, preparing to step into my sleek black Armani evening dress, and both my homegirls walked into my bedroom pleased.

"That's right," Gina said, "show it off!"

"It's beautiful, Tory," Vera said. "But you need to put some pep in your step. We're late as it is."

"What is this?" Gina asked, standing in front of my television set.

"A journalist roundtable discussion."

"C-SPAN *again?*" she asked. "Is this the only channel you watch? Damn. I think you plan your entire existence based on what's on C-SPAN cause if something's good on C-SPAN you ain't going nowhere and you ain't talking on the phone, child, please. You plan your whole day around C-SPAN."

"I do not."

"It seems that way to me, girl."

"I still don't believe it," Vera said. "You actually told Moon everything?"

I nodded and moved over for her to zip me up.

"What did he say?" Gina asked.

"What did he do?" Vera asked.

"He said okay and then he left."

Gina and Vera looked at each other. And then they looked at me. "That's it?" Gina asked.

"Yes," I said regrettably. His response wasn't exactly what I had hoped for either.

"Wait a minute, Tore," Vera said. "He didn't tell you what he was gonna do with Amanda?"

"He didn't have to tell her that, Vera. He's gonna kick her ass out, what you think he's gonna do? I just thought he might give some hints as to what he was gonna do with Tory, if you get my drift."

"Well, he didn't tell me anything. I don't even know if he's canceled the big birthday bash or what's going on. But that's why I've got to go tonight. I'm sure Amanda's out of the picture. But where does that leave me?"

"Right," Gina said, in total agreement.

"I don't know," Vera said. "There should be some cooling-off time—"

"Here we go," Gina said.

"A time of reflection," Vera continued, "for both of you. He needs time to heal from the hurt that Amanda has caused. And you need time too, Tory, to think about what you really want."

"She wants Moon McCalister, Vera, that's what she really wants!"

"Even if he might not want her?"

"Yes!" Gina said.

"No!" I said. "Absolutely not. If he doesn't want me, fine, I've got a life now. I'll live. But I need to know. That's the only reason I'm going tonight."

"And you're ready to be turned down?"

"Vera," I said, "I'm expecting to be turned down."

She looked at me and smiled. "You've come a long way, Victoria," she said.

The party was in full bloom by the time we arrived. The music was performed by a live band and every tune was Motown and old-school R&B. The crowd was wired, talking and laughing and dancing and eating, and I never knew that Moon's quiet home could come so alive.

We hobnobbed with the bigwigs and enjoyed ourselves too. I smiled a lot and sipped sherry, but mostly I watched Moon. He was working the room like a born politician, even posing for photos with excited, blue-haired old ladies. He wore a dark blue, double-breasted tuxedo and seemed to draw energy from the excitement of the crowd.

Me and Vera were hovering around the back of the room, near the library, and the conversation surrounding us was more about the beauty of Moon's home than Moon himself. Gina had left us and was in the thick of the crowd, laughing it up with a group she knew, and Vera was busy asking waiters if she could get a nonalcoholic beverage, preferably lemonade or sweet tea. They always said yes, they would bring it over, but they had yet to do so. When

Moon finally made his way over to our side of the room and came up to us, Vera let him have it.

"I'm very disappointed in the service," she said before he could say hello.

"Are you?" he said and glanced at me.

"I've asked at least four different waiters to bring me a nonalcoholic beverage. I had my preferences but I told them I would take water if that was the best they could do. But all to no avail."

Moon immediately grabbed a waiter walking nearby and pulled him into our group. "What's your name?"

"Raymond, sir," he said.

"Raymond, this young lady has requested a nonalcoholic beverage. Bring her a sample of everything we have and let her choose what she wants. And it will be your job, Raymond, and your job alone to make sure her glass is refilled before it goes empty. Understood?"

"Yes, sir!" Raymond said as if he were a private in boot camp and hurried to obey Moon's command.

Moon smiled. Vera thanked him. And then he looked at me.

"Hey," he said.

"Hey yourself."

"Good to see you again."

"You too."

He stood there, staring at me, making me uncomfortable as hell, and then he looked away. "You ladies are enjoying yourselves, despite the poor service?" he asked.

"Yes," I said.

"It's very nice," Vera added.

"Good," he said, his eyes staring unblinkingly at me once more as if the shock of what I had told him was still sinking in. "Anyway," he said, "nice seeing y'all again."

And he left, giving his other guests a few moments of his much wanted attention too, treating me the same way he was treating everybody else. And suddenly I began to wonder if he believed me

297

when I told him about Amanda's scheme. He may have dismissed my accusations as the babbling nonsense of some spurned woman. It had never even occurred to me that he wouldn't believe me. It wasn't until Gina came over to our group, however, that I realized that in all probability, he didn't.

"She's here," Gina said.

"Who's here?" I asked.

"Amanda is in the house!"

"What?"

"That's right, girl. Miss Trundle up in here!"

I looked around, stunned, and that's when I saw her. She was working the crowd too, but only she was mesmerizing them with her charm and grace. I stared mercilessly at the woman as she moved from one side of the room to the other, squeezing hands, kissing cheeks, and laughing louder than anybody in the room, until she finally came to us.

"This is so nice," she said, hugging all three of us at the same time. "I am absolutely thrilled to see you girls again. I was just telling Derrick that I hoped those sweet people I met at the banquet came tonight. And you came. It is so nice. And each one of you looks so arrestingly beautiful. And, Regina. Oh my. That green is a green to die for. Where did you find such a beautiful color? It's green and it's not green, you know what I mean? I am bountifully impressed. Oh well. You girls have fun now, you hear? Just relax and enjoy yourselves."

She smiled even greater, I didn't think it possible, and moved on. We stared at her as she wormed her way into another group and laid the lies on thick with them too. Gina was so beside herself that she shook her head. "Give me a break," she said, still staring at Amanda, "give me a double-snap-up-and-down-big-time break please!"

"Can you believe her?" Vera said, and then she started mocking Amanda. "Your suit, Regina, you see, is cheap and nothing that I would be caught dead in, but it's to die for, it's arrestingly beautiful!"

"It's green," Gina said, joining in, "but it's not green. It's pink, but it's not pink. It's bullshit, but it's not bullshit."

"Anyway," I said, "I'm bountifully impressed," and then we leaned against each other laughing.

I stayed at the party. I didn't think I could do it, but I did it. It was obvious that Moon did not believe me. Amanda was his lady, no matter what I said about her, and I just simply had to accept it.

The announcement came around eleven P.M. Moon stood in front of the band and asked for the crowd's attention. They all gladly obliged. I was in the back of the room, with my girls by my side, preparing to hear that Moon McCalister would soon become a married man. Amanda was near the front of the crowd, just three rows back, standing like a poised ballerina ready to run onstage and perform.

"It's a wonderful feeling," he said, "to see all of you here tonight. It's not every day that a man gets to turn fifty, or even wants to turn fifty—"

The crowd laughed. I could barely manage a smile.

"But that's the deal. That's what it is. I'm fifty years old today."

Everybody applauded. "That's right," Gina said, "ain't no shame in celebrating the big Five-O!"

"I'm also a very fortunate soul. I'm in love, you see. I'm in love with the most wonderful woman in the world. When the pits of hell would have been more tolerable than another second on this earth, she came to me. She came in beauty and grace and with a dignity no school can teach, and no company can bottle. She walked away from me once and it broke my heart. I thought I had lost her forever. I thought that elusive happiness had eluded me again. But she's back. And I love her. She makes me laugh, and she makes me feel like a kid again. I can survive anything because of her smile. I'll make it, ladies and gentlemen, not because of my business expertise or my political aspirations, but because she walks beside me. She is my compass. She shows me, in her sacrifice, in her goodness, what decent looks like. Politics, like any business, can sometimes be a game of tricks where the people around you don't always have your best interests at heart. They are masters of the mask, using words to tear down others while elevating themselves. They confess love for you when they don't even know what love means. But I have found my soul mate and I cherish her. She's my center and the love of my life. And I say this with every ounce of confidence that I can muster: this world will pass away before anybody, ever, comes between my lady and me."

The applause from the crowd was deafening and Amanda nodded her head and ate it up.

There was no marriage announcement, but that didn't matter to her. His words still rang in her ears like echoing cymbals, those wonderful words that could reduce any romantic to tears. She was his compass, his center, the love of his life. What more could a girl want?

"I want everybody to continue to have fun," Moon said. "I want you to eat, drink, and be merry until your heart's content. In the meantime I am going to have the next dance with my lady and I would suggest that every gentleman in the room grab hold of his lady and do the same."

The band started playing, on Moon's suggestion, "Just My Imagination," and Moon moved down into the crowd and headed toward Amanda. She stood there ready to be swept off her feet, still smiling from ear to ear, still seducing him with every fiber in her being. He was going to dance with his lady, he said, and she could hardly contain her delight.

But he walked right past her. Gina and I looked at each other and Vera grabbed my arm. Amanda's grand smile disappeared so fast that it seemed as if somebody had slapped it off her face. Gina laughed and stomped her feet. "That's what I'm talking about!" she said.

Moon kept walking, past Amanda, past one group after another group, walking faster now, and confident, his unflappable swagger back in force. He walked past everybody in the room until he stood in front of me. Then he extended his hand. My heart got ready.

"May I have this dance?" he asked.

It jumped for joy. "You may," I said. And we danced. We danced all night. Amanda was not his lady, I was. I was his compass, his center, the love of his life. Amanda at first just stood there, silently stewing in her juices, but she didn't make a scene. The world would pass away, Moon said, before he allowed anybody to come between us. There was no scene invented, not even by the queen of scenes, to upstage that.

Amanda Trundle left our life that same night. She packed her suitcase and declined the offer of numerous smitten gentlemen to escort her to the airport. She called for a cab instead.

Moon and I stood outside on the lawn as the last of the guests piled into their automobiles and left. Amanda, with suitcase in tow, came outside too when her cab finally arrived. But she, of course, did not go immediately to her cab. She walked up to Moon instead and announced, as if it were not obvious and long overdue, that she was leaving now.

"I don't know what she told you," she began what she thought was going to be her grand exit speech, but Moon interrupted her.

"Don't, Amanda," he said.

"Don't what?"

"Lie anymore. I don't want to hear another one of your lies."

"Everything I did was for your own good, Derrick."

"I'm sure it was. And if you would have destroyed me because you didn't get your way, that would have been for my own good too."

301

"I was looking out for you, whether you believe it or not. You're going to need somebody like me. You're going to need somebody you can show off and be proud of because of her charm and wit and uniqueness. You deserve the best, Derrick."

"I have the best. And she doesn't have to scheme or connive or manipulate anybody to prove her love."

"But she's not me."

"Yes," he said. "Thank God."

Amanda gave Moon a look something harsh and her hard-earned poise almost cracked. "You know you love me," she said, "and you always will."

"You made one miscalculation, Amanda," Moon said and her attention increased. "You gave yourself too much credit."

Amanda just stood there, realizing wisely that her game was up and all those self-sacrificing lies she was famous for telling were as stale as her threats, and then she picked up her luggage and walked to the cab. She turned, as the taxi driver opened the door, and looked at me. She smiled as if it was all in the game to her and a sister like me should understand that. But I looked away.

Moon placed his arm around me and we watched until she was clean out of sight. It seemed as if we had come to the end of a long, dark day that began the moment she walked into my office and didn't end until now, as the cab turned another corner and was no more to be seen. We came so close, so eerily close to losing each other forever, and the realization scared us. That was why Moon would not let me out of his sight that night. That was why he held me so close to him that it seemed as if he was depending on my arms, my little arms, to hold him up.

We walked, Moon and I, across his estate, ending up in his peaceful backyard. We sat down by the water's edge and allowed the calmness of the trees and lake to calm us down too.

And then he took my hand. His bright brown eyes looked deep into mine.

"Victoria," he said, "will you marry me?"

The words I had longed to hear my entire adult life finally came. And not from some second-rate consolation prize either. But from the Moon. It didn't get any higher than that. I was asked. Victoria Coleman was now among the fortunate ones.

And although my mouth said maybe, my heart screamed hallelujah!

Eleven
My Turn

My heart screamed hallelujah. My workout was finally over. I looked up at Fummi, my personal trainer, who had just run me around the track as if I were some schoolkid and was talking about a double run on Monday, and I wondered if he realized what a grueling taskmaster he really was. He probably did because as soon as he had finished with me he grabbed his gym bag and bottled water and hurried across the field to begin a yelling and complaining and cajoling session with his next customer.

I leaned back on the bench and relaxed. We were at the high school and the track was filled with wannabe track stars like me, and the real ones. The sun was killing us though, it wasn't playing, and my brown face was pouring sweat.

But I basked in it. I popped open my bottle of water, drank up heartily, and chilled. It was Saturday morning, I didn't have anybody's clock to punch or schedule to make or deadline to meet, and I loved it.

But that didn't stop my beeper from going off. I pulled it off of my hip and looked at the number. V again. She'd been blowing up my beeper all morning but Fummi wouldn't let me call her. "I know that game, Tory," he said. "You get your girlfriend to beep you on some phantom emergency and then you all of a sudden gots to go. No, ma'am. I ain't havin' it. You can forget that. Ain't nothing an emergency when you on my time."

I used to argue with Fummi when he came up with those wild accusations of his, but now I just let him talk and have his way. Knowing Vera, it was nothing major. I figured it could probably wait.

But this time your girl was beeping me 911. That was unusual. Girlfriend knew not to bother me 911 unless it was a bona fide, get-your-ass-here-now situation. I grabbed my cell phone from out of my gym bag, which I kept turned off to preserve the battery, and called Vera immediately. Rollie answered the phone.

"V there?" I asked him.

"Is this Tory?"

"Yeah, Ro, what's up?"

"Vera just left. She'd been beeping you all morning."

"I know. What's going on?"

"She's on her way to the hospital."

My heart skipped a beat. "Gina?" I asked.

"Yep. It's time," he said.

I flipped off my cell, grabbed my gym bag and bottled water, and ran so fast across the field that even Fummi had to whip around shocked. "You act like you dying when I try to get you to run like that!" he yelled.

I jumped into my Benz and made a mad dash for TMH, Tallahassee Memorial Hospital. My heart was pumping fast and my shorts and T-shirt were drenched with sweat, and I just couldn't get there fast enough. The traffic was sparse, which was a blessing, but as soon as I thought I had an open pathway to gas it and really be on my way, a train horn sounded, the crossbars dropped down, and I slammed on the brakes within inches of the railroad tracks.

I looked through the rearview. Three cars behind me slammed

on their brakes too, almost running into me and each other, but no one, thankfully, was hit. But the cars did manage to box me in to where I couldn't back up or turn around and try another route.

I leaned back against my headrest and drank more water. The train was one of those long, lumbering freight trains. It was initially moving reasonably fast, given its bulk, but then it started getting slower and slower to almost creeping along. I looked through the rearview, hoping that the cars behind me would decide to back up a little and try to go another way, but they sat patiently as if it was no big deal, so I relaxed too.

I turned on the radio. Betty Wright, in her usual feistiness, was singing about "The Clean-up Woman" and then Patti and her girls put a killing on "Lady Marmalade," a song I couldn't understand for nothing when it first came out. It was all those French words, I guess, that threw me.

Then, seemingly without provocation, the train slowly edged up to a complete stop. I couldn't believe it. Within six freight cars of crossing and it was stopping? Then if that wasn't bad enough it had the nerve to start backing up. I looked in the rearview, certain that the cars behind me would surely take a hike now, but they stayed put as if these slow-behind trains were nothing new to them. I almost got mad. Who needed this? But then The Temptations came on, singing "Just My Imagination," and I smiled.

Three months ago, at his fiftieth birthday party, Moon got the band to play "Just My Imagination" and then he danced with me. It was the most perfect night of my life. Amanda Trundle took her scheming behind back to Baltimore, her threats of ruining Moon if I didn't step aside no longer carrying weight because it didn't matter to us what she did. So she left, knowing that her little trick didn't work, smiling as if she knew it all along.

Moon McCalister proposed to me that night. We walked to the lake behind his house and he asked me those four words I never thought I'd live to hear. What was remarkable to me was that I didn't jump at his offer that night, but I actually gave it some thought.

Any other time and I would have screamed *Yes! Are you kidding? Now! I'll marry you now!* But I actually thought about it this time. For about ten minutes. Then I got real and quickly accepted the brother's offer.

Now the wedding's three weeks away and G and V are driving me nuts with preparations. Which gown am I going to wear, is the reception hall going to be large enough, are my flower girls, brides-maids, bands going to have their acts together, is the caterer reli-able, how many rsvps have been returned, what about the honeymoon? I almost threw my hands in the air on a number of oc-casions and told those sisters to forget it, that Moon and I could just stand before a magistrate and be done with it. But Gina, of course, set me straight immediately. "You better sit down some-where," she said. "You been praying for this day for a hundred long-ass years and now you trying to act like it's nothing? Child, please. We gonna put on a show, you hear me? You ain't never gonna forget your wedding day!"

So I smiled, let them run the show, and called my mother. When I first told her about the proposal she whooped and hollered on the phone so hysterically that my baby brother Ricky thought some-body had died.

Somebody had, in a way. That old desperation died. That old fear of being alone, of never knowing what it felt like to be chosen as somebody's number one, died too. Everybody tells me that I've changed, that I'm nothing like I use to be. They think it was Moon. But Moon and his proposal didn't change me. His love for me didn't make me whole. Experience changed me. Disappointments and knockdowns and high hopes that wilted into crushed dreams changed my life. Now I was ready to see what it was like on the other side. I wanted to appreciate the difference. The night Moon proposed was the best night of my life because I quit trying to force the issue. I let nature, for once in my life, take its course.

Gina cried when I told her the news. She was with me through all of those hapless romances and thought they were just my lot in

308

life, my burden to bear. That's why she cried like a baby when I told her the news. And then she wiped her tears away, cut a jig, and started preparing for the wedding that very night.

She kicked Isaac out two weeks after my announcement and filed for divorce the following day. She could do bad by herself, she said. She was thirty-nine and pregnant, still scared to death of that thing called motherhood, but she was fed up with Isaac's foolishness too. But like always, she bounced right back, even started dating herself an international antique dealer whose routine excursions to Europe to track down original Faberge and other collectibles turned her on.

Vera's happy too. She and Rollie celebrated their ninth wedding anniversary by taking a cruise to the Virgin Islands. Rollie came back rejuvenated. He even started suggesting that he just may allow Vera to do some volunteer work outside of the home. He was thinking about it anyway. But Moon likes Rollie Langston, finding him an interesting kind of man, and he earnestly believes that in time the brother will come around. I'm not so optimistic. But that's Vera's business. And if she can live with it (and she seems to be living just fine), then I may as well too.

And then there's me. Tory. Totally happy and totally content for the first time in my life. They awarded me professor of the year at the graduation ceremony and you couldn't have seen a happier sister. I was grinning so hard that Gina later told me that I was all teeth on that stage. I feel as if it's all coming together for me now, and that old fear that it'll all fall apart isn't there. If it falls, it falls. But at least I'm enjoying the ride. I'm thirty-five and sassy like a twenty-year-old, ready to take on the world, ready to finally, finally get on with it.

My beeper went off again just as the train was a few cars short of getting out of the way. I grabbed the beeper expecting to find V's number again or some foreign number, like the hospital's. But it was Moon.

I slung my car's stick shift into first gear just as the crossbars rose up, and I dialed Moon's number on my cell phone.

"Good morning," he said.

"Hey, babe, what's up?"

"I just called to say I love you."

I smiled. "Oh, I love you too!"

"Where are you?"

"On my way to the hospital. Would have been there too if this goddamn slow-ass train didn't have me stifled all this time."

"Watch your language," he said. "And why are you racing to the hospital?"

"It's Gina. It's time, according to Rollie."

"Tell her I said congratulations. But you drive carefully now."

"I will."

"And slow down, Victoria."

I looked at my car's speedometer as it registered seventy-three with a bullet. "You know me," I said.

"That's what worries me. Now slow down. I wanna see your pretty face again."

My heart melted. He knew exactly what it took to handle me. Just a few sweet, melodic words and I crumbled. And I also slowed down.

I entered the hospital through the emergency room and was finally told how to get to labor and delivery. I wanted to take the elevator but it took its pretty time coming down so I took the stairs instead. I had on my shorts and running shoes, was carrying only my bottled water and my keys, and I was clearing two steps at a time without feeling exhausted or out of breath. Fummi's taxing workouts were finally paying off.

Gina had a private suite near the end of the hall and when I walked in she was handing the baby to Vera. They both were crying, and the baby was too, and I hurried to take my first look at our newest addition.

"Oh my God!" I said as her small, yellow face peered up through the blanket and looked in my direction. "She's beautiful, Gina!" Her hair was jet-black and curly and she squinted and contorted her little face so that Vera and I started laughing. And I started crying too.

"What's her name?"

"Vera Victoria Ridgeway," Gina said. "Better known as VV."

I smiled through my tears. "VV," I said, touching her tiny fingers until they clasped on to mine. "Hey, VV. This is your aunt talking. This is your aunt Victoria. You're named after me."

"And me," Vera said in her deepest voice yet, and Gina and I looked at each other and laughed.

And we had us a big old time with that beautiful baby. Vera held her and I held her and Gina held her and we passed her around like a loving cup. The nurse had to come in twice and tell us to let the baby rest. "She's not even a day old yet," she said.

Vera and I finally obeyed the nurse's wishes and laid the baby in her crib, but then we grabbed chairs and surrounded her, laughing and touching her hair and speculating on what kind of woman she would turn out to be.

"An independent woman," Gina said confidently, and answered her ringing phone.

It was Charles, her antique-dealer boyfriend, calling from Prague, of all places.

"The third time this morning," Vera said. "And Isaac is nowhere to be found with his trifling self."

I looked at Gina as she talked to the new love in her life, smiling and twirling the phone cord with her fingers as if she were some love-struck teenager. I wondered if she understood her history. I wondered if she realized that all of her romances were on the rebound. She would get out of one relationship and immediately fall into another one, no time to regroup, no time to learn.

Now it's Charles's turn. He's the man of the hour now. But you can never underestimate Regina Ridgeway. Either she never cared to understand what she was doing, or she understood it too well.

She just didn't want to be alone. That's her crime. That's her Achilles' heel. That's what drives her down these endlessly darkened roads over and over again.

But VV's here now and she'll brighten up Gina's world. I know she will. She wasn't a day old and already she'd brightened up mine.

"You so crazy!" Gina said to Charles over the phone, and then she giggled. Vera and I looked at each other.

"I'll give it six months," I said.

"No," Vera said, "I think this one is good for at least a year. Or, who knows, maybe even a lifetime."

"Wouldn't that be something," I said, "Gina and Charles growing old together."

"You never know," Vera said.

"True," I said just as the nurse walked in and requested that Gina get off of the telephone.

"You need your rest, Miss Ridgeway," she said.

Gina, of course, ignored her.

"She'll be off soon," I said. "It's long distance."

"What's long distance?" Moon asked as he walked into the room. Vera and I turned quickly in his direction and I jumped up and ran to him. He had flowers for Gina and a big box of chocolates.

"Oh my goodness!" the nurse yelled suddenly and we all looked at the baby. But VV was fine. We then looked at the nurse.

"What's the matter?" I asked her.

She had her hand on her chest and started pointing at Moon. "That's the mayor! That's Mayor McCalister," she said.

"That's right," Gina said, interrupting her phone conversation, "and that beautiful woman beside him is the mayor's wife!"

I smiled and held on to Moon. "Not yet," I said.

"But soon," Moon added.

"I voted for you," the nurse said. "I think you're so wonderful. I think you're going to do so many great things."

Moon actually smiled. "Thank you," he said. And then he looked at me. Tears were streaming down my face. "Honey, what's wrong?" he asked. "You're crying."

"I know. I can't help it." He held on to me and I welcomed his embrace. Then VV started crying too.

"She sounds like Gina," Moon said.

I hit him playfully on his coat lapel. "Come and see the baby," I said and placed my hand in his hand and walked him to the crib. "Her name is VV. Vera Victoria. And she's so precious!"

Moon looked at the newborn child and placed his arm around my waist. He even smiled at her and touched her little fingers. And then he looked at me. "You're next," he said, and I beamed.

That's right, y'all. I got next. A marriage, a baby, the whole nine yards. It's my turn next!